THIN WALLS

ALSO BY KRIS NELSCOTT

A Dangerous Road
Smoke-Filled Rooms

This is Chicago, this is America.
—MAYOR RICHARD J. DALEY, 1968

ACKNOWLEDGMENTS

No one writes a book by herself. I couldn't have written *Thin Walls* without the spectacular collections at Chicago's Museum of Broadcasting and the Harold Washington Library. Also, the Smokey Dalton series would not exist without the support of the wonderful folks at St. Martin's Press, particularly Kelley Ragland, whose keen editorial eye has made each book the best it can be. Paul Higginbotham, Steve and Jenny Braunginn, and my husband, Dean Wesley Smith, helped me fill in details. Thanks for your help, all.

For my nephew,
Knute L. Hofsommer,
with love

THIN WALLS

Kris Nelscott

St. Martin's Minotaur ⚏ New York

www.minotaurbooks.com

Library of Congress Cataloging-in-Publication Data

Nelscott, Kris.
　　Thin walls / Kris Nelscott.—1st ed.
　　　　p.　cm.
　　ISBN 0-312-28783-6
　　1. Dalton, Smokey (Fictitious character)—Fiction.
　　2. Private investigators—Illinois—Chicago—Fiction.
　　3. African American men—Crimes against—Fiction.
　　4. African American men—Fiction.　5. Chicago (Ill.)—Fiction.
　　I. Title.

PS3564.E39 T48　　2002
813'.6—dc21

2002068350

First Edition: September 2002

10　9　8　7　6　5　4　3　2　1

THIN
WALLS

ONE

On the day it all began, I stood in the center of my small apartment, arms crossed, looking at the blank wall behind the door. The radiator clanked beneath the window, pouring in enough heat to make me uncomfortable.

I hated the heating system in this place—an hour of unbearable warmth, followed by a gradual cooling, until Jimmy and I grew chilly enough to grab sweaters. The brick walls were insulated, but the windows were thin and on windy days, a draft came through so strong that the curtains moved. I'd meant to caulk, but I hadn't gotten to it yet. I found that I had an aversion to working on an apartment that wasn't my own.

It was a few minutes after noon on December 6, 1968, and I was feeling out of sorts. I had just had a conversation with Amos Bonet, one of the other fathers in the neighborhood. He'd asked me if I wanted to join him and the rest of the group to get a Christmas tree.

I had been about to say yes when I realized he was talking about stealing one.

"It's no big deal," Amos said. "We do it every year. We've never been caught."

Not being caught wasn't the issue; the issue was the theft, especially of a Christmas tree. I didn't like the symbolism.

But before I could say anything, he added, "It's not like we're

1

hurting anybody. We go up to one of the state parks in Wisconsin, take a few tiny trees. We don't steal from the real tree farmers."

As if that made it better.

"We make a day of it—something to look forward to. Thought you might enjoy it."

Somehow I managed to thank him for his consideration— my judgmental response wasn't going to discourage a neighborhood tradition—and make it up to the apartment.

The place seemed less like home than it had in the summer, when we had been sharing it with all seven members of the Grimshaw family. Althea had managed to keep the living area and half-kitchen clean at all times, despite the crowded conditions. Something was always on the stove, and the place had felt like it was full of love.

It seemed empty now. Part of that was because the Grimshaws had taken most of their furniture with them when they moved to a house more suited to their family's size. The furniture I'd found didn't fill the space nearly as well. We had a dilapidated sofa covered with an afghan Althea had given us, a presswood coffee table that needed refinishing, two floor lamps that didn't match, and the only thing I'd purchased new—a twenty-inch black-and-white television set that dominated the corner beside the door to the hallway.

The whole idea of a tree seemed novel to me. When I lived in Memphis, I had always celebrated Christmas with friends, but I had never made much of an effort myself. I hadn't decorated my home or put up a tree. Usually I helped my friend Henry Davis by running the Christmas dinner for the poor at his church—giving him time to spend at least part of the holiday with his own family.

This year would be very different. I barely had enough money to make the rent. I had no idea how I'd find more cash to spend on presents, a special meal, and all the trimmings a tree required.

A knock on the door made me jump. It was probably Amos. He was trying to be neighborly—the invitation was yet another sign that I was becoming accepted—but I simply couldn't imagine celebrating a holiday of peace and light with a stolen tree in my front room.

I pulled the door open without looking through the peephole and was startled to find a stout, middle-aged woman standing at the threshold. I'd never seen her before.

"Hi," she said, her voice shaking. "Are you Bill Grimshaw?"

Actually, my name is Smokey Dalton, but I had been using the name Bill Grimshaw since I'd come to Chicago in May. Bill was my legal first name and people assumed my last name was Grimshaw because I had been living with Franklin and Althea.

It was safer to use the assumed name, and once I decided to stay in Chicago, I decided to keep it, even having fake identification made out in the name of William S. Grimshaw.

I almost smiled as I realized the irony. I was willing to go to illegal means to get fake identification, but I wasn't willing to have a stolen Christmas tree—an untraceable stolen Christmas tree—in my apartment.

"Yes," I said. "I'm Bill Grimshaw. What can I do for you?"

She licked her lips, then pressed them together as if she were wearing lipstick. She wasn't, although it took a moment to see that. Her cheeks were ruddy with the cold and she had magnificent almond-shaped eyes that needed no enhancement at all.

"I hear you help people find things."

I nodded and stepped aside, letting her into the apartment. Since September, I'd gone back to what I did best—doing odd jobs for people who needed help. Most of the time, those odd jobs involved detective work, although in the early days of the fall, I'd found myself doing truly odd work—a bit of carpentry for people who needed an extra hand on the hammer, helping families move, driving people to the emergency room when there was no one else to help.

That work was becoming less and less common now that I was getting an occasional referral from black area lawyers. It still wasn't enough to make ends meet, and I took way too much work in trade, but it had been a start.

She hovered just inside the door, clutching her cloth coat

closed around her neck. Apparently I made her nervous, which wasn't a surprise. I was six feet tall and broad-shouldered. I made most people nervous, even when I didn't tower over them the way I towered over her.

"We don't have to talk in here if you don't want to," I said. "We can talk outside or go to a restaurant."

She shook her head, then gave me a crooked smile. "That's all right. I just wasn't expecting this."

She was looking at the living room. It was clean, more or less—no dirty dishes or grime on the surfaces. But the afghan was crumpled on the side of the sofa, and yesterday's *Defender* was spread on the coffee table, a large picture of O.J. Simpson with the banner "Player of the Year!" spread across its back cover.

"My office is down the hall." I'd had this reaction from clients before and I wished the apartment was set up differently. If I had lived alone, I would have put the office in the front room and the living area in the back, but I couldn't—not with Jimmy coming in and out. In the back, at least I could close the door for privacy. In the front room, a client and I would have had none.

I led her through the living room to the hallway and turned into the first bedroom. It had once been the boys' bedroom, small and dark, with a single window that overlooked the alley. The heat was even worse in here. I flicked on the overhead light, opened the window, and settled behind my desk.

This room was neat—I tried to keep it as spotless as possible—with old wooden filing cabinets lining one wall. The window filled the other, letting in thin light from the gray, overcast afternoon.

The woman settled into the chair in front of my desk. The chair was wooden and square and looked expensive, even though I'd bought it cheap at the same yard sale where I had gotten the filing cabinets. The chair, cabinets, and desk made me look more prosperous than I was—a good thing, I thought, essential for reassuring clients.

"How can I help you, Miss—"

4

"Mrs.," she said, and to my surprise, teared up. "Mrs. Louis Foster."

I braced myself. Obviously this was going to be a lot more serious than helping her find a lost dog.

She blinked but didn't sniffle, as if she could compose herself through sheer will. "Your cousin, Franklin Grimshaw, told me to come see you. He says you do detective work, even though you don't advertise."

"Yes." Franklin wasn't my cousin, but most people believed he was. It was a fiction we had created when Jimmy and I had arrived last May, when we were running from the Memphis police and the FBI. "I do detective work."

"But you're not one of them agencies?"

I shook my head. I never believed in going through the state—any state—to gain a license to do my own business. I would have had to follow white rules and white regulations, even if I worked for one of the many black detective agencies in Chicago. I preferred working for myself, without submitting to forms and paperwork and tests. There were enough rules in my line of work.

"I work for myself."

"And don't advertise?" The point clearly bothered her.

"I figure that people who need me will find me." I smiled gently, hoping I could reassure her. "You did."

She swallowed and pulled her large black purse onto her lap. Her gloved fingers clutched the clasp, as if she were still debating about using my services.

"Why don't you tell me what happened, Mrs. Foster, and we'll both decide if I'm right for the job?"

She teared up again, then blinked, straightening her spine. I pretended I didn't notice. I didn't want to scare her off, not when something was bothering her like this.

"You didn't know my Louis, did you, Mr. Grimshaw?"

"No, ma'am," I said.

She bit her lip again. "He was a dentist. His offices are in the oldest part of Bronzeville, near the Loop."

5

Her gaze met mine and again I was struck by the beauty of her dark brown eyes.

"Three weeks ago," she said, her voice shaking, "he was murdered."

I had known he was dead from her tone, but somehow I hadn't expected her to say this.

"I'm sorry," I said, and realized how inadequate the words were.

She waved them off with a slight movement of one gloved hand. "The police say he was mugged."

The radiator had stopped clanking. Already a chill was seeping into the room.

"You don't believe the police?" I asked.

"He was a big man, like you, Mr. Grimshaw. People thought twice about doing anything to him."

They thought twice about attacking me, too, but it had happened. "Did you mention that to the police?"

She nodded. "They said that maybe there was more than one mugger."

"But you don't believe that."

"I don't know what to believe." Her voice cracked and this time, a tear strayed down her cheek. She opened her purse, took out an embroidered handkerchief, and wiped her eyes. "I'm sorry."

"It's all right," I said. "It hasn't been that long."

"It has, too, Mr. Grimshaw." She crumpled the handkerchief in her hand. "It's been three weeks, and the police won't even return my calls. They said he should have known better than to be out alone. They said there's too many murders to solve all of them. They gave it enough time, they said, but there aren't any leads."

"These were white cops?" I asked.

She nodded. "I called the Afro-American Patrolmen's League. They said they'd see what they could do, but they said sometimes there weren't any clues and there was nothing to learn."

"They said this the first time you called?"

"And the second. I've spent all my time since he died trying to get help on this, and no one is listening."

I leaned forward so that she knew I was paying attention. I also didn't want her to know that the police were right; often there wasn't enough evidence to gather from a scene to make an arrest.

"Tell me what happened, Mrs. Foster."

Her fingers slipped inside her purse and clutched something, but she didn't pull it out.

"He didn't come home from work that day," she said. "It was the week before Thanksgiving and his mother was coming on Monday. We had a lot of errands to do, and he promised he'd be prompt. When Louis said he'd be prompt, he always was."

"So you knew something was wrong."

She nodded. "I called the police at eight that night, and they said I should wait. He'd come home. Then when he wasn't back the next morning, I called again, and they asked me to describe him. That's when I knew."

Her eyes were dry now and her voice steady. She'd told this part of the story a number of times, and the emotion behind it wasn't sorrow. It was anger.

"I did describe him. They said they'd found a man meeting that description in Washington Park and would I come see if that man was my husband? My Louis had no reason to go to Washington Park, and I told them that, but they insisted."

She stopped and closed her eyes, clearly remembering that morning.

"Was it him?" I asked gently, hoping to move her past what was obviously a painful memory.

"Yes," she whispered. Then she set the folder on my desk. "Here's what happened to him."

I opened the folder. On top were a series of clippings, the largest from the *Chicago Defender* and the rest from the other newspapers in town. A cursory glance told me that most of the clippings were about the discovery of Louis Foster's body, but a few were his obituary, which would be useful in its own way.

I moved the clippings aside and was surprised to find a number of clear black-and-white photographs of a dead body leaning against a tree. Cops moved around it, clearly examining it and the site nearby.

"Where did you get these?" I asked as I turned the top one over, looking for the answer even before she gave it.

"The *Defender*," she said.

That surprised me. The newspaper's stamp wasn't on the back. Instead, someone had written a name and address on a piece of masking tape and pressed it onto the surface.

I closed the folder. I would study the photographs later. She didn't need to see them, a reminder of the horrible way her husband had died. "I don't remember the *Defender* running anything like this."

Her smile was small. "They didn't. They ran an article on his death, though, and it had more information in it than the police told me, so I went there. They gave me the photographs because they had no use for them, but not the notes."

Too bad. I could have used the notes.

"I didn't know newspapers gave away photographs," I said.

She shrugged. "It took a bit of persuading."

I was just beginning to discover how persuasive Mrs. Louis Foster could be. "Mrs. Foster," I said, "there is a good possibility that I won't find out anything more than the police have."

"Of course you'll find out more, Mr. Grimshaw. You'll actually investigate. The newspaper had more information than they did. You'll find out something."

"Maybe," I said. "But it's been weeks. A lot of evidence disappears in that amount of time. We've had rain and some snow, not to mention other people tracking past—"

"Mr. Grimshaw," she said. "I have a lot of questions that no one has been able to answer. Why was my Louis in Washington Park? He was supposed to come home at four. But his receptionist said he had left around noon. His body wasn't discovered until the next morning. Where was he between noon and four? What was he doing?"

My hands were getting cold and so were the tips of my ears. I closed the window and then faced Mrs. Foster again.

This was the part of my job that I didn't like. Prying into someone else's secrets often meant I would disillusion his loved ones. "You might not want me to follow up on this investigation after all."

"Because you might discover that my Louis was having an affair?"

"Possibly." I returned to my desk. "There are a hundred other things that I could find out, none of them pleasant. Are you sure you want to risk learning these things?"

She sat up even straighter. "I thought of that, Mr. Grimshaw. I've thought of everything, and I've decided not knowing is worse than knowing."

"People often have hidden sides, even spouses. You might discover a Louis you never dreamed existed."

She nodded. "I'm prepared for that."

"I hope so," I said. "Investigations like this sometimes bring out the worst, things you never expected, things that could shake you down to your very soul."

"Louis's death was the worst thing that could have happened to me," she said. "I doubt anything else can be worse than that."

I didn't. I knew that surprises had a way of being worse than expected, much worse.

"What do you charge?" Mrs. Foster asked.

I had set rates for the businesses I worked with, but I had learned long ago to be flexible with my individual clients. "What are your circumstances, Mrs. Foster?"

"I'm all right," she said. "Louis had a good salary and I have a good job. We own our home, and he even had a life-insurance policy that paid me fast enough to get him properly buried. I can afford you, Mr. Grimshaw."

I would check on that, just like I always did with clients who claimed they could afford me—and clients who claimed they couldn't.

"All right." I quoted her my weekly rate, which did not

include expenses. For that, she would get an update and a final report. At the end of each week, we both had the option to terminate the job. That way, I wouldn't feel obligated to pursue a case that was going nowhere, and she wouldn't have to pay me if I got too close to a secret she didn't want discovered.

The amount didn't upset her and neither did the fact that our agreement was closed with a handshake. She did insist on writing the rates down, something I wished more clients would do, and she tucked the slip of paper in her purse.

Then she gave me her address and phone number. "I suppose you have questions for me."

"Not yet." I wanted to study the pictures, see if I could find the newspaper article, discover if I agreed with the police—that this was a random act of violence. "I'll call you when I know what questions to ask."

She nodded and stood, shaking my hand again. "Thank you for taking me seriously, Mr. Grimshaw."

"You're welcome," I said, hoping she would still be grateful later. Then I showed her out.

I went to the window that overlooked the street, waiting until she reached the ground floor. I wanted to see how she had gotten here. That alone would tell me a lot about her.

She left the building, walking out purposefully toward a gray sedan new enough to confirm her claims of a middle-class income. I wouldn't use that as my final determination of course, but it was a good start.

The living room was still too hot. I debated opening the window, then decided against it since the outdoor air had chilled my office so fast and there was no way to know when the heat would come back on. I poured myself a glass of water and went back down the hall.

Mrs. Foster had seemed pretty strong, but I couldn't imagine the impact those photographs had on her. She had seen her husband's body in the morgue and that had been bad enough. But I'd learned over the years that seeing the actual murder site, the body in the last position it had assumed in life, the first position it had taken in death, was somehow worse. Seeing the death pose always made the violence come clear.

I sat down and opened the folder, turning first to the newspaper article from the *Defender*. It was from the Monday, November twenty-fifth, edition, two days after the body was discovered.

BODY FOUND IN WASHINGTON PARK
Two teenage boys found the body of Louis Foster around 9:00 A.M. Saturday morning as they walked through Washington Park. Mr. Foster's body lay against a tree in the east end of the park. He had been fatally stabbed and his wallet was missing.

The boys, whose names were not revealed, called the police, who arrived on the scene nearly half an hour later. When asked about the tardiness of the response, the police acknowledged that they first thought the call was a prank. . . .

I set the article aside. The other articles from the *Tribune*, the *Daily News*, and the *Sun-Times* were much shorter, mostly acknowledging that a man had been found stabbed in the park. I skipped the obituaries and turned to the photos.

The first was of two police officers staring at the tree, whose naked limbs twisted crookedly toward the sky. It was an artistic photograph instead of a newsworthy one—the composition clearly something the photographer cared about.

I set that photograph on top of the newspaper articles, knowing I'd comb through all of this later. Then I grabbed the second photograph, and froze.

It was of Louis Foster's body. He was big, as his wife had said, and he was still wearing his coat, a dark cloth coat that covered his long frame. His eyes were open and so was his mouth, the face's slack expression making him look like a caricature of surprise.

But it wasn't the expression that caught me. It was the

position of the body itself. It had been posed against the tree, one arm outstretched, the other across his stomach. His feet were extended and a shoe dangled off his left foot.

I held the photograph up, as if moving it would change the image. My breath caught, and I felt myself shake. I wondered if Truman Johnson had seen these photographs. I would have bet anything that he hadn't.

Johnson was a detective with the Chicago Police Department. Our paths had crossed in August, and he had told me about two cases similar to this one.

The first had occurred in April and another in July. But both of the victims in those cases had been ten-year-old boys, not grown men, men so large that no one thought they'd have trouble defending themselves.

Foster had been stabbed, the newspaper said, and I didn't have to talk to the coroner to know exactly how. Once, through the heart. A quick, sudden movement, guaranteed to kill anyone—no matter how big or how small—in a matter of seconds.

The cops who were photographed at this scene were white. They wouldn't call in a black detective, and they probably hadn't looked up similar killings. Even if they had, they might have missed the boys.

And, I was willing to wager, Johnson hadn't combed the cold-case files for adult victims. He'd told me last summer that he thought the M.O. was for young boys. That was the information he'd given to the FBI as well.

The FBI. The very thought of them made me shudder. They had issued an APB for me and Jimmy last April, after they realized that Jimmy had witnessed Martin Luther King, Jr.'s assassination. Jimmy had seen the sniper who shot King—and it wasn't James Earl Ray, the man they'd arrested in London in June.

It had become very clear, very quickly, that both the Memphis police and the FBI had been involved in Martin's death. They came after Jimmy even before they started looking for the "real assassin." I managed to get Jimmy out of Memphis, and so far, I'd kept us from being caught, but I knew that if I made one mistake, Jimmy would die.

I looked at the photos again. They held a lot of information. The body's position remained the same in all of them. No one had touched it—at least not while the photographer was working.

I closed the file, feeling unsettled. I didn't want to go to Johnson—not yet. The longer I kept the police and the FBI out of the investigation, the better it would be for both me and Jimmy.

But I had a hunch that what was good for us wouldn't be good for others. And I knew I couldn't, in good conscience, be able to keep this quiet for long.

TWO

The slam of the front door made me jump. I looked at the clock on top of one of the filing cabinets. It was after three. Jimmy was home.

I slid the file into the top drawer and turned the lock. Then I came out of the office and into the living room.

Jimmy was in the half-kitchen, getting a Fig Newton from the canister that served as our cookie jar. He still had his coat on.

"Hey, Jim," I said.

He turned quickly, almost guiltily—the cookie already in his mouth. "Hi, Smokey."

He was heavier than he'd been in Memphis, but his face was still thin. Deep shadows outlined his eyes, as they had all year. He had bad dreams almost every night. They woke both of us up and we spent a lot of time watching late movies until one of us fell asleep on the couch.

I scanned the room. No schoolbooks, no notebooks, even though this was Friday and there was a weekend ahead.

"How'd it go?" I asked.

"Okay." He grabbed a glass from the dish rack, shook out some stray water droplets, and set it on the counter. Then he opened the refrigerator and poured himself some milk.

"No homework?"

"Smoke—"

"It's important, Jimmy."

"I gots homework," he said grumpily. We'd been working on his language skills all year and he knew better. He also knew that lapsing into bad grammar was one of the quickest ways to provoke me.

"Oh?" I asked.

"Yeah." He gulped the milk fast, then wiped the milk mustache off his lip with the back of his hand.

"Where is it?"

"I got to report on Black Christmas."

"You have to write a report on Black Christmas?" I couldn't help the lilt in my voice. Jimmy hadn't had a writing assignment since he started school in September.

"No, silly," he said. "I got to report on it. You know—the parade?"

"Your assignment is to go to the parade tomorrow?" I didn't like that at all. "Why?"

"Because the teacher said we should all be thinking about Black Christmas and what it means."

I let out a small sigh. Jesse Jackson had declared this Christmas season a Black Christmas, which meant that all black people should do their Christmas shopping only at black-owned businesses.

The entire Black Belt had caught onto the spirit, leading to articles in the local paper, discussions on the radio, and a few somewhat derisive reports on the local white-run television stations. Jackson's idea did make some economic sense. After all, black-owned businesses couldn't survive without patronage.

But Black Christmas seemed to me the latest attempt by Jesse Jackson to try to take Martin Luther King, Jr.'s fallen mantle and keep it for himself. Jackson had been looking for ways to do that all year.

Jackson was one of Martin's minor lieutenants, and our paths had crossed more than once. I doubted he would remember or recognize me, but I didn't want to give him the chance. Jackson traveled all over the country. The wrong comment to the wrong person might reveal our location.

I'd stayed away from Jackson from the moment I'd come to Chicago, and that wasn't as easy as it sounded. On Tuesday, I'd walked half a mile out of my way to avoid the ground breaking ceremonies at Woodlawn Gardens, the new public housing development, because I'd heard from Franklin that Jackson would be there.

I couldn't go to the parade, especially not with Jimmy. I'd have to find someone else to take him, something I didn't want to do, especially with an event that concerned Christmas.

"What's wrong?" Jimmy asked.

"I just wish you had to write it up," I said.

"Who cares about writing something," Jimmy said, "if you seen it and can talk about it?"

"I care." I was getting more and more disturbed about Jimmy's education. He never had homework. He didn't bring books home, and when I asked him about his day, he always told me what people said, not what he learned.

He shrugged. He still had his coat on and as his shoulders rode up and down, his coat did too. At least he wasn't outgrowing this one yet.

"Maybe I should have you write something—"

"Smoke!"

"—if your teacher's too lazy to do it."

"She's not lazy," Jimmy said, his voice rising. I knew he liked Mrs. Dunbar. I'd met her only once and found her very young, very enthusiastic, and already overwhelmed. "She got too many students and not enough books. She says so all the time. Yesterday, she was talking to the principal—"

The phone rang and Jimmy stopped speaking, as if he were just realizing how much he had said. I hadn't known about the lack of textbooks and the number of students. I'd been so concerned with making money for the two of us that I really hadn't done anything after enrolling Jimmy and speaking to his teacher on the first day. I'd missed the parent/teacher conferences—if there had been any—and I hadn't seen a report card. I had no idea when the things were issued.

The phone rang again.

"You want me to get that?" Jimmy asked. We had agreed that I would handle most of the phone calls, since we couldn't afford a second line for the office.

"I got it," I said, picking up the receiver. "Yes?"

"Smokey?" Laura Hathaway's voice sounded close. Her warm, rich tones always made my breath catch.

"Hi, Laura," I said, trying not to sound as pleased as I felt. "What's up?"

Jimmy grinned at the sound of her name. He liked Laura and she liked him. She made a point of seeing him every week, sometimes twice, and I was grateful for that. He usually didn't get along with women—something I blamed on his mother—so I figured that good female influences, like Laura and Althea, would help him more than I could.

"Want to meet me for some dessert?" she asked. "I have news."

"Good? Bad?"

"Both, actually," she said, but I heard a smile in her voice. "Jimmy just got home from school."

"Bring him. I know a place near the University of Chicago with great pinball machines."

Jimmy adored pinball. I hadn't known that until Laura found out when he had stayed with her in August. When I learned about Jimmy's love of pinball, I realized that his appearance on Mulberry Street the night Martin died had two motivating factors: Jimmy's search for his brother Joe—who had earlier made it clear that he wanted nothing to do with Jimmy—and the pinball machines at the Canipe Amusement Company.

Jimmy had never admitted the pinball to me, even when I'd asked in early September, but his cheeks had flushed. He had probably played a few games that day, and it had taken some time because he was very, very good.

"Sometimes I feel like we're encouraging an addiction," I said.

"Maybe we are." The smile in her voice was dangerously close to a laugh. "But it gives us a chance to talk."

A chance to talk. We'd had so few lately. Laura had been

busy with a court case involving her father's estate, and I'd been trying to hold hearth and home together while setting up my own business.

We were closer than we'd been over the summer, but not as close as we'd been in Memphis before Martin was killed.

"Tell me where and when, and we'll be there," I said.

She did, and we hung up. Jimmy was leaning against the counter, watching me.

"You leaving?" he asked.

"We are," I said, "so I guess you kept your coat on for the right reason."

"Uh-huh," he said, and ducked his head so that I couldn't see his eyes.

He was hiding something. I wasn't going to push at the moment, but I would find out soon enough.

The student hangout Laura had named wasn't that far from the apartment. Jimmy and I walked there partly because I needed to stretch my legs and partly because the Impala was in terrible shape. On cold days, it coughed as it started, and I worried that it wouldn't survive the winter. Rust was flaking off the sides and the undercarriage, affecting heaven knew what. The tires were bald and dangerous in both rain and snow.

Walking also helped me become familiar with the neighborhood and its faces. Last summer, when I was working on my first case in Chicago, I hadn't had a sense of my neighbors and I'd found that to be a handicap. I still wasn't as versed in this city as I had been in Memphis, but I felt more comfortable. I now knew when someone looked out of place.

We walked in the early December twilight, taking a meandering course through the blocks. The air had a chill dampness. The sky was cloudy, and it felt like it was going to snow at any moment.

So far, Chicago's winter wasn't much different from Memphis's, but the locals had been telling me this was a mild year. We'd had snow, but it hadn't stayed. Most days we had a chill rain that turned into black ice by evening.

The main difference was the darkness. It had been overcast for weeks and as the days got shorter, the darkness got more pronounced. It felt as if we never had any daylight at all. I would wake up before dawn, watch the sky turn a hazy gray, and then wait for a brightness that never came.

Despite the cold, Jimmy refused to wear a hat, and I had to struggle to get him to wear his gloves. One of my major expenses this fall had been clothing—neither Jimmy nor I had clothes that would take us through Chicago's vicious winters. I'd been fortunate enough to find some secondhand boy's clothing, including a coat that had a removable lining, but I hadn't been so lucky with my own size.

As a result, I was still wearing Franklin's castoffs, which were old and too bulky around the waist. Sometimes, like now, I wore the windbreaker I brought from Memphis, but it was too thin for the weather.

By the time we got to the hangout, I was very cold.

The hangout was on Fifty-seventh, near a group of bookstores and funky shops that catered to the college students. The nearby neighborhood was mixed—full of student apartments and beautifully apportioned homes for the faculty, as well as other middle-class neighbors who liked the atmosphere.

The most striking part of this area, known as Hyde Park, was that it was the only truly racially mixed area in Chicago. Black and white lived side by side. There was an air of tolerance here that you couldn't find anywhere else in the city, and as a result, Laura and I had taken to meeting here when the students returned in the fall.

The place Laura had chosen this time was a glorified coffee shop. Open twenty-four hours, it was a student gathering place, especially late at night. An on-premise baker made certain there was a large mix of fresh cinnamon rolls, cakes, cookies, and breads available, even in the wee hours. The sandwiches were mediocre and the coffee was burned more often than not, but the desserts were always special.

This afternoon, a sign in the window advertised pumpkin pie—one of Jimmy's favorites—and Christmas cookies.

Someone had hung a single strand of bulbs around the door, and they glowed red, green, and blue in the thin afternoon light.

Through the window, I could see students taking up most of the tables, leaning over books with a dedication that surprised me until I remembered that the term was nearly finished. Even students who spent most of the year protesting had to work hard now—particularly the men, if they wanted to hang onto their student deferments from the draft. No one wanted to end up fighting in Vietnam because he hadn't studied enough.

Jimmy hadn't said anything as we walked, his hands stuck in his pockets, and to my surprise, he didn't say anything now. Usually he would have mentioned the pie or brightened up because he knew this was the place with the pinball machine.

I glanced at him, wondering if he would tell me what was bothering him on his own. I would wait until our meeting with Laura ended. Sometimes she managed to draw things out of him that I didn't even know existed.

The large wooden door opened, and a skinny white student exited, his stocking cap pulled down over his long brown hair. He clutched a book, *Das Kapital*, in his left hand, and a pen in his right. He looked very serious. I supposed I would have, too, if I were forced to read that volume again.

We brushed past him as we stepped inside. The interior smelled of burnt coffee beans and bread—a combination I found seductive. I knew Laura wouldn't be here yet; it took a while to drive down from the Gold Coast, so I found a table near the back.

"This is the place with pinball!" Jimmy said, turning toward the machine as he spoke. It was against the wall near the jukebox, which was silent this afternoon. Someone had the radio on, and disembodied voices discussed the end of the college football season.

"Can I play?" Jimmy asked.

"As soon as Laura gets here."

He wrinkled his nose and sat down, but didn't complain. His patience was one of the things I appreciated about him, even though I didn't like that he'd learned it from the mother and brother who had abandoned him.

"I'm hungry," he said.

"Me, too."

"Do we got to wait to order?"

"No. We can do that now."

He grinned. A waitress, wearing a gingham uniform and a white apron stained with food, approached as if she'd overheard. I ordered pumpkin pie for both of us, coffee for me and milk for Jim.

By the time I was done, Laura had joined us.

"The same," she said as she slipped into the chair nearest the wall.

She looked beautiful. Her cheeks were red with the cold, her blue eyes glowed, and her shoulder-length hair was flipped up in a style I hadn't seen her wear since Memphis. It took me a moment to realize that she also wore lipstick and mascara.

She pulled off her leather gloves and gave Jimmy a quick kiss on the top of the head, which he made a face about even though he didn't try to move out of her way. Then she slipped off her rabbit-fur coat. Beneath it she wore a simple black dress and a strand of pearls. She looked elegant and expensive, out of place in a student hangout.

"What's the occasion?" I asked.

"Court," she said and then smiled at me. I wasn't sure I'd ever seen her so radiant. She seemed alive with joy.

"You get in trouble?" Jimmy asked, and we both turned to him. I understood what he meant almost immediately. His mother had been in and out of court during her last few years in Memphis, mostly on soliciting charges. At one point, the court had tried to find Jimmy's real father, so that Jimmy would have a different home, but his mother had no idea who his father was.

Laura seemed surprised. "No, of course I'm not in trouble."

"Then why'd you go to court?"

She glanced at me, an expression I'd become used to in

dealing with her and Jimmy. She wanted me to explain how a child knew to ask these questions. I'd explain it to her later.

"It was business."

"Yeah?" he said.

"Not like your mother's business," I said.

Laura blushed. "He thought—"

"It is what he knows," I said.

"What kind of business, then?" Jimmy asked.

"It's similar to bank business," she said, "only much more complicated."

"Oh." That ended the discussion for him. He turned toward me. "Can I go play now?"

"After the pie," I said.

"You said I could play when Laura got here."

"I did, didn't I?" I grinned. "All right. But if you're not here when the pie arrives, I'm going to eat it."

He stared at me for a moment. We'd had this discussion before, and once he had called my bluff. I ate his dessert that day, mostly because I felt that I had to live up to what I had said. And because the desserts at that restaurant had been particularly good.

"Guess I'm staying," he said.

Laura grinned. She finger-combed her hair. A ruby-and-sapphire ring I had never seen before glittered on her right hand, and her fingernails were covered with polish.

"You went all out," I said.

"Drew said I had to look like quality." Drew was Drew Mc-Millan, Laura's lawyer.

"You always look like quality to me," I said.

Her gaze met mine, and for a moment, it seemed like we were the only two people in the room. The attraction flowed between us, deep and fine, as if it had never left—which, I guess, it hadn't. We simply had been trying to ignore it.

"Here we go!" The waitress's chirpy voice broke the moment. She set pieces of pie covered in whipped cream in front of all three of us. Then she gave Laura and Jimmy glasses of milk and set down two coffee cups, one for me and one for Laura. "Be right back with the coffee," she said as she disappeared.

Laura looked at her full milk glass and her empty coffee cup. "Wow," she said. "I guess I should have been more specific about my beverage."

Jimmy giggled, his mouth already full of pie. He had a smear of whipped cream along his bottom lip, and he was clutching the fork with his entire fist—a boy prepared to shovel sweets into his mouth quickly so that he could get to the game.

The waitress returned with the coffeepot and a tiny metal pitcher of milk. Laura saw it, her eyes twinkling. We both knew more milk wasn't necessary. But she didn't say anything, waiting until the waitress left before letting out a short laugh.

"What?" Jimmy asked.

Laura shook her head. "Nothing, Jim. It's just been a good day."

"Glad somebody had one," he mumbled, his mouth stuffed with pie.

Her smile faded. "Something happen to you today?"

"Naw," he said and shoved his chair away from the table. "Can I go?"

All that remained of his piece of pie was the crust, beautifully folded and covered with a layer of whipped cream. He never ate the crust, liking the sweet center the best.

"Sure," I said.

He hurried toward the machine, as if he was afraid someone else would get there first. The students were more interested in books this Friday afternoon. Jimmy wouldn't have any competition at all.

"Is he feeling all right?" Laura asked.

"Why?"

"He's still wearing his coat."

I looked. He was, and he hadn't unzipped it. Well, that solved part of the mystery at least. He was hiding something beneath that coat. I'd figure out what it was later.

"So what's your news?" I asked.

Her smile was so bright that it lit the entire room. "We won!"

I smiled, too. I knew how important this case was to her, although I wasn't exactly sure why. "Congratulations."

"This changes everything, Smokey," she said. "That's why I wanted to talk to you. And I wanted a little celebration, too."

My smile softened, became real. I was glad she counted us as part of her celebration. "You'll be busier," I said, "but beside that, I'm not sure how things will change."

The lawsuit had been no surprise to me. Laura and I had initially met because she was trying to resolve problems she'd found in her parents' wills. Her mother had died a year ago, leaving Laura the controlling shares in her father's corporation, Sturdy Investments, Inc.

However, Laura did not have the right to vote those shares. Her father had given the voting proxy to a team of managers he had handpicked to carry out his plans.

That management team had run the company for eight years. Initially, Laura had asked for the voting rights back, something she was entitled to do, but the managers refused. Their argument was a simple one: Her father had left her independently wealthy and she had no need to trouble her pretty little head with business concerns.

Only, Laura's head was more than pretty. It had gotten her through the University of Chicago with a degree in business. She had done so to prove to her father that she could work in his company, but he, like the management team after him, felt that she could live a life of leisure.

But Laura wasn't cut out for a life of leisure. She had taken control of her mother's finances in her mother's last year. Our investigation of her father's personal affairs had raised as many questions as it had answered. I had known it was only a matter of time before Laura would turn her attention to Sturdy Investments.

That she focused on Sturdy after the traumatic events of August made a kind of sense. She was returning to what she knew, and trying to gain control of a life that had been controlled by others from the beginning.

Laura hadn't responded to my statement. Instead, she'd been eating her pie. Her movements were delicate, but they were as focused as Jimmy's had been, as if the pie was something to be gotten through, not enjoyed.

"Laura?" I asked. "Am I missing something?"

She pushed her plate away and picked up her coffee cup, cradling it in her manicured hands. "Do you remember when you met me and Jimmy in the office last summer? I had been going through files."

"Yes," I said, although I hadn't thought of that moment in a long while. A moment when Laura was upset, a moment that she never explained, had seemed unimportant at that chaotic time.

"I found out that there's a lot about my father's company that I don't understand—that I can't understand, really, because the corporation is so diversified." She leaned back, still holding the cup.

I nodded and finally started in on my own pie. I didn't want it as much as I had when I arrived, but I suddenly felt as if I needed something to do.

"I did find out one thing, though," she said. "A lot of Daddy's holdings were in the Black Belt."

"I figured that out when you helped Franklin find a house," I said.

Her smile was bitter. "Do you know what I went through for that? His house is close enough to Hyde Park that the company didn't want to rent to him. They thought they could get— their words now—'a better class of tenant.' I had to vouch for him and offer to pay the rent myself if something happened. Only then would they even consider him for that place."

I'd often wondered how she had found a place big enough for Franklin's family and yet with rent low enough that he could afford it. I'd figured that she had pulled some strings, but I hadn't realized what kind.

"That day," she said, "I had found the files for some of our real estate."

I waited. She set the coffee cup down and looked at me. The joy had left her face.

"I realized that we had a lot of holdings in the Black Belt—and most of those holdings had files inches thick. Logged complaints, letters, requests from the property manager, if there was one, to fix things. Lists of building inspectors. It took me a while to realize what was going on, but I finally got it. Sturdy Investments, through one of its own companies, is one of the biggest slumlords in Chicago."

Her gaze held mine, as if she were daring me to react. But I wasn't as shocked as she had been.

"Laura," I said, "if your father had holdings in the Black Belt, it only makes sense that he was a slumlord. Most landlords here are."

She didn't move. "You don't seem upset."

"Some things are just a fact of life," I said.

"Well, I was shocked," she said, leaning forward. "The money I live on came from screwing people."

"Partly." I was being charitable. Her father had started as a small-time thief and had graduated into a well-connected Chicago businessman. Most, if not all, of his initial business dealings had to have been illegal at best. Being a slumlord was legitimate; I was certain there were a lot of criminal things he had done as well. "What are the rest of the company holdings?"

"I don't know," she said, "and after a while, no one would tell me. I mean, I went through the obvious files—the construction contracts, the other real estate holdings. But Sturdy is a corporation, and we have a lot of partnership agreements with many other businesses. Plus, there are holding companies and dummy corporations and a variety of other things that are simply untraceable to me. Or were."

"But you can trace them now?"

She nodded. "I've been talking to Drew about this—"

I felt a pang. She'd confided in someone else long before she had spoken to me.

"—and he reminded me that if I took action as the majority stockholder, I would be vulnerable. I can't make sweeping changes in the company. They could throw me off the board for mismanaging the assets. Or worse. There could be stockholder lawsuits that would be directed at me. I have to take things one step at a time."

"You have a one-step-at-a-time plan, then?" I asked, not sure if I wanted her to answer yes or no.

"I have to get through the first board meeting. I have to get rid of the team, vote my own shares, and essentially take back the company. I'll put myself in place as chairman of the board and CEO of Sturdy. Then I have to learn how to run it."

I set my fork down. Somewhere along the way, I had stopped eating the pie. My stomach twisted, and I wasn't exactly sure why.

"What's your ultimate goal?" I asked.

"Long term?" she asked.

I nodded.

"To restructure Sturdy, take it out of the business of screwing people and into the business of improving the city—for all the residents."

She looked sincere, sincere and innocent. Her white skin reflected the pale light coming in from the windows. I had seen that fresh-scrubbed, hopeful look before, on the Freedom Summer students who had poured into the South four and a half years before.

"Laura, it—"

"I know," she said, waving a hand. "It's not that easy."

"Actually," I said, "it doesn't work that way."

"Sure it does," she said. "It takes time. I realize that. You asked me for my long-term goals, not my short-term ones."

"Running a company of that size isn't easy."

Her expression froze. "Do you think I'm not capable of it?"

Usually when she asked me questions like that, there was frost in her tone. She got imperious—the rich girl from the Gold Coast talking with an inferior. Only this time, I heard something else. Determination, anger, and a hint of need.

"I didn't say that."

"You think I'm too naïve."

"I didn't say that either, Laura." But she was right; I had thought it.

"Drew thinks so, too. He says my motives are admirable, but I'll learn how the world works soon enough."

That wasn't how I would have phrased things, but the sentiment was the same. I'd seen it before: idealists jumping into a situation they didn't understand and either quitting or becoming co-opted by it. Laura's desire to help was sincere, but I doubted that her passion would sustain her through years of fighting, on both business and personal levels.

Her plucked eyebrows rose. "You agree with him, don't you?"

"You've never run a corporation before," I said.

"Neither have you."

I ignored that. "You're going to have a lot of trouble, Laura."

"I know."

I held up my hand. It was my turn to silence her. "I'm not sure you do."

She pressed her lips together, but didn't say anything.

"Your father showed that he didn't believe you or your mother could handle the company by the way he structured his will. He—"

"Because he wanted—"

"Let me finish." I made sure my voice was soft. I glanced over my shoulder at Jimmy. He was leaning over the pinball machine, his arms gripping it so hard it looked as if he were wrestling a monster.

Laura didn't take her gaze off me. I took a deep breath. "They're not going to look at your brains or your business degree, Laura. To them, you're just a woman. A woman whose father didn't believe she could handle his business."

A flush rose in her cheeks. "So you think I should quit."

"I think you should know what you're up against."

"I do know." Her voice was as low as mine, and her eyes

snapped with anger. "You think I haven't considered this? I'll be the only woman on the board. As far as the stockholders are concerned, the business is being run well. I'll turn it upside down and I won't be doing it to improve profits—although, I think, I will improve them down the road."

"That's a different argument altogether," I said, shoving the pie plate aside and threading my fingers together. "You're never going to get to it. They're going to dismiss you the moment they see you."

"And I should give up because of that?" She was watching me closely.

"It's going to be a hell of a fight, Laura, and you probably won't be able to make the gains you want. You're going to be attacked personally. It's going to be ugly."

She nodded. "I know."

"I wonder if you do."

Her lips thinned. She leaned back in her chair. "It seems to me that in the last year of his life, Dr. King said that poverty was the biggest crisis facing America today, and that eliminating poverty would go a long way toward eliminating racial injustice."

I hated it when people brought Martin up in the middle of an argument. "You think you're going to eliminate poverty by taking over Sturdy Investments?"

"The Reverend Jackson has been saying that people must make a difference in their own communities—black and white."

Black Christmas again. I glanced at Jimmy. He was still wrestling with the pinball machine.

"I'm finally in a position to do something," she said. "I can make a real difference in people's lives."

"For the short term," I said, "you'll still be a slumlord."

She nodded. "The very short term."

"It may not be as easy to change as you think. Just because you'll be in charge of the board and have the majority of shares doesn't mean you can change an entire corporate culture—one that got started on graft and corruption in a town that thrives on graft and corruption—in one lifetime."

29

"So I shouldn't try. Is that what you're saying?" She had crossed her arms.

"You're going to get hurt, Laura."

"I know that," she said. "I don't see why that should stop me."

"It could even be dangerous."

Her eyes narrowed. "So I shouldn't bother my pretty head over this?"

The words hit me with the force of a slap. "I didn't say that."

"You're implying it."

"You're just hearing it that way."

Our voices had gone up. A few people glanced our way.

"Then what are you trying to tell me?" she asked. "That I should duck my head and move on, let someone else deal with the problem? That's not who I am, Smokey."

I was still uncomfortable having my real name bandied about in public. I made a small gesture with my hand, asking her to lower her voice.

"Laura," I said, "you've been protected and pampered your whole life."

"Yeah. And in the last year, I've learned that my entire life has been a lie. I have to do something with all that I've learned. I have to make a difference." She leaned close, so that I was the only one who could hear her. "I nearly died in August, and I realized that I pissed away every chance I'd had to do anything. Every night in that apartment—."

She stopped herself. When it was clear she wasn't going to continue, I said, "Every night in that apartment, what?"

She shook her head.

"Laura, finish."

She swallowed hard and looked away from me. "I don't sleep. I walk around in it, thinking about what would have happened if I had died then. Who would have missed me, who would have even noticed I was gone, and—"

"I would have noticed," I said. "I would miss you."

She looked at me. That openness was there, the same

openness I'd seen that night in Memphis, the night we actually had a chance. I'd seen that look so rarely since then. Only a few times in Chicago, once when she'd asked me if we could try to rekindle the relationship here.

Sometimes I wanted to, no matter how difficult it was. And maybe that was why I was arguing with her—because I knew that this decision, her decision to take over Sturdy, would make an even wider gulf between us.

"Smokey," she said.

I made myself lean back. "Jimmy would miss you, too."

The words put distance between us, just like I intended. She nodded once, swallowed, then looked away.

"I was going to ask for your help with this," she said, "but since you don't support it, I guess that wouldn't be appropriate."

"Ask," I said.

She looked at me again, but the openness was gone. She shook her head slightly. "This is my decision, and—"

"Ask."

"All right." She took a sip of her coffee as if to fortify herself. "I was wondering if, after the board meeting, you would be my spy, for lack of a better word. I need someone I can trust to examine the buildings we own and tell me what condition they're in."

"You can get that from your own people," I said.

She shook her head. "They're going to say everything is fine, and even I know how easy it is to buy off a building inspector. I need someone who'll give me the real information before I request changes in an area. You'd be on my payroll, not Sturdy's."

"Laura, I don't want your money."

"It's a job, Smokey, and I'm paying you for the work because I'm going to demand a lot of you. Will you do this?"

"I'm sure you can find someone else."

"Not someone I trust." Her gaze hadn't left my face. I wondered what she saw there besides reluctance.

31

"All right."

"Good." She grabbed her gloves. "That won't be until January, but I'll talk to you more before that."

She reached for her coat, but I put my hand on it. The rabbit's fur was soft and warm. "When's the board meeting?"

"January second," she said.

"What kind of security do you have?"

"At the meeting? Sturdy's usual—"

"No," I said softly. "I mean you. For the next month."

"I don't need security," she said.

"Does anyone know what you plan to do?" I asked. "Besides your friend Drew, I mean."

"Even he doesn't really know," she said. "I've been purposefully vague."

"Good," I said. "Was anyone surprised that you contested the will?"

"A few people," she said.

"And what was the reaction in court today?"

She put the gloves on top of the coat. "Why? What are you getting at, Smokey?"

"Answer me, Laura."

"They were surprised at the verdict."

"Why? Didn't they fight it hard?"

"My father's will was pretty loose. It's clear that those shares are mine. The proxy was an informal thing, not a formal thing. That's why the case was resolved so easily."

"Was anyone angry?"

"Well, yes, but I expected that—"

"Laura?"

She raised her chin. "They all were."

"And what did your lawyer advise?"

"That I refuse to meet with any of them unless I have a lawyer present."

Thank God for that. The man had some sense. "Well, I'm your security adviser now, Laura. And I want to be present whenever you have a meeting as well, especially if you have an informal one."

32

"Smokey, we're talking about businessmen here, not criminals."

"We're talking about a lot of money here, Laura, and I want to see what you're up against." I took another bite of pie. It tasted better than it had a few minutes before. "Remember, these are people your father trusted."

She studied me for a moment. "Most of these men have known me my whole life."

"You think that'll make a difference with them?"

"Yes," she said.

I sighed. She couldn't afford any illusions now. It didn't matter who shattered them. "You're going to be sticking your neck out, Laura."

"Of course."

"You're not just becoming the first female CEO of Sturdy. You're also going to take on their entire business practice. It'll become clear very fast that you're not going to be a figurehead."

"I'm not going in there with a bulldozer," she said. "I'm going to be careful, play the game, do everything I can to win people over. I promise I'll make the changes subtly. I'll convince the other board members that it's their idea."

"I'm not talking about your changes, Laura," I said softly. "I'm talking about you."

"What about me?"

I studied her for a moment. She didn't get it, not yet. She'd been that protected, that pampered. "You're a woman taking over a world that has been controlled by rich white men. You're asking for a seat anywhere on the bus, a chair at the lunch counter, the right to use any water fountain you want."

"I'm not a national leader," she said. "No one's going to pay attention to me."

"Don't be so sure," I said.

THREE

In the end, Laura agreed to let me accompany her on any meetings that she was going to attend in the next month—formal and informal. I was also supposed to staff part of her security team for the board meeting on January second, something she had planned to ask me to do anyway.

I knew she was doing this to placate me, and I didn't care. I wanted to see for myself how trustworthy these men were, these men who had worked for her father, these men who had known her all her life.

"I don't get it," Jimmy said. "Why'd Laura want to celebrate?"

We had just turned onto our block. The apartment buildings were lit up, curtains drawn against the night. A few people had already strung Christmas lights along their balconies, but I didn't see any trees yet. They would probably all appear after the weekend trip to Wisconsin, stolen, fresh and beautiful.

The air had gone from chill to cold. Jimmy had moved closer to me as we walked. He had been talking the entire way home, but this was the first time he'd mentioned Laura. He had been telling me about pinball. The machine had tilted on him, the first time that had happened in a while. Apparently he blamed the machine.

"And how come she was so dressed up?" Jimmy said. "I never seen her so dressed up."

Actually, he had. He just didn't remember. She was that dressed up the very first time he saw her, in my office in Memphis last February.

"They make you dress up for court," I said.

"I still don't get that," he said. "She was in court because she done what?"

"Did what," I said absently. "She sued someone to get her rights back."

"What's that mean?"

As we walked down the sidewalk, thin flakes of snow floated past, like confetti falling from the ceiling long after a party had ended.

I wasn't sure how to explain any of this to him, but I had to try. Learning the way that Laura lived her life would be as much of an education for him as understanding the roots of Black Christmas. Besides, I had promised myself early on that I would do my best to answer his questions.

"You know that Laura's rich," I said as we walked up the ice-crusted steps toward our front door.

"Yeah. She's white." He reached for the door handle and pulled.

I glanced at him. He had spoken matter-of-factly.

"Not all white people are rich," I said.

He snorted through his nose, pulling off his mittens as he stomped his feet on the brown mat someone had put inside the entry.

"Really, Jimmy. There are some white folks who are very poor."

He shook his head and grinned at me, as if I were teasing him. "That's why we got Black Christmas, so they don't get richer off us."

"Who said that?" I asked. "Your teacher?"

He shrugged and started up the stairs. "Not everybody got white friends like you, you know."

35

Something red flashed inside his coat. I followed him. I was biting back a denial, about to claim that I really didn't have white friends, only Laura. But that was the last thing I wanted to say to him as well.

"What's wrong with white friends?" I asked.

He had one hand on the wooden railing. The other clutched his mittens. "Some people don't like them."

"So you don't like Laura anymore?"

"I didn't say that." He stopped on the landing.

"I'm just trying to understand you."

He frowned at me, his brows forming a single line across his face. "Folks say it's 'coz of white people we all live like this. 'Coz of white people, we ain't got nothing and we ain't got no chance for nothing."

I didn't like that last. The one thing I'd been trying to give Jimmy was a chance. "Who says this?"

He shrugged, turned away and headed up the next flight of stairs.

"Jim? Who says?"

"Folks." He was taking the stairs two at a time, moving beyond me. The glimmer of red caught my eye again. Fabric of some kind, stuffed in his back pocket.

I crossed the landing quickly, quietly. I had a hunch I knew what that red fabric was.

I caught up to him, reached under his coat, and grabbed. My fingers caught soft felt and I pulled.

"Hey!" Jimmy put a hand on his back pocket and turned, all in one movement. Then he froze, his expression a mixture of guilt and terror.

I stuck my fingers in the red felt, pushing it into its normal shape. It formed a small tam—a cousin to the beret—but here it was better known as a sun. The only people who wore a sun were members of the Blackstone Rangers, the largest street gang in Chicago.

"What the hell is this?" I was amazed that I sounded so calm. I wanted to grab Jimmy and, carrying him up the stairs by his arms, throw him into the apartment and never let him out. I

wanted to shred the tam and throw the pieces at him. I wanted to take the railing and rip it in half.

Jimmy's eyes were wide. "Smoke, you don't understand."

"Oh, I understand." I kept my voice soft. "I understand that the Stones love little boys like you. They make you do the work so that Jeff Fort and the Main Twenty-one don't get their hands dirty."

"I ain't done nothing!" His voice rose, and I knew that in a moment my neighbors would be in the hallway. Jimmy and I had never had a public disagreement and we weren't going to start now.

"Inside, quick," I said, nodding toward the apartment.

He ran up the stairs, fumbling for his keys. I had mine out by the time I reached the top. My entire body was cold. I unlocked all three dead bolts and pushed the door open, snapping on the overhead light.

Jimmy scurried past me. I closed the door gently, careful not to slam it like I wanted to.

"Why do you have this?" I asked, trying to be reasonable.

"Because."

"Because why?"

His eyes moved, as if he were trying to think of an answer I would believe. Finally, he said, "You told me I got to try to fit in. You told me not to stand out or nothing, so I—"

"So you joined the Stones?"

"I got to fit in!" He backed away from me and banged into the couch. Suddenly I realized he expected me to hit him. That was probably how his mother had dealt with things.

I was angry enough. Didn't he know what we'd gone through? Didn't he understand how much danger he had put us in? I'd gone to incredible lengths to keep him safe, to keep us safe, and he'd jeopardized it with one single decision.

He looked small now, cringing away from me, like the little boy he truly was. I stared at him for a moment, taking deep breaths to control my anger. Then I tossed the tam on the kitchen table.

His breath hitched, but he didn't move.

"Did you join?" I asked in something that approximated my normal voice.

"I got to fit in," he said again. "You said I got—"

"We established that." I didn't move. I didn't do anything threatening. It unnerved me that he was suddenly so terrified of me, but he had never seen me this angry. "I need to know if you joined."

He glanced at the tam, giving me my answer.

I cursed under my breath, not sure what to do. Yelling at him was the wrong thing. Grounding him would be worse. He had done this in a misguided way to please me. That much was clear—and I should have seen it coming. I should have known what my request that he fit in really meant to a boy who had grown up the way Jimmy had.

"You said they's not a regular gang. That church, they like them."

He meant the First Presbyterian Church in Woodlawn. The minister there supported the Blackstone Rangers and tried to get them to give up their guns. In return, the Rangers used the church as a headquarters, and a few years ago, had a battle with police that shot the entire place up.

"And they do stuff for people, you know," Jimmy was saying. "You told Franklin that gangs got their place. You said they can help sometimes, and the Stones, they help people. You know that."

Jimmy's little speech sounded rehearsed, as if he'd been planning his own defense since he took the tam. Maybe that was why he had kept it hidden, because he had expected my disapproval but hadn't known how to say no and still be part of the group.

"They're not a regular gang." I walked toward the kitchen table and pulled out one of the chairs straddling it and resting my arms on its back. That put me at Jimmy's eye level. It also put a barrier between us so that he might feel protected.

He didn't move. All he did was watch me, still cringing against the couch.

"They're bigger, for one thing, and smarter, and very

dangerous." More dangerous than I wanted to admit, even to myself. The Stones were organized. They had managed to unite twenty-one area gangs, becoming over four thousand strong. They controlled the South Side. And while they did do good things, often with the help of the First Presbyterian Church and the Kenwood-Oakland Community Organization, those things were usually a public-relations move, a cover for their other activities.

"You said that gangs serve a purpose."

I hated hearing all my words echoed back to me. "Yes, I said that."

I had, too, last summer when I helped convince Franklin to take in a teenager, Malcolm Reyner, who had been a member of the Black Machine, one of the few area gangs not yet under the cover of the Stones.

"They do serve a purpose," I said. "A whole bunch of purposes."

They served as a police force in a community where the police were often the enemy. They gave young men a place to go and belong. They taught organization skills, and they filled a power niche that was often empty, especially in the poorer sections of the South Side.

But for every person they helped, they killed five. They took protection money from local businesses and ran drugs throughout the area. They were responsible for a dozen murders that I knew of, and probably a lot more that I didn't.

"The church says they're okay."

"The church is trying to rehabilitate them, Jimmy."

He looked blank at the word.

"It's trying to help them stop breaking the law." And it wasn't working. If anything, the church's help and the legitimacy it had given the Stones had expanded their power, not diminished it.

"So, see? It's okay."

I shook my head. "Sit down. Stop cringing. I'm not going to hit you."

He studied me for a moment, seemed to accept that as truth,

and then levered himself over the couch. The move almost made me smile. He had put another barrier between us, in case I changed my mind.

"Gangs are full of undercover cops and FBI informants," I said.

Jimmy went noticeably pale. "I didn't say nothing to nobody."

"I know," I said. "But it's only a matter of time before they start asking you questions. That's how these groups work."

"But I said I'd join."

I nodded. There wasn't an easy way out of this.

"They won't do nothing to me," Jimmy said. "I'm just a kid. They won't pay attention."

My mind flashed to the photographs of Louis Foster. He had died the same way two little boys had—boys who were Jimmy's age. Boys who, according to the cops, had been killed by gangs.

"Who approached you?" I asked.

He shrugged and looked down, picking at a thread on the bunched-up blanket.

"Jim, who asked you to be in the gang?"

"Different guys." He was mumbling.

"What made you say yes?"

He shrugged again.

"Did Keith join?" Keith was one of Franklin Grimshaw's sons. He was Jimmy's closest friend and they were about the same age.

Jimmy didn't respond.

"Jim?"

He shook his head, the movement so small I almost missed it.

"What did he think of you taking the tam?"

Jimmy picked at the blanket.

"I can just ask him," I said.

He looked up. "Don't."

"Why not?"

"He'll get in trouble."

"Because he joined?"

Jimmy shook his head.

"Then why?"

"He don't know nothing about this," Jimmy said. "Please, Smoke. Don't say nothing to Keith."

He seemed almost frightened.

"What's Keith got to do with this?" I asked.

"Nothing," Jimmy said.

"Are you sure?"

He nodded. "He don't understand how I got to blend in and you said not to tell nobody. But I got to join, Smoke. There's only me and Keith and a couple other guys who don't got suns, and everybody gives us crap about it. They pick on us all the time, and call us names and stuff. If I got a sun, nobody'll pick on me no more."

"No," I said. "They'll just make you run drug packages like you used to do in Memphis."

"I won't," he said.

"You'll say no to these guys?"

"Yeah."

"Do you know what they do to people who say no?"

"That's lies, Smoke. You know it."

"Oh?" I asked. "Did they tell you that?"

He didn't answer.

"Did they also tell you what they do when they want someone dead? The word on the street says they get the twelve-year-olds to do it. You'll be eleven in what—January? That's close enough."

"Smoke—"

"It's all a test, Jim. You graduate to higher and higher levels until you become someone the Main Twenty-one can trust. Unless you die first."

"You're making that up."

"Have I ever lied to you?"

"No." His voice trailed off. He picked at the blanket as if he were trying to pull a thread loose. I wanted to take his hand in my own and hold it still.

The anger was gone, replaced by a sadness that I hadn't

expected. All I had ever wanted for him was an opportunity at a good life. It seemed, since Martin's death, like that was impossible.

"What'm I gonna do, Smoke?" Jimmy's fingers still picked and he hadn't looked up.

"Give the tam back." I wasn't going to call it a sun. I wasn't going to honor the gang name for the hat.

"I can't." His head bent even lower. "They'll beat me up."

Of course they would. "Did they beat you up before?"

He shrugged. It was a yes, then. How had I missed that? What else was he hiding from me? I had been so preoccupied with simple monetary survival and starting the new business that I had let the wrong details go.

Only it wasn't just monetary survival. Since last summer, I'd been distant from everyone, trying to deal with the fact that I had killed someone because I had seen no other choice.

I still didn't, even though I went over the details every single day.

"I got to be a member now, Smoke," Jimmy said. "I'm sorry."

I shook my head. "You're giving the tam back."

"Do I get to stay home then?" For the first time, he looked at me, and there was hope on his face. Did he hate school that much?

I gave him a faint smile. "I thought of that. I don't think running and hiding is the answer."

Although it was what I had taught him—at least in the death of Martin. And I had learned in August that even though standing and fighting could be necessary, they didn't feel any better than running.

"I don't mind," Jimmy said. "I can help you. We can be a team."

"We already are a team," I said. "But you'll keep going to school. Remember what I told you about education. It's how you get ahead."

"You got lots of education," Jimmy said. "You ain't no better than Teddy Lewis's dad and he didn't graduate high school."

He was as good at pulling my strings as I was at pulling his. "I had a good education and a lot of opportunity. I chose to use them differently than most people."

"I don't know nobody here who's gone somewhere because they went to school." Jimmy had let go of the blanket. He was watching me now. I could hear his desperation. He wanted me to tell him it was all right to stay away. He clearly hated school, which was a change from Memphis. There, he had loved his education. He just hadn't had a chance to attend as often as he wanted to.

"Going to school is not up for debate," I said.

"I'm not learning nothing."

"I'm beginning to realize that," I said.

"You got schooling. You can teach me."

"I can't," I said. "I have to work." And even if I didn't, I wasn't sure I could provide the kind of education a ten-year-old needed.

My choices were limited. The schools in the Black Belt were old, overcrowded, and decaying. A handful of students was being bused to white suburban schools, but that was so controversial that white bigots picketed outside and the news cameras were there at even a whisper of trouble. I didn't dare let Jimmy's face appear on television, even if I wanted to subject him to that kind of hatred. And I wasn't sure he'd get a better education in that environment.

I couldn't afford private school and, I suspected, he'd run into the same problems there that he'd face in the white suburban schools. Moving wasn't an option, either. We couldn't go to a small community where we'd be noticed, and as much trouble as Chicago's schools had, schools in other major cities were as bad or worse.

"I goofed up, didn't I?" His voice shook. He was close to tears.

"No." I got up and crossed to the couch, sitting beside him. My weight on the cushion made Jimmy fall toward me and I used that moment to put my arm around him.

He didn't struggle like I expected him to. Somehow, when

I'd taken him from Memphis, I had thought this would be easier. We had an affinity, and he was a good kid.

But he needed time and attention. I hadn't had much of either
in the last year.

"It's my fault," I said. "When I told you to blend in, I didn't
think about things like the Stones. I had forgotten how hard it
is to be ten. Blending in isn't always the right thing to do."

"But now we're in trouble again." He was shaking. "You
gonna send me to Laura's?"

That was what I had done in August. I had hidden him as
deeply as possible, and still I had nearly lost him.

"No," I said.

"She's got schools there, right?"

It would be so easy. Let him stay with Laura and go to a
fancy school in the Gold Coast—where he'd stick out as badly
as he had in her upscale high-rise apartment building.

"Yes, she does. But she's got her own worries right now. I'll
help you through this," I said.

"How?"

"I'm not sure yet," I said. "But I'll figure it out by Sunday
night. I promise."

"I don't want to get beat up," Jimmy said.

"I know," I said. "That's what the Stones are counting on."

44

FOUR

The next morning, I was up early. Sometime during my restless sleep, I'd realized that Franklin's son Keith would also be required to attend the Black Christmas parade. Franklin usually did things like that with his family; if he planned to go, then he could keep an eye on Jimmy for me.

When I called, Franklin agreed to take Jimmy with them. I mentioned the problem with the Stones, not going into detail. He made me promise not to say anything to Althea, because losing her kids to the gangs was one of her greatest fears.

By 9:00 A.M., I had fed Jimmy and left him at Franklin's. Jimmy's tam was locked in my desk drawer, and it was going to stay there until I figured out what to do with it.

I had a lot of legwork to do before I picked up Jimmy at four o'clock. I hoped I could get it all in. I needed to answer Mrs. Foster's questions about her husband, and I needed to start with the photographer and the teenagers who had discovered the body. The newspapers had no idea who the teenagers were, and I didn't want to go to the police, not yet anyway.

But I was willing to bet that the photographer knew. Some of his photographs had clearly been taken before the police arrived. The same name and address was on the back of all of them. I assumed the name belonged to the photographer. He wasn't listed in the Chicago phone book, but that didn't mean much. I wasn't either, although I knew that when the next book came out, it would list the name Bill Grimshaw across from my phone number.

The morning was gray and overcast. The air had an icy crispness that made it an actual presence. A parade in this weather seemed ridiculous. At least it wasn't snowing.

Even though nothing was supposed to start until 10:00 A.M., people were already lined up on the parade route as I drove past. Most of them were wearing thick coats and huddled together against the cold.

I took the Expressway north. I figured the Expressway would be a quicker way to Rogers Park than dodging the parade route. It also kept me out of dangerous areas, where the mere presence of a black man in a rusted car would threaten the white residents.

More than any other place I'd lived, Chicago was a city of neighborhoods. Each one had its own character—and you could tell when you'd moved from one to another even though all you'd done was cross a street. It was almost as if invisible walls divided them, walls you'd learned to sense once you'd spent enough time in the city.

I'd been to Rogers Park only once, and that had been by accident. I'd been heading to a meeting in Uptown, which was just south and east of Rogers Park, and I'd gone a little too far west. Suddenly I found myself in a neighborhood with old, stately trees and once-elegant three-story apartment buildings that dated from the 1920s.

This time, I entered Rogers Park on purpose. The area was as well-tended as I remembered. The address on the back of the photographs was in West Rogers Park, and I was becoming familiar enough with Chicago's particular brand of segregation to know that I was heading into a Jewish neighborhood so old that it made Hyde Park look new.

The address was just off Howard, a two-story house that looked like it dated from the previous century. An ancient oak tree spread its roots onto the sidewalk, and the brown lawn was hidden beneath decaying unraked leaves.

A Studebaker without a spot of rust on its blue exterior sat in the driveway. The one-car garage door was open, revealing a maze of gardening equipment, children's forgotten toys, and rusting tools.

I parked in front of the oak. My heart was beating harder than I wanted it to. I felt out of place on this quiet street with its middle-class homes. Unlike other white neighborhoods in Chicago, no one watched me from the windows and I didn't get a sense of external threat. Instead, the feeling of unease came from me—and I didn't like it.

I got out of the car and headed up the walk, moving with purpose so that I didn't look like a drifter. I had dressed carefully that morning, knowing I was going to be talking with people from various parts of the city. I wore dark pants, a white dress shirt with a button-down collar, and an expensive sweater that Grace Kirkland, one of my neighbors, had given to me after her employer had told her to take it to Goodwill.

I had learned during the fall that dressing down slightly—no suit coat, no suit—made it easier to talk to whites. They didn't seem to think I was trying to step out of my place. I'd stopped wearing a jacket on interviews after I'd been searched by doormen more than once as I'd entered a building.

Someone had recently chipped ice off the steps; broken shards of it littered the ground beside the thin iron railing. The door to the enclosed porch was open, revealing stacks of newspapers and magazines, and boxes of old, mildewing books. Even though it was clear that visitors were supposed to go inside and knock on the main door, I didn't. Instead, I stayed outside the open door and rang the rusted doorbell.

A large chime echoed through the neighborhood. After a moment, the inside door opened. An elderly woman stood there, her right hand, clutching a handkerchief, pressed against her heart.

"You gave me a start, young man," she said, and I resisted the urge to smile. No one had used that tone with me in more than a decade.

"I'm sorry, ma'am."

"It's all right." She pulled the door wide. "Come in, come in. You must be one of Saul's friends."

I didn't move. Her friendliness had unsettled me more than her enmity would have. "Actually, I don't know Saul. But I would like to see him about some of his photographs."

"Well, I'd still like you to come in," she said in a tone that brooked no disagreement. "We're heating half of Chicago, and I simply can't afford it."

"Yes, ma'am." I stepped onto the enclosed porch. It smelled of mildew and wet newspapers. The screen door closed behind me.

She turned around and walked into the house. I had no choice but to follow her, pulling the main door closed. The house had been decorated fifty years ago and not much had changed. A console television stood next to a claw-footed couch, and a transistor radio sat on top of a bookshelf. Otherwise, I saw little evidence of the 1960s in the main room.

"Come on," she said, heading into the kitchen. "I don't bite."

"No, ma'am," I said as gently as I could. "But have you considered that I might?"

She laughed, a youthful sound that made me see how beautiful she must have been decades ago. She was lovely now, with skin as fine as parchment and brown eyes that twinkled with merriment.

"I've never been afraid of anyone, young man, and if that gets me in trouble someday, so be it. I've had a good long life." She waited until I joined her in the kitchen and then she closed the kitchen door behind me.

This room was hot where the others hadn't been, and I realized she was conserving on her heating bill by keeping the heating ducts open only in the room she was in.

"I suppose you should tell me who you are just in case someone asks." She stopped at the stove and picked up an ancient coffeepot. "Want some?"

"No, thank you, ma'am."

"Well?" she asked and I blinked, realizing I wanted to tell

her my real name. I hadn't felt this comfortable with a white woman before. She made it seem easy.

"I'm Bill Grimshaw, ma'am. I'm here about some photographs that your son—"

"Grandson," she said.

"—left with the *Chicago Defender*."

"Well, of course you are," she said. "I knew you weren't with the *Tribune*."

Her eyes twinkled even more at that and she swept her hand toward the table. "Are you sure I can't offer you something?"

"No, ma'am. I really can't stay." I found I was oddly flattered by her attention. It wasn't the needy attention of a lonely person, but the warmth of someone who was interested in others.

"Are you going to buy something from my Saul?"

"No, ma'am. I'm just following up on a story." I knew that made me sound like a reporter, and I didn't care. It was easier to let people assume they knew what I was doing than to actually explain my work. "I'm interested in some photographs he took in Washington Park."

The smile left her face and she nodded. "The murder."

"Yes," I said.

"It upset him something awful." She leaned on a kitchen chair as if she suddenly needed support. "I told him he has to get used to that sort of thing if he wants to be a real reporter, but he said the best reporters were still people, too. Is that right, Mr. Grimshaw?"

"That's a hard one, ma'am."

"It is," she said. "He doesn't want to be just any reporter. He wants to break that really big story, be a man who makes a difference. I say there are rungs to the ladder, and he just shakes his head. Says all he needs is something to hang his hat on. Is that how you got started, Mr. Grimshaw?"

"My experiences aren't typical, ma'am."

"Mrs. Weisman," she said. "You ma'am me and I feel a hundred years old."

I smiled because she sounded so annoyed. "When will Saul be back, Mrs. Weisman?"

"Who knows?" she said. "He's an adult now, makes his own schedule. We barely see each other."

"Perhaps I could call him, then."

"Perhaps," she said. "But it might be easier if you just go to the speech."

"The speech?" I sounded like a parrot, but I felt a bit like Alice in Wonderland. "What speech?"

"Oh, I don't know. Some young man who's making quite a ruckus with his political statements, I understand. Saul's taken a fancy to him, wants photographs, a record. Says it'll be important." She sighed. "Young men are always making a ruckus, it seems to me. If it's not about one thing, it's another."

I was about to speak, but she raised a finger at me. "Don't yes-ma'am me."

"No, ma'am," I said, and we both laughed.

She smiled at me. "I like you, Mr. Grimshaw. You can come back here any time. You don't need my Saul as an excuse."

"Thank you," I said.

"He's at the University of Illinois Circle Campus. You know where that is?"

"Yes, I do."

"I don't know what building. Sometimes these speeches, they happen outside. But it's cold for that. You'll have to look for signs."

"Advertising a young man making a ruckus?" I asked, unable to resist.

"A bit of the devil in you, Mr. Grimshaw," she said, smiling. Then her smile faded. "The speech is on civil rights. The speaker belongs to one of the splinter groups that I can't keep track of. The ones in berets."

"The Black Panthers?" I asked, feeling cold. The last time I'd had any contact with the Panthers, it had been in Memphis.

"That's the group." Those sharp eyes must have caught something in my expression. "I take it you don't approve."

I shrugged. "Sometimes people go too far."

"That they do," Mrs. Weisman said. "But my Saul is quite taken with them. Says they're not what they seem. And I trust him. He's a good boy who thinks about things."

I made myself smile and nod, since I couldn't disagree with her about a boy I'd never met. But I knew that sometimes people thought too much about things and rationalized experiences that only served to harm someone else.

Everything I'd heard about the Panthers I disliked, from their fake military bearing to their off-the-pigs attitude. I didn't want to go into a Panther enclave searching for a nice Jewish boy, but I would.

I'd been in worse places. Just not voluntarily.

The University of Illinois Chicago Circle Campus stood just west of the Loop. The campus was only three years old, the result of years of campaigning to get a University of Illinois branch in Chicago proper.

To make way for the university, the Daley regime had destroyed one of the city's most racially mixed—and renowned—neighborhoods, the place where famous Chicagoan Jane Addams had defeated one of the city's worst slums with her innovative Hull House. Hull House itself had to be razed to make way for the new university, and only the building's façade remained.

I had learned all of this from Franklin, who had taken one of his night classes there—under protest because he had fought the destruction of the neighborhood.

The university and the expressways formed a sterile barrier between the Loop and the black neighborhoods to the west. Fences and walls rose all around the campus, making it look more like a modern prison than a place of learning. All that was missing were barbed wire and the guard tower.

I parked near the thirty-three-story concrete monolith called University Hall and walked into the center of campus. Someone had planted young trees that weren't thriving well in the Illinois climate. Raised sidewalks, flanked by chain-link fences meant to keep undesirables from getting in and students from falling to the ground below, led to newly constructed buildings, done in a modern and somewhat tasteless steel-and-concrete design.

Except for a few students hurrying toward the physical plant, the campus seemed empty.

There were no signs anywhere, no street lamps with posters stapled to them, no wallboards with papers fluttering in the breeze. I'd never been in such an empty and unscholarly atmosphere. In the distance, the buildings of the Loop rose like ghosts in the morning's gray light.

It had gotten colder, or maybe it just seemed that way. I shoved my hands in my pockets, wishing I had taken my coat out of the car, and hurried down the sidewalk, looking for signs of life.

I finally caught it—two young men with afros, standing outside a large, curiously flat building that seemed to go on forever. They stood near a concrete column, smoking cigarettes and having a serious discussion.

"Panthers still here?" I asked as I hurried toward them, pretending I was late.

"Yeah," one of the men said, cigarette bobbing with the movement of his lips. He inclined his head toward the door and I nodded my thanks.

The door had been propped open, a piece of wood jammed beneath the steel bottom. Even the floor was concrete, purposefully bare and ugly. A carpet might have improved the look, but a carpet would get dirty over time. Concrete looked dirty from the beginning.

A male voice echoed in the hallway, faint but insistent, speaking with the rhythm of the best Baptist ministers. I recognized the cadence, but couldn't make out the words. I followed the sound around a corner and into a room with double blond-wood doors, a sliver of glass running down the center of each.

These doors were closed. I pushed on one and slipped inside as applause and shouting erupted, and found myself in a whole new world. The room was full of people on their feet, some shouting, "Panther Power!" Others were just cheering.

There had to be a hundred people or more in a room

designed for far fewer. Most were black, but some whites were scattered throughout, surprising me. A number of men were wearing black leather jackets and black berets, but those who didn't had bushy afros.

A lot of women were scattered throughout, most wearing scarves over afros that matched the men's. It seemed, from my vantage, that I was the oldest person there.

"So we say," an amplified male voice shouted over the cheers. The cheering faded and the crowd sat back down, and I found myself staring at someone I didn't expect. A young man, dressed like I was—white shirt, expensive sweater, and dark pants—clutched a microphone and paced.

Behind him, men wearing black leather jackets and berets stood with their arms crossed, guns strapped ostentatiously over their shoulders.

"So we say," the young man said again. He was tall and broad-shouldered, with a clean-shaven face and shorter hair than any other black male in the room. "We've always said at the Black Panther Party that they can do anything they want to us."

He had the thick accent particular to this region of Illinois and he spoke fast, like most Northerners. But something in that deep voice was compelling, pulling me forward.

"We might not be back."

"Right on!" someone yelled, just as if they were in church.

"I might not be back."

There were mumbles.

"I might be in jail."

Moans.

"I might be anywhere."

Sudden silence. The crowd looked worried.

"But when I leave, you can remember I said with the last words on my lips, 'I'm a revolutionary.' And you're going to have to keep saying that."

The crowd murmured, "I'm a revolutionary."

His voice rose. "You're going to have to say, 'I am the pro-letariat. I am the people. I am not the pig.'"

53

Voices repeated his words, softly, and people swayed like they were at a revival meeting.

"You're going to have to make a distinction." He leaned toward the crowd. I leaned toward him, as everyone else did. "And the people are going to have to attack the pigs."

I found myself nodding even though I disagreed.

"The people are going to have to stand up against the pigs."

"Amen!" someone shouted.

"That's what the Panthers are doing. That's what the Panthers are doing all over the world."

His presence seemed to fill the room, and it seemed like he was talking directly to me. I'd had that experience with only a few other speakers before, and only once with a speaker that young.

Martin, when he gave a sermon at Boston University. I'd gone and listened to him speak just before I left for Korea, and I knew he had a gift. An amazing gift to rally and unite people behind whatever cause he wanted them to hear.

This young man, this teenager, had the same gift. And he was using it for a completely different purpose.

"Now," he said, lowering his voice, bringing down the level of emotion, "we got to talk about the main man. The main man in the Black Panther Party. Your Minister of Defense and mine, Huey P. Newton."

I made myself turn away and study the crowd, looking at the whites. Most of them sat in groups of two and three, as enthralled as everyone else. Only one sat alone.

He was leaning against the back wall. Instead of guns strapped around his shoulders, he had cameras—two of them that looked as if they weighed more than he did. His hair was as bushy as some of the afros in the room, but his curls exploded from his head as if he were a cartoon character who had put his finger in a light socket. He was wearing a blue sweater and a white turtleneck, and on the floor, tangled around his feet, was a thick jacket—the kind that a guy carried with him only because his grandmother had nagged him to do so.

". . . we say let him go. Let him free . . ."

I made my way around others sitting on the floor and leaning against the back wall. Most of them were so focused on the speaker that they didn't seem to notice me. A few glared because I had interrupted their enjoyment of the speech.

". . . this is our relentless demand . . ."

I made it to the photographer's side. He and I were probably the only people in the room not looking at the speaker. The photographer's head was bowed and he was writing furiously in a pocket-sized spiral notebook. I was half a head taller than he was and able to look down at his cramped handwriting, but I couldn't make out the words.

". . . as the vanguard leader, he took us down the correct road of revolution . . ."

"You Saul Epstein?" I whispered.

The photographer whipped his head up so fast I thought he was going to hurt himself. "Who wants to know?"

"I'd like to talk to you for a few minutes outside if I could."

He frowned at me, gave me a once-over that made it clear he didn't think I belonged. "About what?"

"Some of your photographs."

"Shhh," a woman beside me hissed.

Epstein's pale cheeks flushed bright red. He glanced at the stage as if the speaker had heard her. But the young man was on the other side of the room, using the microphone to punctuate his point.

". . . Marxist-Leninist theory. We put it into practice . . ."

"What pictures?" Epstein whispered.

"Some you took in November. You left them at the *Defender* offices."

"Shhh!" the woman said again, louder this time.

". . . that's what the Black Panther Party is all about . . ."

Epstein flipped his notebook closed and tucked it in his back pocket. He bent down to grab his coat, his cameras swinging perilously close to the floor. Then he wove his way out of the room, looking over his shoulder every few seconds to make certain I was following.

". . . we say All Power to the People. Black Power to Black

People. Brown Power to Brown People, and Red Power to Red People, Yellow Power to Yellow People . . ."

We reached the door. He pushed it open and we slipped through.

". . . and even White Power to White People . . ."

The door closed and the voice became indistinct. I could still feel the effects of it tingling through me, the way it drew me toward an argument I didn't want to hear.

"Who was that?" I asked Epstein as we headed down the hall to the main doors.

He looked at me as if I hadn't recognized Muhammad Ali. "That's Fred Hampton. You don't know who Fred Hampton is, man?"

I did know. I just had never seen him before. The newspapers didn't cover the Panthers if they could avoid it, and no one had given him airtime. I'd only heard some of my neighbors talking about him, and I'd thought he was much older.

"So that's the chairman of the Illinois Panthers," I said. "Is he even out of high school?"

"Don't mock, man. He's cool and smart. You should listen to him sometime."

"I just did," I said. "He was talking about killing cops."

"No he wasn't," Epstein said. "If you'd really paid attention, you'd know he was talking about self-defense. That was the original name of the party, don't you know? The Black Panther Party for Self-defense."

I hadn't, and I really didn't care. I wasn't interested in militant politics. I wanted to know more about Louis Foster's death.

"Let's talk here," I said, stopping beside a built-in alcove. A long seat, made of wood, topped the shortened brick wall. Behind it, more wood hung in a decorative pattern. Dying plants clung to the dirt behind the wooden seat—obviously placed there as decoration and then forgotten. A cylindrical ashtray, filled with sand and cigarette butts, had been placed within easy arm's reach of the alcove.

We sat down. Epstein dumped his coat beside him, not caring that it trailed in the dirt. "So you're with the *Defender*?"

He didn't look at me as he spoke, but I could sense the eagerness. He was looking for a break, any kind of break, and he had come with me because he thought I would provide it.

"No," I said.

He raised his shadowed gray eyes toward me. "Then how did you know about my photographs?"

"I'm working with Mrs. Louis Foster."

It took a moment for the name to register. When it did, his skin grew even paler. He shook his head. "I'm so sorry, man."

I didn't know if he thought I was a relative or a friend. I didn't care. I wanted the information from him and that was all. "I need you to tell me about that day."

He fiddled with one of the cameras. It was expensive, high-end, a professional's camera. "How'd you know I'd be here?"

"Your grandmother."

For the first time, he looked fierce. "You didn't bother her, did you?"

"No," I said. "Why would you think that?"

A flush rose from beneath his turtleneck. He shrugged. "How'd you find her?"

"You put an address on the back of your photographs. I assumed that's where you lived. Turned out I was right." I didn't try to keep the sarcasm from my voice.

Shouts, whistles, and the stomping of feet came from the room we'd just left, followed by applause.

"I don't get it," he said. "If you don't work for the *Defender*, how'd you see my photographs?"

"Mrs. Foster can be very persuasive."

"And how are you involved?" His questions were perceptive and cautious. I realized then that he was older than he seemed.

"I'm looking into her husband's death, since no one else is."

"You're some kind of private eye?"

"Something like that," I said.

"I don't believe I caught your name."

"That's because I didn't throw it." I extended my right hand, willing to make this a meeting of equals. "Bill Grimshaw."

"Saul Epstein," he said as he took my hand, his innate

politeness reiterating what we'd already established. "What do you need to know?"

"When did you get to the park?"

He frowned. "Just before dawn."

"Why?"

"The park's busy that time of day. It's amazing what you can record with a telephoto lens."

He said this last so softly I could barely hear him. People were pouring into the hallway, gesturing, talking about the speech, seeming excited.

"What are you trying to record, Mr. Epstein?"

He shrugged. "I'm a photographer. I get what I can."

"Your grandmother says you're looking for a big story."

"Every reporter does."

"I thought you were a photographer."

His gaze met mine, held it for a moment, and then he said, "What do you want, Grimshaw?"

No "Mister" and the tone had changed, as if he could push me away just by being rude.

"I told you," I said. "I need to know about that day. I'm trying to find out what happened to Louis Foster."

"Then you don't need to know about me, do you?"

"It would help," I said.

Most of the crowd from the speech was filling the hallway. We were speaking louder and louder just so we could hear each other. No one seemed to notice us. One young man flicked a cigarette butt into the ashtray without even looking our way.

"I'm freelance," he said.

"I gathered that."

He ignored my comment, watching the crowd as if he were searching for a face. "I got some nibbles from some major New York magazines for pieces on Chicago."

"Pieces that require you to go to the South Side?"

"A few." He ran a hand over his camera. "They want profiles of Chicago during the year after the Convention, to see if it made permanent changes."

The Democratic National Convention had made an impact nationwide in a year that had had a dozen amazing events. The Walker Report, an official government study that called the Convention a "police riot," had been issued on the first of December. In Chicago, Daley dismissed the entire report, but the rest of the country was using it as a spearhead for debate.

"You must have some credentials to get a gig like that," I said.

"I do." He sat up straighter. "Real credentials, not hippy-dippy ones. I've been a stringer for Reuters, had some pieces in the *New York Times*, sold some photographs to *Life*. I was offered a job at *Look*, but I like picking my own stories. That way, you have a chance to stumble on something no one else has."

"What have you stumbled on here?"

He shook his head slightly. "Nice try, but I'm not convinced you are who you say you are. You got I.D.?"

"I don't have press credentials. I'm not a reporter. I told you that. Whatever your great story is, it's safe with me."

The crowd had thinned. A few stragglers passed us, some looking our way as if searching for someone.

"That morning," he said firmly, making sure I knew he wasn't going to tell me what he was working on, "the park was pretty quiet. It was cold—the beginning of that damp cold that lets you know winter is getting serious."

I nodded, encouraging him, and at the same time, wondering if he was quoting from something he'd written.

"I was changing my film when I heard shrieking—it wasn't screaming, you know. There's a difference."

I wanted to ask him why he was changing the film. What had he been shooting before the screams began? But I figured he could tell his story, then I'd ask more questions.

"These kids come running past me. They couldn't've been more than thirteen, fourteen. They see me and one of them grabs my arm. 'Mister, there's a guy. He needs help.' "

His words had the polished familiarity of a story that had

59

been told a hundred times. A cop would have interrupted the flow, but I didn't. Sometimes I found the stories as revealing as the truth.

"So I let them take me to the guy. Big guy, like you, on his side in front of a tree, not too far from where I'd been sitting. Only, he was beyond help. That was clear right from the start. I sent the kids to call the cops, and then I started taking pictures."

I was just beginning to take in the details. His description was interesting. Most white guys would have mentioned that Foster was black. Had he avoided it out of sensitivity toward me?

"How many pictures did you take?" I asked.

"My last three rolls. I left the best ones with the *Defender*."

"And the *Tribune* and the *Daily News*, and the *Sun-Times*, right?" I asked.

He grinned. "Hey, you go legit first."

I winced. The *Defender* was legit, at least in my community. "Do you still have the other photographs?"

"Sure."

"May I see them?"

"I suppose it wouldn't hurt," he said.

A woman stopped beside him and put her hand on his shoulder. Her skin was mahogany dark, her lips full, and her hair in the beginnings of an afro. It was thin on top and wispy on the sides, the way women's hair got when they'd left the straightener in too long or burned it beneath a hot iron. She wore a pale pink mohair sweater, dark blue pants, and high-heeled boots.

She smiled at Epstein. The look warmed her face, giving her a radiance that she didn't have in repose. "You didn't stay."

He shook his head and nodded toward me. "Been talking to Mr. Grimshaw here about that dead guy in the park."

I noted that he had used the "Mister" this time.

"Oh?" Her gaze turned toward me. Her dark eyes were as intelligent as Hampton's. "What's your interest?"

"I'm investigating for the family."

She nodded. I didn't have to explain to her. "Learning any-thing?"

"I just started."

"He found me," Epstein said.

"You gotta show him the pictures," she said.

"He has those."

"Not all of them."

"I was promised the rest," I said.

"Good." She shoved Epstein aside with her hips, sat next to him, and then draped her legs across his lap. He flushed, but didn't move her. After a moment, he rested a hand on her thigh.

The ease between them made me uncomfortable and she knew it. I made myself look away from his hand.

"Were you with him?" I asked.

"All night." She gave me another radiant smile. "But I stayed in bed when he went out into the cold morning air."

"Elaine!" Epstein's flush grew deeper.

She was watching me closely. I wondered how much of her relationship with Epstein was designed to provoke other people and how much of it was just for her.

"So you don't know anything about the murder," I said.

"Only what Saul has told me."

I nodded and turned my gaze back to Epstein. His face was bright red, the embarrassment painfully obvious. His hand had moved off Elaine's thigh and was toying with the cameras again.

"Tell me about the teenagers."

"I did," he said. "About thirteen, fourteen. They were scared."

"What did they look like? What were they wearing? Why were they there?"

His face closed down, and I realized I was onto the reason he was in the park.

"Gang kids," Elaine said.

"Goddammit, Elaine," Epstein said.

She shrugged and leaned into him. "You may as well tell him. The cops never bothered to ask you."

"They didn't follow up?"

Epstein shook his head. "I kept expecting them to, you know. I gave them all my information, but no one called. No one ever got back to me. I watched the papers, figuring maybe they'd solved it, but I never saw anything."

"They didn't solve it," I said, "and they don't seem to be trying. That's why Mrs. Foster asked for my help."

Elaine's face lit up. "You one of those detectives the cops been harassing?"

The police had been stopping employees of black private-detective agencies and arresting them if they had guns, even if they had licenses for those guns. A lot of cops just sat outside the agencies waiting for someone to leave—usually headed for a security job—and then arrested them once they got outside the Black Belt. It was so egregious that the agencies were thinking of banding together and filing a complaint with the state.

I had looked at the entire affair as one more reason why I didn't have an official license.

"I don't carry a gun," I said, although I had one. I kept it locked in the glove box of my car.

"I thought all you guys did," she said.

"Sorry to disappoint." I looked at Epstein. "Did you get the teenagers' names?"

"Yeah." He shifted forward, unsettling Elaine, who took her legs off his lap. He took the notebook out of his back pocket, thumbed through the pages, and stopped near the front. "Names and addresses. I'll copy them for you."

"Thanks," I said.

He wrote the names down on another sheet of paper. I watched him. Elaine stared at the floor as if the conversation were already over.

I took the moment to study her face. There were premature lines and shadows in it, and I got a sense that she was not as content as she pretended.

When Epstein finished, he handed me the paper. I didn't look at it, but I didn't pocket it either. I didn't want to give any signals that we were done. "So your story's about gangs."

"Mostly," he said.

"The Blackstone Rangers?"

"They call themselves the Black P. Stone Nation now."

"Some of them do," I said. "They're pretty dangerous."

"I know," he said. "I'm careful."

"What were you watching? A drug deal?"

"Just a meet between rivals trying to broker a truce." He sounded sad that I knew what he was doing.

"I'd like those photos, too," I said.

"I don't think so," he said. "They're part of the story."

"How about you let me look at them when I pick up the remains of those three rolls?"

"You don't give up, do you?"

"No," I said.

"You want to share what you learn with me?"

"Maybe," I said. "If it'll do any good."

"Who decides that?"

"Me," I said.

Elaine smiled to herself and leaned against the wall, watching me sideways.

"You think it was a gang hit?" I asked.

"No," Epstein said. "That's not how they do things. They got a whole system, usually, and they leave the body somewhere more obvious. That part of the park isn't anyone's special turf. If he was a hit, he'd've been left on the side of the street. You know, like maybe Sixty-third if he was a warning for the Stones, or west of Cottage Grove for the Disciples. But he was just there by that tree—and it wasn't messy. Gang killings're usually messy, just for a lesson."

"And he was too old." Elaine was still studying me. "Like you."

"You don't think he was just in the wrong place at the wrong time and the gangs took him out?"

"Stones don't let that happen anywhere near their turf, man," Epstein said. "Killings happen for a reason. They send a message. All they have to do with a guy like that is scare the shit out of him, maybe beat him up. They don't need to kill him."

That had been my sense of it, too. "So who was out of place in the park that morning?"

"You mean besides me?" Epstein asked.

"Yeah," I said.

"No one so far as I could tell."

"Did the kids call the cops or did you?"

"I told you," he said. "The kids did."

"Gang kids?"

"I didn't say that they were." He tilted his head toward Elaine. "She did."

She wasn't paying attention. She was staring down the hall. "There's Fred."

And without a good-bye, she got up and walked away. Epstein watched her go, his face a painful mix of desire and wariness.

The speaker and his bodyguards had stopped near the doorway. They were talking with some people I didn't recognize. Elaine joined the group, leaned forward and caught Hampton's arm. He gave her a dismissive smile, moved away slightly, and continued the conversation.

"So they're not gang kids," I said, "and they did call the cops."

"Why're you having trouble with that?" Epstein asked.

"Just trying to get the story straight, that's all."

"They're not gang kids. They did call the cops. And it took a while for the cops to get there, too. I sent the kids back twice."

"They came back to the body?"

He sighed and nodded. I finally had his attention. "I made them stay away as best I could. They didn't need to see that. But I get the sense they'd seen a lot more than that over the years."

"How?"

He shrugged. "Just some things they were saying, you know, like how it was amazing a guy could be dead and not be bloody."

"Do you think they touched the body?"

"No. They kept their distance."

"Did you touch it? Move it?"

He grimaced. "What do you think I am, man?"

"Have you ever seen any other body like that?"

His eyes narrowed. "It was my very first. Are we done yet?"

"Not yet," I said. "You only took three rolls even though you were alone with the body for some time?"

"I ran out of film." He said this slowly, as if explaining to a stupid person. But I had a very real sense that he was lying. Why would he lie about the number of rolls he shot of the body?

"How much film do you usually carry?"

"Enough," he said.

"Cooperate with me," I said. "I'm not the cops, I'm not a reporter out to get your story. All I want to do is find out what happened to Louis Foster."

He glanced at Elaine. She had moved as close to Hampton as she could, her head tilted back as she listened to him speak. But he didn't seem to notice her at all.

"I got eight rolls from that morning. Most are pretty useless to you."

"Let me judge that," I said.

"I'm not letting you have them," he said. "You can just look at them."

"Fine with me. Tomorrow afternoon suit you? At your grandmother's?"

"I'll be there at three," he said. "If you're late, I'm gone."

"All right." I was willing to wait. He might be more cooperative at his grandmother's house, without the distraction of Elaine.

Epstein stood and started to walk away, his gaze focused on Elaine. She saw him and smiled at him, extending her hand. He put up a finger, turned around, and came back for his coat.

As he grabbed it, he paused. "Look," he said to me, "I'm really sorry that guy is dead. But I told you everything I know."

"No," I said as I stood. "You told me everything you think you know."

He looked at me, surprised.

"See you tomorrow," I said, and left him.

FIVE

The addresses Saul Epstein gave me were on the University of Chicago side of Washington Park. I slowly made my way back toward my own neighborhood, almost as if I'd planned my route in advance.

When I got south of Thirty-fifth, I found myself in a traffic jam on the Dan Ryan Expressway. As I looked over the freeway walls toward the city, I saw crowds of people moving along the sidewalks and cars backed up on the side roads. Apparently the parade had ended.

The afternoon was still gray, and the clouds hung thick overhead. They seemed heavy with moisture, but so far, nothing had happened. I was beginning to think this was what Chicago's winters were like—continually overcast, always promising but never really delivering serious snow.

I exited the Dan Ryan near the Amphitheater and headed into the heaviest traffic. Cars sat bumper to bumper, some in the middle of the road, while people walked by, laughing and having a good time. Several adults carried children on their shoulders. Others held hands like a human chain, so that no one would get lost.

I didn't see Jimmy, Franklin, or any of the Grimshaw children, although I doubted I would this far north on the route. I also didn't see any red tams. Maybe the Stones had stayed away from the parade.

It took fifteen minutes for the traffic to clear. I continued toward the lake, then turned south, finally ending up on the correct street.

The block was filled with single-family dwellings, nice houses with what had to be, in the summer, nice lawns. Even now, the yards were well-kept, leaves raked and the grass clipped close before the winter began. I hadn't expected it; I had thought that the neighborhood would be full of apartment buildings like the one I lived in.

These streets were empty. Apparently, they were far enough from the parade route that they didn't get the traffic or the pedestrians. Most of the houses looked occupied: cars parked in driveways, lights on inside despite the early hour. One house, in the middle of the block, already had its Christmas decorations up. A battered, white-flocked sign wished everyone who passed "Happy Holidays."

I squinted at the addresses, most of them marked clearly beside the doorbells. The numbers moved logically, unlike in some parts of the city, and I found the first address with ease. It belonged to a large brown house on a corner lot. Even though the second address had a different street name, I realized that the houses were directly across from each other. The boys were neighbors.

A woman stood on the porch of the second house as if she were waiting for someone. She wore a heavy, floor-length sweater over a pantsuit. The sweater was unbuttoned and she clutched it closed with one hand. The other hand was cupped at her side.

I parked the car in front of the house, checked Epstein's crabbed handwriting, then slipped the note into my pants pocket. Then I opened the car door and slid out.

"Excuse me, ma'am," I said. "I'm looking for Gus Foley."

Her eyes seemed pale in the thin afternoon light. "You the police?"

The question surprised me. Why would she think the police would show up in front of her home in a rusted Impala? "No, ma'am."

She grunted softly, an eloquent comment of disgust. "What do you want with August?"

It took me a second to realize that Gus was a nickname for August. "I'm following up on the death of Louis Foster. I understand your son found the body."

"He and his friend Van, yes."

I had continued walking forward. I was most of the way up the sidewalk toward the porch. She hadn't moved.

"I'd like to talk to one or both of them if I could," I said.

"But you're not a police officer."

"No, ma'am."

"Who do you work for?"

"The victim's family, ma'am. The police aren't doing much investigation."

"Don't I know it." She sighed. "The boys are in the basement. I'll take you there."

That surprised me, too. I figured she'd bring them outside, if she would let me speak to them at all.

From her cupped hand, she flicked a cigarette over the porch rail. I put out the still-smoldering tip as I mounted the steps. She waited until I was beside her before opening the front door.

The house smelled of lemon-scented furniture polish. A bouquet of dried flowers stood on an occasional table beside the door. A curved wooden staircase, leading to an upstairs floor and to the basement, was on my right. To my left was the neatest living room I'd ever seen in an inhabited house.

"Down there," she said, gesturing with her thumb. As she moved, she released the scent of fresh cigarette smoke like perfume.

The steps were bare wood, polished to a gleam. The banister shone, too, and I didn't touch it as I walked down. A deep and irregular *tick-tick* greeted me as I went farther; it took me a moment to recognize the sound of a Ping-Pong game in progress.

The basement was another world. An old ratty carpet covered the floor. A round leather ottoman, at least twenty years old, was pushed against the paneled wall. The matching chair had a split across the back that someone had tried to repair with cellophane tape.

A couch, covered with several mismatched blankets, was pushed against the far wall, and a black-and-white television nattered to itself from a crudely built-in bar. The Ping-Pong table wasn't visible until I was nearly to the bottom of the staircase.

The table dominated the room. The furniture had been pushed aside to accommodate it. Two teenage boys, still reed-thin and not yet into their growth, concentrated on the match. Both stood as far from the table as possible and gripped their paddles like weapons.

"Boys," the woman said from behind me. "This gentleman would like to talk to you."

It was then I realized that we hadn't even gone through the ritual of getting each other's names.

The boy closest to the couch glanced up and the Ping-Pong ball sailed past him.

"Mo-om," he said, making the word two syllables long to show his irritation.

"You can take a break," she said.

"Yeah," the other boy said. "You need one. That's two in a row I got."

"We replay this point," said the first boy, who had to be Gus.

"Nope," said the second. "You're not supposed to lose concentration."

"Boys," the woman said.

Gus looked at me. His eyes were as pale as his mother's, and I realized with a start that they were blue. They gave his face an artificial cast, his dark skin making his eyes seem almost pure white in the right light.

"Who're you?" he asked, a question his mother had

neglected. She remained on the middle step, watching, as if she weren't allowed in the basement.

I walked toward him. The basement smelled of mildew and unwashed clothes. "Bill Grimshaw. I work for the family of Louis Foster."

"The dead guy." The other boy breathed the words, almost reverently.

I glanced at him, gave him what I hoped was a reassuring look. "Yes."

"What do you do for them?" Gus had crossed his arms, his eyes narrowed. He stood straighter, as if he were prepared to defend his home against me.

"I'm investigating Mr. Foster's death."

"You a cop?" the second boy asked.

"No."

"Why'd you come here?" Gus asked.

"Because the police haven't," I said.

"How'd you know?" the second boy asked.

"Are you Van?" I asked.

He nodded. "Hey, you're, like, Mannix, only black, right?"

I smiled at the way he was trying to put me in context. "Something like that."

"There's no such thing as a private eye in real life," Gus said. "That's just TV."

"Actually," I said, "there are a lot of private eyes in Chicago."

"Really? Neato." Van squeezed his way between the Ping-Pong table and the wall so he could come close to me. "You got like a gun and everything?"

"I don't carry a gun," I said, and I heard Gus's mother let out a small breath.

"If you're not a cop, we don't got to talk to you," Gus said.

"No, you don't have to," I said, "but it would be nice if you did."

"Why?" He raised his chin. I got the sense he didn't like looking up at me.

"Because no one is investigating his death except me." I glanced at Van, keeping him in the conversation. "His family would like to know what happened to him."

"We just found him," Gus said. "We had nothing to do with it."

"I know that," I said. "All I want to do is find out what you remember."

Gus turned his head toward Van and studied him for a moment. I was tempted to look, too, but didn't. I didn't want to seem too eager.

"Mom," Gus said after a moment. "Can we have some of that cider?"

"Whatever you have to say to Mr. Grimshaw, you can say in front of me." She had one hand on the railing, but she had come no farther down the stairs. "He's a stranger, and your father would be upset if I left you alone with him."

I bit back irritation. Too bad her caution had finally arrived.

"He's not my father," Gus said.

"It's okay," Van said. "We weren't supposed to be in the park. We already got grounded for it. We can't get into more trouble."

I frowned. "I thought you lived across the street."

"He does," Gus's mother said. "We grounded them together. The friendship's a good one, and we want to encourage it, even if they do make mistakes."

I understood what she meant, but probably wouldn't have before Jimmy. The memory of that red tam locked in my desk floated through my mind, and I pushed the thought away.

"When did you get to the park?" I felt awkward, still standing at the bottom of the stairs. Van was six inches too close to me, and Gus was too far away. All of us stood, like people posing for a portrait.

"About eight," Gus said.

"Early on a Saturday."

He shrugged.

"What were you doing there?" I asked.

"Hanging out," Gus said.

"There's this girl Gus likes," Van said. "She lives across the park. We were—"

"Shut up," Gus snapped.

"August," his mother said, her tone warning.

"It's all right," I said. The vehemence of Gus's response was confirmation of everything Van had said. "Tell me what happened when you got to the park."

"Nothing," Gus said. "We were just crossing it."

"Then I saw this foot," Van said. "The shoe, actually, hanging there. I thought it was weird, so we go around and—"

"There's the dead guy." Gus's pale gaze turned to me. "Van starts screaming like a baby—"

"You screamed, too," Van said.

"—and we take off running until we see this guy, the photographer. He's the one who told you about us, isn't he? Asshole."

"August," his mother said again.

"He is, Mom. He said he wouldn't tell anyone who we were."

"He said he wouldn't tell the cops who we were," Van said.

"Why not?" I asked.

"Cops like white people better," Gus said. "Or haven't you noticed?"

I didn't answer that. "Then what?"

"Van takes him over to the dead guy."

"You didn't want to go?"

"He was dead," Gus said. "There was nothing we could do."

"You didn't know that," Van said, with the indignation of a thousand arguments.

"Yeah, I did."

"How?" I asked.

"I seen a dead guy before."

His mother sat down on the stairs and rested her elbows on her knees, her hands covering her mouth.

"Really?" I asked. "Where?"

"Woodlawn," he said. "Near the Castle Church. We used to go there."

The First Presbyterian Church in Woodlawn. "The Castle Church" was the Blackstone Rangers' nickname for it.

"You saw the dead guy at a funeral?" I asked, being deliberately naïve.

"No." Gus's voice remained the same but his eyes were bleak. "This kid I went to school with. Someone shot him. They stuck his tam in his mouth. It was weird, all that yellow cloth poking out."

"Yellow?" I asked, expecting to hear red.

"The Vice Lords." Gus's mother sounded tired. "The boy wore his hat in the wrong neighborhood."

"Yeah." Gus spit out the word. "That's what all the grown-ups think."

"What do you think?"

"I think he was carrying a message. Then they left him on the Gaza Strip as a warning."

"The Gaza Strip?" I looked at Gus's mother.

"Sixty-fifth and Woodlawn," she said. "It's the dividing line between the Disciples and the Stones. Or it used to be."

There was history here, in this family, that was just below the surface. Van was looking down at his feet.

"We got out of there just in time, I think." Her gaze met her son's.

He ignored her. "Skin looks different when you're dead. Like it's not real. That's what this Foster guy looked like, even though there was no blood."

"So you wanted to leave."

He nodded. "But Van didn't believe he was dead. So he gets this white guy—"

"His name was Saul." Van still sounded defensive.

"—and takes him over. The guy looks like he's gonna puke. Then he tells us to call the cops. Like it'll do any good."

"Did you?" I asked.

"Yeah," he said. "Twice. I gave the white guy's address the

second time, like I was from that neighborhood and just stumbled on the body, and they showed up right after that."

Van twirled his paddle. Gus's mother watched her son.

"What did the police do?" I asked.

"Looked around. Asked stupid questions."

"They wanted to know what gang we were in," Van said.

"Like we would've told them that," Gus said.

"They're not in a gang," his mother said.

"I know." My tone was gentle, but dismissive. I didn't look at her. I continued to concentrate on the boys. "What else did the cops want to know?"

"If we knew the guy. If we'd seen the mugging. I don't know how they knew it was a mugging. I mean, you couldn't even see any blood. I think if a guy got shot in a mugging, there'd be blood."

"He wasn't shot," I said. "He was knifed."

I had Gus's attention for the first time. "Then there should have been more blood."

"I didn't say he was in a knife fight."

"Was he still alive, Mister?" Van asked, his voice small. "I mean, should we have got him to the hospital? I thought maybe we should."

I shook my head. "He'd been dead for hours."

"The skin," Gus said to Van.

"What else did the cops do?"

"Made us go home," Van said.

"They said they were going to come talk to us, but they never did." Gus looked angriest about that. He probably was. In anticipation of a police visit that had never come, he'd probably confessed to his parents that he'd gone to the park.

"Anything else about that morning stand out?"

"What do you mean?" Van asked.

"Besides the body, was there anything unusual in the park?"

"The white guy," Van said.

"The photographer," I said.

"No." Gus rolled his eyes. "He's there all the time. He's

seeing some girl. She's got an apartment near the park."

"They spent the whole summer necking near that tree." Van sounded both embarrassed and fascinated.

Gus's mother looked appalled. I had a hunch her son was going to face another upsetting conversation after I left.

"There was another white man in the park?" I asked, trying to keep the conversation focused.

"Yeah," Van said.

"I thought a lot of white folk used the park," I said.

"They do," Gus said, "but this guy was just sitting in his car at the curb, like he was waiting for something."

"Where?" I asked.

"Not far from the dead guy," Van said.

"He peeled out when Van started screaming," Gus said.

I frowned. The man's behavior might not mean anything, but it was odd to drive away the moment someone started screaming. "What kind of car was he driving?"

"I dunno," Van said.

"An old guy's car," Gus said.

"What's that?" I asked.

"I can tell you what it's not," Gus's mother said. "It's not a sports car or a rich man's car. The boys know everything to know about those."

Which left sedans, station wagons, and a dozen others. "What color was it?" I asked the boys.

"Dark blue," Van said.

"Kind of a green," Gus said at the same time.

"Station wagon?" I asked.

"Naw," Gus said. "It was a boat."

A big car, then.

"Fins?"

"Newer," Van said.

"Can you remember anything else about it?" I asked, not sure if what they did remember helped me.

Gus looked at Van. Then they shrugged together.

"It was really clean," Van said.

"Clean?"

"Yeah." Gus sounded excited. "You know. Most cars got stuff on them by now."

After the rains started, cars in Chicago were usually covered with a thin layer of dirt and grime. Most folks didn't wash their cars again until the weather warmed up.

"Shiny clean," Van said.

"Like it was new?"

"No," Gus said. "Tires looked used."

"You got a good look at it, then," I said.

"I don't like being watched by white guys," Gus said.

I understood that sentiment. "Did you get a good look at him?"

"The white guy? Not really. He was inside the whole time."

"Was he old, young? Fat, thin?"

Van shrugged. "He was just a white guy."

"Like the photographer, then," I said, hoping for a basis of comparison.

"No. They were different," Gus said. "The guy in the car didn't have as much hair."

"And he looked meaner," Van said.

"Meaner?"

He nodded. "I wouldn't want to mess with him, you know?"

I didn't know. That wasn't a picture. "Was he older than the photographer?"

"He never got out of his car," Gus said with emphasis in an attempt to end this part of the conversation.

"Would you recognize him if you saw him again?" I asked.

"If he was parked in the same place," Van said.

So the man and the car were one package to them. That might be helpful, if Epstein had taken a picture of the car before the boys found the body.

"Is that all?" Gus asked. "Because we got stuff to do."

"August," his mother said.

"I have only a few more questions," I said. "The dead guy. Had you seen him before?"

"In the park?" Van asked.

"Anywhere."

Both boys thought. After a long moment, they shook their heads.

"Never," Van said.

"Nope. Not in the park, not around here," Gus said.

"Would you have remembered him if you had seen him?" I asked.

"He was a big guy," Gus said. "Nice clothes, expensive shoes. I'd've noticed him."

"We would have," Van said. "Like maybe he was Gayle Sayers or something."

In other words, even in this neighborhood, they weren't used to seeing a man like Foster dressed so nicely unless he was a famous football player.

"I had heard," I said, moving in a different direction, "that there was gang activity in the park that morning."

Gus's mother raised her head. I had caught her attention at least.

"No," Gus said too quickly.

Van had opened his mouth to answer, but stopped when Gus spoke.

"I know you weren't involved," I said, even though I didn't know that. I was trying to cover for them so they would answer me. "I just need to know the entire picture."

Neither boy answered me.

Gus's mother studied me for a moment, as if she were measuring my character, and then she stood up. "I think I hear the phone," she said, and went up the stairs.

We all watched her go. I think the boys were more surprised at her sudden departure than I was. I was grateful. She gave me a chance to ask some questions they might not want to answer in front of her.

"I won't tell anyone else what you say to me," I said. "This will be between us."

Van watched Gus. Gus's eyes held mine. "My mom worries," he said. "She thinks I'm stupid enough to join the Stones."

"You know a lot about them," I said.

"Hard not to, growing up where I did. A lot of my friends . . ." His words trailed off.

I nodded. "Was it a girl that brought you to the park?"

"Mostly," Gus said.

"It was my fault," Van said, his voice little more than a whisper. "I brought him."

That surprised me. "Why?"

"I missed my stop on the El. I got off in Woodlawn thinking I could catch a train back. Some guys—" his eyes filled with tears "—they took my money and my grandpa's watch. As a lesson, they said. My mom didn't know I had it. The watch."

Now the morning was beginning to make sense.

"Gus, he said he knew some guys who could maybe get it back."

I looked at Gus. His gaze no longer met mine. "I told you. A lot of the kids I grew up with are in the Stones."

"Did you get the watch?" I asked.

He shook his head, a small movement, speaking of a great failure. "They wanted too much money."

"Or to join," Van said, so softly I had to strain to hear him. "They'd give it back if we joined."

"Like we'd do that," Gus said, bringing his head up. "I'm not going to end up like those guys. I seen one friend shot. That's enough."

Van was watching him with the same kind of awe he had shown when he realized I worked as a detective. Van would do whatever Gus did. Fortunately, Gus was making the right choice.

"Does your mom know the watch is missing?" I asked Van.

"Not yet." His small frame rose and fell in a great sigh. "I just took it the once. She wasn't supposed to know."

"They probably wouldn't have gotten it back for you anyway," I said. "Whoever took it probably pawned it the same day."

"You think the pawnshop still has it?" Gus seemed interested for the first time since we started the conversation.

"It might," I said. "It'll still cost money to get it back."

"But only money," Gus said.

"Yeah," I said. "Tell you what. Give me a description of the watch and I'll keep an eye out."

"You'd do that?" Van asked.

"For nothing?" Gus said.

"You've already given me information. That's something." I tried to pay attention to both boys, but it was Gus I was really speaking to. "All I ask in return is that if you remember something else, you tell me."

"Okay," he said.

"The watch," Van said. "It's a pocket watch. All silver. My grandfather got it when this guy he worked for on the Gold Coast died."

The Gold Coast. Where Laura lived.

"Anything distinctive about it?" I asked.

"It's got a E and a G twisted together on the back, and it's old."

I wanted to ask what Van was doing with something like that, but I suspected I knew. He had had someone he wanted to impress—and it had backfired on him. "It doesn't sound like something like that would move too quickly around here. I'll see if I can find it."

"Thanks, Mister," Van said.

"Mr. Grimshaw," I said. "I'll write my number down and leave it upstairs. Call me if you remember any more."

"We will," Gus said, and since the promise came from him, I knew they would.

I mounted the stairs, half expecting to find Gus's mother at the top, listening. But she sat on an upholstered bench near the door, her hands clutched together and her head bowed. She had taken off the heavy sweater, revealing a body that was cigarette-smoker thin.

"How bad is it?" she asked, not looking at me.

"It's fine," I said. "You've got a good son. You've managed to keep him away from some bad elements."

She shook her head. "We were just lucky. I married a man with a good job and we were able to move here. It got August out of that neighborhood."

"It takes more than just a move to get a kid out of a gang," I said. "You did something right."

"I suppose." She stood up, stretched, and smoothed her hair with one hand. "He's seen some things that no boy should see. He talks tough, but I don't think he's slept much since November. He blames himself for taking Van down there. Van was raised here. He's not as mature as Gus."

"I know," I said.

She gave me a half smile. "What do you think your chances are of finding out what happened to that man?"

The question surprised me. I never thought about percentages. I never had. "I'll find out what happened to him that day," I said. "I just may not find out why."

SIX

It was twilight by the time I got to my car. The shortest day of the year was fast approaching and that, mixed with the gray weather, made it feel as if we'd been in perpetual darkness since November. I hadn't realized I was inside so long. Fortunately, I wasn't far from the Grimshaws'. I drove there in less than ten minutes.

I expected to find Jimmy on the Grimshaws' front porch. He usually waited for me there whenever I was late. Althea once told me there was nothing they could do to keep him inside. Jimmy got restless about half an hour before I was due, and at that point, no walls could hold him.

But the porch was empty. The light over the front door was on, and so were the interior lights, but Jimmy wasn't hovering behind the solid wood railing. It had been a cold day and it was getting colder. Maybe Althea had talked him into staying inside.

I hurried up the walk, took the steps two at a time, and opened the front door as I knocked. The smell of cooking beef greeted me; Althea was making a brisket. The dining-room table hadn't been set yet, and that room was empty.

The whistles and thuds of a televised football game came from the living room. As I walked in, I found the Grimshaws' oldest son, Jonathan, sprawled across the couch, watching. The two youngest girls, Norene and Michele, whom we all called

Mikie, were playing with a group of dolls on the floor beside the television set.

"Hey, guys," I said. "Where's Jim?"

"Uncle Bill!" Norene ran across the floor and hugged my leg. She had turned six in September.

I bent down and picked her up, grunting as I did so. "You're getting too big for this, kiddo."

"What're you gonna do to Jimmy?" she asked me, twirling one of her braids.

"What do you mean, what am I going to do?"

"Keith hit him," she said in a spray of bubble-gum breath.

"Norene, Mom wanted to tell," Mikie said. She was eight and trying hard to act older than her sister.

"Keith hit him?" I asked that of Jonathan, who hadn't taken his gaze from the television screen.

"They're in the kitchen," he said in a deep voice that still startled me. When I'd moved in with the Grimshaws in May, Jonathan's voice hadn't changed yet. Puberty was coming on fast. He was at least four inches taller than he'd been six months ago as well.

"So you're not going to tell me either," I said, adjusting Norene in my arms.

"I think Mom's dying to tell you." Jonathan kept staring at the TV.

In spite of myself, my gaze wandered over there. The camera had pulled back to show both teams, huddled in a time-out. "Was there a problem at the parade?"

"Santa was wearing a dishi," Norene said.

"A what?"

"A dashiki." Jonathan sounded bored. "It was weak."

The kitchen door swung open and Malcolm Reyner backed out, carefully balancing four glasses of juice in his large hands. Malcolm had moved in with the Grimshaws in September. I'd found out, after he helped me on a case, that he had been living on the streets for the better part of the year.

He was still tall and rangy, but he'd thickened up some under Althea's watchful care. He was doing well in other ways, too.

He had a part-time job now as a short-order cook, thanks to Franklin, and he was taking night classes to prepare him for his GED.

He grinned at me. "Hey, Bill. Fancy seeing you here. I think you're wanted in the kitchen."

"I understand there's a problem."

"Understatement of the century. Good luck." He carried the glasses toward the stained coffee table.

I set Norene down, and she hurried over to Malcolm, unwilling to miss the treat.

"Malcolm," I said, reluctant to venture into the war zone just yet. "You want to pick up a few extra bucks?"

He grabbed his own glass of juice and wandered back to me. Occasionally, I hired him to help me, sometimes as extra muscle, sometimes to be my eyes and ears in places I couldn't go. "Is it something fun or something dangerous?"

"Probably neither, although you'll have to keep your eyes open."

"What is it?"

"Norene," Jonathan said irritably, "you're in my way. Move, and while you're at it, turn up the TV."

We got the message. We moved deeper into the dining room.

"What do you need?" Malcolm asked, his voice softer now. The television volume went up, and I doubted that anyone could hear us.

"I want you to hit pawnshops for me, looking for a pocket watch. If you find it, let me know right away, but don't pick it up."

"Sounds easy," he said.

"It might not be. Some of these places can be rough."

"Okay," Malcolm said. "How will I know this watch?"

I described it to him. He repeated the description back to me, word for word.

"I'll let you know when I find it," he said.

"Thanks." I smiled at him, then squared my shoulders and headed into the kitchen.

Althea was standing beside the stove, stirring something that was boiling in a pot. Her face was flushed and her arms were dusted with flour. She wore an apron over a pantsuit that didn't flatter her bulk, but had probably kept her warm during the parade.

Keith sat directly behind her, facing the corner. His hands were clutched together and he looked like he'd been crying.

"Something smells good," I said as I walked in.

" 'Bout time you showed up." Althea waved a wooden spoon for emphasis.

"I hear the parade wasn't what you expected."

"Santa wearing black velvet and riding on a black sleigh," she said with a touch of disgust. "You'd think somebody died."

"No jolly old fat white guy, huh?" I stopped by the kitchen table. It was covered with flour and in the center, a bowl with a towel over it told me that Althea was making bread.

"I expected a black Santa. I hoped for one. I could've done without the dashiki done in the national colors of the Republic of Ghana. Give me the red suit any old day."

I laughed, looking for Jimmy. I finally saw him in the corner beside the sink. He was facing the wall, too, his arms crossed and his lower lip set in a familiar way.

"So you want to tell me what happened here?" I asked. "Looks like the boys are forbidden to speak."

"They don't *breathe* without me giving them permission." Althea glared at them over her shoulder. "Lacey, you come out here and mind the stove."

"Mo-om!" The voice came from the bathroom.

"I'm not in the mood, missy."

The bathroom door slammed. Lacey stomped out. She was wearing a pink terry-cloth bathrobe over a pair of black pants, and her hair was pulled back in a makeshift ponytail.

She faced me, and I had to concentrate so that I didn't laugh. One eye was completely made up—blue eye shadow, a fake eyelash so large it looked like clown makeup, and black eyeliner applied too thick. The other eye hadn't been touched, except for a smudge of eyeliner at the bottom of the lower lid.

"Uncle Bill, tell her I got to finish."

"Honey, if you were my daughter, I wouldn't let you wear that goop until you were married and out of the house."

She snorted at me and stalked toward the stove. She grabbed the wooden spoon from Althea and started stirring.

"Any more attitude, missy, and you aren't going anywhere tonight," Althea said.

Lacey glared at the pots, but didn't say another word. Althea led me out of the kitchen and down the hall toward the bedrooms. We stopped near the small alcove built in for the telephone.

"It wasn't the Stones, was it?" I asked, unable to wait any longer.

"It wasn't that serious, thank the Lord," Althea said, "but I don't want those boys fighting in my house, and this one came to blows."

"I heard Keith threw a punch."

"He was provoked," Althea said. "Seems Jimmy believes Santa Claus is for babies."

"Really?" That surprised me. "We hadn't discussed it."

"Well, he made his opinions known when we got back. Santa is for babies, Christmas is for rich foolish people who only think about material things, and the rest of it's just a pile of hogwash."

"He said all that?" It wasn't like Jimmy to express himself so eloquently.

"And more. It started in the car on the way back, and by the time we got home, Mikie was in tears, Norene was asking questions she's too young to know the answers to, and Keith was getting pretty upset. He told Jimmy to shut up, and when Jimmy didn't, Keith hauled off and hit him. I expect he'll have quite a shiner tonight."

I nodded, uncertain whether the smile building inside me was appropriate or not.

"So I pulled Jimmy aside for a talking-to and told him it's not right to make fun of other people's beliefs. He apologized, but still said he thought the whole thing was stupid. So I reminded him that Christmas was about the Christ child and he said he didn't know nothing about that, except the lip service people pay it on the radio."

The urge to smile was fading. Apparently, Jimmy had insulted Althea as well.

"So I asked him about his churchgoing habits, and he said the only time he's been in a church was when you made him see a minister in Memphis."

Althea put her hands on her hips. I backed away. Obviously, I wasn't going to be spared in this tirade either.

"Now I know, Smokey Dalton, that you were raised a good God-fearing man, and that your parents, bless them, took you to church every Sunday. I also know, because of your upbringing and your friendship with the ministers in Memphis, that you understand how important church is to our community."

I found myself braced against the telephone alcove.

She leaned toward me, lowering her voice. "If I've ever seen a boy in need of a community, it's this child. He has lost his home, his family, and his friends. Keith tells me he provokes fights in school, and now Franklin tells me about the sun you found. You don't give this boy something to hold onto, he'll make that something himself."

"I know that, Althea." Somehow, I found my voice. "I'm trying. I've only been a parent for eight months."

"Yes, and then you go and resume your work instead of getting a regular job—"

"I'm not cut out for a regular job."

"—and I think he's afraid you're just going to up and die on him. Some thug'll shoot you or the cops'll come after you thinking you done something you haven't, and he'll lose you, too."

"I already tried a job, Althea. It didn't work."

Her expression softened. "I'm not telling you to change. I'm telling you to find ways to help this boy."

I sighed. I was doing everything I could to help Jimmy. It just didn't seem like enough. "I'm willing to take advice."

"Good," she said, "because I'm going to give it. Better yet, I'm going to help you."

My shoulders sagged a little. I felt a tinge of relief. I hadn't been lying to her; I was in new waters here—both in Chicago and with the boy.

She wiped her hands on her apron. "I think there's no better time to introduce a child to the wonders of the Lord than the holiday season. The church is pretty, the music is special, and everyone's in a festive mood."

"Althea—"

She held up a hand to silence me. "I know you have your own troubles with the Almighty, but this boy should be entitled to make up his own mind. Even if he decides, like you, to turn his back on his upbringing, he needs to understand the community. He needs to know it's there for him, no matter what happens, no matter what he does. You know that, Smokey. You need to give that to him, too."

"Althea—"

She raised a single finger and silenced me again. "I made this offer before and you didn't take me up on it. You're going to now. Sunday School starts at eight-thirty. We leave here at eight sharp. You get him here at a quarter to in his best clothes and we'll take him with us. You don't have to go unless you want to."

"Althea—"

"In return," she said, glaring at me, "you are invited to join us every Sunday for dinner. We eat about four. You don't even have to dress for it like the rest of us do."

"I appreciate it, Althea, but—"

"I'm not going to let you say no this time, Smokey." Her dark eyes flashed. "This is how it's going to be."

"All right," I said.

"All right?" She seemed surprised. Apparently she had expected more of a fight.

"He needs more than I can give him. I'm glad you're willing to help." I leaned forward and kissed her cheek. It was warm and brushed lightly with flour. "In fact, I appreciate it more than I can say."

She blushed and laughed, pushing me away, reminding me of the girl she had once been. "Don't you let Franklin see you kissing me in the hallway."

"What?" I asked, pointing toward the overhead light. "You mean that isn't mistletoe?"

She laughed harder and walked down the hall, her dark mood broken. I stayed near the alcove for a moment and caught my breath.

Finding that tam on Jimmy had disturbed me deeply and I hadn't figured out a way to deal with the problem. Taking him to church wasn't the solution, but Althea reminded me of something I had forgotten. I wasn't completely alone; I had a community to draw on.

It was time I did.

We stayed for supper. Much as I appreciated my privacy, I had missed being part of this large, rambunctious family. The Sunday dinners would be good for both Jimmy and me. I did warn Althea that I would be late the following day; I also promised to help pay for the meal since she couldn't afford two more mouths to feed. She accepted the first statement and refused the second, just as I expected. I would simply have to find another way to repay her kindness, as I had done when Jimmy and I lived with them.

Jimmy and I arrived at our own apartment building around eight. As I pulled open the downstairs door, female laughter filled the public hallway. We stepped inside, and a woman's voice said, "Stop right there."

We did. I looked up the staircase and saw my neighbor Marvella Walker flanked by two other women. Marvella was wearing a long dress beneath her fake-fur coat. Her hair was piled on top of her head, accentuating her high cheekbones and classic features. Dangling gold earrings drew attention to her long, supple neck.

"Stay right there, Bill," she said, "and tell me what you think of this."

She took off the coat and dropped it over the railing. It

landed in front of Jimmy, sending up a waft of perfume.

The gown she wore wasn't formal like I had expected. It was white, done in an Egyptian style, with gold bands beneath her breasts, wrapped around her waist and trailing over her hips. Her magnificent legs were hidden, but her arms were bare, except for the gold bracelets around her wrist and the strange snakelike gold coil over her biceps. She came down one step, revealing matching gold sandals on her feet.

"Well?" she asked, her voice husky.

"You're going to freeze," I said, not willing to admit that my mouth had gone dry at the sight of her. She was, as I had noted before, the most beautiful woman I had ever seen, and I wished I could be as attracted to her as I was to Laura.

She laughed. "I'm not going to be alone. Ladies, show the man your outfits."

The two women behind her removed their coats as well, but neither of them had the flare Marvella did. Both women clutched the coats, letting them drag on the steps, which ruined the effect of their Egyptian gowns. Their outfits were a variation on Marvella's, but neither woman looked as stunning as she did.

"Bill," Marvella said, "meet my sister Paulette Shipley . . ."

The woman on the right dipped her head slightly. She had Marvella's bone structure and I would have considered her stunning if she hadn't been standing next to her gorgeous sister.

". . . and my sort-of cousin, Valentina Wilson."

"Val," the third woman said softly. She seemed almost embarrassed to be in the costume, which did not flatter her. She was petite where the other two women were statuesque, and she seemed lost in the white gown.

"Ladies," Marvella said, "this is the man I told you about, Bill Grimshaw."

I wondered what she had told them. She'd been angling to get into my bed since August. I'd refused her more than once, which apparently was something she wasn't used to.

The women flowed down the stairs as if they were entering a ballroom.

"Did you dress up just for me, or am I missing some important social event?" I asked.

"I'd like to say it's for you, Bill." Marvella's fingers brushed my face as she passed me on the way to her coat. "But we're heading to the Grand Ball of Nefertiti. Remember? I asked you about it last month."

She had and I had forgotten, partly because I turned her down and partly because I thought nothing sounded duller than a charity costume ball held at a brauhaus.

"You don't have to dress up," Paulette said. "I suspect most of the men there won't be wearing togas."

"Egyptian men didn't wear togas," Val said. "Roman men did."

Marvella handed me her coat, and I draped it over her shoulders. She smiled back at me, her gaze catching mine. "Sure you don't want to come? A beer or two won't hurt on a Saturday night."

"It's for the South Side Community Art Center," Paulette said.

"Thanks," I said, edging toward the stairs, "but Jim and I have a quiet night planned."

"Someone could watch your boy," Val said, and I got the sense that she would have had I given her the chance. She apparently wanted to go about as much as I did.

"Sorry." I smiled at her. "Maybe next time."

She looked away, nodded, the smile on her face small. On an impulse, I picked up her coat and held it out for her the way I had done for Marvella.

As she slipped into the coat, I said quietly so that only she could hear me, "Chin up. You look lovely."

"I look silly," she said just as quietly, "but thank you."

"Come on, ladies." Marvella's voice had an edge that it hadn't had a moment earlier. "We're going to be late."

She opened the door and stepped outside, shivering theatrically.

"Sorry you can't join us, Mr. Grimshaw," Paulette said, heading into the frosty night.

"You're the smart one, not letting them talk you into this."
Val gave me an impish grin and then followed her cousins into
the cold.

The door swung shut behind them and Jimmy shook his
head. "How come you let them go out like that and you don't
let me go out without mittens?"

"If I were in charge of them, they'd be wearing mittens, too,"
I said as I started up the stairs.

"They'd still get cold," he said, and I grinned at him.

As we got closer to our apartment, I could hear the phone
ring inside. I sprinted up the last few steps and unlocked the
door. I managed to get inside and picked up the phone in the
middle of a ring.

"Yeah?" I said, sounding as out of breath as I felt.

"Smokey?" Laura.

Jimmy walked in and closed the door, locking all three dead
bolts before taking off his coat.

"Hey, Laura. We just got in."

"I know. I've been calling."

Jimmy hung his coat on the back of a chair and went into
the half-kitchen—his coming-home ritual.

I turned my back so that he couldn't see my face. I figured
if she'd been trying to call all day, she had bad news. "What's
up?"

Behind me, glasses clanked.

"I was wondering if you're still serious about that security
thing."

"Yeah, I am." I shook off my coat, one arm at a time, and
let it drop on the couch.

"Good." She sounded hesitant. "Because Drew thinks that,
um, we need you tomorrow."

"You told Drew about my offer?" My voice sounded funny,
strained, not quite my own.

In the kitchen, water ran for a moment and then stopped.

"Yesterday, after I talked to you. He thinks it's a good idea.
He wants to know if you have the same sense of these guys as
he does."

"What guys?"

Jimmy wandered into my line of sight, drifting in front of the coffee table, pretending to look at days-old copies of the *Defender*.

"The ones who've been running Sturdy. They want to have brunch tomorrow."

"On Sunday? Isn't that strange?"

Jimmy set his glass of water on top of the pile, then sat cross-legged on the floor, no longer pretending he wasn't listening.

"Drew says no. He says they're going to approach me informally to see how serious I am about voting my stock." She still sounded hesitant. "I told him if it was informal, we really didn't need security, and he says we do, just to let them know that we're serious."

Something in her tone alerted me. "You were going to go alone?"

"Well, initially," she said. "I think I should be able to handle this."

Now her voice sounded more confident. The hesitation came from parroting her lawyer's words, words she wasn't sure she believed in.

"Is he coming?" I asked.

"Drew? He insisted on it. He was here when they called."

"At your office?" I asked before I could stop myself.

"At the apartment. He brought champagne."

And I had fought with her over pumpkin pie that I didn't even spring for. "That was kind of him."

"He does things like that."

Jimmy was frowning at me. I pushed my jacket aside and sat on the couch, bowing my head so he couldn't study my face.

"So," she said, "can you come to brunch tomorrow?"

"I have an appointment at three."

"We should be done by then. We're meeting them at twelve-thirty."

"Where?" I asked.

"The Walnut Room. You'll have to dress."

"Laura," I said, "this is just a hunch, but I doubt this place will let me in on a busy Sunday."

Or any day, for that matter. My best suit wasn't that nice and my color was all wrong.

She laughed. "They'll take you, Smokey. It's in Marshall Field's."

I didn't think that would make much of a difference, but I'd already registered my complaint. "Do I need to bring a team?"

"A team?" She paused for a moment before understanding sank in. "A team of security people? No, I wouldn't think so. I can't imagine these men, no matter how angry they got, leaping across tables in a public restaurant."

I hated asking the next question, but I did anyway. "Does Drew agree?"

"I didn't ask him. It's not his choice anyway. It's mine. And I think one security person is enough, don't you?"

"He's more familiar with the situation than I am, Laura."

Jimmy had his elbows on the table. He was staring at me. He was getting a black eye. I wondered if Althea had put ice on it. The swelling didn't seem that bad.

"Just you, Smokey," she said. "And I'll pay double your average rate since it's a weekend."

"Laura, in my job, there is no such thing as overtime."

"There should be." She paused, so that I could argue with her. It seemed that we were always fighting about money. About her money. I didn't give her my usual response. I was too tired to fight tonight. It could wait until she wanted to settle the bill.

When I didn't say anything, she added, "I'm looking forward to seeing you, Smokey."

"I'm coming tomorrow as the person heading your security team, Laura. You'll only complicate matters if you let these people know we're friends."

She sighed. "I don't like all these rules."

"You'll have to get used to them if you're going to run Sturdy's management team."

Jimmy frowned, as if what I said made no sense to him.

"How do you know, Smoke?" Laura asked. "You don't work in a corporate environment."

"And now you know why," I said, and hung up.

SEVEN

The next morning, I arrived later than I expected. I reached the Loop with half an hour to spare, but spent most of it searching for a place to park. I finally found an empty spot four blocks away from the huge Marshall Field building at the corner of State and Washington.

I didn't expect State Street to be so busy on a Sunday, but it was bustling. People hurried from department store to department store, carrying packages and bags, and dragging children by the hand. If Christmas was a religious holiday, as Althea said, I wasn't seeing much evidence of it here.

The entire Loop was decked for the holiday. Garlands hung from the light poles, and miniature Christmas trees stood in fake shelves specially built for that purpose on each pole's base. Real evergreen trees, about three feet high, grew in pots that lined the edges of the sidewalks.

A manger scene that looked like it had been stolen from the façade of a Roman Catholic church sat on the balcony above the elaborate cast-iron entrance of Carson Pirie Scott. Two blocks north of me, I could see long, gold trumpets sticking out over the pedestrians. Marshall Field's wasn't too far away.

Still, it took me a while to negotiate the crowd, which grew worse the closer I got to Field's famous windows. People were lined up eight deep to see the displays, and employees were working politely to keep the lines away from the entrances. Adults dressed as elves handed out Frango mints as customers entered the store, and Christmas carols blared from speakers mounted nearby.

I made it inside only to feel even more overwhelmed. The main aisles were clogged. Signs pointed toward Santa's Village and the Toy Center. White women bent over perfume displays and men waited behind them, arms crossed. Children cried and pulled at their parents, and more than one shopper crouched, taking display items from a toddler's hands.

The noise was deafening—conversation and the *whoo-whoo* of an unseen toy train, "White Christmas" blending with music boxes playing "Jingle Bells," sales clerks promoting a special, while children shouted and ran through the aisles. The smells were overwhelming, too—a jumble of perfumes mixing with the scent of the evergreen boughs that hung from every display case, the pungent odor of discarded mints that had been crushed against the tile floor.

It took me a while to find the escalators, even longer to find the directory that told me where the Walnut Room was. I managed to make my way up, staring at displays strategically placed in front of the escalators, and wishing I had money this year. I saw serving dishes that Althea needed, and bookends that would help Franklin's desk.

As I passed the Toy Center, my eye caught a distant display that made me do a double take. I thought at first that I was looking at black Barbie dolls, and then I read the sign explaining that I was looking at Barbie's new friend Crissy. I wondered if Mikie and Norene would be willing to share one, and doubted I had the money for that either.

The line outside the Walnut Room went halfway around the seventh floor, and I knew I was going to have to bully my way inside to see if my party was already there. That was going to be a trick; the restaurant was as fancy as I had feared it would be.

I was about to go up to the hostess when someone caught my arm. "Smokey."

I turned. It was Laura. I was relieved to see her. I hadn't realized how besieged I felt.

"Hey." I smiled at her, then caught my breath.

She, at least, looked like she belonged in this store. She wore a conservative blue-wool dress that flowed over her hips and fell to her knees. The dress accentuated the blue of her eyes. Her hair was pulled away from her face, and large teardrop pearls hung from her ears. Her makeup was light, but noticeable, since she hadn't been wearing any most of the year.

With her other hand, she pulled a white man closer to us. He was as tall as I was, but not as broad. He looked like he was in his early thirties, which I thought young for a lawyer, but he radiated intelligence. His black suit was a little hip for Chicago—the jacket was longer than I'd seen and cut square at the bottom so that it flared slightly. He wore a striped shirt and a black tie that looked like silk.

"Smokey," she said, "I'd like you to meet my lawyer, Drew McMillan. Drew, this is Bill Grimshaw."

His gaze took in my ill-fitting secondhand suit, more than a decade out of style, and then returned to my face. He nodded without smiling or extending his hand.

"Smokey?" he asked in a Boston Brahmin accent that almost made it sound as if he'd said "Smo-kah."

"It's a nickname," I said, with a cautionary glance at Laura.

He raised his eyebrows slightly, then said, "They're already inside. I scouted out the dining area before you arrived. I don't believe they saw me."

"I suppose you'll want me at a separate table?"

"It's not necessary this time," he said. "Laura trusts your opinion, and we do need a good security man with no ties to the city. Just listen and we'll take it from there."

I nodded.

"Shall we?" He held out his arm for Laura to take, but she ignored it. Instead, she kept pace with me, as if she were making certain that people knew I was with their party.

McMillan told the hostess which party we were meeting, and she led us into the Walnut Room. I stopped in astonishment, unable to help myself. Before me was the largest Christmas tree I had ever seen.

It went up at least two stories, its peak lost in an atrium that covered the room. It was decorated with thousands of white bulbs, all of which were on, and more ornaments than I could take in. The room, which was circular, surrounded the tree, and diners sat beside it as if nothing were out of the ordinary.

Laura smiled at me. "Eating here at Christmas is a Chicago tradition."

McMillan didn't notice. He continued to follow the hostess. From the back, he looked even younger; his dark hair and stylish suit gave him an air of expensive elegance.

Laura followed my gaze, apparently sensing my discomfort. "Come on."

She touched my arm, and for a moment I thought she was going to take it, the way that she should have taken McMillan's. But she didn't, and we walked in companionable silence to a large, square table on the far side of the room. Four men were already seated there. They stood as Laura approached.

"Miss Hathaway," said the one nearest us with a slight bob that was the Midwestern equivalent of a bow. None of us were fooled, though. He was only pretending at subservience.

"Mr. Cronk," she said, smiling at him. "Gentlemen."

They all murmured their hellos.

"Let me introduce you to my companions," she said, still standing, which meant that they had to stand as well. "I'm sure you recognize Andrew McMillan, the head of my legal team, and this is Bill Grimshaw, who heads my security."

"Security, Miss Laura?" one of the men asked. "I'm sure we don't need security today."

He didn't even look at me as he spoke, but his message was clear enough. I wasn't welcome here.

"Perhaps *we* don't," she said, "but *I* do."

"This is just a friendly lunch, Miss Hathaway," said a third.

"Why, who would think it was anything else?" Her smile was beautiful and gracious. "I don't believe I finished the introductions."

She turned first to the man who objected to my presence. He was portly and short, his hair so thin on top that he didn't even bother with a comb-over. "This is Walter Donoghue, who has been with the company since Daddy started it."

Donoghue extended a hand to McMillan, who shook it. He ignored me.

"Next to him is Victor Recknagel, who has been with the company almost as long." He was the other objector, taller, with an angular face and a thin blond mustache that made him look vaguely Prussian. He also shook McMillan's hand, then looked my way, but his pale blue eyes wouldn't meet mine.

"Then we have Eugene Parti, who is my godfather."

She indicated the stoop-shouldered, white-haired man to Recknagel's right. Parti shook McMillan's hand, then smiled at Laura, his face softening as if he were applying for the job of Santa Claus.

"I'm remiss in my duties," he said in a gravelly voice. "We should be in church, child."

She laughed and his eyes twinkled. It was clearly an old joke between them. He winked at her, but she didn't wink back, obviously pretending not to see it as she turned toward the man who had spoken first.

"And this is my father's right-hand man, Marshall Cronk."

Cronk was the only one who looked directly at me. His eyes were a startling green on his too-thin face, and they were cold, cold and dangerous.

He extended his hand, first to McMillan and then, surprisingly, to me. I took it, felt calluses as old as I was and a strength undiminished despite the years, and got the message. He was not afraid of anything, whether it was hard physical labor, other people, or threats from the outside.

We measured each other, and then relinquished the grip at the same time.

Laura sat down, and we all followed suit. I eased my chair closer to the table, careful not to snag the linen tablecloth. An elegant holiday bouquet of holly, complete with berries and trimmed evergreen boughs, graced the center of the table. The plate before me was real china with the Marshall Field's logo, and the utensils were highly polished silver.

It had been a long time since I had had a meal in a place like this.

Waiters surrounded us almost instantly, pouring water into the long-stemmed goblets, removing the plates before our seats and setting bread plates in their stead. Two bread baskets found their way to the table as Cronk ordered two bottles of wine without consulting any of us.

The menus were on calligraphed linen cards and we studied them as an excuse to avoid conversation. I made my choice quickly and used the rest of the time to watch the others surreptitiously.

Laura was nervous. She kept moving the card from hand to hand. McMillan pretended an ease he didn't have. After making his decision, he leaned back in his chair almost as if he were detaching himself from the meeting. The other men betrayed their tension in the jerkiness of their movements, the way they snuck glances at each other as if everything were operating by a prearranged script.

We ordered food, drank wine, and the conversation was casual—the weather, the cost-of-living increase, and, briefly, the Bears. I didn't say a word and neither did McMillan, although Laura held up her end beautifully.

We were halfway through the salads when the conversation turned.

"Did you get a chance to see the windows downstairs, Laura?" Parti asked.

"Not yet, Uncle Gene."

"I remembered how much you liked them, so that's why we came here."

Her smile froze. McMillan didn't move. I picked up my wine, but didn't drink it so that I could watch.

"I figured you were too busy to do much holiday shopping."

"One always finds time to fit it in," Laura said.

"Precisely," Parti said. "The meeting won't take long, so you have the afternoon to catch up on all you've missed."

"I take it your wives like to come here," Laura said in a flat tone.

"My wife insists on it every year," said Donoghue, with a grin to the others.

"Mine, too," said Recknagel.

"My mother always enjoyed it, but my father never did." Laura dabbed her mouth with her linen napkin. "I'm a lot more like my father."

She said it so blandly that I thought no one else caught the barb and the warning. But Cronk did. He tilted his head slightly.

So, apparently, did McMillan.

"Why did you call this meeting?" he asked, moving the conversation from its polite Midwestern rhythm.

Parti glanced at his companions. "Perhaps we should wait for the entrée . . ."

Which had probably been the plan. Have a short conversation over food and then flee.

"I don't think so," McMillan said. "There's a line outside that extends halfway around the floor. When we're done eating, the restaurant will want this table. But you knew that when you planned the meal here, didn't you?"

"I'd forgotten how busy the place is at the holiday season," said Cronk, who hadn't answered Laura's wife question. "If I'd remembered, I would have made the reservation somewhere else."

He sounded so innocent that anyone who wasn't practiced in business would have believed him. But clearly McMillan heard the sentence for what it was, the admission of Cronk's first calculated move.

A waiter cleared my salad while another set a large plate in front of me. A smooth brown crust covered the entire top of my chicken potpie. Some of the gravy bubbled through one small hole toward the center. It smelled wonderful and my stomach growled.

No one spoke while the waiters set the rest of the meals down. Then, as they left, McMillan said, "The meal's here. I guess we're on your timetable after all. What's this about?"

I stabbed through the crust with my fork and fragrant steam rose. Parti pushed his own plate aside.

"Laura," he said in his grandfatherly way, "I know that this past year has been a difficult one for you. Losing a parent always causes reflection. Dora Jean told me just before she died that you felt you had to step into your father's shoes and be strong for her. But he did design everything so that you're taken care of. You know that, don't you, honey?"

I was glad I hadn't put any food in my mouth, because I wasn't sure I would have been able to swallow after that speech. I kept my head down so that the anger which was starting to build wasn't visible. I was Laura's bodyguard, not her advocate. She had another man for that.

"What do you want?" Laura asked, but she didn't speak to Parti. She spoke to Cronk.

"Miss Hathaway." Donoghue spoke instead of Cronk. It was clear they were operating from a script. "Are you dissatisfied with the way we've been running Sturdy?"

"I don't know how you've been running Sturdy," she snapped. "I don't have access to all the books."

"All you had to do was ask," said Recknagel.

"I did ask," she said.

"It must have been an oversight, then," he said, as if her abruptness did not upset him. "Come into the office tomorrow and I'll give you everything you ask for."

I took a bite of the potpie, determined to keep myself busy so that I wouldn't be tempted to get involved in the conversation. The meat was tender, the gravy delicious. Lots of carrots, peas, and potatoes floated in the mix.

"Everything?" Laura asked sweetly.

"Of course, ma'am. You're a part of the business, after all."

"A substantial part, after Friday," McMillan said.

"I understand that this was a personal victory for you, honey," Parti said. "You need to feel like you're in control. Well, you have control now, dear, but you will need advisers and no one is more familiar with the company than we are."

I could feel Laura's fury. I made the mistake of looking up and realized that I was the only one who was eating. I set my fork down.

"Eugene," she said, her body trembling so slightly I wasn't sure if the others could see it. "I'm nearly thirty years old. It's time we drop the pretense. I'm Laura, not honey. Yes, we have a relationship and yes, we have a history, but it's a superficial one, and not relevant here."

She was getting sidetracked, just like they wanted her to.

"Now," she said. "I've asked a simple question and I would like an answer from you, Mr. Cronk. Why did you call this meeting?"

He stopped in the process of buttering bread. "We were getting to that, Miss Hathaway."

"Well, get to it now."

"It would be better if we explain our thinking," Donoghue said.

"I asked Mr. Cronk." Laura's spine was straight and her face was pale. Her eyes glittered as if they were the only part of her that she allowed to show emotion. "Marshall?"

He blinked at her use of his first name. I had a hunch that was the first time she had ever used it.

"Laura," he said emphasizing her name with just a hint of sarcasm, "your father went to great pains to make certain that Sturdy Investments would operate smoothly after his death. We have had significant growth in the past eight years, even more than other construction firms in the city, and as you know, they've all done quite well. We believe that any changes now would be harmful to the company."

McMillan smiled as if he had expected this. Laura didn't move. I took another bite of the potpie, unable to let it go to waste.

"We think it would be best for all concerned if we continue to vote your shares and act in your stead on the board of directors." He resumed buttering the bread. "Of course, we will work more closely with you, keeping you informed of the overall business concerns."

"We should have done that from the beginning, hon—Laura," Parti said. "That's my fault. I still think of you as that darling girl who would come up here with me Christmas week and—"

"Cut the crap," McMillan said. "It's insulting and it wastes our time."

I silently cheered him. He deflected Laura from the minor argument and kept her on the important one.

"The books will be open to you," Cronk said, "and we'll have someone available to explain them to you should you need it. You'll be welcome in my office at any time, and I will gladly listen to any advice you have on Sturdy's operations."

Laura was so still she looked as if she were carved in stone. She stared at Cronk.

He smiled at her. "If a good portion of my wealth were tied into a single company, I would want a say in that company's operations. I think your lawsuit was wise and I'm sorry we didn't think to discuss your proxy with you before we had to go to the courts."

"We gave you ample opportunity," McMillan said.

"It was our oversight," Cronk continued as if McMillan hadn't spoken. "And for that, we owe you our deepest apologies."

"I don't care about apologies," Laura said, "and I don't care for the tone I've heard during this meeting. In fact, I don't like any part of this gathering today. From now on, if you want to see me, you make an appointment with my secretary and we'll meet in my office at Sturdy."

The men stared at her. I had to work hard to keep a smile of approval off my face.

"I do want to see the books. I'll be studying them between now and the board meeting on January second. I expect each of you to be available to answer my questions if and when I have them." She leaned forward slightly, and I saw a hardness in her face that I'd never seen before.

Donoghue and Recknagel leaned back. Parti's eyes were wide. Only Cronk didn't move.

104

"As you can tell," she said, "I plan to vote my own shares. That should have been plain to you in September when Mr. McMillan first contacted you. The fact that you missed something so obvious worries me. If this is how you've run Sturdy, then clearly you are not upholding my father's legacy."

She stood, dropping her napkin on her full plate as she did so. McMillan stood and so did I. The other men were so astonished that they forgot their manners and remained seated.

"Thank you for lunch," she said. "I wish I could say that it was a pleasure. Meals here should be festive. I'm sure that in the future, should you feel the need for a business lunch, you will choose a more appropriate venue."

Then she turned and walked away. McMillan's smile grew. He nodded his head toward the men. "Gentlemen," he said and followed her.

I stayed for a beat longer, ostensibly pushing my chair in. The men were staring after Laura as if they had never encountered anything like her before. Perhaps they hadn't. Cronk's gaze met mine and his eyes narrowed.

I nodded my head, acknowledging the glance, then headed out of the restaurant.

It took me a few steps to catch up to Laura and McMillan. Laura was stalking out, her head high, that familiar autocratic pose she used when she was most upset. She made it to the escalators before she checked to see if we were following her.

Her skin was flushed, her eyes too bright. Her lower lip trembled as she looked at McMillan, then she saw me and held out her hand.

I took it and she pulled me close. McMillan watched, missing nothing.

"Do you believe the way they treated me in there?" she said, her voice shaking.

"You should have expected it, Laura," McMillan said. "We discussed it."

"We didn't discuss the honeys and the dears and the have you seen the windows, little girl? I expected to be treated as an equal, not a featherbrain who didn't know what she was getting into." Laura's voice rose enough to catch the attention of several shoppers getting off the escalator.

"They've been running the business a long time," McMillan said. "They're not going to see you as an equal."

"That's not what she's talking about," I said.

McMillan looked at me in surprise. Laura's hand was still clutched in mine and I felt her grip tighten.

"They belittled her," I said. "First with the choice of restaurants, and then allowing Parti to treat her like a child. They made it clear that she is nothing to them and they did it in a personal way, guaranteed to shake anyone's confidence. A weak person would have caved in during that meeting. Fortunately, Laura's anything but weak."

McMillan glanced toward the restaurant, then back at me, as if assessing my words. "Good point," he said after a moment. "I'm usually better at nuance than that."

"That's not nuance," I said, squeezing Laura's fingers and then letting go. "That was blatant. Nuance is much more subtle, like refusing to shake someone's hand during an introduction."

A thin line of color appeared in his cheeks. "I'm sorry," he said. "I underestimated you."

"People tend to do that," I said.

He turned to Laura, his cheeks a deep red. "I think we should find another place to have lunch. I'd like to hear your take on what happened in there—and I'd like to hear the rest of Mr. Grimshaw's analysis. He clearly sees things that I do not."

Laura looked up at me. Her skin was pale. She looked drained. "Does that work for you, Smoke?"

"I'm sorry, Laura," I said. "I can't. I'm working on another case—"

"That's right," she said a little too quickly. "You told me." She gave me a small smile. "We'll talk later."

I hurried through the crowd of shoppers, wondering why I felt so guilty. I did have another case and it would take time for me to get to Rogers Park. But that lost look on Laura's face twisted my stomach. Only, I couldn't make her feel better. Maybe McMillan could.

Or maybe she would just have to realize that things were different now. Maybe that was why I felt so unsettled. I knew just how difficult such changes were.

EIGHT

It was five to three when I turned onto Epstein's block. I was so focused on arriving on time that it took me a moment to realize something was out of place.

Three cars were parked haphazardly in front of Mrs. Weisman's house. A rusted white Cadillac with long fins jutted into the street, as did a dented blue Thunderbird. A dark blue Volkswagen bug was trapped between them, the other cars parked so close that there was no way the VW could pull out.

No one was on the street. The sidewalks were bare, and it seemed like most of the houses were empty. Cars were gone, garage doors were open. The folks who lived here had gone shopping or visiting, taking care of Sunday errands.

The only thing that seemed out of place were those three cars.

The VW's driver's door wasn't closed tight, and its passenger door hung open. I didn't like the looks of this at all.

I parked two houses away and got out of my car, easing my door closed so the sound wouldn't alarm anyone. I thought I heard a scream, but I wasn't certain. I hurried toward the Weisman place.

The door to the enclosed porch swung on its hinges, and as I climbed the steps, I realized the interior door was open. From inside, I heard thuds and the sound of breaking glass.

I hurried across the porch and into the house. On the floor

of the living room, a man hunched over another man, holding him up by his shirt and repeatedly punching him in the face. I recognized the curly mop of hair; the victim was Epstein.

I couldn't see anything that would serve as a weapon—all of the furniture was heavy and covered with small knickknacks. So as I ran into the living room, I grabbed the assailant and, using my forward momentum, propelled him toward the wall. His head hit with a resounding thwack and he collapsed.

I dropped him and turned toward Epstein. His lips were moving, but I couldn't make out the words. He raised a hand weakly. As he did, I heard more glass break in the kitchen.

"Where's your grandmother?" I asked.

He shook his head ever so slightly. I glanced at his assailant, who was out cold. At least I hoped so. That blow had had a lot of power in it. I didn't want to think about the other possibilities.

"I'll be right back," I said. "You'll be safe for the moment."

This time, he nodded, then winced. His face was bloody and swollen, his features nearly hidden by the blossoming bruises. I hurried toward the kitchen, pulling open the door as I ran inside.

Elaine was sprawled across the table, a man holding her in place with a single hand to her throat. She clawed at his fingers while he used the other hand to brace himself between her legs. Her shirt was ripped in pieces and her skirt was pooled around her waist. Broken dishware littered the floor.

Neither of them saw me. I grabbed the ancient coffeepot that Mrs. Weisman kept on the stove. Coffee sloshed inside, and the handle burned my palm, but the pot was hefty.

The man saw me before I had time to bring the pot down on his head. He let go of Elaine as I swung the pot sideways, catching him in the cheek with the hot metal. Steaming coffee spilled from the spout, scalding him.

He screamed. Elaine scrambled backward, adjusting her clothing as she did. She tumbled off the table onto the glass shards.

At that moment, a door beside me opened. I caught a glimpse

of a staircase before the muzzle of a hunting rifle pushed itself against my face. I stepped away, putting my hands up, and then I saw who wielded the gun—Mrs. Weisman, looking angry and competent.

"It's me, ma'am," I said. "Bill Grimshaw."

Elaine's assailant staggered out the back door, still screaming, clawing at his face and arm. Elaine huddled on the floor.

"Mr. Grimshaw?" Mrs. Weisman's voice shook.

"Yes, ma'am. Mind if I lock the back door?"

"No, son." She lowered the rifle. "Where are those men?"

I stepped over broken glass and locked the back door. "I only saw two. One's in the living room unconscious, and you saw what happened to the second."

"There's clothesline in the top drawer next to the sink," she said, still holding the gun.

I took the rifle from her. It was old and looked like it hadn't been used or cleaned in fifty years. "Call the police," I said. "And I think we're going to need an ambulance, too."

She nodded. I set the gun on one of the stairs and closed that door. Then I went into the living room, closing and locking the front door. I could hear Mrs. Weisman's voice in the kitchen as she spoke on the phone to the authorities.

For a moment, I hesitated. If I left now, I wouldn't have to face the police and all the inevitable questions. But Mrs. Weisman knew who I was.

I glanced into the living room. Saul hadn't moved and neither had his assailant. The floor was spattered with blood.

I went back into the kitchen and got the clothesline. Elaine remained on the floor, rocking back and forth on the glass. I wasn't certain she even knew it was there.

Mrs. Weisman's hand shook as she held the phone. "Please hurry," she was saying. "I'm not sure if they'll be back."

I took the clothesline into the living room and knelt beside the assailant. He was young, in his twenties maybe, but large and strong. I was lucky I had taken him by surprise.

His back was going up and down. He was breathing, which

I was more thankful for than I could say, but his blond crewcut was matted with blood.

I yanked his hands back and tied them behind his waist. Then I tied his feet for good measure. As I finished, Mrs. Weisman came in the room. She gasped when she saw Epstein.

"Saulie," she said, kneeling beside him. He turned his head toward her. I moved to his other side.

He was badly beaten. It was lucky I had come when I did. It looked like part of his face had been smashed in.

"What happened?" I asked.

Epstein's lips moved, but he still didn't say anything.

"I was upstairs changing the bed linen," Mrs. Weisman said. "I heard the cars pull up, and shouting. I looked out the window and saw Saulie and Elaine running for the house, those two after them. I knew I had my rifle somewhere. I found it fast enough, but not the bullets. I had no idea anyone could do so much damage so quickly . . ."

Her voice trailed off. I patted her shoulder. "He'll be all right," I said, although I wasn't entirely sure of that. "I'm going to check on Elaine."

Mrs. Weisman nodded absently. She was smoothing the hair off Epstein's forehead, which seemed like the only part of his face that wasn't injured.

I got up and went into the kitchen. It was a mess. Coffee mixed with the broken glass. The tablecloth hung sideways off the table, and it looked like most of the items on the counters had been swept aside.

Elaine had put up quite a fight.

She had stopped rocking and was huddled in a fetal position where she had fallen. I stepped across broken glass to reach her.

"Elaine," I said, knowing better than to touch her. "It's Bill Grimshaw. We met yesterday at the Circle Campus."

A shudder ran through her. There were white dish shards in her afro, and trailing down her back.

"You're lying on glass," I said gently. "I'm going to help you up before you get cut."

"No!" The word was quick, breathy and forceful. Outside, sirens echoed, still a few blocks away.

"You need to stand, Elaine." I kept my voice even and calm. "We have to get the glass off you."

"No," she said again, but she moved, glass crunching beneath her weight. She moaned with sudden pain.

"It would be easier if I helped you," I said.

This time, she didn't respond, and I wasn't sure if she had heard me. Then her hand, scratched and bloody, reached for the counter. She gripped it and sat up slowly, the glass crackling. I winced, uncertain how much more she was grinding into her flesh, but knew that right now, she found the glass preferable to a man's touch.

Still, I kept a hand behind her in case she fell.

The sirens got closer, their wails filling the room. It took Elaine an excruciatingly long time to stand, and she tottered as she did. She kept one hand on the counter, used the other to hold the remains of her shirt in place, and then turned toward me, her feet sliding on the broken glass.

Her left eye was swelling shut and her lower lip was covered with dried blood. Her face was turning black and blue, but she wasn't as badly beaten as Epstein was. Her skin was littered with cuts. Shards of glass clung to her cheeks and hair. She didn't seem to notice.

I didn't let my shock at her appearance show. I'd dealt with rape before and I knew better. Right now, the best thing I could do was to get her to a hospital and see if she needed treatment.

The sirens invaded the room and then stopped. My ears rang.

I extended my hand. "Crossing that glass will be tricky."

She stared at my fingers, then at my face, as if she were trying to remember me. Then she looked at my fingers again. I heard a door open in the living room, followed by voices, the banging of equipment, and Mrs. Weisman directing people to her grandson.

The ambulance must have arrived first.

Elaine didn't seem to hear any of it. Slowly she reached her hand to mine, and her fingers, colder than any living fingers I'd ever touched, grabbed on hard. I didn't move for a moment, knowing the slightest sudden movement could send her back into that near-catatonic state. I waited until she let go of the counter, until she started across the pile of glass, before increasing my grip so that she wouldn't fall.

More voices, the squawk of radios, and Mrs. Weisman's high-pitched tones rising above the rest. Another door and some banging almost made me wince, but Elaine didn't seem to notice. She still focused on me.

We made it to the bare tile before she stopped walking. She was dripping glass pieces, leaving a little trail of them behind her as she moved, and I wondered how I could convince her to wipe them off. Part of her skirt was caught in the waistband, showing her left thigh and buttock. Her underwear was ripped as well, and hanging from her like her shirt was.

She clutched her shirt closed, but it covered nothing. I could see all the bruises and cuts from the glass. She opened her mouth just a little and I thought she was going to say something, when the kitchen door banged open.

Elaine cringed as if a gun had gone off, but she didn't let go of my hand. Two uniformed police officers came in, both white, burly, and red-faced.

"What the hell's going on in here?" the first one asked, glaring at me, and I knew what he was thinking. I remembered that moment in the living room when I'd had my chance to escape. I should have taken it.

"We need an ambulance," I said as calmly as I could. Elaine was cringing again, as if she were trying to shrink into nothing. Her hand slipped out of mine, and I felt as if I'd lost a major fight. She pulled at her clothes with both hands, as if she were just beginning to realize that she wasn't covered.

"We're looking for a Bill Grimshaw," the second cop said. "Where is he?"

A rage flared inside me, warming my cheeks. I took a breath before speaking, hoping I sounded calmer than I felt. "This woman needs medical attention. Now."

Something in my voice made them look at her. "Jesus," one of the cops said.

The other pivoted and left the room, saying as he did so, "We got another vic in here."

"Get away from her," the first cop said to me.

"I'm not your perpetrator," I said. "He's tied up in the living room. The second guy got out the back door, but I'm not sure if he went far. He'd been hit in the head and scalded with hot coffee. If his car's still here, he's somewhere around."

"Nice try, boy, but it don't wash." He pulled out his gun. "Get away from her. Now."

Two guns in one hour. I didn't like my odds. I turned my hands so that the cop could see them and started to move away.

"No," Elaine said.

"I told you to step away!" The cop was getting nervous. He still thought I was doing something to her, even though I was too far away to reach her now.

"What is the meaning of this?" Mrs. Weisman came into the room, her voice as powerful as a drill sergeant's. "Put that gun down, young man. I told you to find Bill Grimshaw, not shoot him."

His gun shook. For a moment, I thought the cop was going to pull the trigger out of sheer surprise.

"No!" Elaine lunged for me. The tattered remains of her blouse fell off. She wrapped her arms around me, and I could feel her trembling. I knew what this cost her. "Don't hurt him."

The cop looked confused. "Where's Grimshaw?"

"Are you blind, young man?" Mrs. Weisman snapped. "You're pointing a gun at him."

The other cop had come into the room, followed by one of the ambulance attendants. They stopped when they saw the gun.

"What the hell are you doing, Speer?" the second cop asked. "Put the gun down."

Speer stared at me. "You're Grimshaw?"

"My I.D.'s in my back pocket." I tried not to sound sarcastic. "You want to see it?"

"But the old lady said Grimshaw saved everyone." Speer lowered the gun slightly.

"The old lady," Mrs. Weisman said, "is standing behind you."

"Don't hurt him," Elaine said again, still clinging to me. I could feel the heat of her bare skin through my suit.

"Put the gun down, Speer," the other cop said again. "Now."

Speer holstered his weapon. He looked like he was the one who'd been attacked. "What the hell happened here?"

The ambulance attendant came forward, reaching for Elaine, who cringed as she let go of me.

"Oh, dear," Mrs. Weisman said.

I slipped off my suit coat and wrapped it around Elaine's shoulders. I'd wrapped a coat around a woman's shoulders just the night before, and she had smiled at me. I wondered if Elaine would smile again.

Elaine clutched the coat. The ambulance attendant took a step back, obviously understanding the situation.

"We need to get you to the ambulance, honey."

She shook her head once, an eloquent no.

"We'll get a cot and you can ride in with your friend." Then the ambulance attendant looked at me. "He is her friend, isn't he?"

"Her boyfriend," I said, keeping my tone even.

"You're going to want to know how he is, aren't you?" the ambulance attendant asked Elaine.

The mention of Epstein seemed to reach her. "Saul?" she asked me.

"He got beat up pretty badly," I said. "I don't know how he is, but this gentleman'll take you to him."

"You, too," she said, and I realized then that I had become the only safe thing in the world for her. I would have to stay until she was through part of this process.

"All right." I eased my arm around her shoulder, moving so slowly that she could have stopped me at any point. She didn't. She leaned into me, letting me help her toward the kitchen door.

"You're not going," Speer said. "We have to talk to you."

115

"I'll give my statement at the hospital," I said as I passed him. The other cop was standing close. I let him see my fury. "There was a second man. He's the one who attacked Miss Young. He got out the back door about fifteen minutes ago, but I managed to do some damage before he did. I don't think he got far. You should look for him. You certainly don't want him doing this again."

The other cop flushed and nodded. "You heard him, Speer. Check the backyard."

Mrs. Weisman reached toward Elaine, then brought her hand back. "I had no idea," she said, more to herself than to anyone else.

The ambulance attendant hurried ahead of her and disappeared out the front door. He was going for the other cot. They must have already loaded Saul into the ambulance.

Elaine walked slowly but with determination through the kitchen door. She stared straight ahead, as if she were moving by sheer will alone.

I glanced into the living room. There was blood on the floor where Epstein had been and another pool near the perpetrator. He was gone, and for a brief, terrified moment, I thought he had escaped.

Then we stepped into the cold afternoon air, and I saw the other attacker, sitting up in the back of the police car. He looked bleary-eyed, but all right.

Now there were neighbors on the street, dozens of them, crowded around, watching. They stared at Elaine and I as if we were the ones at fault. Only two cars were parked haphazardly—the bug, with its door still open, and the Cadillac. The Thunderbird was missing.

Apparently the second guy had gotten away after all.

The attendant pulled the cot down. "Lie here, miss."

Elaine looked at it, the thick mattress pad, the restraints to hold her in place, and shook her head.

"Miss, to ride with us—"

"I don't think she can lie down," I said. "All that glass."

"Oh." The attendant flushed. "Right. Let's see if we can get you comfortable inside."

Epstein was already inside, his cot pushed against the far wall. It always amazed me how empty the back of ambulances were. A first-aid kit hung from the wall, extra restraints and towels were in a small container near the back, and there was nothing else except room for cots and some seats built over the wheel wells.

I helped Elaine into the back of the ambulance. The attendant took one look at her, started to reach for her, and I shook my head.

He nodded once and said, "There's not a lot of room back here. Can your friend follow us in his own car?"

She looked at me, her eyes wild. "Don't leave—"

"I'll ride with you," I said, wishing this weren't happening.

The attendant placed some towels on the wheel well. I climbed in as Elaine sat down, then I helped the attendant put the other cot inside.

I took a seat on the floor. The attendant closed the doors, then rapped on the roof.

The ambulance pulled forward. We all swayed. The attendant grabbed Epstein's cot so that it wouldn't slam into the walls of the van.

Elaine was watching Epstein. "We weren't doing anything. Isn't that crazy? We weren't doing anything."

She was speaking as if she were alone. Or talking to Epstein, who looked like he had passed out from the pain.

"What do you mean, miss?" the attendant asked.

"In the park." She turned toward me. "We weren't doing anything."

"I know," I said, even though I didn't.

The siren came on. Oddly, it didn't sound as loud from inside.

She turned back to Epstein. "He's the nicest man. He didn't deserve this. It's my fault."

I wanted her to stop, but I wasn't sure how to silence her.

"What is, miss?" the attendant asked.

"This whole thing. If he hadn't met me . . ."

"You don't have to talk now," I said.

She didn't seem to hear me. A tear ran down one cheek, hit a small piece of glass sticking out of a cut and divided in two. "We didn't even know them, that's the thing. They saw us together and they went nuts, and Saul, he had no idea—I mean, he knows intellectually, but he doesn't *know*—you know?"

She turned to me for that last and I nodded. I was beginning to get a picture of what happened.

"Did they follow you from the park?" I asked, unable to help myself.

"I thought we'd made it when we reached the car." She leaned forward. She let go of my coat and it gaped, but she didn't seem to notice. She was looking at Epstein. "I had no idea he'd drive home. I thought he'd—I don't know. I'm used to—most men, they—like you . . ."

She looked at me again as her voice trailed off. She was right. If I'd been being harassed by two white men in a park, I wouldn't have led them to my house.

Then I leaned back slightly. Two white men in a park. What had they been doing?

"What park was this?" I asked her.

But she didn't answer. She was staring at Epstein. The attendant frowned at me. The ambulance hit a bump and we all slid to the right.

The ambulance seemed to be going extremely fast. I leaned forward so I could catch a glimpse of Epstein. His cot slid, despite the efforts of the attendant to hold it. I held it, too, and felt the cool metal cut into my palm.

We rounded another corner. The vehicle slowed, turned again, and eased to a stop. The siren sounded louder now. The doors in the back were flung open and medical personnel, wearing scrubs and lab coats, reached inside.

They removed Epstein first. Someone told Elaine to lie down and she shook her head. A man reached for her and she cringed.

"Let's go in, Elaine," I said, putting a hand on her arm,

slowly, so that she could object if she wanted to.

She looked at me for a moment, then nodded. A member of the medical team reached for her as she stepped down and she flinched away, losing her balance. I caught her from behind and kept her moving.

"She's covered with glass," I said to a young white man wearing a lab coat. "And she's got injuries I haven't seen. She'll need attention."

"Then let us—"

"No," I said, brushing him off. "She's in shock. You're going to need my help."

And they did. When they asked Elaine to do something, she refused. When I asked, she at least considered it. She wouldn't lie down on any cots and she didn't want to be left alone.

An emergency-room doctor did a cursory examination of her while I sat in a nearby chair, talking to her, trying to keep her calm. When he was done, he pulled me aside as if I were the one responsible for her.

"Your daughter—" he said, and I started at the assumption, but I didn't correct it. As long as they thought I was family, I could help. "—is going to need surgery. Glass is ground into those cuts. I'm not sure I can save her looks. She'll need stitches all over, especially her back. It's ruined. You said she was attacked. Was she raped?"

"I'm not sure," I said. "When I came in, he had her by the throat and he was between her legs. I couldn't tell if he was beginning or ending."

The doctor nodded. "We'll put her under, see what we can find. The cops want to talk to her first, though. It's my inclination to make them wait. This is a very traumatized woman. But I know they haven't caught the guy. If you think it's best—"

"Take her to surgery," I said. "The cops can wait."

NINE

I waited, too. I had to hold Elaine's hand while the anesthesiologist worked, but once she was under, I was free to go.

Instead, I found Mrs. Weisman sitting in the waiting room. The place was large, done in orange and gold, obviously someone's idea of happy colors. Newspapers had been abandoned on the plastic seats, and a child's doll lay on a table, forgotten.

Mrs. Weisman was the only person in the room. She sat with her head bowed, her hands clasped together. It seemed like she had aged fifteen years. When she heard my footsteps, she looked up. Anxiety and fear filled her face and then faded into a small smile when she realized it was me and not a doctor.

"I don't know what we would have done without you, Mr. Grimshaw," she said, her voice shaking.

I sat down across from her. "Looked like you were about to take control."

She shook her head. "I hadn't used that rifle since my honeymoon, and even then I was afraid of it. Creatures like that, they sense fear. They'd've knocked it out of my hands and hurt me as bad as they hurt my Saul."

"No, they wouldn't have," I said. "Creatures like that are afraid of everything. They don't like surprises and you would have been a big one. You'd have scared them off."

"You're a kind man." A bit of the old twinkle returned to her eyes. "And a good liar."

"I just call it like I see it, ma'am."

"There you go, ma'aming me again." She patted the seat next to her. "I'm Ruth."

"Bill," I said, as the impulse to tell her who I was rose again. I supposed it wouldn't hurt. "But my closest friends call me Smokey."

"Smokey," she repeated, and nodded. "It suits you better than Bill. I thought the name a little too bland for you. Come. Sit." She patted the space beside her again, and I moved.

"How's Saul?" I asked, knowing only because she was still sitting here that he was alive.

The twinkle faded. She sighed. "They broke some ribs and smashed most of the bones on the left side of his face. He might lose his eye."

Her voice wobbled, and she had to take a deep breath before continuing.

"He had trouble breathing. They think it was the blood, but they weren't sure. They said they won't know the extent of the damage until they get him into surgery."

"He's there now?" I asked.

"They don't know how long it'll take." She turned toward me. "What was wrong with those boys? Why did they come into my house? Why did they want my Saul?"

"I'm sure the police will find that out."

"They have only the one boy, and they nearly blamed you. Why would they do that?"

I took her hand in mine. Her bones were fragile, her skin soft and papery. She was right; those boys would have destroyed her, maybe killed her.

"I think you know why they did it," I said.

"If you're saying they did that because you and Elaine are Negroes, then no, I don't." Her hand tightened on mine. "People are people, Mr. Grimshaw."

"Yes, they are." In all their bigoted, narrow-minded and

hate-filled glory. I wiped a tear from her cheek. "Unfortu-
nately."

I stayed at the hospital for five hours. Epstein's surgery ended
in three hours. They rebuilt part of his face and tried to save
his eye, although whether that took remained to be seen. His
lungs hadn't been punctured by the broken ribs like they feared,
so they taped him up. Before they finished, they removed teeth
that had become lodged in the back of his throat.

One more blow to the head, the doctor said, and he might
have died.

Elaine's surgery took longer because they had to painstak-
ingly clean tiny bits of glass out of each cut and scrape. She
received over one hundred stitches on various places all over
her body. I sat at Elaine's side for a while, but she didn't wake
up before visiting hours ended. Neither did Epstein, which I
considered a blessing.

During the afternoon, a different set of police officers took
our statements, but we didn't have a lot of light to shed on the
circumstances. The guy they'd caught wasn't talking and the
second one had eluded capture. I didn't figure that would last.

At one point, I excused myself to call Franklin, explaining
my situation briefly so that he'd tell Althea and Jimmy why I
was late. When I finished, I looked up Elaine's phone number
and tried her apartment, hoping she had a roommate who
would tell me how to locate her family. But the phone rang and
rang. I would have to contact the school. Mrs. Weisman had
no memory of ever discussing Elaine's next of kin.

Then I went back to emergency and pulled aside one of the
black nurses. She was heavyset and pretty. Her name tag read
"Marge Evenrud." She had been very helpful with Elaine, so I
sensed I could trust her.

I asked her to keep an eye out for any young white male
admitted to the hospital in the next few days with burns along
his right side, particularly on his face and shoulders. I expected
the burns would be old and festering before he came in.

I didn't have to ask twice. She took my name and number, and promised she would.

The hospital called Mrs. Weisman a cab and she asked me to wait with her, knowing that my car was near her house. As we rode back, I asked her if someone could stay with her. I wasn't sure I wanted her to stay in the house.

She patted my knee. "Mr. Grimshaw, that boy isn't coming back, and I have good locks. Besides, my rifle's not getting put away."

I wasn't sure if that reassured me or not. What eventually did reassure me were the lights that were on in her home when we arrived. Her neighbors were there, still cleaning up the mess.

Mrs. Weisman introduced me to all of them as the man who had saved her Saul, and all of them treated me with a warmth that surprised me. Many apologized to Mrs. Weisman for not calling the police. Most hadn't even noticed the disturbance until they heard the sirens.

As soon as I could, I left her with them and drove to Franklin's. I was halfway there before I realized I had never gotten the photographs that Epstein had promised me. I wondered if Mrs. Weisman even knew where they were.

Jimmy's worried face was pressed against the living-room window as I pulled up to Franklin's house. It was nearly ten o'clock and I was exhausted, the adrenaline from the fight long gone. I was also cold; the police had taken my suit coat as evidence when they took Elaine's ripped and bloody clothing.

I hurried inside, glad for the warmth, the light, and the familiar place. Jimmy wrapped himself around me, which surprised me. Lately, he'd been trying to act grown up. But he was still ten, still a child at heart. I rubbed a hand along his small head.

"I'm sorry," I said, but Jimmy didn't answer. He just clung to me.

Franklin watched from the dining-room table, his law books spread before him. "The boy was all right until the last hour or so. How're your friends?"

"They'll make it," I said, letting my tone tell him how serious it all was.

Althea came through the kitchen door. She still wore an apron over her Sunday dress. "My heavens, Smokey. No one's tended to you, have they?"

"Me?" I looked down. My white shirt was streaked with dried blood, and a few small shards of glass still clung to the hems of my trousers. "I'll be all right."

"It's just like you. Take care of everyone else and pay no attention to yourself. I saved some food for you. It's warming in the oven."

"There's no need, Althea."

She ignored me, putting a hand on Jimmy's shoulder. "Come on, Jim. Let's take your father into the kitchen."

Reluctantly, Jimmy let me go. He shook Althea off. He whirled toward me, hands on his hips. "You nearly died, didn't you?"

The depth of his anger surprised me. "No, Jim," I said. "I wasn't the one who got hurt."

"That's blood." He stabbed my shirt with his finger.

"Someone else's," I said.

"They could've hurt you."

I suppose they could have if they had known I was coming, but I didn't tell him that. "No, they couldn't, Jim. It happened too fast."

"Your friends got hurt."

"Yes," I said, "they did. They were already being hurt when I arrived. I just got them out of the situation, like I got you out of trouble in Memphis."

He didn't move for a moment. Then he reached out and grabbed my hand. "C'mon. I made everyone save you some gravy. It's the best."

I let him pull me toward the kitchen, where everything was clean and bright and there wasn't a spot of broken glass.

We stayed longer than we should have. Jimmy fell asleep at the table, head resting on his arms. I took the time to talk with

124

Franklin about the next morning. I still hadn't come up with anything I liked for dealing with Jimmy's involvement with the Stones, but what I did come up with would work for a while.

Franklin and I would take turns driving the kids to and from school. We'd walk the boys inside, even though they would probably protest, and we'd pick them up the same way.

I took the first shift, driving Jimmy and the four youngest Grimshaw children to school the following morning. The distance was short and the kids were pretty subdued, maybe because they sensed my mood. In the pocket of my jacket, I had Jimmy's tam, and it felt like a lead weight.

Before we left, I had told Jimmy what I planned to do. It made him angry.

"I thought you said I got to fight my own battles, Smoke," he had said.

"I did."

"But now you're doing it."

"Sometimes other people have to stand up for us, particularly on difficult things."

"I'm not gonna do it," he said. "I'm not gonna tell them I'm afraid of you. I'm not, Smoke."

"Yes you are," I said. "When they approach you again, you have to remember to call me your father. You have to tell them you're more afraid of me than them. Believe me, a lot of them will understand this."

"But it's a lie, Smoke." He shook his head. "Yesterday they told us that lying was bad."

Church. I had forgotten about all of its rules. "Sometimes lies save lives, Jim. You know that."

"Then why would they tell me I can't?"

"Because they're luckier than we are," I said. "They have the luxury to make hard and fast rules. We don't."

He had frowned at me then, but hadn't said any more. In fact, he had barely managed a hello when the Grimshaw children got in the car.

I pulled into the school parking lot and turned off the engine. The school was smaller and shabbier than I remembered, the brick walls covered with graffiti that someone had tried in vain to clean off. The windows on the first floor had burglar bars, and a rusted chain-link fence enclosed the brown yard. Children crowded the swing-set area, and among the knit caps and fur hats, I saw dabs of red.

I sighed and got out with the kids. A number of parents had pulled into the parking lot and they were eyeing the yard with the same suspicion I was. They had their children by the hand and walked them toward a side entrance to the building.

I let the kids lead the way. Lacey walked ahead of us, head bowed, as if she weren't part of the group. She was in her last year of grade school and already considered herself a woman. She was beginning to look like one, too. The makeup she had worn on Saturday night was in her tiny purse; lipstick and eye-shadow had spilled out when she opened it inside the car.

The little girls held my hand, happy to be with their Uncle Bill. They wanted to show me off like a new toy, but I promised they could do that some other time. Jim and Keith walked close to me because I had told them to, but they wanted to hurry. They were embarrassed by my presence.

We reached the back door. The faint odors of chalk and processed air flowed out with the heat. A teacher stood there, monitoring the children as they came in. She smiled at Lacey, who smiled back, then said a friendly hello to the little girls. The boys hung back.

"Go on, Keith," I said after a moment.

"Jim asked me to stay."

I hadn't heard that, but it didn't surprise me. "And I'm telling you to go into the school."

Keith looked at Jimmy, then shrugged and went in. Jimmy didn't move.

I put my hand on his shoulder and turned him toward the playground. "Who gave you the tam?"

"I don't like this, Smoke."

"Dad," I said, correcting him. "And I don't care that you don't like it. We're doing it."

He nodded toward a group of boys who stood just outside

126

the fence. They were older, in the early stages of puberty, and much bigger than Jimmy. But not bigger than me.

"Come on, then."

"Smoke, can't I stay here?"

"No," I said. "But you don't speak a word and you don't make eye contact. Look down, like I gave you a good talking-to."

"You did."

Not as good as my father would have given me. Or even my adopted father, for that matter. I sometimes wondered if their harshness was better than this logical approach I tried to take with Jim.

I kept my hand on his shoulder, propelling him forward. We walked around the fence to the clump of boys. A cloud of smoke rose from the center of the group, and the stench of cheap cigarettes filled the air.

"Hey, Pops," one of the boys said. He was the largest, about half a foot shorter than I was. "Come to join our little group?"

They had stepped forward, hands at their sides. At least one boy was palming a switchblade. A few had on thick coats a size too big, coats that could have hidden anything.

"I came to return something you gave to my son by mistake," I said.

"Ooo," said the leader. "Tough guy. Should we be impressed, Pops?"

I reached into my pocket and pulled out the tam, holding it between my thumb and forefinger as if it smelled bad. "We don't want filth like this in our home."

The teasing looks faded. The boys' mood changed as if they were all one person. They glared at me. Jimmy flinched.

"So even though my son appreciates the offer to join your cozy little group, he's turning you down. And I'd thank you to leave him alone."

"What you think of that, kid?" the leader asked Jimmy. A shiver ran through Jimmy, but he didn't move.

"It doesn't matter what he thinks. All that matters in our house is what I think." I dropped the tam on the ground.

The group murmured and I heard the snick of a blade. Jimmy twitched ever so slightly, but I ignored it.

"If I find out you boys have been harassing my son, I will come after you personally."

"You think you can take us on, Pops?"

"No." I paused, and Jimmy glanced up at me in surprise. "I don't think I can. I know I can."

"You don't scare me, old man," the leader said.

"I'm not trying to," I said. "I'm just telling you how it will be."

"You be doing a mighty stupid thing, taking us on, Pops," said the leader.

"Let's be clear." I kept my hand on Jimmy's shoulder. He felt like he was going to bolt. "I'm not taking you on. I think your organization serves a purpose. I'm not threatening that purpose, nor am I saying that I will. I'm simply establishing my boundaries. Think of me as a gang of one. My son is my turf. Cross into my turf and we'll have conflict. Stay away from my turf and we'll ignore each other forever. Is that clear?"

"What do we get if we respect your turf?" he asked.

"It's what you don't get," I said. "You don't get me in your face every minute of every day."

"We should be afraid of that? Hell, man. Cops can't do nothing to us, why you think you can?"

I smiled slowly, let him see the menace in my eyes. "Because cops have rules they have to follow. I don't."

The leader stared at me. His skin was acne-scarred, and a few scraggly whiskers grew on his chin. He was still too young to grow a beard.

"Pops," he said, "you be one strange motherfucker."

As he spoke, he made a small swirling motion with his right hand. The rest of the group backed away. The leader reached into his pocket and Jimmy stiffened. I didn't move at all.

The leader pulled out a pack of cigarettes, tapped it, and slid one forward. I hadn't smoked in almost twenty years, but I remembered the drill.

I took the cigarette. "Got a light?"

Jimmy looked at me in astonishment. The leader tossed me a book of matches. I opened it with one hand, isolated a single match and lit it with my thumbnail, a trick I'd learned in Korea. Then I put the cigarette in my mouth and lit it, shaking out the match.

"Thanks," I said. My lungs strained to cough out the nicotine, but I wouldn't let them. I gave the group a nod, then steered Jimmy back toward the school.

As soon as we were out of earshot, he said, "You don't smoke."

I let out a lungful of smoke. My eyes burned. I'd forgotten what this felt like. "No, I don't, and I don't plan to start."

"Then what—?"

"You never refuse a peace offering, Jim, no matter what you think of it."

He frowned at me. Inside the school, a bell rang. "That's the warning."

The kids on the playground looked up. Some ran toward the door. Others took their time. I led Jim to the back door where I'd brought the other children. I held the cigarette in my hand, letting it burn down without putting it out.

"You remember what to do if you have problems," I said.

He was developing the most elaborate array of frowns. This was a new one. "I ain't tattling to no one."

"You're going to the principal if you have trouble." I spoke firmly. "He'll call me or Franklin."

"Everyone'll call me a baby."

"If that's the worst that happens, I'll be pleased," I said. "We can live with that."

"I can't," Jimmy said.

I took a fake puff off the cigarette in case we were still being watched. Then I tossed it on the pavement and ground it out with my foot. "Last year, Jim, you came to me because you didn't like the group your brother Joe was hanging out with."

"That's different," Jimmy said.

I nodded. "Yes, it is. That group wasn't nearly as tough or mean as this one. And you saw what happened to Joe."

Jimmy's eyes filled with tears. He wiped at them angrily.

"I don't want anything to happen to you," I said. "You're all I've got."

"I can take care of myself," he said, but the words held no conviction.

"Humor me," I said. "Go to the principal if there's trouble. And wait here at the door after school. One of us will be here to pick you and the others up."

The last of the children were trailing inside. The teacher at the door met my gaze. *Hurry up*, she mouthed.

"How come it got to be so hard, Smoke?"

"I don't know, Jim," I said, touching his cheek lightly. "Sometimes it just is."

TEN

I went back to my car and stuck my keys in the ignition, waiting for the school doors to close. As they did, the gang of kids outside the fence tossed their cigarettes and headed for Woodlawn. The dismal building looked even smaller and dingier in the gray light.

My heart was beating hard. The confrontation had taken more out of me than I expected. I had been as worried about it as Jimmy, maybe more so. I still wasn't sure it was going to work, but I had to try. I was going to help Jim lead a productive life no matter what it took.

I reached for my swinging keys when someone pounded on the driver's side window. I jumped, startled, and turned. A man I'd never seen before pressed a policeman's shield against the glass. He was wearing civilian clothing and his skin was darker than mine.

I rolled down the window a few inches, enough to speak to him, but not enough for him to get a hand through.

"Help you?" I asked in my coldest voice.

"Chaz Yancy, Gang Intelligence Unit." He nodded toward an unmarked van parked across the street. I hadn't even noticed it, which showed just how preoccupied I had been. "What were you talking to the Stones for?"

I kept my hands on my lap so he could see them. "They gave my son a hat. I returned it."

"Do you have any idea who those boys are, Mr.—"

"Of course I do," I said, ignoring his not-so-subtle attempt to fish for my name. "I'm not real fond of the Blackstone Rangers. Why do you think I want to keep my kid away from them?"

"If you're so hot to keep your kid away, why'd you talk so long?"

"And take a smoke from them?"

"That, too." He had a gold front tooth. It caught the thin morning light.

"We came to an agreement. The cigarette sealed the bargain."

"An agreement?"

"If they left my kid alone, I'd leave them alone."

"You're such a big tough guy that they're all afraid of you?"

I shook my head slightly. "I just convinced them it wasn't worth their time to deal with me."

He let out a small snort. "What's your name?"

This time, I couldn't ignore the question. "Bill Grimshaw."

"Well, Mr. Grimshaw, these boys aren't afraid of anything. All you probably did was call attention to yourself and your little boy. You probably made things a lot worse for him."

"You think so?" I kept my voice bland, but he was beginning to anger me.

"Whenever parents get involved, things get much worse. You people have no idea what you're messing with."

"So you think I should've let my kid keep the tam, join the gang, get into trouble?"

"I'm not saying that."

"What are you saying?" This time, I let him hear just a bit of the anger.

His eyes widened slightly. "I'm saying you should have let us deal with it."

"You." I nodded, pretending to be thoughtful. "The group of men hanging out in that van over there, watching little kids smoke cigarettes, carry dangerous weapons, and recruit other little kids into activities we all know are illegal."

"Yeah," he said. "Us."

"They gave my boy the tam on Friday. What did you do about it?"

"We'd talk to him."

"Eventually."

He nodded.

"Make him feed you information."

"Maybe."

"Put him in even more danger."

"Listen, Grimshaw, you're out of your depth."

"No, Yancy. You are. No one uses my son for anything. Gangs or cops. You got that?"

"You threatening a police officer?"

"I don't see a uniform," I said. "So far as I'm concerned, this is one man talking to another."

I turned the key in the ignition and the car rumbled to life. Yancy backed away. I shoved the gearshift into drive and peeled out as if I were a teenager in a drag race.

By now, my hands were shaking. If I had stayed a moment longer, I'd have been the one getting in trouble for harassing a police officer. My temper was snapping. A gang intelligence unit watching a grade school, seeing the recruitment and doing nothing about it—that was as criminal to me as the recruitment itself.

I drove north and east. My plan had been to do as much research as I could into Foster's life before I hit the libraries. Sometime that day, I'd also go to the hospital and see how Epstein and Elaine were doing.

By the time I reached State Street, I was a little calmer. If I'd had Laura's clout, I would have called the police commissioner and complained about his idle Intelligence Unit. Of course, if I had Laura's clout, Jimmy and I wouldn't have been in this situation in the first place.

I drove up State Street toward the Loop. Foster's dental office was near the old Black Metropolis, which had once been the center of Bronzeville, the black neighborhood. Much of that had been gutted for housing projects and so-called urban renewal, but some of it was left. The office, which Foster shared with two other dentists, was on a block filled with business offices and private medical services that catered to the black community.

Foster's address was in a brown brick building in the center of a block. The building had its own parking lot off an alley. The alley was full of broken glass, but the lot itself was clean and well-tended.

I parked near a new Mustang and got out, noting that it seemed even chillier this much closer to the lake. I stuck my hands in my jacket pockets and hurried into the building.

The interior reminded me of my old offices in Memphis. I hoped that by now, Henry Davis had cleared out my files and stopped paying rent on the office space. Still, losing it gave me a pang. I tried not to think of that old life; it was gone for good. As long as I had Jimmy, I had no way of returning home.

I shook off the thoughts, checked the black board that listed the office names in little white plastic letters, 1930s' style. Foster's office was on the third floor. I took the marble stairs two at a time, using exercise to shake off the last of the anger, and found myself feeling calmer when I reached the top.

The entire floor had a sharp medicinal scent. The overhead lights had been replaced with bad fluorescents sometime in the last ten years, washing everything in a sickly glow. Foster's office was the first one on the left. The sign on the door read simply DENTAL OFFICES. To find the dentists' names, I had to look beside the call bell to the door's right.

The knob turned easily in my hand and as I stepped inside, the medicinal smell grew. The high-pitched whine of a dentist's drill came from down the hall, as did the murmur of voices. Overhead, the radio advertised the newest show at Mr. Kelly's—Flip Wilson for two full weeks.

The waiting area was small and furnished with old wooden chairs. On a scarred coffee table, ripped and torn copies of *Ebony*, *Time*, and *Reader's Digest* were lined up next to that day's edition of the *Defender* and the *Daily News*.

A phone rang behind the receptionist's desk, but no one answered it. After a moment, the ringing stopped. I couldn't tell if someone had picked up an extension or if the caller had just given up.

I walked to the desk and leaned on it. Beside my elbow, a new patient information form rested on a clipboard, a pen tucked into the metal clasp. Behind the desk were shelves holding patients' files, carefully arranged alphabetically. A number of the files littered the desk, one resting kitty-corner on top of an electric typewriter that someone had forgotten to shut off. Its hum was barely audible over the whine of the drill.

I toyed with hitting the little silver bell that sat on the edge of the counter, but decided that wouldn't ingratiate me with the staff.

After a moment, the drill shut off, a woman laughed, and the minty scent of mouthwash filtered toward me from the back. The laughter grew closer until a woman came into view.

She was heavyset, with a round face and coal-black eyes. She wore a white smock over a dark blue dress, and on her left hand she wore a flashy diamond engagement ring. Her laughter shook her entire body. When she saw me, she stopped, but the mirth was still apparent in the twitching of her full lips.

"Fill out the patient information chart," she said, tapping the clipboard, "and I'll be right with you."

"I'm not a patient," I said. "I'm investigating the death of Louis Foster."

Immediately the laughter vanished from her face. "You with the police?"

She asked the question with hope. Apparently the police hadn't been here, either.

"No," I said. "I'm working for the family."

"Oh, you must be Mr. Grimshaw," she said. "Alice told us you'd be coming by."

I wished she hadn't. I wanted to catch them all before they had time to coordinate their stories—if, indeed, there was a need to coordinate stories.

But I made myself smile. "Yes. I'm Bill Grimshaw."

"I'll get Dr. Wright. He's been wanting to talk with you."

"I'd like to talk to you first, if I could."

"I don't have a lot to say." She sank into her green office chair. It squeaked, needing oil.

"That's all right," I said. "I just wanted to check the information I have. I understand Mr. Foster left here at noon that Friday."

She nodded, and didn't meet my gaze.

"His wife thought he was leaving at four."

The receptionist shrugged. "He often left early on Fridays."

"Do you know why?"

"No." She moved the file off the electric typewriter, then grabbed a sheet of white paper and put it in the platen. "That's all I can tell you."

It clearly wasn't. "Mrs.—"

"Miss," she said. "Paula Firness."

"Miss Firness, was Dr. Foster seeing another woman?"

"What he did in his own time wasn't my business." She used the return key to wind the paper into the typewriter.

"I had a long talk with Mrs. Foster." I kept my voice low. "She says it's worse not knowing who killed her husband than it is thinking that he had an affair."

Paula Firness sighed. She shook her head. For a moment, I thought she wasn't going to answer. Then she said, "A woman called him a lot. I was always to put her directly through unless he was with a patient."

"Do you remember her name?"

"Jane Sarton."

"Did she ever come to the office?"

"Not that I know of," Paula said.

"Did you ever meet her?"

"No." She sounded indignant.

"Did he go to meet her on Friday?"

She didn't answer for a long time. She arranged papers before her, then set one on a typing stand. It became clear she wasn't going to answer that question at all.

136

"Miss Firness," I said in a polite but firm voice. "Did he meet her on Friday?"

"I don't know for sure."

"But you think so."

She closed her eyes. "He usually saw her on Friday afternoons."

"How long had he been seeing her?"

Her eyes flew open and this time, she turned to me. "Dr. Foster was a good man. He was kind to all of us here, and we miss him a lot. You're not going to make him out to be a horrible person."

"No, I'm not. But I need to know everything I can about him so I can figure out what happened that day."

"He never hurt anyone."

"By having an affair with this woman?"

"No, I mean at all." She leaned toward me. "I always sent the frightened patients to him. He did his best to treat them light. He was a big man, but he had slender hands—long fingers like a piano player. He was good. Our business's dropped off by almost half since he's been gone."

I caught the implication. The others weren't nearly as good as he had been. He brought in most of the revenue, and now that he was gone, she was worried about her job.

"Do you have a phone number for her?"

"For Miss Sarton?" She started to shake her head and then stopped. She opened a desk drawer and pulled out an appointment calendar for the front half of the year.

She thumbed through it until she reached a Friday in May. There was Jane Sarton's name, with a phone number beneath it. Unlike the rest of the entries, this one was in a slashing, masculine hand.

Miss Firness copied the phone number onto a piece of paper and handed it to me.

"Thanks," I said, putting it in my shirt pocket. "I only have a few more questions."

She glanced toward the back. The whine of the drill had

started again, followed by a deep masculine voice trying to sound soothing.

I asked, "Was there anything else unusual about him? Strange friends? Abnormal behavior before he died? Unusually moody or preoccupied?"

Miss Firness turned toward me again. Someone said "Ouch!" rather loudly down the hall and she didn't even seem to notice.

"His mother-in-law was coming to visit. He hated that. But he seemed like he was in a good mood. He told me that he'd finally hit his savings goal. He said he had to tell someone that because—." She stopped herself.

"Because what?"

"Because he couldn't tell his wife."

Now we were getting somewhere. "Why not?"

"It was going to be a surprise."

"What was?"

She shrugged. "He never said. He just laughed and told me it was better to save my money than spend it on frivolous things. He was real frugal, Dr. Foster was."

"Anything else?"

"He always had candy for the little kids. The other dentists, they frowned on that, but he said any little kid could have candy in moderation, so long as they brushed. If the kid didn't take care of his teeth, he didn't get any candy on the way out." She twisted her engagement ring. "Him and Mrs. Foster, they couldn't have kids. I always thought maybe he treated kids so good because that was the only contact he'd have with them."

"Were there ever any gang troubles here, Miss Firness?"

"Gangs?" She looked at me in confusion.

"You know, like the Blackstone Rangers or the Vice Lords? Did he have any of them as patients?"

"Heavens, no, Mr. Grimshaw. It was always peaceful here. The people who brought in their children, well, you'd recognize them from some of the finest families in Bronzeville."

"Did he have trouble with gangs at home?"

She frowned. "Why're you asking this?"

"Because the police think his killing might have been gang-related. They might have targeted him."

"Dr. Foster?" She shook her head. "I'm not even sure he was really aware that the gangs existed, Mr. Grimshaw. He lived his own life on his own path and rarely strayed from it."

"Until the weeks before his death."

She pursed her lips. "Until that Jane Sarton started to call."

My meeting with the rest of the office staff proved less helpful. The other two dentists took time from their busy round of patients to talk with me, but all they could add was that they would both miss Foster's handling of the office's financial affairs. He had been frugal to a fault, and had invested some of their income to a profit, something the others hadn't realized until he died. Neither of them had a head for business and they were thinking of hiring an office manager to take over that part of Foster's role.

The dental assistants talked about his patients, and I heard nothing unusual. Some of the biggest names in Bronzeville brought their children to him because of his reputation with kids. Again, no gang connection and no reported troubles, either at home or at work. The other dentists weren't even certain if he carried large amounts of cash with him.

I left the office with Jane Sarton as my only lead, although I got a list of friends and acquaintances who might be able to help. I exited by the front of the building, hoping to find a pay phone. The closest one was two blocks down. Graffiti stained its exterior, and someone had ripped out the phone book.

I slipped a dime into the slot, listened to it clang, and then dialed. After a single ring, someone picked up.

"Jane Sarton," a cultured female voice answered.

I was a bit startled by the greeting. I'd never heard anyone answer their home phone like that. "Miss Sarton?"

"Yes?" Practiced patience.

"My name is Bill Grimshaw. I'm investigating the death of Louis Foster and I was wondering if I could speak to you."

There was a long silence on the other end. I waited, listening to background noises, but hearing little over the traffic noise of South State Street.

"The . . . what?" she said after a moment, all confidence gone from her voice.

"The death of Louis Foster."

"Lou is dead?" she asked.

I leaned against the booth's glass wall. Of course no one had told her. She was the mistress that no one knew about. Why would anyone tell her?

I doubted that anyone could fake this kind of surprise. Which made the events of the last afternoon of his life even more important.

"I'm sorry," I said. "I thought you knew. It was in the papers."

"It was?" She sounded numb.

"Yes. Last month. I was wondering if I could talk with you."

"Last month." She repeated that as if I were asking for an appointment in the past. "When?"

"The weekend before Thanksgiving."

"How?"

"That's what I'd like to talk with you about, ma'am. Could I come and see you? It's easier to do this face-to-face."

"I—" She hesitated. "I have a lunch meeting. Can we do it at one-thirty?"

She had startled me again. If I had just discovered that my lover died, I would have wanted to find out more immediately.

"One-thirty's fine," I said. "Where are you located?"

She gave me an address in Old Town. "I'll look for you at one-thirty, then," she said and hung up.

I stared at the phone. She was the coolest woman I'd ever heard. I'd broken the news to others about their loved ones before and no one, no one had ever reacted so strangely.

I'd find out what caused this odd reaction when I saw her. I had about two hours to kill before our meeting. Since she was north of the Loop, it wasn't that much farther for me to go to the hospital. I'd wanted to check on Epstein and Elaine anyway; this was my chance.

The hospital looked different than it had the day before, busier, more structured, as if it had acquired a sense of purpose. Perhaps part of the difference was that I entered through the front doors instead of the emergency entrance and had to play twenty questions at the Information Desk before I was allowed upstairs.

The other reason, of course, was that it was Monday, and hospitals, like all other businesses, sprang to life after the silence of the weekend.

I took a clunky old elevator to the third floor where Epstein's room was. I wanted to see him first because part of me wasn't certain he was going to make it through the night. The cautious way the doctor and the surgeons had spoken about him made me worry that more was wrong than they were letting on.

His room was halfway down a long corridor. It was a quiet wing; even the overhead speaker, announcing doctors' names and codes, seemed muted. No one appeared to stir in their rooms, although a number had televisions on. The hospital smell—sickness mixed with cleaning solvents and greasy, unappetizing food—was nearly enough to drive me out of the building.

But I finally found the door with the right number and wasn't surprised to find Mrs. Weisman inside, her purse on the end table and an unopened bag of knitting beside her chair. Someone had pulled the privacy curtain closed behind her, and against that yellow backdrop, she looked even frailer than she had the day before.

I cleared my throat as I walked into the room. The medicinal smell was stronger here, along with a faint trace of urine.

"Mr. Grimshaw!" she said with real pleasure. Even though we had exchanged first names, we seemed loath to use them.

"Mrs. Weisman," I said, grabbing a chair from the far wall and placing it beside hers. "How is he today?"

So far, I had managed to avoid the immobile figure on the bed, but as I asked the question, I looked down. Epstein's face was wrapped in gauze, with extra bandages over his left eye. His right peeked out, closed, his long lashes resting on the white material. Part of his forehead remained unbandaged and his hair cascaded over the pillow, giving the impression that he was a young girl instead of an adult male.

Intravenous tubes were taped to the inside of his elbow, and a drip unit sat near the wall. The call button was within reach of his right hand, but looked like no one had even tried to touch it. His knuckles were scraped, a detail I hadn't noticed the day before. He must have tried to defend himself.

"They're keeping him sedated," she said. "The longer he remains still, the better off he is."

I nodded as I sat down beside her.

"They said they'd call me before they woke him up, but I couldn't sit home and just wait."

"I understand." I took her hand and patted it.

"I don't know what we would have done without you, Mr. Grimshaw," she said.

"You'd have found a way."

She shook her head. "There's no phone upstairs. I keep going over and over this in my mind. What if I had come down and you hadn't been there? What then?"

"Both men were busy. They wouldn't have noticed you. You could have gotten out."

"But would I? That's what I keep wondering."

I took her hand. It felt small beneath mine. "Focus forward. Saul's going to need your help for a while."

"For a long while." She shook her head. "They're still not sure about his eye. We have to wait until he wakes up, and even then we might not know for a while. I'm so afraid to tell him that he might lose it, Mr. Grimshaw. His photography is what he lives for."

I wasn't sure how much effect losing an eye would have on a photographer. Perhaps not a lot for a photojournalist, but some of those shots I had seen were artistic. The loss of an eye might make a difference there.

I looked at Epstein, so small beneath the covers. He hadn't been a big man as it was. The fact that he survived such a beating was a testament to something, although I wasn't sure what.

"What have the police found out?"

Mrs. Weisman's lips thinned, an expression I was beginning to learn was one of disapproval. "They're charging the boy who beat my Saul with aggravated assault and breaking and entering. They may add more charges later. But he won't say who his friend was, and now he has a lawyer, so he's not talking to anyone."

The news didn't surprise me. I had expected the lawyer almost immediately. Not that it mattered to me. The boy had become inaccessible to me the moment he went into police custody.

"Does he have a name?"

"Gilbert Mattiotti. Apparently they call him Bruiser."

"Why doesn't that surprise me," I said.

"That was my first thought." She plucked at the blanket with her free hand.

"No discussion of motivation?"

She shook her head once.

I wished I'd had the opportunity to talk with Bruiser Mattiotti. I had spent the night wondering if these two were the ones I'd been searching for—although the beatings didn't seem to fit. Foster's murder and the matching murders of the young boys had a cleanliness to them, a precision.

Still, I wanted to question him about it. I only hoped I got to the second perpetrator before the police did. If I didn't, I might have to enlist Truman Johnson's help sooner than I'd expected to.

"I tell you what," I said, squeezing her hand and then letting go. "I want to see Elaine, but when I'm done, I'm coming back here and dragging you to lunch."

"I don't want to leave—"

"You won't leave the hospital. I'll suffer through cafeteria food for the honor of your company."

She smiled. "You're such a flatterer, Mr. Grimshaw."

I smiled back and stood. "I'll take that for a yes."

A bit of the old twinkle returned to her eyes, and I was glad to see it. I left, promising to return shortly.

Elaine was on another floor. Her room wasn't as nice, but she had a window and Epstein did not. Of course he wouldn't have had any use for it yet, and I shuddered, thinking about his eye.

The bed closest to the door was empty and had been stripped of its sheets. The smell of bleach was strong in the room, and the window was open slightly to compensate. It was chilly inside, but someone had tucked two extra blankets around Elaine's bed.

Her television set was on, blaring a soap opera, but she didn't seem to be paying attention. Instead, she stared out the window at the gray Chicago skyline.

"Elaine?" I said as I took the seat beside her bed.

She blinked, then sighed, turning toward me. The right side of her face was covered with small stitched wounds. She looked like a doll that had been shredded, a doll that some well-meaning parent had tried to sew together in vain.

There was no smile or relief when she saw me. Just a bleakness that hadn't been in her eyes two days before.

"I'm sorry for yesterday." Her voice was raspy, and her words surprised me.

"Sorry? You didn't do anything wrong."

"I'm not usually clingy."

"You're not usually attacked by a complete stranger."

She nodded, as if dismissing my words, and then said, "Mind turning down the sound?"

I grabbed the volume knob and twisted it all the way down.

"What were you doing there yesterday?" She was covered to her chin. Not even her hands were visible. I thought I had seen them as I walked in. I got the sense she had covered up while my back was turned.

"I had a meeting with Saul."

"Oh," she said with disinterest. "You were the meeting he wanted to come home for."

"Is that why he drove you there?"

She shook her head slightly. "He was running. He just didn't know where to go. He wasn't thinking it through."

"Had you ever seen those guys before?"

"You and the police." Her dark eyes flashed. "That's all you care about. Had we seen them before? Did I know them? What did I do to provoke them?"

"I didn't ask you that," I said, returning to the chair. "And I actually hadn't intended to ask any questions at all, just to see how you were doing."

"I'm fine," she snapped.

"You're still here," I said gently.

"Five hours of surgery. They insist that I stay." She made it sound as if she would rather be doing anything else.

"Did they reach your family?"

For the first time, a slight smile touched her face. Every movement looked painful as it tugged at the swollen wounds. "They think you're my father."

"I know," I said. "I tried to tell them—"

"It's all right. I don't have a father, and my mother's dead. I called my sister. She lives in Detroit. She'll be here tomorrow to take me home."

"Home to Detroit?"

The smile faded. "I can't take care of myself for a while. Too many stitches. The doctor's afraid I'll pop them. Besides, I've had enough of Chicago."

After all this, I could understand why.

She slipped a hand out from under the covers. Her palm was bandaged, and more bandages covered her arm. With her fingers, she brushed away a strand of hair.

"How's Saul?" she asked in a completely different voice.

Needy, worried. The same voice she had used yesterday when she was in shock.

"They beat him up pretty badly. His ribs are broken and so are a lot of bones in his face. They did some reconstruction, but he'll probably need more. He might lose an eye."

She winced. "I thought the worst thing that happened to him was the loss of that camera."

"What camera?"

"Both, actually. Those bastards ripped the cameras off his neck and smashed them. I had to hold him back. He wanted to stay and fight then."

I didn't move. She wanted to tell part of this, but she didn't want anyone to ask questions. Somehow, I understood the contradiction.

"He was crying on the drive to the house. The old one had belonged to his father."

Anger rose inside me and I had to struggle to suppress it. Part of me believed I should be used to it by now—that vicious, unreasoning hatred that seemed to come at us just because we walked the same earth as white people. But I wasn't used to it. I would never be used to it. And while I knew it existed, I was still stunned by it.

"You know," she was saying, "if I had been with anybody else, we'd've gotten out of there the minute the guys looked our way. But I didn't see them at first, and Saul wasn't used to the warning signs. In the car, he told me they'd been watching us for a half an hour. You wouldn't have let guys like that stare at us for a half an hour."

"No, I wouldn't." I'd learned the look, learned how to be wary of it, learned how to dodge it.

"He didn't know. I should've known." Her eyes were dry, but her voice shook. "I'd like to see him before I go. I want to apologize."

I leaned forward, surprised at the depth of her guilt and wishing that I knew how to deal with it. If we were in Memphis, I'd ask Henry to see her, or one of the other ministers, someone trained in the art of listening, of consoling, of counseling. But

I knew no one here, and I wondered if Elaine did either.

"You think this is your fault?" I asked.

"I'm the one who knows how people are. Saul's naïve. He was protected. I liked that about him. . . ." Her voice trailed off.

"You didn't see those men," I said.

"Not until it was too late." She brushed her face again, and I realized that she had no hair in the way. It was a nervous gesture, something for her to do. "But I used to check, you know."

I did know. I was always more vigilant when I was around Laura than I was without her.

"I forgot this time." She sighed. "It was his neighborhood and the people there were so nice. I stopped worrying."

"We can't always prevent these things from happening, even if you were paying attention."

She shrugged, then winced. The movement must have hurt her stitches. "I should have seen them, felt them. The things they yelled . . ."

I didn't say anything.

"Saul's not going to understand why I have to go." Her voice was quiet.

"Yes he will. You're going to need help healing, just like he will."

She shook her head slightly. "He's so—taken with me. So serious."

"You're not, are you?"

For the first time, her eyes teared. "He's nice. He's different. I like him."

"But he's not the only one, is he?"

"I'm not like that!" Her voice rose. "I'm not!"

I held out my hands, trying to calm her down. "I just meant—"

"You are like the police. They think it's all my fault. If I hadn't let him kiss me in the park—"

"Elaine." I said her name firmly and that caught her attention. "I know this isn't your fault. I know it. I saw what was happening. No one asks for that. No one invites it. I wasn't suggesting that you were."

She struggled to grab control of her emotions, but her lower lip still trembled. She had seemed so calm that the outburst surprised me. I wondered what other emotions were lurking beneath the surface.

"All I was asking was if you had fallen in love with Saul."

Tears filled her eyes again. "I wish I had," she whispered. "You don't know how much I wish I had."

ELEVEN

Elaine and I talked a little longer, mostly about inconsequential things. I managed to get her sister's name, address, and phone number before I left, ostensibly for Saul, but for myself as well. I wanted to keep track of her, make certain she was all right. I also wanted to talk to her sister and let her know the severity of the attack. Elaine would need someone to talk to— and if she couldn't find that person at home, she might have to see some kind of professional to help her through. I knew the doctor wouldn't suggest it, so I would, especially given the way her emotions had fluctuated in the short time I had spent with her.

After I left Elaine, I stopped in the emergency room. I saw Marge Evenrud, the nurse I had spoken with the night before. She waved at me, held up a finger asking me to wait, and disappeared behind a door. After a few moments, she joined me.

"Nothing yet, Mr. Grimshaw," she said quietly. "But I did some askin' about you, found out you're related to Franklin Grimshaw, and how you done work for people."

"Yes," I said.

"They still not sure they got all that glass outta that girl," she said in a low voice. "They watching her tonight, hoping she don't get infected. And the police, they just treated her like dirt, thinking she ask for the whole thing, kissing a white boy like that."

"He nearly died for it," I said.

"And what'd he do 'cept follow his—" She waved a hand in front of her hips, the gesture almost eloquent. "So I got myself thinking, we don't know who her attacker is or where he lives or what he was doing in the park on a Sunday. He coulda been from anywhere."

I hadn't thought of that, and I should have. It showed how tired and preoccupied I had been the day before.

"Ain't no guarantee he's even coming here. There's dozens of hospitals in this city, maybe more."

"I'm sorry," I said. "That hadn't occurred to me."

"Well," she said, "I got it all solved. I got friends all over the city, nurses I used to work with, folks I went to school with, and we're all keepin' an eye out for you. He shows up anywhere in Chicago, we got him."

"Bless you, Marge," I said, feeling a relief I hadn't expected. "That's more than I could have hoped for."

"Got enough white boys like that in this world. Be good to take a few off the streets." She smiled. "I gotta be getting back, but I thought you'd want to know. Stay by the phone. I'm wagering if the burns is as bad as you say, we'll be hearing from him any minute now."

After that, my lunch with Mrs. Weisman was uneventful. We purposely discussed light topics—the football season, the upcoming Davis Cup, which I'd learned more about thanks to Arthur Ashe's great year, and our worries about the country after the recent election. We never mentioned the attack or its consequences, and she seemed more relaxed when I said goodbye to her half an hour later.

The address Jane Sarton gave me turned out to be right across the street from Lincoln Park. The neighborhood was old and run-down, though it had clearly been upscale once upon a time. A handful of respectable businesses remained—a dress shop, a Nordstrom's department store, a once-classy restaurant.

But not half a block away were head shops and adult book-stores, business offices that were now empty or had posters advertising rock concerts in their windows.

The last time I had seen this neighborhood, it had been over-run with hippies and college students, all protesting the war. Now the park seemed empty. No one walked its brown grass, and unraked fall leaves blew across the deserted streets. I wondered where Elaine and Saul Epstein had gone to neck, if the area was private as so many areas in the park were, or if it was as public as the curb across the street from me. Not that it mattered. What mattered was that someone saw them.

The address turned out to be a realty office. The sign above the store, manufactured in the 1920s at the latest, read S&S REALTY, promising me excellent service at excellent prices.

I pushed open the glass door and was hit by a wave of heat, followed by the scents of Emeraude and cigarettes. A beige carpet that had seen better days covered the floor of the waiting area, and an elderly white secretary guarded the big desk that stood in front of the doors leading to the realtor's offices.

Somehow I'd had the sense that Jane Sarton was a woman who didn't work, who had Friday afternoons free to meet her lover because she was a stay-at-home wife. The address prepared me to meet a white woman, but it hadn't prepared me for this ancient business, the feeling as if I'd walked into someone else's past.

I approached the desk. "Hello," I said in my warmest voice. "I'm here to see Jane Sarton."

"You must be Mr. Grimshaw." The elderly woman stood up. She had on a red suit with a narrow skirt, and wore more costume jewelry than I'd seen on one person. The smell of Emeraude was stronger here. She extended a hand. Her wrist, hidden by a series of gold bracelets, jingled as she moved. "I'm Jane Sarton."

The voice was the same—that upscale, clipped Chicago accent that I'd heard on the phone. I took her hand and shook it, something I'd rarely done with a woman.

"Bill Grimshaw," I said, hoping my surprise didn't show. "I wanted to talk with you about Louis Foster."

"I remember." She made her way around the desk and put a "closed" sign in the window. "Quite a shock you gave me this morning. I had no idea why Lou hadn't kept our appointments, but I figured he'd simply found a new agent or changed his mind."

"Changed his mind?"

"About the house." She frowned at me. "Didn't they tell you?"

"They?" I asked.

"Of course they didn't," she said, answering her own question. "No one knew. It was going to be a surprise."

"A surprise?"

"You poor dear." She sat on an antique chair that needed reupholstering and patted another chair next to her. "You did say you're investigating Lou's death."

"Yes." I took a different chair, a sturdier wooden chair across from her. I wanted to be able to see her face.

"So I take it that there was, as they say, foul play?"

She had to be at least seventy. The steely gray hair, piled in a beehive on top of her head, moved as a single unit. It was a wig. I tried not to stare at it.

"He was murdered."

"Oh." She let out the word as a single breath. "Was it for the money?"

"Money?" Why did I feel as if this woman would do better investigating the case than I would?

"The stocks. Now surely someone told you about them."

"No, ma'am," I said, hoping we were discussing the same person.

"That Lou." She shook her head. "If my husband had left me as well off as Lou Foster left his wife, well then, I wouldn't have to try to keep these doors open. Not that I'm much of a businesswoman. I'm simply too interested in people and not interested enough in sales. And I seem to be the only realtor in the city who believes in the Fair Housing Act. Well, the only white one anyway."

She grinned at me as if we shared a secret. I was still struggling to catch up. I had checked out Foster's finances, using the information that his wife had given me to discover his bank balances and the value of his home. I had heard nothing about other investments—although the dentists did mention that he had managed their money extremely well.

"How did you know about the stocks?" I asked.

"He told me, of course. I've been burned a few times. I get the client ready, the homeowner moves, and then the financing falls through or the check bounces. Since I depend on those commissions for my own rent, I check out everything clients tell me—white, black, or purple clients. It doesn't matter to me, so long as their money's good."

And so long as they could put up with her. I wondered how Foster had done it. She seemed well-intentioned, but something about her attitude told me that her liberalism had come upon her at the same time her financial woes had. "What did he tell you about the stocks?"

"Not enough, actually. He seemed to have a nose for the right investment. International Business Machines and Coca-Cola, all bought when he got out of college in the late forties. He had other stocks as well, some he wanted to get rid of because of the war—Dow Chemical, Morrison-Knudsen, a few others. When he sold those, he'd have a windfall—his word, of course—and he wanted to use it to find the perfect home to grow old and retire in. His words again, actually. He wanted to have a house purchased and the deal closed before his wedding anniversary in February. It was going to be a surprise to his wife."

It would be, too. I wasn't sure how I was going to tell her this. We had both considered the possibility of an affair. The idea that he had been about to do something both grandiose and magnanimous actually might be harder to take.

"How much was he worth?" I asked.

"I don't know exactly, but he was going to pay cash for whatever we found. That opened a lot of our options, you know. We could deal directly with some sellers, and we had the chance of getting into neighborhoods that traditionally—well, you know, of course, since you've probably encountered the same problem yourself, Mr. Grimshaw."

She had her legs tucked to one side and crossed at the ankles like a debutante. Her feet were swollen inside her red pumps. Despite her nonstop conversation, I got a sense of deep exhaustion from her, and not-so-well-hidden desperation.

"If you don't mind my asking," she said into my silence, "when did he die?"

"They found his body on November twenty-third in Washington Park, but they think he died the day before. That day was a Friday."

"Oh, dear," she said. "No one's spoken to me before now. Are you a police officer, Mr. Grimshaw?"

"No, ma'am. I work for his wife. The police aren't really following up on anything."

"Such a tragedy. He was such a young man. I'm stunned that I didn't know." She twisted her fingers together. "Apparently it was something more than a mugging or you wouldn't be here."

"You may have been the last person to see him, Mrs. Sarton."

"I know for a fact that isn't so, Mr. Grimshaw." She stood up in a wave of perfume and walked to her desk.

For a moment, I thought she'd continue with the cliché—that his killer had been the last to see him—but she didn't say anything more. Instead, she rummaged through her desk drawer, finally removing the pages of a calendar.

"I thought so," she said, more to herself than to me. Then she looked up and gave me an apologetic smile. "My memory isn't what it used to be, Mr. Grimshaw. Thought I'd refresh it before I continued."

"I appreciate that," I said.

She left the desk and came back to the chair, still carrying the pages from the calendar. They had been pulled out when they were completed, each day marked off with a slash through it. She sat across from me and handed me a page.

"See there?" she said, pointing to her one-o'clock appointment. It was marked with an LF and an address. "I took him to see this house for the fifth time. He was real interested, but real nervous about it. It's in what we call a transition neighborhood. Upper-class Negroes are moving in—"

Blacks, I mentally corrected her, the voice in my head so loud that I thought she might have heard it.

"—and of course whites are moving out."

"Of course," I said.

"Oh, I'm sorry, Mr. Grimshaw." She looked appalled. "I didn't mean to insult you, but it's just a fact of life in some of these neighborhoods. I didn't even show Dr. Foster some of my houses. We agreed we wouldn't see places in Cicero and some of the suburbs. He wanted a nice home without all the problems. This neighborhood was as troubled as he wanted to get."

I stared at the address. It was on a small side street nearly forty blocks south of my neighborhood. I had no idea there was even a black community there.

"This is a white neighborhood?" I asked.

"Transitional," she said again.

"What, exactly, does that mean?"

She met my gaze for a moment, then looked away. "Um, well, a few families moved into the neighborhood before the riots last April, and since, well, others have wanted to leave."

It took me a moment to figure out what she was saying. "Black families moved in and now the neighborhood is experiencing white flight?"

"Crudely put," she said, still not meeting my gaze.

"That sounds like a gold mine for real estate agents."

"Some," she said. "But it can also be quite a headache. I had no idea that banks have preferred customers when I got into this, or that financing could be so difficult to come by. I've been searching for good rates for your people, but I've had difficulties. Rates quoted me are quite different than rates that would be quoted to you."

155

"I'm aware of that," I said.

Of course I was. It was a fact of life that the Jane Sartons of the world never had to deal with. Blacks usually got charged a higher interest rate, and sometimes even a higher asking price, than whites. Banks skimmed profits off the deal, so white-owned, blacks-only mortgage lenders had gotten into the business. They charged higher rates than banks and had terrible restrictions. On some, even one late payment could result in foreclosure.

"I often warn my clients of this problem up front. Some accept it, and others find a way around it, the way Dr. Foster was doing. Paying cash for the house gave him a measure of control that I found unprecedented, and I was trying to convince him to let me broker the deal. That way, the seller wouldn't know that he was selling to a colored man and the price would remain fair."

Her language made it difficult to concentrate on what she was saying. She was trying to serve her clients as best she could, even in the face of her prejudices.

"So he was interested in this house—"

"Oh, it's beautiful," she said. "Large bedrooms, a second bathroom, and a living room that has picture windows on two sides, a marvelous garden in the spring, and even a fence for privacy. I adore the house, and I think Lou did, too."

"But?"

"No buts. I expected him to come in the following week with an offer. The house wasn't moving quickly, since it's in a transitional neighborhood, and the seller was motivated, at least when he spoke to me."

I caught the hesitation in her voice. "The seller had met Dr. Foster before, hadn't he?"

"Oh, no. The house was usually unattended when I showed it. The owner had already found a new home in Lake Forest, and had moved. It's so much easier to show an empty house."

The hair rose on the back of my neck. "So the owner met Dr. Foster for the first time that day?"

"Yes, and they seemed to get along." She pushed the bangles

higher up on her arm. They disappeared under her sleeve. "He did want to speak to the other neighbors, but he told me it was just a formality. He said it's his house to sell, after all."

"Was he surprised that Foster was black?"

"Who knows? He didn't act surprised, but then many of my clients don't when they meet someone. I only hear later. They'll call or ask me not to bring anyone like that around again. Or they'll take their home off the market. That's happened a few times. And more than once, the neighbors have banded together to buy the house." She spoke so matter-of-factly that I got even more chilled.

"Did the owner call you?"

"No, not about Dr. Foster. We'd had some problems in the summer—the owner wasn't sure he wanted to sell to your people then—but his house wasn't moving and he changed his mind."

I made note of that. "You're sure?"

"Oh, yes," she said. "I don't like to subject my clients to the prejudices of others."

She said that so primly that it almost made me smile.

"So you never heard from the owner again?"

"I did," she said. "He called after Thanksgiving, wanting to know what happened to the deal. I left a message with Lou's service, but no one called me back."

Because they all thought he was having an affair with her. I almost laughed at the irony.

"That's a bit rude, come to think of it," she said. "After all, how was I to know what happened? Not everyone reads the papers every day."

"I think his office was stunned to lose him," I said.

"I couldn't very well call his wife, since this was supposed to be a surprise. So I called his office again the following week and got the service again—they should have instructed the service to say something."

"Yes, they should have." I was being polite. I had no idea how these things worked.

"And then I put him on my tickler. I was going to call at the end of the week." She sighed. "Well, I guess that's that."

"Is the house still for sale?" I asked.

She brightened. "Are you interested?"

"I'm not in the market to buy," I said. "I was just curious."

"Oh, yes. I spoke to the owner just last week. He's getting a bit desperate. I could get you a good price, particularly if you have your own financing."

I smiled. The idea of my being able to afford a house was ludicrous. "So you and Dr. Foster met with the owner, and then what?"

"I drove back here. Dr. Foster stayed there. He wanted to meet a few of the neighbors. Mr. Delevan—that's the owner—offered to show him around. That's the last I saw of him."

I nodded. "You drove separately to the house?"

"We always did."

"Really?" I asked, feeling uncomfortable. "Dr. Foster didn't take public transportation?"

"No." She looked appalled. "He had a beautiful car. It looked new."

No one had spoken to me about the car. It wasn't in the newspaper reports, and his wife had never mentioned it.

"He drove it that day?"

"Oh, yes," she said. "I wouldn't have left him without transportation."

"What's Mr. Delevan's first name?"

She tilted her head and her wig slipped slightly. "Now, you're not going to tell him you heard from me, are you? He's already upset about this sale falling through."

"When he hears what happened, he won't be angry at you," I said, not making any promises.

"I suppose." She took the appointment page back from me, as if she were afraid I was going to keep it. "His first name is Oscar."

I nodded, then glanced at the clock on her desk. I would have to leave soon if I wanted to pick up the kids on time. "Would the Fosters have been the first black family on the block?"

"On the block, yes, but not in the area. That was why so many other families left. I've shown a number of houses in that neighborhood."

"Would Mr. Delevan take kindly to answering questions from me?"

"He was very polite with Lou. They both knew what was going on."

Still, I took it as a caution. "Is there anything else you remember, Mrs. Sarton? Did Dr. Foster tell you what his plans were for the rest of the day? Did he seem nervous or upset? Was there anything out of the ordinary?"

She frowned, taking my question seriously. Then she shook her head. "He seemed fine. I was more nervous about the meeting than he was. He said he'd have to get used to the neighborhood, and I didn't disagree."

Then she got up and walked back to her desk, setting the appointment pages down. "As for his plans, he didn't really mention them. We weren't friends, you know. Just business acquaintances. I'm sure he didn't say much to me at all."

"So you had no idea what he was going to do when he left the house? Even though you thought he might make an offer?"

"He told me that it depended on timing." She looked at me, obviously startled that she remembered. "His mother-in-law was coming, and he would be very busy the next week. He wasn't sure when he would get away."

I nodded.

"He had some things to pick up at the store on his way home, and thought maybe he'd shop in the neighborhood, since he might be moving there. He was going to ask Mr. Delevan where the nearest grocery store was." She shrugged. "That's it. That's all I remember."

"That's plenty, Mrs. Sarton." I stood. "Let me give you my number in case you remember anything else."

"All right," she said. "But might I call you if I see the perfect house for you?"

"I doubt I'll be in the housing market for a long time,

ma'am," I said as I scrawled my name and phone number on a notepad. "Do you by chance have Mr. Delevan's phone number?"

"His new address, too." She opened a desk drawer to reveal several Rolodexes, stuffed full of cards. She pulled one out. I copied the information off of it.

As I wrote, I asked, "You didn't take Dr. Foster anywhere else that day, did you?"

"No," she said. "I was convinced he was going to buy the Delevan house. We had done all our searching the previous Fridays. He was very particular, Dr. Foster was. I'm going to miss him. Do you think it's too late to send a condolence to the family?"

I tucked the address in my pocket. "It's never too late," I said.

TWELVE

As instructed, the kids were waiting inside the school when I arrived. I managed to be on time, which was amazing, considering how late I'd left the north part of the city.

The little girls chattered all the way to Franklin's. Lacey pretended to be cool by staring out the window, and the boys were unusually silent. When I'd dropped off the Grimshaw children, I asked Jimmy if he'd had any more problems that day.

He'd shaken his head. I wasn't sure I believed him, so I decided to ask again later.

We got to the apartment around four. The street was quiet and the December dark had settled in. The air felt heavy, and forecasters were predicting snow.

Jimmy got the mail from our little hole-in-the-wall mailbox while I trudged up the stairs, feeling like the day had been longer than it really was. A note was thumbtacked to our door.

Grimshaw, it read in a childlike scrawl. *Mind your own goddamn business—or else!*

It was, of course, unsigned.

I removed it and the thumbtack and stuck them in my pocket, relieved that Jimmy hadn't seen it. Anger that had been beneath the surface all day flared, but I tamped it down.

The note could have been left by anyone, but the crudeness of the threat and the childishness of the handwriting suggested the Stones. I had been expecting some kind of reprisal for the morning's confrontation. I just hadn't expected it to be directed so clearly at me.

The apartment was too warm, the radiator cranking so hard it felt as if we had stepped into a sauna. I opened a window and sent Jimmy in search of the landlord. Of course, no one was in the building except us. I suppose I should have been grateful; the *Defender* was full of articles about renters who weren't getting enough heat this winter.

I cooked us an early dinner—I'd learned in September that Jimmy always came home hungry, even when I gave him extra lunch money—and left Jimmy with the dishes while I went into my office to make some phone calls. I tried Delevan first, but there was no answer at his Lake Forest home. I searched the phone book for his South Side phone number, found it, and learned that it had been disconnected.

Next, I tried Alice Foster. She answered on the second ring, her voice wary. She relaxed slightly when I introduced myself.

"Are you making any progress, Mr. Grimshaw?" she asked.

"I'm not sure yet, although I am covering ground that the police didn't."

"That's not a surprise," she said.

I wrapped the phone cord around my hand. "I have a few questions, Mrs. Foster. Things that have come up in the investigation. I was wondering if you could clarify them."

"I'll try," she said.

"Whatever happened to your husband's car?"

"It vanished," she said. "The police found no trace of it near the park, and no abandoned vehicle was picked up anywhere. His receptionist said he'd taken it when he left the office, but no one's seen it since. The police believe that's confirmation of the mugging. They think the car was stripped and sold for parts when it was left in the Washington Park neighborhood."

"Washington Park isn't usually that bad a neighborhood," I said.

"I told them that." Frustration filled her voice. "I told them a lot of things."

162

"What kind of car was it?"

"It was a brand-new Oldsmobile."

"What color was it?"

"Brown."

"Let me know if the car turns up, will you?"

"Of course, Mr. Grimshaw. You'll be the first to know."

She sounded sincere. Part of me wished I had done this second interview in person, but I wanted to get the information that night. I felt it more important to stay home with Jimmy than to run all over the city chasing clues.

"When was the last time you spoke to your husband?" I asked.

"Shortly before he left the office, around noon. He said he'd be home by four."

I nodded. That was consistent with what she had told me before. "Finally, Mrs. Foster, when you were going through your husband's things, did you find any stock certificates?"

"A number of them," she said. "They were in his desk at work. Why?"

"Have you verified them?"

"What do you mean?"

"Have you checked with a broker to discover their current value?"

"Oh, no," she said. "I figured they were something to do with work and I'd get to them eventually. Louis handled the finances for the office, and I wasn't ready to deal with all that paperwork until someone from there offered to help me. So far, no one has."

"Are you sure the certificates belong to the office? Or are they in your husband's name?"

"I'll check the file," she said. "I wasn't really paying attention. I feel like I've been in a fog, Mr. Grimshaw."

"Where did he keep your personal finances?"

"At the office," she said. "Everything was locked in his desk."

"Where are the certificates now?"

"In a box in our spare bedroom."

I shook my head, now glad that she couldn't see me. "Mrs. Foster, stock certificates can be extremely valuable. I suggest you take care of them as soon as you possibly can."

"I doubt that we have anything of great value, Mr. Grimshaw. Only rich people have valuable stocks. Louis left me well off, but only because he was a frugal man. There were times he'd rather save a penny than he enjoy himself."

The kind of man who hoarded fortunes and invested wisely. The kind of man I wished I was, but had never been. If I had been that kind of man, Jimmy and I wouldn't be having the financial problems we were having now.

"Do me a favor and check, Mrs. Foster. And do it quickly."

"How did you learn about the stock certificates, Mr. Grimshaw?"

"One of your husband's business associates mentioned it," I said, not willing to tell her the whole thing until I knew that Jane Sarton had been telling the truth. I didn't want to get Alice Foster's hopes up only to have them dashed. "If you check this out for me, I'll know whether I can believe that person or not."

"Oh." Mrs. Foster sounded a lot more interested. "I'll do so first thing in the morning."

"Thanks," I said. "Let me know what you find out."

Then I hung up the phone and headed back into the living room. As I settled on the couch with Jimmy to watch television, I wondered why some husbands kept the family finances secret from their wives. I'd encountered it twice that day, implied in Jane Sarton's annoyance at being left without enough money for her golden years, and directly from Alice Foster.

It wasn't the first time I'd run into this strange phenomenon. Somehow, I doubted it would be the last.

The next morning, our well-oiled routine collapsed. Jimmy was still in his pajamas, finishing his oatmeal, when Franklin arrived to take him to school, and I was lost in the mess that was Jimmy's room, searching for a clean shirt. I abandoned the search and Jimmy abandoned his oatmeal. We managed to get him out the door only five minutes late, looking rumpled and food-stained, but presentable enough.

I was left with a pile of laundry, a mass of dirty breakfast dishes, and an empty larder, realizing, not for the first time, why nature's model for parenthood included both a mother and a father.

The chores would have to wait until after school. Jimmy and I would tackle them together. Jimmy and Smokey's big night out at the Laundromat. Maybe I could scramble enough cash together to buy us dinner at the nearby A&W as a treat.

I closed the door on Jimmy's room, put the dishes in the sink, and went into my office, the only neat room in the house. There I tried Delevan again, but had no luck. I even called the operator to make certain I had the right number. I did. I found it odd that he didn't answer at night or in the morning, and hoped it only meant that he was out of town.

I had a number of stops that day. I wanted to check out the house that Foster had visited on his last day, and investigate the neighborhood as well. Maybe if I timed everything right, I would be able to pick up much-needed groceries before moving on to my next stop.

I also wanted to do some library research. Aspects of this case bothered me. I still hadn't found what tied Foster to last summer's two dead boys, aside from the circumstances of their death. What I was most afraid of was that they'd all been killed by a random stranger, like the victims of the Boston Strangler had been a few years before.

But so far, this case didn't seem like the Strangler. He seemed to have acted on impulse, going into women's apartments and raping them late at night. The position of these three bodies suggested deliberation, which pointed to some kind of plan.

Maybe I would find that plan when I learned why Foster was in Washington Park. His real estate broker, if I could believe her, said he was looking at a home several miles south of that location. His car was nowhere to be found, and no one had seen him there—at least no one had come forward to say so.

The presence of the white man in the car bothered me—why would anyone drive away when a child started screaming?—and I wished I could get my hands on Epstein's photographs. Maybe when he was out of the woods, I would ask Mrs. Weisman if she could find the pictures for me. Even pictures without Epstein's descriptions and memories would be better than nothing.

I hated murder cases for just this reason. There were always too many questions and not enough answers.

I was still chewing over the various possibilities when I grabbed my jacket and headed out the front door. I locked all three dead bolts, a habit I'd started again, and headed down the stairs, sticking my hand in my pocket to grab my gloves.

Instead, my fingers brushed paper. The note. I had forgotten all about it. I had gotten threatening notes in the past, and they were often harmless, but I always did track them down.

I headed back up the stairs and knocked on Marvella's door. She was usually home during the day. She didn't work much, thanks to a lump-sum alimony payment from one of her many ex-husbands.

It took a moment for the door to open, and then it opened only partway. A chain held it in place.

"Oh, it's you," she said, sounding sleepy. She closed the door and I heard the chain rattle. A moment later, the door opened all the way.

She was wearing a loosely tied satin floor-length robe and obviously nothing underneath it. Her hair, usually styled, was frizzed around her face. She stifled a yawn.

I couldn't help myself. I smiled. "Sorry to wake you, Marvella."

"You could have at least brought coffee," she said, holding the door open. "Come on in. I'll make us some."

"I don't have much time." I didn't want to go into that apartment with a beautiful, barely dressed woman. "I have a question for you."

She rubbed the sleep out of her right eye with her fist. "Shoot."

166

"Yesterday, before three, did you see anyone tack a note on my door?"

"I don't spy on your door, Bill," she said.

"I know," I said. "It's just that there aren't many people here during the day."

"You usually are."

"I've been working a job." I was always careful not to use the word "case" even around Marvella, who had found me my first legitimate case in Chicago last August.

"A real one?"

"For me," I said.

She smiled. I liked her face without all the makeup. It didn't seem so imposingly beautiful.

"I didn't see anyone in the hall yesterday," she said. "Just a couple of kids."

That didn't surprise me. "Near my door?"

"They were out here laughing. Must have been just before three or just after. I didn't see them put a note on your door, but I did tell them to scram. I figured they were here to see Jimmy."

"Yet you told them to leave."

"Well, you weren't here. He wasn't here. They didn't belong in the building, and they were noisy. I don't like strangers in here."

I didn't either. "How old were they?"

She shrugged. "How'm I supposed to know? They looked like they could be friends of Jim. Their voices hadn't changed."

"Would you recognize them if you see them again?"

"Maybe," she said. "If they're wearing the same jackets."

"Were any of them wearing red tams?"

"Stones?" That woke her up. "No. At least not that I noticed. They weren't wearing hats at all, and their jackets were un-zipped. That I do remember."

So the hats could have been in their pockets. "Thanks, Marvella."

"You having some kid troubles?"

"I don't know yet," I said. "Get their names if you see them again, will you?"

"Sure," she said. "Anything to help the most handsome single man in the building."

"The only single man in the building," I said.

She raised her eyebrows. "Sure you don't want to come in?"

This time, the invitation was unmistakable. "Next time, Marvella."

She pouted. "You always say that."

"And I always mean it," I lied.

I drove south to the address Jane Sarton had given me. The neighborhood seemed to be a good one, filled with small, plain Chicago-style bungalows—sturdy but undemanding houses that could handle the city's severe weather.

Six blocks north of the address, on Eighty-ninth Street, was another park. Stoney Island Park, small by Chicago standards— only two blocks long—caught my attention. If someone had murdered a man down here and wanted to leave him in a park, why not Stoney Island? Why take him—or anyone—farther north?

The drive took me deep into the heart of Chicago's steel country. The address I had was significantly south of the U.S. Steelworks, although the company remained a dominant presence, its processing plant belching foul-smelling smoke that stayed beneath the clouds.

But other tall chimneys rose just south of the neighborhood, also trailing smoke into the already thick air. I guessed they belonged to either Republic or Wisconsin Steel or maybe both, but I wasn't about to drive down there to check.

On my way, I passed an elementary school and a number of churches. A synagogue dominated a nearby corner, its façade shabby with age. There were several business districts, looking like downtowns of places that had once been miles from Chicago's city limits.

The nearby blocks were well-tended, the houses in good shape. Most had young trees out front and the remains of nice summer gardens. There was a lot of evidence of children, from basketball hoops on garage doors to swing sets in backyards.

There was also a startling number of FOR SALE signs and a complete lack of people on the streets.

I pulled in front of the house that Foster had wanted to buy. It was older than the others in the neighborhood, and larger. The house rested in the center of a short block. A low fence enclosed the yard. Two oak trees towered over the street and over the smaller, newly planted trees in front of the neighbors' homes. What I could see of the yard was covered with brown leaves, and so was the sidewalk.

The house was clearly empty.

I got out of the car and shivered in the morning chill. The snow that had fallen the night before had only been a dusting. Traces remained on the leaves, but nowhere else.

I started up the walk and then I saw the lockbox hanging from the front door. I wouldn't be able to investigate this house without a real estate agent. I wasn't really sure I wanted to. I had just been curious about where Foster had spent his final day.

The house seemed bigger than Jane Sarton had prepared me for, and she hadn't told me about the large enclosed porch. The house had been remodeled in the last year or two, and I thought it odd that someone would put so much work into a place only to sell it a short time later.

I turned around to return to my car, and shivered again. Someone was watching me. Elaine Young had been right. There was a sense a black person developed, especially when he was outside his community, a sense that kept him awake and alert.

I didn't move, hoping the person who watched would reveal himself, but I saw nothing. The windows of the houses across the street were covered with curtains, and no one moved in the houses nearby. I couldn't hear the sound of a car's engine, nor did I see anyone on the various lawns.

Had Foster felt this? Had it made him nervous, or had he seen it as a challenge? In spite of all the digging I'd been doing into this man's life, I had no real sense yet of him as a person.

I had no idea how he'd react in a situation in which his life was threatened.

I walked to my car slowly, giving whomever it was time to reveal himself. No one did. I got inside and sat in the remaining warmth from the heater, debating whether or not I wanted to go door-to-door.

In the end, I decided against it. I would talk to Delevan first, see what he said about his afternoon with Foster, and then I'd see if I needed to speak to the neighbors. I wasn't relishing the idea much.

I started the car and drove north, back to a corner grocery store I had seen just a block away. I parked outside, plugged the last of my pennies into a nearby meter, and went in the store.

If Foster had been investigating the neighborhood, he probably would have stopped at this grocery store. It was close and large, although that wasn't saying much.

It was a full-service grocery. I pushed open the double doors and stepped inside. The place was warm and smelled of fresh bread. A row of carts was lined near the door and I grabbed one, heading down the closest aisle while I made a mental list of the things I needed.

Right away, I knew I was outside my neighborhood. The prices were lower than they were in the groceries in the Black Belt. The produce—what there was of it this deep into winter—looked fresh. The apples weren't bruised and the oranges were actually orange, not the sickly yellow color I'd been seeing since I arrived in Chicago. The onions were big and juicy, the potatoes all fresh.

I resisted the urge to load up the cart—I had a small budget, after all—but I had a giddy sense of freedom as I went from aisle to aisle, looking at things that were as much as fifty cents cheaper than they were at home.

It wasn't until I reached the back, where the meat department was, that I realized I wasn't welcome here. Behind the signs that advertised fresh-ground hamburger and sirloin steaks, a white man in a bloody butcher's apron watched me.

He was short and balding, with thick arms and a narrow mouth. He watched as I looked at the chicken. At thirty-nine cents a pound, it was almost twenty cents cheaper than it was in the Black Belt.

He stared at me as I browsed. Finally, I grabbed a pound of hamburger, enough to last me and Jimmy to the end of the week, and put it in my cart with the rest of my items. I didn't buy anything else, even though the chicken was tempting. I didn't want to stay beneath that stare a moment longer.

"Excuse me," the butcher said, "but you might want to re-think that."

I gripped the cart tighter. "Really?" I asked, trying to keep my voice level. "Why is that?"

He nodded and leaned over the meat case, indicating that I should, too. But I knew better.

"If I were you, I'd shop somewhere else." And so it started.

"Well, I'm here now," I said.

"No, no." His tone was gentle. "That's not what I mean. I'm not threatening you. But there's no reason that you should fill up your cart. They'll send someone to chase you out. I've seen it happen before."

I studied him for a moment. I wasn't sure how to place him. He'd felt menacing a minute ago, and now he was giving me something that could be taken as friendly advice.

"I keep trying to change our policies," he said into my silence, "but it does no good."

"The neighborhood is in transition," I said, using Jane Sarton's word. "Maybe someone else should try to change the policy."

The butcher sighed. "You wouldn't be the first."

"Who else tried?" I asked, thinking of Foster. Maybe he had been here on his way home, just like I was.

"There's been a number, but—" The butcher stopped and looked toward his right. A slender clerk, a tuft of hair sticking up on the back of his head, came up the aisle. He was frowning at me.

"You new to the neighborhood?" the clerk asked.

"I've been looking at houses this morning," I said, sounding friendly even though I didn't feel that way.

"Been a lot of you people here lately."

I bristled, but didn't let it show. "In the store or in the neighborhood?"

"In the neighborhood," he said, "driving nice folk out."

I didn't respond to the man. I glanced at the butcher, but he had disappeared into the back, as if he hadn't wanted anyone to see him talking to a black customer.

The slender clerk stared at me. He seemed to expect some kind of response. I was tempted to leave the cart and walk away, like they wanted me to. Instead, I went down the chilly frozen-foods aisle and got some orange-juice concentrate, my hand shaking.

I made myself continue shopping. I had every right to be there, but that clerk had made me feel as if I had crossed an invisible line. Had this happened to Foster as well? I didn't see anyone I felt like asking.

The checkout clerks wouldn't meet my gaze as I headed toward the line. I was the only man pushing a cart. Every other customer was a white woman, most of whom gave me startled looks.

Their carts were overflowing with food, except for the woman ahead of me. She had two expensive sirloin steaks, some frozen broccoli, and a package of Minnesota wild rice. By the time her bill was totaled, it would probably equal mine.

When I settled on a line, the checkout girl looked over the magazine rack and shook her head at me, making it clear she wasn't about to let me pay for my food. I was tempted to leave the cart in the middle of the store and walk out just like the butcher had advised, but I didn't. I'd had enough of subtle looks and vaguely worded threats.

I waited until my turn. No one got in line behind me; a few middle-aged housewives took one glance at me and got in a longer line.

When the checkout girl finally finished with the woman ahead of me—and she took her time on purpose—she put a

CLOSED sign on the counter in front of her register.

I handed the sign back to her.

"No you don't," I said in my softest, calmest voice. "I was patient just like everyone else. You can show me the courtesy of waiting on me."

She gave me a look that was one part fear and another part anger.

"I'm not getting in another line," I said. "You will wait on me."

She raised a hand, signaling for the manager. Apparently he had been watching me, because he arrived almost immediately.

He was a short man with a receding hairline. What hair remained had been greased and slicked back against his skull. His black horn-rimmed glasses magnified his pale blue eyes.

"This register's closed," he said. "Miss Nelson needs her break."

"She can't wait on one more customer?"

"No," he said.

"Then I guess you'll have to make room for me in another line."

The entire store was watching now. Checkout girls had stopped halfway through other customers' groceries and were turned in my direction. The other customers were clutching their handbags to the handles of their grocery carts as if I were going to run through the aisles snatching every wallet.

"The other lines are closed," the manager said.

"They don't look closed," I said.

"They are." He crossed his arms over his thin chest. The checkout girl had moved behind him, as if his slight frame would offer her protection from me.

The anger I'd been feeling all week was coming back, magnified by the frustration I'd felt since the attack on Saul and Elaine. "Let me get this straight," I said carefully. "The lines are closed . . . to me?"

"Yes." The manager looked relieved that I finally understood.

"You want me to leave my groceries and walk out?"

"That would be best for all involved, I think."

He was right; it probably would. Creating a scene would do me no good at all, and would probably make this group of friendly white people call the police. Still, I couldn't stop.

"This is how you treat all your black customers?"

"We don't have such customers," the manager said.

"You run them all out?" I asked.

"People usually don't go where they're not wanted." The manager kept his arms crossed. The checkout girl in the aisle behind him nodded.

"I'm the only black man you've had in this store?" I asked, getting my questions about Foster in anyway.

"Usually your—girls—show up. We politely ask them to leave." He was staring at me.

"Like you're politely asking me?"

"Yes."

The tuft-haired clerk had come down an aisle, along with another man who wore a black suit. They watched from a distance. So far, no one was near a phone.

The butcher hadn't come at all. He had known this was going to happen, and he had warned me. Had I heard a friendly warning as a threat because I was uncomfortable here? I couldn't tell.

"I don't think this is very polite," I said. "I have as much right to be in this store as anyone else."

"Well," said the manager, "it's a privately owned business, and we have the right to choose our customers."

"My money is as green as theirs," I said, nodding at the women standing in nearby lines.

"We don't want it."

Of course they didn't. Just like they didn't want Saul Epstein to kiss Elaine Young, or Louis Foster to buy a house in their neighborhood. They didn't want me to buy groceries at a reasonable price or send Jimmy to a well-financed public school.

"Well," I said, "you are going to get my money whether you

like it or not. You can wait on me or not, that's your choice, but I'm taking these groceries home."

He watched in horror as I reached behind the counter and grabbed a bag. I shook it open, and set it in front of him. Then I reached into my cart. My fingers found the hamburger first.

I read the price sticker to him, then set the hamburger in the bag. Then I picked up the orange-juice concentrate, read that price sticker, added that price to the hamburger's price, and set the concentrate in the bag.

I took out each item, added its price to my verbal total, and placed it in the bag. The work took me only a minute or two. The total came to $15.95. I dug into my back pocket, pulled out my wallet and opened it, finding a ten, a five, and a one. I set them on the counter, picked up my grocery bag, and left the cart.

"Keep the change," I said as I walked out the door, shaking with fury.

Even though I knew I had to hurry—someone would have called the police by now—I didn't run. I wasn't going to let them see how deeply they'd shaken me.

I got to the car, set my groceries inside, and started it up. Then I backed out of my parking spot, turning around so that I wouldn't drive past the big windows advertising FAIR PRICES. In the distance, I heard the wail of a siren.

Why Louis Foster would want to live in that neighborhood was beyond me. I wouldn't want to face that every day, or have Jimmy face it either.

The sirens grew closer. I glanced in my rearview mirror, but no cop car was following me yet. I turned off on a couple of side streets, then headed north, toward home.

I parked in front of the apartment building and got out. Even though it was the middle of the day, this street had signs of life: a car motor running in a driveway; a woman carrying evergreen boughs out of her apartment building; an old man sipping a cup of steaming liquid while he stood on his porch, watching me as I watched him. Maybe they'd seen something yesterday—my little note-carriers. Maybe my neighbors knew more than I thought they did.

I took the groceries inside. Marvella's door was closed and locked, a rolled-up newspaper on the mat. I was disappointed; part of me wanted to talk to her, to tell someone else about the experience I'd just gone through, to get that poison out of my system. Or maybe I'd just been thinking about her all morning, no makeup, the satin robe loosely tied over her long, powerful body.

It had been a long time since I'd been with anyone. The last time was in March with Laura. It was beginning to show.

No note waited for me on my door. I was surprised that I had looked for it, and even more surprised at my relief when I discovered it wasn't there. I unlocked the door and went inside.

The place was a mess, and smelled of curdling milk from that morning's breakfast. I set the groceries on the counter, then took a deep breath to calm myself.

I hadn't encountered that kind of overt racism since I'd come to Chicago. Usually, in Chicago, people smiled at you and then denied your rental application. Or they looked at you, a warning gaze that seemed well-intentioned, when you walked into a restaurant that didn't like "your kind." Sometimes, in Chicago, I couldn't tell if people were really discriminating against me or if I was being paranoid.

I'd once said to Franklin that I preferred overt racism. At least then you knew where you stood.

I now regretted those words. Either kind of discrimination felt bad. Even now, I felt nauseous, a sense of helplessness filling me. My protest hadn't meant much to anyone, least of all to the store manager. I'd barely gotten out of there ahead of the police.

What I needed to do now, besides calm down, was to finish my research, maybe do some library work, something that kept me away from other people until my surliness passed.

I had just put the perishables away when the phone rang.

"What?" I said as I picked it up, not caring how the person on the other end responded.

"Um . . ." That person was a woman with an unfamiliar voice. "I'm calling for Bill Grimshaw."

My name is Smokey Dalton, I wanted to snap. *I use the other name because a childhood friend was murdered in cold blood by white bigots and I'm hiding one of the witnesses.*

"That's me." I wasn't making the conversation easy for her. Part of me regretted it, and part of me didn't care at all.

"I'm, um, Marge Evenrud. I work in the emergency room at—"

"Miss Evenrud," I said, pouring warmth into my voice. "I'm sorry. I was expecting another call."

She let out a nervous laugh. "Someone you don't like."

I wasn't sure I liked many people at the moment. "You could say that."

"Listen," she said, sounding more confident, "you wanted to know if someone with infected burns on his face and shoulder come in. Well, we got someone."

My hand tightened on the receiver. "Really?"

"He meets your description. He's twentyish, white, and he's got a long burn on his cheek. That one's not infected. In fact, it's beginning to heal. But his shoulder and arm show definite signs of scalding, so bad that some fabric from his shirt got mixed into the flesh. He's got a raging infection there."

"Is he in the hospital?"

"Oh, yes. He has a fever, which the doctors are trying to bring down, and he's on penicillin to stop the infection. We got a call in to one of our burn specialists to see what the next step is."

"What could that step be?" I asked.

"Surgery, possibly. Or they might just wait until the infection lessens before they make a decision."

"Is he being sent home?" My heart was pounding. This sounded right.

"Possibly. Right now he has a room, but his mother made it clear when she brought him in that they don't got a lot of money. We told her that we'd take care of him, but she didn't seem all that interested. She said she was tired of his whining."

"Can I see him?"

"If you get here soon," she said. "He'll probably see the burn specialist around two, and then I have no idea what will happen."

"I'll be there shortly," I said.

"Should I be calling the police, Mr. Grimshaw?"

"Let me see him first," I said. "Let's make sure this is the right guy."

"All right. His name is Bruce Owens and he's in room four-eleven."

The fourth floor. Not far from Elaine. I wondered what genius did that until I remembered that no one else realized who he was—if indeed he was the person who attacked her.

"I can get in trouble for giving you this information, Mr. Grimshaw. Please don't tell nobody about my call."

"I won't," I said. "And thanks."

I made it to the hospital in record time. The place looked as busy as it had the day before. This time, I didn't have to argue with the woman at the information desk, and no one looked askance as I hurried across the lobby.

The elevator seemed even slower than it had the day before. My entire body was humming and I couldn't seem to keep still. I rocked back and forth on the balls of my feet, as jittery as an addict in need of a fix.

This was the break I had needed. I wanted to question one or both of these attackers about their other activities. I didn't think they had killed Foster or the boys, but I couldn't be certain. Maybe this attack had spiraled out of control. Or maybe a single killer had gotten tired of working alone.

Once I identified him, I would ask Marge Evenrud to call the police. I wouldn't wait for them, of course. Instead, I'd tell her to lie, saying that she had been told to call them if anyone with these burns had come into the ward.

I wasn't even sure I'd be able to ask questions. He had a fever, and his side was infected. He might be asleep, or incoherent.

He was neither.

Bruce Owens watched television from his bed beside his room's window. The privacy curtain was open, revealing a second bed, unmade, a lunch tray with half-eaten food beside it. The chart at the foot of that bed was missing.

I stayed back, studying Owens' face. He had a long red burn that ran from his eyebrow to his jaw. His arm and shoulder were not bandaged, but rested on top of the covers, the swollen skin red, pus-filled and cracked.

An untouched lunch tray sat on the end table beside his bed. Near his right hand was the nurse's call button.

The sight of his face brought back that afternoon—the leer he had, the way he held Elaine by the throat as he braced himself between her legs, the bleakness in her eyes.

I strode inside the room and closed the door.

"Hey!" he said.

Then I closed the curtain over the window. "Remember me?"

His face paled, and he reached for the call button.

I pulled it out of his grasp before he was able to press it. "We're going to have a little conversation."

"I have nothing to say to you." He sounded defiant, but his eyes were large, a little dilated—probably from his fever—and his right hand shook.

"No 'I'm sorry'? No 'I didn't mean it'? No 'Things got out of hand'?"

His eyes narrowed. "They got what they deserved. He was necking with that monkey."

"Woman," I said, sitting on the side of the bed closest to his injured arm. "She's a woman. And you did a lot worse to her."

"That bitch needed to learn her place, man."

"Really?" I bumped his hand with my hip. He yelped. "She deserved everything she got?"

His eyes filled with tears, but I was under no illusion. They were tears of pain, not remorse.

"I'm sorry," he whispered. "Things got out of hand."

"Uh-huh." I was surprised I could sound so calm when what I really wanted to do was grab his fork and burst each pus-filled blister. "I suppose your attack on Louis Foster got out of hand, too."

"What?"

"You and your friend left him in Washington Park so no one could trace him to you. Or did you observe him there doing something you didn't like? Was he in need of a lesson, like Saul and Elaine?"

"I don't know no Foster." He reached for the call button again, wincing as he did.

I shoved it onto the floor. "And what about those little boys? What did they do? Look at a white woman wrong, like Emmett Till?"

"I don't know no Emmett Till."

"That doesn't surprise me. Why should you know anything about the history of the civil-rights movement?"

He had shoved himself away from me, his head pressed against the bed's headboard. "You're crazy, man."

"Am I? I'm not the one who attacked a couple because their skin colors didn't match."

"So what?" he said. "They were spreading their filth all over the park. But I don't know these other people."

"Louis Foster. Built like I am, well-dressed? You left his body in Washington Park the weekend before Thanksgiving."

"The weekend before Thanksgiving I was in Springfield with my friggin' grandmother, man. Ask my whole family."

I stopped. He looked as terrified as a man could get. "You didn't attack anyone else?"

"I didn't say that." He glanced at the door, but no one came in to rescue him. "I didn't kill no one, though."

"Saul Epstein nearly died."

"And I didn't touch him. That was Bruiser."

"You thought you'd teach the girl a lesson."

"It got out of hand, man, like you said. Okay? But I didn't leave no bodies in Coontown." His eyes widened as soon as the word came out of his mouth.

It took every ounce of my self-control not to hit him. I stood up, and without saying another word, walked out.

I was shaking and I wanted to put my fist through the wall. Actually, I wanted to put my fist through his face, tear him up the way his friend had torn up Saul Epstein.

But I made myself keep walking until I found the stairs. I went down them two at a time, my steps echoing on the metal floor, until I reached the main level. Then I walked to the emergency room.

It was astonishingly quiet. A nurse sat at reception and an ambulance was parked outside the door. Through the open door to the back, I could see another nurse reading a magazine.

I walked around the desk and through the door. The receptionist was yelling at me, but I didn't care. I kept walking until I saw Marge Evenrud.

"That's him," I said as I crossed the tile floor.

She hurried toward me, making little shushing motions with her hands.

"Did you recognize him?" she asked when she reached me.

"Oh, yeah. Call the cops."

"Great. You can wait—"

"I'm not waiting for them. You tell them that they asked to see anyone who was burned. Elaine, Saul, Mrs. Weisman—any one of them can identify him."

"But—"

"Thanks, Marge. I'll talk to you again when I'm calmer."

Then I pushed open the emergency-room doors and stepped into the cold, gray afternoon, knowing that if I didn't get out of there quickly, I'd head back up to the fourth floor and vent all of the rage that I'd been feeling on one wretched little bigot's face.

THIRTEEN

I calmed down some on the drive back to the apartment, which was good, because the moment I pulled in front of the building, a police car pulled in behind me.

I cursed, then put my hands on top of the wheel, keeping them in plain sight. I had no idea how long the cop car had been tailing me. I'd glanced in my rearview mirror as I drove home, but I hadn't seen anything. Of course I'd been so furious that it was entirely possible that I missed the car altogether.

Footsteps approached and then a cop in plainclothes blocked the light through the driver's side window.

"Grimshaw," a familiar voice said, "you are the most paranoid son of a bitch I ever saw."

I looked up. Jack Sinkovich was peering into my window. His pale skin was ruddy with cold and his nose dripped. He'd grown a thin mustache since I'd seen him last. It didn't flatter him.

"Come on out," he said. "I gotta talk to you."

I glanced in the rearview mirror at the patrol car. No one else was in it. I grabbed the handle and opened the door slowly. I didn't entirely trust Sinkovich. We'd worked together on a murder case the previous summer, but I knew he'd also spent the nights of the Democratic National Convention with birdshot in his gloves, beating college students for exercising their constitutional right to free assembly.

I stood up, towering over him slightly. The last thing I wanted to see right now was a white man, particularly a white cop. "What is it, Sinkovich?"

"Ain't you prickly," he said. "You see the Walker Report?"

He was referring to Daniel Walker's report on the Convention, the one that called the events a police riot.

"It seemed pretty fair to me," I said.

"Me, too." He didn't meet my gaze.

I studied him, surprised. Those two words were a peace offering. The last time I had seen him, I had yelled at him for his part in the riots.

Still, I wasn't going to give him much ground. "What do you want, Sinkovich?"

He tilted his head to one side, gave me an aw-shucks shrug. "Hear you're a big hero."

"Where'd you hear that?"

"Word gets around. You saved some old lady and her kid in Rogers Park."

"That's what they're saying, huh?" I asked, feeling the anger start to swirl again.

"Yeah."

" 'They' being cops?"

"Yeah." He grinned, as if he approved of what I did.

"I saved an old lady, her grandson, and his girlfriend." I spoke softly. "His black girlfriend."

Sinkovich whistled. "No one mentioned that part."

"That doesn't surprise me." I slipped my hands in my jacket pocket, felt the note crinkle, and said again, "What do you want?"

His smile disappeared. "Can we talk somewhere?"

"This is good enough," I said, not wanting to take him into the apartment.

"I been thinking a lot about this and it's just not right." He shoved his hands in his pockets. "Only, I'm in that proverbial—

you know—rock. Hard place. So I thought of you."

The afternoon's chill increased. "You're going to have tell me more than that, Sinkovich."

He nodded, then glanced down the street. "Look, can we go inside? I am damn cold."

Then I realized what his problem was. He didn't want anyone to know we'd had a conversation. Now I was curious.

"All right," I said, "but the lobby echoes. We're going up to my apartment. It's been a hell of a day, so no cracks about the mess, huh?"

"Deal." He almost sprinted inside. I followed more slowly, wondering what I was getting myself into.

He waited by the door. I pulled it open and let us both in. The lobby lights were on, giving the place a yellow look. No one was on the stairs, but I heard a television set blaring a soap opera from a nearby apartment. It felt like I'd lived a week since Jimmy left this morning. It was hard to believe that it was only the middle of the afternoon.

I led Sinkovich to the apartment. I unlocked all three dead bolts and shoved the door open, the scent of sour milk even worse than it had been before. I flicked on the overhead light and pulled off my coat.

The radiator clanked in the corner, giving off too much heat, just like it always did in the afternoon. I opened the window leading to the fire escape, and then leaned against the back of the couch, arms crossed.

Sinkovich closed the door and looked around. "Nice place," he said with no irony at all. "No offense, but I'd heard most of the apartments in this part of town were holes."

"Most of them are," I said.

He nodded, then looked away again.

"So what's this problem?"

"You been down to my neighborhood, right?"

"Oh, yeah," I said. "I've been to your neighborhood. Remember? Your wife wanted to throw me out and one of your friends called to make sure I wasn't robbing you blind. I like your neighborhood, Sinkovich. It's got such community pride."

His flush deepened. "That's just it. Things are changing down there. Lots of houses being sold."

"Lots of white people are moving out?" Of course they were. If they were moving out in Delevan's neighborhood, they were moving out of Sinkovich's, too, which was a mile or more to the north.

"Yeah." He hadn't met my gaze since he came into the apartment. "We got ourselves a neighborhood association and everything."

I almost made a sarcastic comment; then I stopped myself because I actually heard him. Was he going to talk to me about Foster? If so, how did he know I was working on the case?

He ran a hand over his blond crewcut. "I don't like what I been hearing, you know, Grimshaw?"

He was serious and upset. I knew there was a good cop mixed in with the bad in Sinkovich. I'd felt, ever since I'd met him, that the two of them were at war.

"There's this new family," he said, "just a few doors down from me. One of yours."

"Mine?" I asked, raising my eyebrows.

"Shit, you know. Colored. Black. Whatever I'm supposed to say nowadays."

"Black, Sinkovich. You're white. I'm black. See how simple that is?"

"Who put a bug up your ass?" he snapped suddenly.

"Oh, I think it's been there a while," I said.

"Forget it." He spun, headed for the door, then stopped, bowed his head and sighed. "Goddammit, Grimshaw, you're not making this easy."

"I don't know what I'm supposed to make easy, Sinkovich."

"That family." He turned, leaned against the door as if it gave him strength. "The neighborhood association, they been telling them to get out, you know. Tried to buy them out, tried to talk them out of the deal. Tried to keep them from moving in."

I was cold, despite the clanging radiator. "Are you a member of the neighborhood association, Sinkovich?"

He shook his head. "Believe it or not, Grimshaw, I kinda have a live-and-let-live attitude. Figured it was the Olsons' right to sell the house to whoever they wanted. Sometimes you get neighbors you don't want, and sometimes they turn out okay. You can't predict this stuff in advance."

He sounded sincere enough and he looked troubled. I sighed. "What brought you here, Sinkovich?" I asked, without the edge this time.

"I got word—I know folks in the association. I mean, I lived there my whole life. My family's been on that street forever. I grew up in that house."

It had been painfully obvious the one time I had been there. Sinkovich's house had been filled with furniture older than he was, furniture that hadn't been moved in generations. And there were photographs of Sinkoviches on the wall that seemed to go back half a century or more. At the time, I had found it reassuring, proof that Sinkovich wasn't living beyond his means, wasn't a cop on the take.

I still believed that, as angry as I had gotten at him last August. He'd always seemed honest at his core.

He leaned his head against the door, the pain evident on his face. "They're planning to burn them out, Grimshaw. Make it look like a Christmas-tree fire or something."

I didn't move.

"We're talking a family here," he said, his voice pleading. "They got little kids."

"Who's planning to burn them out?" I asked.

"The association." He blinked, then looked up at the ceiling as if he had to focus somewhere else. "They say they warned them. But I don't think you give warnings for this kind of thing, Grimshaw. I think the fire's the warning. They're trying to let your people know to stay out of the neighborhood."

This time, I let the "your people" pass. "What do you want me to do?"

"Talk to the family," he said. "Get them out of there. That's what you're good at, right? Taking care of things? I thought maybe if you got involved, then no one'd get hurt."

I was so dumbfounded that for a moment, I couldn't say anything. I shook my head once, let my arms fall to my sides, and then shook my head again.

"What's wrong with this picture, Sinkovich?"

He frowned at me. "What do you mean?"

"Which one of us in this room is the cop?"

He smoothed his mustache with his finger. His eyes were shadow-lined, and his lips were chapped. He'd been biting them.

"Look, I don't dare get involved," he said. "This is the best I can do."

I snorted and shook my head. "Having me tell them to forfeit the house or get burned out? That's the best you can do?"

"The association, most of them are friends and family. And at work, you know, there ain't much sympathy for guys who cross over."

"Cross over the color line?" I asked, not sure I understood him.

He nodded. "Guys with you guys as partners get shit all the time. And then there's the whole rat-fink aspect."

"Of telling on your friends."

"They're gonna know it was me. I was at the last meeting, begging them to reconsider everything, telling them it wasn't right. I had to sleep on the couch for a week after that. My wife, she don't like the changes at all."

My stomach was churning. I felt no sympathy for him. I wasn't sure if that was because of the day I'd had or if it was because I didn't completely understand his dilemma. The answer to it seemed very clear to me.

"You were at the meeting," I said.

"Yeah." His flush had grown deeper.

"Where they planned the arson."

"I didn't have nothing to do with it, Grimshaw, I'm telling you."

"What does the law say, Sinkovich? If someone dies in a fire, and that fire was arson, what happens to the folks who were there for the planning session?"

"I keep telling you! I didn't plan it."

"But if you didn't stop it, what would the law say then?"

"I'm trying to stop it," he said.

"No you're not," I said. "You want *me* to stop it by giving the association what they want."

"Come on, Grimshaw, this is serious. There's kids in that house."

"Yeah, there are," I said. "In their home."

He stared at me.

"If this were a white family, what would you do?"

"If it was a white family, this wouldn't be happening and you know it."

"But use that limited imagination of yours, Sinkovich," I said. "What if it was?"

"Shit, Grimshaw," he said. "It must be easy to be you. So fucking holier than thou. I come here for help."

"And I'm giving it to you. You heard a group of people plan arson. That's illegal. Do something about it."

"I'm telling you, I can't."

"Because you put your own standing in the community ahead of people's lives, Sinkovich."

He closed his eyes and tilted his head sideways, his lips pursed. After a moment, he managed, "That ain't fair."

"The truth usually isn't."

He opened his eyes. He looked small and trapped. "You ain't gonna help me, are you?"

"You can handle this better than I can," I said. "Catch them in the act. Send out a squad, some cops you don't know."

He let out a small sigh. "You know how many of these things happen with the force's approval? Huh? They go by, they see what's going on, they stop, find out what it's about, and drive the fuck away. Like I'm supposed to trust them."

"Welcome to my world, Sinkovich," I said softly.

"Son of a bitch," he said. "Son of a fucking bitch. If I do this, I won't be able to go home no more."

"Yeah." I nodded, remembering the driving that Jimmy and I did after Martin died, looking for somewhere to go, gradually realizing that Memphis would no longer be home. "I know."

He yanked my door open and pointed at me. "If that family dies, Grimshaw, it's on your head."

Then he slammed his way out. I leaned against the couch, sliding it on the thin carpet. Maybe it *would* be on my head. I hadn't even asked the family's name. I had no idea who they were.

I was about to go after Sinkovich when I heard a car start. I looked out the open window. The patrol car was driving away.

"Son of a bitch," I said, echoing Sinkovich.

I went to the phone and dialed the Grimshaws'. Althea answered. "Franklin in?" I asked.

She must have recognized something in my tone, because she got him immediately.

"Smokey?"

"Franklin, I just got word there's a black family who moved into the Bush who are being harassed by a neighborhood association. The association is planning to burn them out."

"Who are they, Smoke?"

"I don't know," I said. "I didn't get their names. But they moved in somewhere around Eighty-seventh. Can you use your connections, find out who they are?"

"I'll do what I can," he said, and hung up.

I'd done all that I could as well. I sank onto the couch, put my face in my hands, and wished that this long, ugly day would finally come to an end.

FOURTEEN

The next morning, we were nearly done with breakfast when Jimmy told me that school had been pushed back half an hour. I didn't believe him, of course. I thought it would be a good way for him to avoid the Stones and being seen by his friends as he was escorted to school.

It wasn't until he found a crumpled and battered note in his school clothes informing parents of the changes that I accepted what he had to say. He got mad at me, and I didn't blame him.

I was still furious from the day before. I'd spent half the night awake, trying to figure out if there was somewhere else I could take Jimmy, somewhere safe where we wouldn't have to watch our backs every moment of every day.

I couldn't come up with anyplace. Small towns were too small, too white. And every large city in the country had problems like Chicago's.

I used the extra half hour to clean up the apartment and make a few phone calls. Delevan still didn't answer, and neither did Mrs. Weisman. I had wanted an update on Epstein.

So I called Marge Evenrud at the hospital. I apologized for my attitude the day before, and she said she understood. The police, on the word of Mrs. Weisman, had arrested Owens and moved him to the hospital wing of the Cook County jail.

At least that problem had been taken care of.

Even with all of that, Jimmy and I still got to Franklin's fifteen minutes early. The exterior of the house was covered in Christmas lights. Malcolm was wrapping an evergreen shrub in even more lights, looking like he was having the time of his life.

"Hi, guys," he said as we came up the sidewalk. "They're finishing breakfast inside, Jim. I bet if you hurry, you can get some sausage."

"Thanks!" Jimmy said and ran for the door. As he pulled it open, I said to Malcolm, "That was the most effective dismissal I've ever seen."

Malcolm grinned at me. "I'm still young enough to know how to appeal to a kid."

"I'll ignore that," I said.

He put the last few lights on two boughs, then let the electric cord trail to the sidewalk.

"I don't want to know how you're going to attach that," I said, thinking of Sinkovich's mention of fire.

"I don't either," he said. "I'm just following Franklin's orders. Guess Althea's always wanted a house at Christmastime."

I hadn't known that, but it didn't surprise me. After being so cramped in our apartment, the Grimshaws must have felt as if they were in heaven in their large house.

"I've been tracking down the watch," Malcolm said. "I haven't found anything yet, but I've been doing some asking. There's a pawnshop the Stones use, but no one'll tell me which one it is."

"If you don't feel comfortable going there," I said, "I'll do it."

He grinned at me. "You gave me this task, boss. I'm following it through. I'm not afraid of those guys."

"You should be," I said.

"Nothing wrong with looking at the merchandise in a pawnshop," he said. "In fact, without customers, it would be out of business."

I nodded. "Just be careful, okay?"

"Okay." He wrapped the last of the lights. We both went inside.

The interior of the house smelled of sausage, pancakes and syrup. I was full from my own breakfast, but the smells made my mouth water all the same.

The little girls were still at the table, along with Althea and Franklin. Jimmy had a plate before him and was happily munching on a piece of sausage. Keith was sitting by the door clutching his jacket and looking impatient, and Lacey was nowhere to be seen.

"Smokey," Franklin said. "You've got a few minutes. Come with me."

Keith glared at us. Althea smiled and said, "Girls, time to clean up. Tell your sister she's pretty enough."

Franklin led me to his study. As we went by the bathroom, he pounded once on the door with his fist. "Finish up, Lace. Your sisters need to get in here before we go."

"Da-ad," Lacey said.

"No arguing, girl." He rolled his eyes at me, then led me into the study. It was a cozy room, not much bigger than a closet, and it smelled faintly of pipe tobacco.

He closed the door. "I'm not sure I'm ready for a teenage daughter."

I smiled. "And you're going to have three of them."

"Don't remind me." He rummaged around on his desk. "I put some feelers out last night. There are half a dozen candidates for your arson, maybe more."

He stopped moving papers, then handed me a copy of the *Defender*. It was yesterday's. I hadn't seen it.

"Could this be them?" he asked.

I stared at the headline. FAMILY TERRORIZED IN ALL WHITE AREA. I shook the paper open and read.

A woman who had moved into the 1500 block of West Eighty-second Street called the *Defender* to complain that she and her son, a Vietnam vet, were being terrorized by their neighbors. She had called the police repeatedly, but the police had refused to do anything.

Just like Sinkovich had said would happen.

I handed the paper back to Franklin. "No. This is a family with little children. And they live closer to Eighty-seventh."

"Just checking," he said. "One of my contacts suggested that maybe you'd heard from this woman, too. She's spreading the news of the harassment everywhere she can, trying to hang onto her home."

"I don't know why. It's not a great neighborhood." Then I sighed. "I'll try to reach my contact again, and I'll get the family's name this time."

Even though the thought of stepping into that mess made my stomach twist.

"Don't know why you didn't in the first place," Franklin said.

"Long story." I glanced at the wind-up clock on his desk. We still had a few minutes. I could hear girls arguing in the nearby bathroom. "Any problems yesterday?"

"The boys are pretty quiet," Franklin said. "They haven't said anything, but I get the sense that they're not happy with this."

"Think the Stones are bothering them?"

"I have no idea, Smokey, and that has me worried. I'm out of my depth here."

"Yeah," I said softly. "So am I."

My conversation with Franklin didn't help my mood. I dropped the kids off at school and escorted them in. A gang of young boys wearing red Stones' tams watched from the playground, but didn't do or say anything.

Their acquiescence to my little plan was making me nervous.

I thought about driving back down to the house Foster had been looking at, but I wasn't sure I could tolerate more of yesterday's problems. I hadn't been able to reach Delevan, and I didn't want to interrupt Mrs. Weisman yet to ask for the photographs. So I went to the library instead.

The main branch of the Chicago Public Library was a five-story stone building that took up the entire block from

Washington to Randolph streets. Its eastern side flanked Michigan Avenue and fit in beautifully with the other turn-of-the century buildings along that street.

I used to hate going into the library, because I got a lot of stares, but the employees were getting used to me now. The interior itself was stunning, with two Tiffany domes and wide, flat marble staircases. I found that being inside, surrounded by all the books and the beautiful architecture, calmed me.

The task I'd set for myself was a daunting one, and I'd been putting it off since Alice Foster had come to see me the Friday before.

I wanted to find out two things: I wanted to learn if the previous victims and Foster were connected. If they were, then these killings were part of the same pattern.

What I also had to check for was whether or not there were more victims. I hoped not. Three was three too many, but I would look all the same.

In fact, I planned to start there, since that was the scenario I wanted most to rule out. So I decided to trace the year backward through the newspapers, looking at each page, especially taking note of the one-paragraph stories about deaths on the South Side. It was going to be long, tedious work, and I'd have to be sharp for it.

I started with the *Defender* because it was most likely to carry stories about the South Side. From there, I'd look through the other main dailies to see if they covered anything as well.

When I broke for lunch, my hands were covered with newspaper ink, and I felt like I had bathed in dust. I'd managed to go through the entire year's worth of *Defender*s, taking notes on the previous two cases I knew about—and realizing my worst fear.

It looked like there were at least two more.

The first killing seemed to have occurred in February. The body of a young woman had been found in Lincoln Cemetery in Blue Island, which was close enough to the city to be considered part of it by a lot of residents. The woman had been stabbed, found with one shoe off and posed against Bessie Coleman's gravestone.

Bessie Coleman, the *Defender* article informed me, was the first black woman to get a pilot's license. She died in 1926 during a barnstorming run. In fact, the *Defender* article told me more about Bessie Coleman—and Lincoln Cemetery, one of the Chicago area's two all-black cemeteries—than it did about the woman who had died.

That woman, Violet Stamps, seemed to have lived a quiet life. Stamps was a schoolteacher who lived in Bronzeville. Her family said she had never been to Blue Island in her life, and they had no idea what she was doing there.

Her purse was missing, but she wore a valuable diamond engagement ring. The police believed robbery was the motive, but her family believed otherwise because her ring remained, and she never carried money in her purse, preferring to clip it inside her coat pockets. Someone who had gone to the trouble of killing her, her family contended, would also have taken that ring and gone through her pockets.

I was inclined to agree.

The other killing occurred in late September, and the body was found in Garfield Park, propped against a tree, much like the other three. This time, the deceased was an elderly man, Otis Washington, whom the police had thought died of exposure, until the coroner found a single stab wound to his heart. Washington was an alcoholic who lived on the streets—although he tended to be seen more often in Jefferson Park than Garfield Park, which was quite a distance away. The police believed his death had been caused by a brawl with another vagrant, one who was carrying a knife.

I wasn't so sure, but it was hard to be certain about anything from the vague news reports. What I found most discouraging were the number of unsolved deaths reported—from teenagers found in the gutter to middle-aged black people—all crime victims. The *Defender* always printed a story or two about them, and then the case was dropped, with no more explanation at all.

Probably the cases were left open and no more explanation was to be had. I counted over a hundred random killings on the South Side alone, and most of the dead were teenage boys.

But that didn't help. If anything, it made me feel worse. Violet Stamps' death was clearly linked to Louis Foster's, and I suspected Otis Washington's was as well.

Five deaths, all linked, meant that a killer had been systematically working his way through an agenda of some sort. Since Foster's death happened less than a month before, I had to believe that the killer was still out there, still planning someone else's death.

My problem was finding that killer before he had time to kill again.

I didn't have the personal resources, but I also didn't have enough information to go to the police. The white officers who handled these cases wouldn't care about the deaths in the Black Belt—and one that occurred outside the city.

Truman Johnson would care, but he might not be able to work on the cases. He'd given the first two to the FBI, and I didn't want them involved.

I'd go to him as soon as I had enough solid information. I still didn't know the extent of the killings or what the link between the victims was. I'd have to do more research to find out.

I only hoped I would get to it all before the killer found his next victim.

I still hadn't gone through the other newspapers, nor had I looked at 1967, but I had to leave to pick up the kids. Even though it was still early afternoon, an accident on Michigan backed up traffic, and I had to wait for a quarter of an hour before I could inch forward a block and get an alternate route.

I arrived ten minutes after the school's closing bell to find chaos.

On the playground, a dozen boys in tams—none of them over twelve—formed a half-circle around two other boys. They were playing a game of keep away with one of Norene Grimshaw's dolls, a pale, blond Barbie. Norene was crying as she reached for it, her face a mask of agony.

Keith held Mikie back. Jimmy hovered near the edge of the group, looking out of his depth. Lacey stood in front of the boys, screaming at them.

A teacher peered out of a half-open door. She slammed the door shut as I pulled into the parking lot.

I had known it had been too quiet. And I knew how this game worked. Jimmy was supposed to get the doll back for Norene. If he fought for it, he would probably get hurt—knifed or worse. If he didn't, he would have to make a bargain with them—a bargain he wouldn't be able to tell me about. And these boys would force him into their group because he had the best of motives: to protect little Norene.

I got out of the car and strode into the playground. Only Keith and Mikie noticed me. The other kids were yelling too loudly. I put a finger to my lips.

Norene was sobbing so hard that I could hear her over the shouts of the boys. The crowd quieted as they saw me, all except Norene, whose tears wouldn't stop. She kept reaching for the doll, which was being held over the head of one of the taller boys.

Jimmy shook his head at me, but I ignored him.

"Uncle Bill, thank God," Lacey said as she ran toward me.

"Step out of the way, Lace," I said. "Let me take care of this."

She moved to one side, close to Jimmy. Norene still cried and jumped for her doll.

The boys expected me to talk to them. That's what adults did. Adults tried to reason with these irrational children, forcing them to think in good, ethical terms.

I was past good, ethical, and polite. I didn't feel like reasoning with anyone.

I picked up the boy with the doll, holding him by the collar until we were face-to-face. My anger helped my natural strength.

"You want to know how it feels to be bullied?" I asked.

He glared at me. I didn't like the way he looked, so I slammed him toward the ground with as much force as I could

197

muster. At the same time, I raised my knee. We connected—my knee into his groin—and he screamed. I let go of his collar and he toppled backward.

As he fell, I snatched the doll from his hand. The junior Stones were so surprised they didn't make a move toward me, even though several switchblades had come out.

"Go ahead," I said, meeting each of their gazes, one by one. "Try something. I'll gladly break each and every one of you in half."

"It was just a game, Gramps," one of the kids said. He spoke from the back.

"It's a game you're not ever going to play again," I said. "I made a deal with you all. You don't mess with anything that's mine. That includes this little girl here and her doll, as well as her sisters and her brother and my son. You got that? You guys touch anyone in my family again and I swear, you won't know what hit you. Now get the hell out of here."

I didn't have to tell them twice. They backed away, and when they thought they were out of my sight, they ran. The boy I'd hurt was still on the ground, clutching his crotch and moaning. None of his friends bothered to help him.

I knew that this kind of challenge would only work once. In the future, if they went after anyone named Grimshaw, they'd either bring guns or older kids, and eventually I'd find someone or something I couldn't out-fight. I had to find a way to settle this once and for all.

Norene snuffled beside me. I crouched, handed her the Barbie, and then pulled her close.

"Uncle Bill," she said and burst into fresh tears. Her whole body was vibrating with sobs. I picked her up and cradled her.

"I don't know what we would've done if you hadn't shown up, Uncle Bill," Lacey said. "No one was helping us."

"Yeah," Keith said. "I even ran for the principal, but he was already gone and none of the teachers wanted to come outside."

They were as afraid of the Stones as I should have been. But I was tired, tired of seeing innocent people getting picked on for no real reason. Tired of making it from one day to the next bottling all my rage inside and not taking any action. I had acted in August when I'd decided that nothing was going to force Jimmy and me from Chicago, but that action, however defensive, had been violent. It seemed like this week was just an extension of that.

My gaze met Jimmy's. His eyes were filled with unshed tears. He knew why this was happening. It was happening because I had returned his tam, and the gang wanted him, for whatever reason.

"Let's go," I said.

We walked toward the car. I saw a few faces peeking out the school windows. Teachers, frightened of their students, terrified to do the right thing.

Like Sinkovich.

How did we come to this? A place where people turned a blind eye to the violence around them because it didn't involve them. It didn't matter that it involved a sweet six-year-old girl who had never hurt anyone.

Norene's tears had soaked through my jacket. I could feel the warm dampness against my shoulder. She clung to me and her doll as if she were afraid to let go.

As we reached the car, I saw a familiar van parked against the curb. The anger, which had exploded just a few moments ago and then receded, built again.

The boys and Mikie got in the back seat. Lacey headed for the front, but I stopped her, handing Norene to her. Norene resisted, and Lacey looked at me in surprise.

"I'll be right back," I said. "You all get in the car and wait."

They did, locking the doors even though I hadn't told them to. I crossed the street, heading directly for the van. I could hear Franklin's voice in my head. *Smokey. You know better than this.* And I did. But I couldn't stop.

I reached the van. The windows were covered with condensation and smudge marks where hands had tried to rub it away.

I pounded on the driver's window with my fist. The window rolled down and I found myself face-to-face with Chaz Yancy.

"You feel good beating up little boys?" he asked me.

"You feel good watching innocent children get trashed by these thugs?"

"They weren't doing anything illegal," he said.

"Really? I counted half a dozen switchblades there. What counts as illegal in your book?"

"Can't comment on that."

"I hope to God you're here for a good reason," I said, "because if your assignment is to watch and listen and not get involved—"

"I think I should stop you now. Threatening a police officer isn't the wisest thing in the world."

We stared at each other for a moment. The white guy in the passenger seat shifted uncomfortably and I heard a radio squawk in the back of the van.

I broke the silence first. "Why are you sitting here day after day? What's going on at this school that needs your watchful eye?"

"Same thing as goes on at all the other schools down here," Yancy said. "This is where it all starts."

"And you just let it."

He shrugged. "We're taking care of things."

"Not from my vantage. That little girl didn't deserve any of that treatment."

"Then maybe you shouldn't have thrown that sun in the Stones' faces," he said.

"My fault, huh?" I asked.

"More yours than mine," he said. "We're trying to close down the entire shop. You haven't even touched the edges of the problem yet."

"So you're giving me the same advice you gave me before. Give up and let my kid run with the gang."

"You got six beautiful kids there, Grimshaw," Yancy said. "Better to lose one than all of them."

"You son of a bitch."

"You wanna keep them all?" Yancy said. "Stop making things worse. Eventually they'll come after you. And you're no match for the nine millimeter that Jeff Fort prefers."

The thing was, he was right, and I knew it. But I wasn't going to let him know that I agreed. "Don't you feel odd, sitting here watching schoolchildren while Jeff Fort turns the Stones into the Black P. Stone Nation, more than four thousand strong?"

"We're doing what we can, Grimshaw," Yancy said. "The only way to kill this body is to cut off the head. We haven't figured out how to do that yet."

I stared at him for a moment, not sure he'd actually said that to me, admitted that they were willing to do what they could to get rid of Fort and the other leaders of the Stones.

"The body's pretty lethal all by itself," I said. "Especially if you keep letting it grow one kid at a time."

"We don't got control of that," he said. "It's concerned parents like you that have all the cards."

Then he rolled up the window. I felt as if he'd struck me a blow as hard as the one I'd just dealt that kid. Concerned parents. I'd enlisted Franklin, but that was it. How many others were handling this same thing, and doing it all alone? And what happened if we did it together?

The idea held me all the way to the car. I unlocked the driver's door and climbed in. Norene was still sniffling as she sat on Lacey's lap and stroked her Barbie's blond hair. Mikie's face had turned gray. Keith held her hand. Jimmy was staring out the back window, his face turned away from me.

I was afraid for him, afraid for all of them. I wanted to protect them, make the world perfect for them, and I couldn't. I couldn't even keep them safe for an afternoon. I had no idea how to do it for a lifetime.

"Let's go home, kids," I said and we did, because there was nothing else we could do.

FIFTEEN

That night I got three phone calls. The first, just after Jimmy and I finished our early dinner, was from the owner of a South Side insurance company that catered to blacks. He'd heard that I did good work and he wanted to talk with me about doing occasional claims investigation for him. We talked for a little while and I found I was interested. We agreed to meet after the holidays, to see if we were compatible.

The second call came from Alice Foster. She was ecstatic. She and a newly hired lawyer went through the stock certificates. She was rich and she hadn't even known it.

"Mr. Grimshaw," she said, "how did you learn about the stocks?"

"A business partner of your husband's—"

"I spoke to the other dentists," she said. "They didn't know a thing."

"It wasn't them," I said, deciding it was time to tell her the truth, since the news panned out. "Your husband was going to buy you a nice home as an anniversary present. Something like the kind of home you'd always dreamed of. He told the real estate agent he was working with that he planned to use money from a proposed stock sale. She double-checked the information before showing him some of the more expensive houses."

There was a long silence. I wished I had waited to tell her when we were face-to-face.

"Was this what got him killed?" Mrs. Foster asked.

Honesty, I reminded myself, even though I didn't like breaking her good mood. "I don't know yet."

More silence.

I finally said, "Remember the gesture, Mrs. Foster. I found no traces of another woman or anything suspicious. Your husband loved you. He wanted to surprise you by giving you one of your dreams."

She gave a weak laugh. "I would rather have him alive, Mr. Grimshaw."

"I know that," I said gently and promised her a report by Friday before I ended the conversation.

When I hung up, the phone rang again. This time it was Laura.

"Smokey," she said. "Do you have a minute? I need to talk to you about Sturdy."

I suppressed a sigh. I didn't care about her problems at the moment, although I probably should have. She was paying me to. "All right," I said.

She told me about Sturdy's latest move—contacting her old attorney with the same plan the men had proposed on Sunday, as if her old attorney could explain it to her more clearly and convince her to take the deal. McMillan had gotten angry, informing the management team they were out of line, but they responded again to the old attorney, not him. They seemed to think he was the problem, a puppetmaster controlling Laura.

I paid only partial attention to the story. While she was talking, I watched Jimmy do the dishes. His shoulders were slumped and he moved slower than usual.

"So anyway, Smokey," Laura was saying, "we still haven't gotten the requested documents. I need to go into Sturdy tomorrow and get them. Drew said he'd accompany me, but I figure he's a lightning rod right now. It's better if you come. Can you?"

"How long will it take?"

"Not too long," she said. "A couple hours at most."

"I need to be home by three or so." I no longer intended to leave Jimmy alone after school.

"Maybe we should go in the morning, then," Laura said. "Just in case they keep us waiting."

"All right," I said. "Meet me at the Randolph Street entrance to the public library at ten-thirty."

"We could meet here," she said, "have some breakfast, talk a little."

"I'm on a case, Laura. I need to do library work and my time is pretty limited right now."

"All right." She sounded disappointed. "I'll see you at the library at ten-thirty."

When she hung up, I went to Jim's side and grabbed a towel, drying the dishes he'd already placed in the rack.

"You don't gotta do that," he said. "I can get it."

"I know," I said.

We worked in silence for a while. He had gotten good at his chores, when he chose to do them. The dishes sparkled.

"You think those guys'd hurt Norie?" he asked.

"No," I said. "They were trying to get to you."

"I figured." He rinsed the final pan and handed it to me, then let the water out of the sink. "I didn't mean for none of this to happen, Smoke."

"I know that, too," I said. "They threatened you right from the start, didn't they?"

He shrugged.

"Tell me about it, Jim."

He wiped out the sink, then wrung out the dishrag before hanging it over the faucet. "Can't."

"This'll just be between us. You know I can keep a secret."

He nodded once, but kept his head bowed. I could see the tight muscles in the back of his neck. One of them twitched slightly. I hadn't realized how much strain he'd been under.

"It was Keith." He finally spoke so softly I had to strain to hear.

"Keith?" I asked, surprised.

"He was hanging out with those guys. I told him he didn't know what he was doing, but he said he grew up with them and they was all fine. Then they started asking him to take stuff for them, you know, wrapped stuff that he wasn't supposed to look at."

Jimmy understood all of that. His real brother, Joe, had used the same trick to get Jimmy to deliver drugs in Memphis.

"I said this ain't right, and I told him to stop. He was getting scared, so he did. He give the sun back, just like you done. Only then they threatened to do stuff to Mikie. They didn't know about Norie or Lacey. I asked 'em what they really wanted and they said it don't matter so long as they had a body to do their stuff. They asked me if I wanted to volunteer, and I said yes just to get them off Keith's back."

I put my hand on his shoulder. That was something I would have done. Maybe he had been observing me a little too closely.

"That was Friday. They give me the sun, and then you found it. I wasn't going to say nothing, figuring they'd just pick on me and leave Keith alone. But they're not, Smoke."

"That wasn't the first time they went after you guys this week, was it?" I asked.

He shrugged again. "It was okay. They couldn't do nothing until today."

His matter-of-fact tone hurt a lot worse than an accusation would have. They didn't try anything until I arrived late, unable to protect the boys like I had promised.

"What do you think we should do?" I asked him.

"I dunno," he said with such quiet conviction that I knew he'd been thinking about it for some time.

"We'll figure something out," I said, and hoped it was true.

I was up several times that night, awakened by dreams, voices and memories that were mingling together. Sinkovich's description of his neighborhood association, Yancy's mention of concerned parents like me, and my own memories of school haunted me.

After my parents died, my adopted parents sent me to an

excellent school, and there was a focus on learning at home. There were kids who ran with a bad crowd, as we used to say, but they did so because they couldn't keep up or because they had nothing else. I was so busy with my studies I never had time to be idle.

By the time Franklin arrived the next morning, I had the beginnings of a plan. I wanted to assemble all of the concerned parents together and form a group that protected our kids like Franklin and I were doing, and one that educated them as well. I even knew who we could ask to run after-school sessions that included homework and a focus on reading.

Grace Kirkland, who'd hired me in August, had a son who was attending Yale, and it looked like her youngest son would go to a good college as well. She'd managed all of this as a single parent, sending her children to the same schools Jimmy went to. She knew how to emphasize learning.

I presented all of this to Franklin, without telling him about Keith's involvement. Jimmy listened silently.

"There's less than two weeks until Christmas," Franklin said. "I doubt anyone has enough time for a meeting-and-planning session."

"This is important," I said. "I think concerned parents would make the time."

Concerned parents. It seemed so logical, but they could be a loaded weapon. Concerned parents tried to stop the busing of black students into white schools. Concerned parents were probably behind the attempted arson that Sinkovich had been talking about.

And here I was considering putting together more concerned parents. Still, I couldn't think of anything else.

Franklin studied me for a moment, then nodded. "We'll do it at my house. I'll find a time—probably next Wednesday night—then send a notice to the *Defender*. We'll have to talk to the parents in the neighborhood ourselves. I think Althea has a list from last year's fund-raiser."

"Good," I said.

"But I'm not doing this one alone, Smokey," he said. "If we get people there, you'll run the meeting."

"Deal." I had hoped to do that anyway. I had some clear ideas on what I wanted to do. "I'll talk to Grace, too."

"We'll have to pay her."

"I know," I said, and hoped the other parents agreed on a way to pay her what she was worth.

"Until then, we've got to be on time for those kids." It was the only time since the incident that he'd blamed me.

"Is Norene all right?"

"She didn't want to go to school this morning," he said. "It's a good thing I'm driving today."

I nodded. "I'm sorry, Franklin."

He gave me a halfhearted smile, then led Jimmy out the door. I stood in the silence for a long moment, realizing that for the first time in our friendship, Franklin hadn't accepted an apology. He saw all of this as the fault of me and Jimmy, without really understanding how very complicated it all was.

I made it to the library with more than an hour to spare before I had to meet Laura. I used that time to look through the *Daily News*, which, along with the *Sun-Times*, were the only white papers in the city that had a chance of covering the kind of news I was looking for. I hoped that their reporters might have better access to the police than the *Defender*'s did.

This time, I went directly to the weeks of the murders, finding all but the killing of Violet Stamps in the *Daily News* and no mention of three of the killings in the *Sun-Times*. They only bothered to report Foster's death because he was a well-known dentist.

I got no new information from those papers, and I resigned myself to an afternoon searching through the 1967 version of the *Defender*, most of which was on microfiche. I finished with the main dailies just in time to meet Laura on the front steps of the library.

She was already there, huddled against the wind. The

temperature, according to the radio, was only in the fifties, but it felt colder. The wind had a damp chill to it, a way of clawing through clothing and promising severe weather to come.

Her hair was down but not styled, and she wore casual pants beneath her rabbit-fur coat. She hadn't worn any makeup, but she didn't need any. Her cheeks were red with cold, and her eyes were a warm, vivacious blue.

"Thanks for meeting me, Smokey," she said as she slipped her hand through my arm.

I put my cold, bare hand over her warm, leather-gloved one. "I said I would."

"I know," she said, "but you've seemed preoccupied lately. This is really my fight."

That it was, although I didn't say anything as we walked down Randolph toward Dearborn. I'd never walked through the Loop with Laura, certainly not arm in arm, and it felt oddly comfortable. Since people were wrapped in their winter coats, faces and skin color weren't clearly visible. No one gave us a second glance.

As if we'd made a mutual pact, we drew apart outside the eight-story building that housed Sturdy Investments. We walked into the main entrance and crossed the dingy two-story lobby.

This building had once been grand, like many of Chicago's downtown buildings, but as with most of them, the grandeur was covered in decades of grime and filth. The atrium, which was supposed to have a skylight effect, made the lobby seem dark.

We entered the only open elevator and Laura greeted the attendant by name. He was an elderly black man, like most of the elevator attendants in the city. He didn't look at me as he shoved the lever toward the seventh floor, pretending, just like white people did, that a black person was beneath his notice.

Laura and I watched the red lights behind the metallic scroll numbers light up, indicating each floor. When we reached seven, she exited and I waited half a beat until I could walk a step behind.

The clear glass doors with STURDY INVESTMENTS, INC. written on them in gold were closed. Laura gripped the glass handle on one and pulled, letting herself in.

I'd been here only once before, on a weekend in midsummer, and the building had been empty. Now the reception area was full. People read newspapers on the blue plastic couches, and a receptionist, sitting behind a blond wooden desk, struggled to answer the constantly ringing phone.

When she saw Laura, she smiled and ignored the phone altogether. "Miss Hathaway, were we expecting you?"

Without the smile, the question would have been rude. As it was, it seemed like an innocent query, with just a hint of the trouble underneath.

"In a way, Darlene. Is Marshall in?"

"No, ma'am. He stepped out for an early lunch. Is there anything I can do for you?"

"Do you have papers for me? I've been requesting them now for most of the week."

"Papers." She patted her clean desktop as if the papers could be invisible. "No, ma'am. Let me get Mr. Parti for you."

"No need, Darlene," Laura said. "I'll see Marshall's secretary instead."

Then, without waiting for the receptionist to summon the secretary, Laura walked around the desk and down a narrow hallway. I followed, feeling the gaze of everyone in the waiting room on my back.

We reached a large office area with a separate secretary's desk. The office door was closed, and it had Marshall Cronk's name posted on a gold plate against the wood. Before the door was another blond wooden desk. The woman behind it was heavyset. She wore her hair in a black beehive whose color could not have been natural.

When she saw Laura, she smiled. "Miss Hathaway! To what do we owe this honor?"

Again, I thought I heard an undercurrent of discord, but it was too subtle for me to be certain.

"I've come for the papers that Marshall promised me."

"Mr. Cronk hasn't sent any papers by me," the secretary said. "Are you sure you requested them?"

"No games, Henrietta. You've received multiple requests from my attorney and from me for the monthly statements and the annual reports. I'm entitled to all of it as a stockholder."

"This isn't my area, Miss Hathaway, you know that—"

"I know that everything that happens in Sturdy goes past you," Laura said with admirable toughness. "You know about the requests and you know why I haven't gotten the papers."

"Oh, Miss Laura, You're in over your head, dear." The secretary had a look of concern on her round face. Her gray eyes darted back and forth, as if making certain they were all alone. "Some of the old-timers here don't like what's been going on."

"So?" Laura asked.

"They're going to make things as difficult as possible for you. I say continue things the way they are. The team is making you a mountain of money. No need altering that."

Laura's smile faded. "Do you believe that, Henrietta?"

"Honey, if I had as much money as you, do you think I'd be sitting in a stuffy old office?"

"No," Laura said, her voice cold. "I don't believe you would."

I wanted to put a hand on her arm, to remind her to stay calm, but that wasn't my place. My place was to guard her, although at the moment, it didn't seem like she needed me at all.

"Tell Marshall," Laura said, "that if I don't receive the papers to which I am legally entitled by the close of business tomorrow, I will see him back in court on Monday. Can you see beyond your loyalty to give him that message, Henrietta, or should I write him a note and slip it under the door myself?"

"Miss Laura, there's no need—"

"Miss Hathaway," Laura said. "I am no longer ten and you are no longer my father's secretary."

The secretary leaned back as if she'd been slapped. "I'll give him the message, Miss Hathaway."

"Good." Laura looked at me. "Let's go."

She led the way toward the hall, but stopped before she entered it. I almost walked into her, stepping aside at the last moment.

"Henrietta," she said in a tone I recognized. It was filled with deceptive warmth. "How many years do you have left until retirement?"

"I'm a fixture here, Miss Hathaway," the secretary said with a smile. "No one's ever mentioned retirement to me."

"Really?" Laura let the chill back into her voice. "How very odd."

Then she continued down the hallway. Some of my worries about her ability to handle herself in the corporate world evaporated at that moment. Maybe she would be able to achieve her goals at Sturdy Investments—if if she managed to get through this month without too many troubles.

By the time we reached the reception area, two white security guards stood next to the door, arms crossed. They hadn't been in the room before. They glared at Laura, but let her pass. One of them extended an arm as I tried to follow her through the glass doors.

"What's your business here?" he said.

"I'm here with Miss Hathaway," I said.

"Sturdy Investments would prefer it if you did not return to this building ever again," he said, so softly I was the only one who could hear him.

"Well," I said, "if I worked for Sturdy, then it would have the ability to order me around. I work for Miss Hathaway, and she asked me to accompany her here. You want to take this up with her?"

Laura was waiting by the bank of elevators, watching, concern on her face.

"I know only what I've been told," the guard said.

"Who asked you to speak to me?" I said.

"I'm not at liberty to say." The guard hadn't taken his hand from my arm.

"Really?" I said, imitating Laura's tone. "I'd hate to have

Miss Hathaway blame the messenger for the message."

Then I shrugged off his hand, walked out the door and joined her.

"What was that about?" she asked.

"Tell you outside," I said as we stepped into the far elevator together.

Drew McMillan was waiting for us in the lobby, leaning against a stone column. When he saw us getting off the elevator, he stood slowly.

"Well?" he asked Laura as we got close.

"Nothing," she said, her irritation showing. "Just like we expected. I don't like these games, Drew."

"They're designed to upset you," he said. "I warned you about that when you decided to demand the reports."

"After going through Daddy's lawyer like that, I had to do something." She shook her head. "I hate this."

"It'll be over in January," McMillan said. Then he turned to me, surprising me. "How did it go?"

I shrugged. "Fine."

"Smokey ended up talking to a security guard," Laura said. "He won't tell me why."

McMillan raised his eyebrows in an implied question.

"Sturdy doesn't seem to like the idea that Laura brought protection."

"They said that?" Laura asked.

I gave her a thin smile. "It's either that or they don't want people of color in the office."

"Or both," McMillan said.

"Or both," I conceded.

Laura's lips thinned. "I'm going to—"

"You're going to wait until January," McMillan said. "If they can intimidate you, they win."

"He's right," I said, "and from the thumbnail you gave me last night, it sounds like they're trying every trick in the playbook."

Laura glanced at the elevator and shook her head. "You'd

think they'd try a real negotiation with me instead of this stuff."

"They don't think you're the real threat, Laura," McMillan said. "They think someone else is manipulating you. Me, or maybe Mr. Grimshaw here. This stuff is aimed at us, not you."

He was right; the way they sent material to the previous lawyer discounted him, and that little scene upstairs was meant to intimidate me.

"They're still underestimating you," McMillan said to Laura.

I smiled. "Wait until they realize the magnitude of the mistake they're making."

She gave me the first genuine smile of the morning. "Thanks, Smokey."

McMillan glanced at the silver watch on his wrist. "That didn't take as much time as I expected. I suspect that if we hurry, we can still find a table at any restaurant down here. Join us, Grimshaw?"

"No, thanks," I said. "I've got some pressing work today."

"Smokey—" Laura started, but I shook my head.

"Sorry," I said. I probably would have stayed if nothing had happened the day before. But too much had, and I needed to focus on my work, not Laura's.

I said my good-byes and slipped through the doors before Laura had a chance to call after me. I hurried down Randolph Street, heading back to the library. As I crossed State, I glanced down at the clock on the Marshall Field building. It wasn't quite noon. I had nearly three hours to go through the rest of the *Defender*.

I intended to make the most of them.

SIXTEEN

Three hours later, I left the library feeling disconcerted. I found four more possibles in 1967. All were adults, all were left in parks or cemeteries mostly on the South Side, and none had a previous history of violence or gang involvement. I wondered how many I was missing, and wasn't sure there was any way I could find out.

The number of deaths disturbed me greatly, as did their randomness. These victims had so little that was obviously in common that I could count the factors on one hand: they were stabbed; they were left in a park or cemetery in a black area of the city; and they were black. A couple had been left in the same park, but in different areas. I'd have to see police reports and talk to the survivors to know if there were any more factors that the victims shared.

The sheer number of victims was daunting and so was the amount of work. I hadn't found a pattern in timing—the killer didn't seem to strike every three weeks or every Friday—but I couldn't rule out something like that. I didn't have enough information.

And it was clear that the person who was doing these killings would continue until caught, which meant that there would be other victims if I didn't act quickly.

But I was one man. I wouldn't be able to investigate all of these cases, continue to care for Jimmy, and earn a living. I needed help, even though I didn't want it.

I had to go to Truman Johnson, the policeman who had discovered the pattern in the first place, and he might have to go to the FBI, since they had been brought in on the cases of the two boys. If he went to the FBI, I had to leave the cases behind.

I'd never done that before. I'd even wrapped up my cases in Memphis before I left. I'd never abandoned anything in mid-investigation.

I was also worried that the FBI would shuffle these cases to the bottom of their cold-case file and nothing would ever get resolved. The killer would remain free, and more people would die. I couldn't have that on my conscience and neither, I suspected, could Johnson. I'd have to trust him, something I didn't do easily with anyone.

I got home before Jimmy, made some coffee to take off the day's chill, and then called the precinct, asking for Johnson. The dispatch informed me that Johnson was out on a case, so I left a message asking him to get in touch with me, telling him it was urgent, that I had new information about our unfinished business.

I knew he would understand.

Then I tried Delevan again. The phone rang ten times. The fact that I couldn't reach him bothered me, but I didn't want to drive to Lake Forest to see him, especially after all I'd been through lately. I didn't really want to venture into white Chicago without a backup.

Finally, I did a few things I'd forgotten to do the day before. I called the hospital and asked for Saul Epstein's room. Mrs. Weisman answered, just as I expected she would. Saul was awake, she told me, and in a lot of pain. He had given a statement to the police, and had even identified both Mattiotti and Owens from a photo array. She also said Saul's spirits were low, and asked me to visit as soon as I could.

I promised I would.

Then I called the hospital back and asked for Elaine's room. As she had predicted, she had been released on Tuesday, leaving with her sister.

I pulled the phone number out of my wallet and called Elaine's sister in Detroit. I wanted an update, and I wanted to tell the sister that Elaine would need emotional support as much or more than she would need physical support. I'd been through this with clients in Memphis, and I knew that with attacks like this, the emotional scars were the last to heal.

On the fifth ring, a woman's voice answered.

"Kit Young?" I asked.

"Who's askin'?" the woman said.

I identified myself.

"Oh," she said. "You're the guy who busted in and broke up the fight. Elaine talked about you."

"I was wondering how she's doing."

"She seemed okay when I left her on Tuesday. A little down, but you gotta expect that."

I leaned against the couch. "You left her?"

"Yeah. She didn't want to come back to Detroit. No matter how much we talked, I couldn't change her mind."

I was cold. "The doctors said she couldn't be alone. She would need help so that her stitches would heal."

"She's got it," Kit said. "She's got some friend taking care of her."

"Really?" I asked. Elaine had told me she'd be with her sister. "Is she with that friend now?"

"I suppose so," Kit said. "I didn't call her when I got home last night. I was too tired. I was going to do it when the rates went down tonight."

"So where's she staying?" I asked.

"At home. I left her at her apartment."

"Alone?" The coffee churned in my stomach.

"She said her friend was coming. She said it was all right to leave." Her sister was beginning to sound defensive.

"Who? Who's the friend who's going to take care of her?" I asked, hoping Kit would list a name I didn't recognize.

"I dunno," Kit said. "I didn't exactly give her the third degree."

Which, she was implying, I was giving her. "I'd like to know who it was. I'd like to know who to talk to about her."

"Some guy. Saul something? He was her boyfriend. Guess he got hurt, too, but not as bad."

"Not as bad?" I said. "He's still in the hospital. I just spoke to his grandmother."

"I'm sure she said it was this Saul guy who got attacked, too." Kit sounded confused. "Why would she say that he was taking care of her when he wasn't?"

"I don't know." I didn't like the way this was going. "What was her mood like when you left her?"

"She seemed okay. Pretty upbeat, which surprised me. I thought she'd be more upset."

"Upbeat?" That surprised me, too.

"Yeah. She said she loved me, would miss me, and was grateful that I came, wished it was under better circumstances. I wished that, too. We would've hugged, but you know."

"She was saying good-bye," I said softly.

"Of course she was. I was leaving—"

"Did she always treat you that warmly when you parted?"

"Hell, no. Elaine and I, we had our disagreements, you know. It was better to keep a couple hundred miles between us. That's why I wasn't surprised she decided to stay."

That sounded logical, but it didn't ease the feeling in the pit of my stomach. "Thanks for your time, Kit."

"You've scared me now, mister. You think she's all right?"

"She's not all right," I said. "She was beaten, badly injured, and most likely raped. She's in about as bad shape as a person can be. I only hope she was lying to us both for a good reason."

"You think I should've stayed," her sister said defensively.

"Yeah, I do," I said and hung up.

First, I called Elaine's apartment. I let the phone ring so many times that anyone would have picked up the receiver just to stop the annoying sound. When I realized no one was going to pick up, I tried the number again to make certain I had dialed correctly. No one answered that time either.

I immediately went to Marvella's apartment to ask her to stay with Jimmy until I got back. Fortunately, she was home.

Elaine's apartment was close to Washington Park, in one of the nicer sections of the South Side. Her building was a three-story white brick, indistinguishable from a single-family dwelling unless you looked closely at it and saw the six mailboxes outside.

Her apartment was on the third floor. I hurried up the wooden stairs—obviously this place had once been a home and these stairs had been part of the grand entry—and knocked. There was no answer.

Then I tried the knob. It turned, but the dead bolt was locked. I had a couple of choices. I could search for the resident manager, if there was one, or I could open the door myself. First, I felt along the door frame for a key. My fingers encountered only dust. Then I looked under the mat she had placed in front of the door. Still nothing.

I scanned the hallway, looking for another place where a single woman living alone would hide an extra key. I saw nothing. Then I glanced at the staircase. The knob at the top of the banister hung crookedly.

I touched it and it swiveled. I twisted it off, and found a key taped to the base. It looked like a dead-bolt key. I took the key out, put the knob back, and tried the key in the door.

The dead bolt turned.

I knocked again. "Elaine?" I kept knocking and calling as I pushed the door open. Then I stopped. A familiar smell greeted me, one I had hoped I wouldn't find here—the smell of feces, mixed with the stale stench of vomit.

The apartment was cool, almost cold. The baseboard heaters were shut off. It was dark. Curtains on the windows lining the eastern wall were pulled tight. I fumbled for a switch beside the door, found it, and flicked it on.

The main room was tiny—one large box with the kitchen in

the upper corner. A door led into a darkened area, and I could see the edges of two doors, probably the bathroom and a bedroom. An ancient folding couch dominated the middle of the room. A small television set rested on top of a pile of boxes, and a chair was pushed up against the spotless kitchen counter.

Books were piled on the floor, all in neat stacks, and all away from the baseboard heaters. Most were best-selling novels, but another pile were books like Frantz Fanon's *The Wretched of the Earth* and political texts. Another pile contained the *Kama Sutra* and books on free love.

Several posters were taped to the wall, some of them on free love as well, and one showing a naked woman having sex with a number of unseen partners. All that was showing were their hands, caressing—and covering—parts of her body.

I left the door open and went farther inside. The apartment had the untouched sense of a place where the owner had been on vacation. The dishes were done, the counters spotless. There wasn't a drop of water in the sink or a speck of dried food on the stove.

The smell got worse the deeper into the apartment I went.

The dark area was too small to be called a hallway. The door to my right led to a tiny bathroom, and the door directly ahead of me led to a single bedroom.

I pushed that door open all the way. The light from the living room fell across the bottom of a bed and on it, I could see two immobile feet.

I felt for the light switch here, too, and finally found it. I hesitated for just a moment before turning it on, not sure I wanted to see what was in front of me. Then I hit the switch.

Elaine lay on top of the bed, which was still neatly made. She was completely naked, her body covered with stitched wounds on almost every visible piece of flesh. The area around her thighs was bruised and she had been shaved, probably for surgical reasons.

Her head was back, her eyes partially open. Vomit trailed out of her mouth and onto the pillow. Her lips were blue.

It was so clear that she was dead—and that she had been dead for a while—that I didn't even have to touch her to see if she was cold.

I stepped farther inside. Bottles of pills—some of them prescription painkillers and penicillin, others sleeping pills—were open on the bedside table next to an empty bottle of Scotch.

I stood there for what seemed like forever, wishing I didn't understand the scene. She had said good-bye to me, too, and I hadn't heard her, hadn't understood her. *Tell Saul I'm sorry*, she had said. *It's my fault*—for what? Believing she had the freedom to be with any man she wanted, when she wanted?

There was no note, which didn't surprise me. From the look of Elaine's hands, just opening the bottles had been difficult enough; there was blood on her right hand. The stitches on her palm had pulled free, and the skin still bore the imprint of the bottle caps.

Holding a pen would have been almost impossible. Besides, I think she gave her explanation by remaining naked on top of the covers. She didn't want to live with that body anymore, not after what had happened to it.

"Ah, honey," I whispered, wishing she could hear me. "If only you'd given it a little time."

If only she hadn't let the bastards win.

SEVENTEEN

I used the phone in Elaine's living room to call for help. I requested an ambulance as well as the police, even though I knew the ambulance wasn't necessary. Part of me wanted to be wrong, to have misjudged with that simple look in that dismal room what my heart knew to be true.

Everything seemed to take a long time. I waited with her, wishing she hadn't been alone in the end. Wishing that her sister and I had remembered to call the day before. Wishing that I had listened more closely on Monday when I'd visited her in the hospital.

The ambulance arrived first. The attendants came in the open door. They didn't look around the apartment, as I had—not a single glance. Instead, they went straight into the bedroom, and knew without touching her that she was gone.

They treated me like a friend who had been too blinded by grief to realize she wasn't breathing anymore. They didn't even seem to notice that I had done nothing to try to revive her. They used the radio to request police presence again, and this time, it came within minutes.

The patrolmen might have seen this as a drug-related hippie death, despite her sutures, if I hadn't told them about the attack on her the weekend before. She still had the hospital bracelet on her right wrist, giving credence to my story, and most of the pills had come from the hospital pharmacy.

I didn't tell them my role the Sunday before. In fact, I told them little about myself, except that I had spoken to her sister because I was worried about her, and got even more concerned when I realized that she had lied to both of us about who was going to care for her. I gave the police Kit Young's phone number in Detroit.

They didn't ask for my phone number or my full name, and I gave neither. If someone figured out later who I was, then fine. I would say I'd forgotten to give them my name because I had been in shock.

After the questioning was done, I asked if I was needed any longer. One of the cops said I wasn't, and promised to call me if they had any more questions, apparently not realizing they didn't really know who I was.

I stepped into the hallway, saw Elaine's neighbors—college students mostly—staring into the apartment as if they could understand what was going on. I didn't look at any of them as I walked down the stairs and exited the building into the growing darkness.

I didn't say anything when I got back, but I must have seemed shaken. Marvella didn't try to cheer me up. She didn't even flirt.

The apartment smelled of roast pork and fresh biscuits. Sweet potatoes steamed on the table and green beans were boiling on the stove. Jimmy was watching the news on television, the sound turned up so that Marvella could hear.

"Is everything all right?" she asked me as I closed the door.

Of course it wasn't. But I didn't know how to tell her what had happened. I wasn't certain how to deal with it myself.

"It was what I expected," I said and heard the defeat in my own words. I had known it deep down from the moment I realized that Elaine wasn't with her sister. Maybe I had even known it sooner.

What was my responsibility to a woman I had met only three times? I had thought she would be well taken care of, but if I had known her family situation, perhaps I would have made other choices. I hadn't, and I felt guilty, even though when I

222

looked at this logically, I doubted I could have prevented her suicide.

Elaine Young had been determined to kill herself—perhaps from the moment in the ambulance when she stared at Saul Epstein and wondered if he would live. She had been an intelligent woman, and she had used all of that intelligence to guarantee her own success. There wasn't even a phone in her bedroom. Once she had taken all the drugs she'd been given and chased them down with Scotch, she couldn't have called for help if she wanted to.

"Smoke?" Jimmy twisted on the couch, his arms resting on its back so he could face me. "What happened?"

For a moment, I debated telling him. Then I remembered what Althea had said to me, that Jimmy was afraid I would die. He didn't need to know how closely death had touched us yet again.

"Tough day," I said. Then I made myself smile at Marvella. "Sure smells good. You didn't have to do this, you know."

She smiled back. "Yes I did. I don't get the chance to cook for people very often. Go clean up. Dinner will be ready in a few minutes."

The situation seemed oddly surreal to me as I walked to the bathroom. For perhaps the first time in my life, my homecoming mimicked the ideal American one—I came home from my demanding job to find a beautiful woman cooking a sumptuous meal in my kitchen, and a bright, good-looking child interested in what happened in my life. It was a Norman Rockwell moment, if you didn't look at what was underneath it.

I came back out to find the table set, the television off, and Jimmy already in his chair. I joined him, and Marvella put gravy-covered pork slices on the table, followed by a bowl of green beans.

I had no stomach for food, but I ate anyway. To refuse would have been churlish, and would have called attention to my mood. Marvella carried the conversation, although I tried. Jimmy watched me from the corner of his eyes, as if he were trying to figure out exactly what I wouldn't tell him.

Jimmy went to bed without a fuss. Marvella left after she finished the dishes—she insisted on cleaning up her own mess. When I told her I didn't know how to repay her, she finally flashed her flirtatious grin.

"I'll think of something," she said, but her heart wasn't in it and she left quietly, telling me that I could ask for her help at any time.

Her departure left a gloomy apartment, and I was restless. The familiar opening chords to *Dragnet '68* sounded on the television and I shut it off, not wanting to watch the supposed heroics of white cops in the big city.

Finally, I picked up the phone. I didn't call Kit Young; I couldn't face that conversation. Instead, I made one that was, in some ways, even harder.

I called Ruth Weisman.

It was after visiting hours had ended at the hospital, so I knew she would be home. She answered on the second ring, sounding breathless and worried.

I introduced myself and she calmed immediately. She was probably still on edge, worrying about her grandson.

"I have bad news," I said, "and I thought I'd better tell you in case it airs on television tonight."

"The police didn't let those hoodlums out, did they?" she asked with such ferocity that I could see her again, hunting rifle in hand, her eyes wild.

"No, ma'am," I said. "In some ways, this is worse. You might want to sit down."

"What is it?" she asked.

"Elaine Young," I said. "She killed herself today."

"What?" Mrs. Weisman breathed the word, long and empty, her voice filled with disbelief. "She was such a vibrant girl. Are you sure she did it to herself?"

"Yes, ma'am," I said. "I'm the one who found the body."

I didn't want to describe it to her, and to my relief, she didn't ask any more questions.

"This will destroy Saul."

"I thought it might hurt him," I said. "You may want to call the hospital and make sure he isn't listening to the news. I doubt the death of a black woman will make the local channels, but sometimes they surprise me. If we count on their lack of coverage, they'll break the story tonight."

"Yes, I'll call," she said, and I thought she was going to hang up. Instead, she said, "Mr. Grimshaw?"

"Yeah?" I said.

"Will there be a service?"

I hadn't even thought about it. I wasn't sure I wanted to attend a memorial. "I don't know," I said. "I can find out for you."

"I'm sure I can find out that information myself," she said. "It's just that—Saul loved her so. If I tell him, he'll be devastated, and if I don't tell him, he'll be angry when he finds out, especially if he missed the service."

"I don't know what to tell you, Mrs. Weisman."

"Of course." She paused, then changed direction. "What about you, Mr. Grimshaw? Certainly this can't be easy for you."

Her concern touched me. Every once in a while things seemed so bleak to me, and then someone like Mrs. Weisman—or even Marvella, with her marvelous dinner—would remind me that there was compassion in this world after all.

"It's not easy," I said. "But I'm okay. I just wanted to make sure that you and Saul would be, too."

"We'll get through this," she said. "No matter what. I promise you that."

EIGHTEEN

I didn't even try to go to bed. I knew if I closed my eyes, I would see that stitches-covered body naked on the bed, hear Elaine's voice saying *I wish I could see Saul before I go. I want to apologize.* I had thought she wanted to apologize for not seeing the attack coming. Now I was wondering if she wanted to apologize for leaving him for good.

I was sitting on the couch, the *Defender* open on my lap and the television playing an old movie that I only had on for noise. I was trying to read an editorial on Black Christmas, but I couldn't wrap my mind around the words.

Awake or asleep, I was haunted by Elaine.

I might have dozed off. The television was playing a test pattern when I heard the front door to the apartment building slam open and someone shout my name. At first, I thought I was dreaming, but then the shout came again:

"Grimshaaaaaaw!"

It was a man with a voice I recognized, but couldn't place. Footsteps sounded against the stairs, loud in the late-night silence, and my name got shouted again.

"Grimshaaaaaaw!"

I set down the paper and went to the door, opening it just a crack to peer through. Sinkovich was on the stairs, swaying, his face red. He was wearing a T-shirt not suited to the cold, a pair of blue jeans, and sneakers.

"There you are, you holier-than-thou son of a bitch!" He pointed at me, still shouting. "I hope you're fucking proud of yourself."

"Shut up, Jack. It's the middle of the night."

"What're you going to do? Call the cops?" He laughed at his own joke, but I didn't find it funny.

"What do you want, Sinkovich?"

He pointed at me again, the movement uncertain. He was drunk. I could smell him even at a distance.

"I figure you owe me," he said loudly. "It's all your fault anyway."

"I don't owe you anything, Sinkovich."

"Sure you do. I listened to your piece of shit advice, and now look at me. I don't even got a fucking shirt." He started up the stairs, slipped and nearly fell, catching himself at the last moment.

"Go home, Sinkovich."

"I would if I could." He laughed again. "Like a stinking Dr. Seuss book. I would if I could but I can't so I shan't."

His laughter had become raucous and obnoxious. A door opened upstairs. "What's going on?" someone shouted.

"Nothing!" Sinkovich shouted back. "Just some drunk in the hall. We'll get rid of him."

Then he looked at me and said softly, "Right, Grimshaw?"

I was always conscious of the burden my work put on my neighbors. Strangers coming in and out, occasional problems like the one with the notes on my door. The last thing I needed was to get on my neighbors' nerves.

I held the door open. "Get in here."

Sinkovich didn't have to be asked twice. He hurried up the stairs, swaying as he moved, but not falling like I expected, then belched as he came through the door. Beer. Lots of it, and something with onions as well.

I closed the door behind him. "Now tell me quietly what's

going on. I've got a sleeping kid in the back room."

"I got a sleeping kid, too, like anybody cares." Sinkovich opened my refrigerator, the light making his face look sickly green. "Just like I thought. You're not a real American, Grimshaw. No beer. You got any booze?"

I did, but I wasn't about to give it to him. "You don't need any more."

"You never need booze," he said, giving me a lopsided grin. "But you want it. And this is one of those times I want it."

He grabbed a piece of pork off the tinfoil-covered plate Marvella had put in the refrigerator, then let the door close. He chewed with his mouth open as he sank into one of my kitchen chairs.

"So, you got a guest room?"

"What?" I asked.

"It's your fault. I can't go home. None of my friends is talking to me. My mom says I'm a disgrace to the family, and my wife, well, she says she always knew I was a nigger-loving bastard."

I winced.

"Neighbors, now they don't like me much neither, considering a whole lot of them paid bail this afternoon. The judge said he understood the frustration, but he said arson ain't the answer."

The picture was becoming clearer now. "Did they burn down the house?"

"Damn near." He leaned the chair back on two legs. I had the sense he wasn't as drunk as he was pretending to be. "I figured the best way to get them was to catch them in the act. So I knew when it was coming down, and I got there, saw some folks with gasoline cans, and called for backup. It arrived soon enough, but everyone still knew I was the one who ratted on them. Makes me the most popular person in the neighborhood, next to that nice Negro family that nearly got burnt out."

"Smokey?" Jimmy came out of the bedroom, rubbing his eyes with his fist. When he saw Sinkovich, he frowned. "What do you want?"

228

"You ever teach that kid to respect his elders?" Sinkovich asked me.

"He's not real fond of white people," I said.

"Well, well, well. Bigotry runs both ways," Sinkovich said.

"Go back to bed, Jim," I said. "Officer Sinkovich was just leaving."

"You're throwing a homeless man on the street?" Sinkovich asked.

"You've got a home," I said.

"My wife changed the locks." He kept rocking on the chair. The legs groaned. "Which is a real fu—" he glanced at Jimmy "—friggin' piece of work if you ask me since the house has been in my family, not hers. So I call her and beg her to let me in. She says her folks are coming for her and my son on Sunday, and until then, I can go sleep with the—well, you know."

"So you thought you'd take her up on that."

He slammed the chair down on all four legs. "No, actually. I thought maybe you'd understand. I saved some lives last night, whether or not anyone cares."

Which was more than I had done.

Jimmy was watching me. I sighed. "Does the family know what nearly happened to them?"

"They know. I talked to them. They can't move. They can't afford it. They're locked in. Dumb Polack that I am, I promised to help 'em if they had any more trouble. I was feeling magnanimous, don't you know?"

I did know, very well. "Do you think they're going to be attacked again?"

"Not by nothing illegal. The judge set normal bail for arson on these folks. Then he pulls me aside and says that next time I should maybe just, you know, tell people this ain't done, because my actions left him no choice but to do this by the book— as if what they all done was my fault, not theirs. Then he says I'm damn lucky none of them had a precinct captain or an alderman in their pocket, because I'd be out of a job for arresting decent people that way. Decent people."

He snorted, then wiped his nose with the back of his hand.

"Decent people. You know, I'm beginning to think the definition of decent people ain't what I was raised to think it was. Because to me, decent people is the people who have a nice house that they're real happy with who don't bother nobody and go about their business, not people who try to friggin' burn out their neighbors. And then I'm the one who gets punished for it. I told my wife, the b—"

He glanced at Jimmy again.

"Jim," I said, "could you get some sheets and a blanket for Officer Sinkovich? I think he's staying the night."

"Thanks, sport," he said to Jimmy and winked. Jimmy rolled his eyes at me and headed down the hall.

"I told my wife," Sinkovich said, softer now that Jimmy wasn't in the room, "that decent people do nice things. She's a Christian lady, so she thinks. She goes to mass. She tithes ten percent whether we can afford it or not, and the things she said to me about what I done, it was as if I was the devil incarnate. Which she's been thinking anyway because I been thinking, too, doing some reading. Wondering if things ain't quite so simple, you know. And she hates it. She says I ain't the guy she married. But she married a cop. Which is, by definition, I think, a guy who believes in right and wrong and doing things by the book. Not that most guys think that way."

He patted his T-shirt, then burped again. "What a friggin' time to quit smoking. Got a cigarette?"

"No," I said.

Jimmy came back, carrying sheets, a blanket, and a racecar pillow from his bed. He set them on the couch, then crossed his arms and looked at Sinkovich. "How come you think I'm a bigot, mister?"

"I didn't say that, sport."

"Yes you did."

"Your dad said you don't like white people."

Jimmy looked at me. "He just said that to make you mad."

Sinkovich raised his eyebrows. "Kid's got your number."

"He'll have yours inside of an hour, too," I said.

"I don't know a lot of white people," Jimmy said, apparently

230

stung by Sinkovich's remark. "But I know one who's the best person in the whole world."

"Really, sport? Who's that?"

"Laura Hathaway."

Sinkovich laughed. "Yeah, like you hang out in those circles, kid."

Jimmy just stared at him. After a few seconds, Sinkovich's smile faded.

"You really know Laura Hathaway, of the Gold Coast Hathaways? Dame who changed her name back to Hathaway when she gets divorced because that name has more clout than Godzuki or whatever the hell her husband's name was?" he said.

I had forgotten that Laura had been married before. But of course she had. And it must have been quite a scandal on the society pages when she insisted on returning to her maiden name.

"She and my dad are best friends," Jimmy was saying.

"That's enough, Jim," I said.

Sinkovich shook his head. "You know, just when I think I got you figured, Grimshaw, you throw some kind of weird curve at me. Laura Hathaway. Next thing you know, you're gonna tell me you play cards with Mayor Daley."

"Daley and I aren't on the same page," I said.

"Now that makes sense." Sinkovich slapped his hand on the table. In that moment, all his bravado seemed to leave him. He looked smaller, as if in a matter of seconds he shrank. "I'm sorry to put you out. I just didn't have nowhere else to go and I don't got enough money for a hotel. Even the guys at the precinct, you know, they think I should've handled it different. I get the next few days off so that 'emotions can cool down.' "

Jimmy yawned. "Can I go back to bed?"

I nodded and he padded his way down the hall. Sinkovich didn't seem to notice.

"So I think Grimshaw'll take me in. He knows what it's like. He calls it like he sees it. He'll maybe—"

"You need to get some sleep, Jack," I said, interrupting him. He was beginning to repeat himself, like drunks usually did.

"Yeah, I guess so." He stood up and wiped his face. Then his eyes met mine. His were bloodshot. "You know what was hardest for me today, Grimshaw?"

"What?" I asked.

He gave me a confused little smile. "Knowing that the mother of my kid ain't a woman I like much. I think maybe I knew that, but it come real clear tonight, the stuff she said. I got to wondering how I could've even thought she was something, you know? I can't even blame it on my dick. I'm kinda afraid that I used to be—ah, hell."

He shook his head and sank onto the couch.

"I don't know nothing anymore," he said.

I recognized that feeling, too. I put a hand on his shoulder. It was thinner and bonier than I expected. "There's aspirin and Alka-Seltzer in the medicine cabinet."

He gave a short laugh. "Think I'll need that, huh?"

"You just might," I said and headed toward my room. I finally felt like I could sleep without dreaming. Instead of being annoyed by Sinkovich's arrival, I was grateful. He had distracted me just enough to let me relax.

In the morning, however, Jimmy and I felt as if we'd been invaded. Sinkovich's snoring dominated the entire living room. I made breakfast, trying to be quiet, but it made no difference. If a brass band had been playing in front of Sinkovich, I doubted he would have awakened.

As Jimmy and I shared some cold cereal and toast, Jimmy said, "You know, Smoke, I forgot to tell you that some guy named Johnson called last night."

"Truman Johnson?"

Jimmy nodded.

"Good," I said. "I was wondering why he hadn't called back."

I would try to reach him again after I took the kids to school. Getting them there on time was turning out to be something I wasn't as good at as I thought I'd be. And I found that irritating.

232

I'd always thought I'd been punctual, but apparently it had never mattered like it did now.

The kids were subdued, and as we drove, I realized I hadn't asked Jimmy about the day before. The fact that I was letting things drop was a sign of how overwhelmed I'd been feeling. The thought made me think of Elaine, and brought my mood even lower.

Even though there were a lot of young kids with tams in the playground when I arrived, no one gave us any trouble as we walked inside. When I came out, I noticed that the Gang Intelligence Unit van was gone, and I wondered if whatever they were looking for had happened or if another crisis was occurring elsewhere.

The silence on the playground was unnerving. I hadn't seen the street this empty all week. Part of the change might have been the weather. It was still gray, and the air's damp bite seemed even chillier than it had before. The wind had come up, slicing through my coat.

I felt like we were caught in a twilight between fall and winter. A part of me, a less rational part, felt that if it would only snow, everything would improve—and not just the occasional dusting of flakes we'd been having, but a good, heavy storm, the kind Chicago was famous for.

But there were no storms forecast, and the radio station was bemoaning the fact that there wouldn't be a white Christmas this year. There wouldn't be a black one either, at least not in our house unless I got busy.

When I turned onto our street, I noted a squad car parked across from my apartment building. Sinkovich's white Ford was still in front, so I knew the squad didn't belong to him. I supposed someone had finally tracked him down, or that the squad was here investigating something completely unrelated to me or my friends.

As I parked behind the Ford, the squad car's door opened. A cop in plainclothes got out.

I recognized his shape before I recognized him—big, burly,

the beginnings of fat. A lot of height and an athlete's grace. Truman Johnson shoved his hands in the pockets of his great-coat and crossed the street.

I got out of my car, the bits of moisture in the wind stinging my cheeks like miniature needles. "I was just getting ready to call you again."

"Like minds, I guess." He turned up the collar of his coat to protect his nonexistent neck. Like most former football players, his shoulders seemed to blend into his chin. He didn't wear a hat, and his ears were tipped red with the cold. "I figured since you didn't call me back, I'd come see you. They said it was urgent."

"It is." I led him down the sidewalk. It was slick. The temperature had gone down in just the last hour. If things didn't change soon, ice would coat every damp surface.

As we crossed the threshold to the main door, Johnson looked at the steps. I knew he was remembering the boy's body that had been dumped on those steps the night we met, and the way that the case—for him—had never really been solved.

He let me lead him up the steps and waited patiently while I unlocked the dead bolts. The sounds echoed in the hallway. The building felt nearly deserted. Everyone but me—and maybe Marvella, who was probably still asleep—was at work.

I opened the apartment door and was assailed by the smell of coffee and burnt toast. Sinkovich sat at my kitchen table, looking like death. His eyes were red-rimmed, his skin grayish green, and his clothes wrinkled from having been slept in. He had wrapped both hands around a brown coffee cup he'd taken from the top shelf. A plate covered with blackened crumbs sat in the middle of the table.

Johnson stopped beside me. The door slowly closed behind him. When it clicked shut, he looked at me and said softly, "I can't believe you're associating with him."

Sinkovich raised his head as if he hadn't noticed us before. He raised his eyebrows, probably in an attempt at irony, but the look only managed to accentuate his miserable condition.

234

"Don't tell me," he said to Johnson. "You think I did something wrong, too?"

"No." Johnson didn't move. "I think you were remarkably heroic. Amazingly so."

Sinkovich stared at him. "Didn't expect it of me, did you?"

"No, I didn't," Johnson said.

Sinkovich snorted, then sipped his coffee and shook his head. "I suppose you two got some kind of meeting. I'll leave you to it."

But he didn't move. I unzipped my coat, pulled it off, and hung it on the coatrack. "Want something?" I asked Johnson.

"Coffee would be nice." He took my words as indication to take off his coat.

"It's cold out there, Jack," I said as I walked into the half kitchen. "You don't have the clothes for this weather."

"I'll live," he said.

"You might as well stay." As the words came out of my mouth, I realized I'd been toying with telling Sinkovich about the case all morning. "This concerns you, too."

He frowned, and so did Johnson. Their expressions were so similar that it was almost comical.

I set milk and sugar on the table, along with cups for me and Johnson. Then I took the percolator off the stove and poured. I offered to refill Sinkovich's cup, but he put his hand over the rim.

Johnson gave Sinkovich a wary look, then sat down. "What's this about, Bill?"

Someday, I realized, I would tell him my real name. I wanted to trust him more than I already did. But I knew it wasn't wise.

Before I sat down, I went into the my office and grabbed the photographs that Saul Epstein had taken of Louis Foster's body. I brought them out as the radiator clanked on. The apartment was about to enter its warm phase.

"Last Friday," I said, "I got hired on to investigate a murder case. Take a look at these pictures."

I tossed them on the table. Johnson took them first, looking at each one. His expression revealed nothing, but his intensity did. He saw exactly what I had seen.

Without a word, he passed the photographs to Sinkovich. Sinkovich looked at the first, then set it faceup on the table. He patted his T-shirt pocket, but failed to find cigarettes. His hands shook. Then he got up, poured himself more coffee, and sat back down.

For a long time, neither man said anything. They studied the photos. I drank my coffee, wincing at the bitter, burned taste.

When I got up to make fresh, Johnson said, "Last Friday?"

"Yeah," I said, knowing what was coming.

"And you didn't contact me?"

"There's already a police file on it," I said as I poured out the remains of the coffee that Sinkovich had made. He was still staring at the photos as if no one had spoken.

"So?" Johnson said.

"The investigating officers thought it was robbery. Gang-related." I rinsed the percolator, then filled it with water.

"White cops," Johnson said with contempt.

"Hey!" Sinkovich said.

"I don't know if they were white," I said, hoping to keep peace between the two. "I didn't talk to them."

"You found this and you didn't talk to anyone?" Johnson asked.

"What, you think you can do better than we can?" Sinkovich asked, suddenly all cop.

"Who noticed the connection, Jack?" I put the metal filter and its holder into the percolator, then filled the top with coffee grounds. The rich scent of the grounds was like a balm. "It wasn't the Chicago PD."

"Not everyone knows what's going on there," he said sullenly.

"You'd think they'd know about cases that are so important they've been sent to the FBI." I was referring to the murder of the first two boys.

"I told you," Johnson said. "Those cases were ignored."

"Except by our copycat."

236

"What copycat?" Sinkovich asked.

I waited for Johnson to answer. He didn't say anything, probably hoping I would. But I wasn't going to talk about the case. I'd made that clear in August. Not even Johnson knew what I had done and I meant to keep it that way. He had his suspicions, and he knew that sometimes we had to operate outside of the law.

Ironic, then, that Sinkovich was in trouble for preventing that very thing. His unit believed that he should have ignored what his neighbors were doing; his conscience hadn't let him.

"What copycat?" Sinkovich asked again.

Finally Johnson answered him. "The boy we found last August was killed by a copycat."

"You know that for a fact?" Sinkovich asked.

Johnson nodded.

"You catch the son of a bitch?"

I could feel the silence. I knew that Johnson was looking at me. I put the percolator on the burner and turned on the gas, then kept busy so that I wouldn't have to turn around and face him.

"I think so," Johnson said after a moment.

I turned around then. Both men were looking at me.

"That true, Grimshaw?" Sinkovich asked.

"If Truman says so." I sat down.

A small smile touched the corner of Johnson's lips. This was a game we'd play for the rest of our lives, and we both knew it.

"Let me get this straight," Sinkovich said, leaning forward and resting his forearms on the table. "We got two little boys who died this way, and one grown man."

"No," I said. "We have seven others."

"Seven!" Johnson looked stunned.

I nodded. "That's why I called you. I've found possible victims that go back to February of sixty-seven, maybe farther. The M.O. seems to be the same in all of them, but I can't tell just from the newspaper records."

"Seven?" Sinkovich frowned. "How's that possible?"

I slipped a piece of paper with the pertinent facts of the cases to Johnson. "I'd like to see the police files on these cases."

"Civilians can't—"

"Stop," I said, my fingers still on the piece of paper. "You wouldn't have these names without me. You wouldn't have anything except those two boys, whose cases are getting colder by the second. You can share this."

"Hell, I'd share it," Sinkovich said, "except I can't even get into the precinct right now."

Johnson was staring at me.

"Your choice," I said to him.

"You'd let a creep get away because of your pride?" Johnson said.

I pulled the paper back. "I didn't say he'd get away. It'll just take me longer to catch him, that's all."

"How do you know these cases are connected?" Sinkovich had the same look on his face that he'd had when I had talked to him about the Richardson case last summer—a look of great curiosity mixed with fear.

"All of them were found in cemeteries or parks or other public places," I said. "All of them appeared to be out of context. Most were thought to be victims of robberies, yet their most valuable possessions remained on their bodies. All of them had been stabbed."

"That's it?" Sinkovich asked. "What about the shoe? What about the position of the bodies? You can't make a connection like that without some kind of confirming evidence."

"I know." I kept my voice calm. "That's why I want to see the police files. The newspaper didn't have any of that information."

"Why don't you just let me handle it from here?" Johnson asked. "You got us going. You'll get credit."

"Handle it like you've been handling the other two cases?" I asked. "All you managed to do was leak enough information for a copycat to hear about them. You're the one who told me that those cases would be ignored."

Sinkovich turned his head toward Johnson. "You said that?"

"Two little black boys dying near the ghetto," Johnson said. "What do you think?"

"Why'd you give up the cases, then?" Sinkovich asked.

"My superior sent them to the FBI, just like they're supposed to do when there are multiple homicides with the same M.O."

"So that's where these are going?" Sinkovich asked.

Johnson didn't answer.

"Probably," I said.

"You think with nine possibles behind this guy that the cops will continue to ignore him? I mean, stuff like this, it's like the Strangler case. Nine possibles and we got some nut running around the city killing people at random." Sinkovich was looking back and forth between me and Johnson as he spoke. "Shit, Richard Speck went on a spree here two summers ago and the whole city was living in terror. We caught him pretty damn fast, but I remember those days. Everyone was scared. And Speck did all his killings on one night. I can't imagine how this city'll react when it learns there's been nine victims over the space of years."

"It probably won't react at all," I said.

"What?" Sinkovich turned so fast he almost knocked over his coffee cup. It wobbled and he stopped it with one hand.

"Speck's victims were white," I said.

Johnson raised his head slightly. I had his attention now.

"There's so much killing down here that no one really pays attention. How many murders go unsolved or are attributed to gang violence?" I looked at both of them.

Neither answered me. Their silence was answer enough.

"I'll wager that the only reason those two boys' cases got sent to the feebies was because Truman here pushed for help, saying that these didn't look like typical gang killings."

"I didn't push for help." Johnson's voice was soft. "I just wanted to combine the cases. My commander looked at the files, realized that these weren't typical gang killings, and sent them on. It was a smart way to make sure I wouldn't waste my time on unimportant homicides."

He managed to say the last with only a minimum of bitterness.

"They can't ignore this many cases," Sinkovich said.

"Why not?" Johnson put one elbow on the back of his chair so he could see Sinkovich clearly.

"Because if Grimshaw's right, we got some kind of mass murderer working the streets of Chicago."

"Killing black people." Johnson seemed perfectly relaxed. I was beginning to realize that when he seemed relaxed, he was the most dangerous. "Didn't you just say that you can't go to work today? Is that because you betrayed your neighbors for doing the right thing, even though it was against the law?"

Sinkovich flushed. "I never said they did the right thing."

"I know you didn't," Johnson said. "But I heard a rumor this morning that a judge chastised you for handling the case improperly. And there's talk all through the city that you're going to be given a desk because you're not fit to be on the street."

"What?" Sinkovich's eyes widened. "Is that true?"

Johnson nodded.

"Oh, shit." Sinkovich bowed his head and ran his hands through his hair. It was too long to be called a crewcut now, and his fingers made it stick out in tufts. "They're going to try to chase me out."

"You don't play nice anymore," Johnson said.

Water started to boil in the percolator. Its first little pop made me jump.

"I been a cop my whole life," Sinkovich said. "My dad was a cop."

"Then you know the code." Somewhere in this conversation, Johnson's hostility had disappeared and he was speaking to Sinkovich with sympathy now.

"What was I supposed to do?" Sinkovich's voice rose. "You tell me. What was I supposed to do?"

"What you did," Johnson said.

"But I'm paying for it now. And that means if something else comes up, I can't do nothing about it. If I lose this, I don't got nothing left."

Johnson looked at me over Sinkovich's head.

"His wife locked him out yesterday," I said.

Johnson nodded. I didn't need to explain any more.

Sinkovich threaded his hands over the back of his neck. Last night's drunk act had been a good mask for the despair that was obvious now. And Elaine had reminded me how lethal such despair could be.

"If you're at a desk," I said, "you'll be in a good position to help us on this."

Sinkovich shook his head. "They'll want to know what I'm doing. They'll look for anything to bust me out of the department."

"Then you may as well go out following the law." Johnson was still watching me as he spoke. I liked him more and more each time I talked to him. Johnson got subtlety.

"Then what?" Sinkovich asked, raising his head. His pale skin was blotchy. "When they kick me out, then what do I do?"

"We'll figure it out from there," I said.

"Oh, yeah," Sinkovich said. "I recognize that one. We'll cross that bridge and all that. I just like to know ahead of time."

"There's no way to know," Johnson said. "We have access to more files than Grimshaw here does. Who knows? This sick fuck might be killing white people, too."

"I gotta hope for that so that if we catch him, I'm a hero?" Sinkovich shook his head. "That's fuckin wrong, man, and you know it."

"Of course I know it," Johnson said. "Doesn't make it any less true."

Sinkovich stood up and took the percolator off the burner. I hadn't even noticed that the coffee was done. He stood there with his back to us for a long time.

"Nine victims, maybe more," he said after a while.

"Yeah," I said.

"And this guy's been getting away with it for two years."

"That I found," I said. "I haven't had time to go back farther than that."

"Shit." Sinkovich still had his back to us.

Johnson was watching him, expression unreadable.

"What the hell. In for a penny, in for a pound, my mom used to say." Sinkovich sighed. Then he turned, his face grim. "Give me a copy of that goddamn list."

NINETEEN

With that, the investigation became an unofficial police project. Because Sinkovich wasn't allowed near his precinct until Monday, we agreed that Johnson would dig up the files and we'd meet at my apartment on Sunday to review them. Sinkovich would do the library work I'd been doing, to see if he could find more victims.

Even though I had their help, I kept a few things from them. I didn't tell them about Delevan or Saul Epstein's remaining photographs. I also didn't tell them about the two boys I'd interviewed or the car that had driven away from the crime scene.

All I wanted them to do was work on the connections between the victims. I wanted to keep Louis Foster for myself.

After they left, I typed a report for the newly rich Mrs. Foster. I didn't tell her everything. I left out the fact that her husband might be one of many victims, and I also didn't tell her about the leads I hadn't followed yet. Without that information, the report was only two pages long, single-spaced, and it felt like I hadn't had as busy a week as I had.

Still, I paper-clipped my weekly expenses bill to the back of the report, as we had agreed. I hoped she'd pay me quickly. I needed the extra cash for Christmas. I still hadn't figured out how Jimmy and I would celebrate, but I did know that we would. Jimmy needed at least one happy Christmas in his young life.

By the time I finished, I had to pick the kids up from school. I put Mrs. Foster's bill in an envelope, meaning to drop it off along the way. As I left the apartment, I hesitated near the door. I hadn't given Sinkovich a key, but I had a hunch he'd be back. No amount of cajoling was going to change his wife's mind, no matter what he thought.

I'd loaned him one of my jackets, but he'd need more than a grimy T-shirt and a single pair of pants to get through the next few days. My clothes wouldn't fit him, and besides, I didn't have enough to share.

When he got back, I'd direct him to a nearby thrift store. Between the two of us, we could probably scrounge up enough cash to get him a change of clothes for the weekend.

The junior members of the Blackstone Rangers were back in the playground when I returned to the school. I recognized some of the faces, although others were new. They made a point of watching me park and walk to the front door. I was on their list, and they were making sure I knew it.

I entered the school just as the final bell rang. Kids poured out of classroom doors, and the hallway, which had been empty a moment before, was full of children. Slowly my flock gathered around me, only Lacey holding back until I beckoned her to us. We managed to walk out with a large group of students and get to the car with no problems at all.

My shoulders relaxed as I backed out of the parking lot. I hadn't realized how tense even that little ritual had made me.

The children were silent on the drive, and I didn't ask any questions. I dropped the Grimshaws at their house and continued home. Jimmy stared out the passenger-seat window, answering any question I asked him with a nod or a grunt.

Sinkovich's car wasn't in front of the apartment building when I parked, and I was grateful. I wanted to talk with Jim, see how the week went, see why everyone had been so silent. I was trying to figure out how to approach the subject when I opened the building's front door.

Marvella was leaning against the banister, her legs crossed at the ankles. Her elegant feet were bare, and the pedal pushers she wore revealed equally elegant ankles. Her hair was wrapped in a towel, and she wore a Roosevelt University sweatshirt two sizes too big, the sleeves pushed up.

In her right hand she held a single piece of paper, and she was slapping it against the palm of her left. "I saw your little visitors again today, Bill."

"Little visitors?" Jimmy asked.

"Nothing important," I said. "Go on upstairs and I'll join you in a minute."

"No." He crossed his arms. "I got as much right to know what you're doing as you do."

Marvella's mouth quirked upward. "I hope you understood that," she said to me, "because I sure didn't."

"He seems to think this is a completely equal relationship." I looked down at Jimmy. "It's not, Jim. I'm the adult and I make the rules. You're heading upstairs."

He glared at me, then ran up the steps, avoiding Marvella as he did. She didn't move or say anything until we heard my door slam shut.

"Another note?" I asked.

She nodded. "I caught them pinning it up about a half hour ago."

"Same kids?"

"No," she said. "This time, I recognized one of them. You know Sonny Bonet?"

"Amos Bonet's son?" Amos Bonet was the man who had invited me to steal Christmas trees last weekend. His son was also named Amos, but everyone called him Sonny. "Yeah, I know him. He seems like a good kid."

"That's what I thought." Marvella handed me the note. "But he says he wrote this."

I took the paper. It was a lined sheet that had been ripped from a notebook. In a different childlike scrawl, it read: "Grimshaw!!! Stay out of stuff you don't understand."

"Sonny Bonet wrote this?" I asked, unable to understand why. "Is it for Jimmy?"

"I don't think so," Marvella said. "He said that some man asked him to write the note and tape it to your door."

"Did you see the man?"

She shook her head. "He stopped Sonny a few blocks from here. I didn't even try to look for him."

"And you got Sonny to tell you all this?"

"It wasn't hard," she said. "A soft voice and cookies go a long way toward dispelling a kid's fear."

I smiled at her. "Thanks."

"That's it?" she said, smiling back. "Just thanks?"

"Is there anything else?" I asked, deliberately misunderstanding her. "Other kids, more information?"

"No." Her smile widened. "But I should get more than thanks for fending off the mighty note-writer."

"How about thanks a lot?"

She sighed, but her smile remained. "Someday I'm going to meet this woman."

"What woman?" I asked.

"The one who has such a hold on your heart." She came down the stairs, wincing as her bare feet touched the tile floor. Then she leaned in and kissed me on the mouth. "That's the kind of thanks I meant."

"Mmm," I said, wishing I felt more for her than I did. "I'll remember that next time."

"No you won't," she said, her eyes twinkling. "But that's all right. I'll be happy to remind you."

"I'm sure you will," I said, and hurried up the stairs to my apartment, note in hand.

Jimmy was as confused by the note as I was. He and Sonny Bonet got along; they had just seen each other that morning in school, although Sonny had left early to help his mom with her shopping.

Welfare checks arrived around the beginning and middle of every month. Even though prices at the markets always went up at this time, some families had no choice but to shop then. Usually they went in pairs because thieves were out as well. In fact, I'd seen more than one mailman travel with a guard on check days.

The Bonets weren't the only family on the block receiving some kind of assistance. A lot of families were just unable to make their bills. When I'd moved into the neighborhood, Franklin had warned me not to tell the authorities who lived in an apartment. Social Services did spot checks, and families couldn't receive Aid to Families with Dependent Children if a man lived in the household. So there were a lot of shadow households— intact families that pretended to be run by single parents when the government showed up.

I'd had several interactions with Amos Bonet before he told me that he lived with his family several buildings down from mine. The fact that he mentioned it at all was a sign of trust.

Their apartment building was older than ours. The brickwork was crumbling, and the iron banister leading up the front steps was rusted. Two of the windows had been broken since I moved into the neighborhood in May. Someone had stuffed blankets in them to keep the wind out.

Jimmy led me to the Bonets' apartment, on the first floor. This building was built before the turn of the century, and except for the addition of electricity and modern plumbing, it hadn't been remodeled since. He knocked on a solid wooden door that had a metal Number 1 held on by only one nail.

The door opened almost immediately, sending the distinctive odor of boiling ham hocks into the hallway. My stomach growled, and I realized I had forgotten to eat lunch.

The person holding the door open was a little girl, no more than five. She saw us, then turned and ran deeper into the apartment, leaving the door ajar.

A radio played in the background and I recognized the rich, warm tones of Sam Cooke. Children's laughter echoed, followed by a woman's voice, hard and angry.

"Hello?" Jimmy pushed the door open farther. "Is Sonny here?"

"Son, one of yer friends is here," the woman shouted.

"I'm coming!"

Someone ran toward the door, then pulled it open all the way. A boy, taller and thinner than Jimmy, stared at both of us.

"Dang it," he said.

"It's all right—" I started to say, but Jimmy held up his hand to silence me. That was a trick I used. I'd never seen Jimmy do it before.

He took the note from me and waved it at Sonny. "You wanna say something?"

Sonny glanced at the note, then at me, before looking at Jimmy. His lower lip trembled. "I didn't mean nothing."

"I thought you and me was friends," Jimmy said.

I watched him with admiration. I hadn't realized how well he could stand up for himself.

"We are," Sonny said.

"Then why'd you do this?"

Sonny put a finger to his lips, then stepped into the hallway. He pulled the door closed. "This's kinda private," he said to me.

"This's my dad," Jimmy said. "Anything you say to me you can say to him."

"You're not gonna say nothing to my dad, are you?" Sonny asked me.

This was the moment of truth. We'd get no information out of him if I let him know I was going to act like a grown-up. "I wasn't planning to," I said, not making any real promise, but not lying either.

Sonny stared at me a moment longer, as if taking my measure. Then he slid a grimy hand into the right-hand pocket of his too-small pants. After a bit of a struggle, he pulled out a crumpled twenty-dollar bill.

"Some guy gave me this to write the note. I didn't think nothing was wrong with it." But the quiver in his voice told a different story.

"What guy?" Jimmy asked.

Sonny shrugged. "I dunno. Some white guy."

That stunned me. It stunned Jimmy, too, because he gave me a quick glance over his shoulder. I nodded at him. This was his interrogation, not mine.

"You let some white guy tell you what to do?" Jimmy asked.

"Twenty bucks!" Sonny held up the bill. "It's just a note."

"It's a mean note," Jimmy said.

"I thought it was a joke." Even though he didn't. He had backed against the door. "It's Christmas, Jim. I can get my mom something now."

Jimmy's eyes narrowed. I recognized the look, and remembering the argument he'd had with Keith over the importance of Christmas, I put my hand on his shoulder, reminding him to stay calm.

"Who was this white guy?" Jimmy asked.

"I dunno," Sonny said. "I never seen him before."

"But you took his money?"

"Jim, I told you—"

"How did he approach you?" I asked.

Sonny looked up at me as if he'd forgotten I was there. "He yelled at me from his car, asked me if I wanted to make a quick twenty."

"What did you say?" I asked.

"I went over to him. What'd you think, I'm dumb?"

I didn't answer that, not yet. I needed more information first. "Then what happened?"

"He asked me if I had some school paper and a pencil. I said sure." Sonny shifted from one stocking-covered foot to the other. "Then he asked if I knew a Bill Grimshaw. I said no. So he said this Bill Grimshaw lived down the block, and I said, 'Oh, you mean Jimmy's dad.' "

Jimmy's body went rigid beneath my hand. I didn't like the sound of that either.

"He said that seemed right. Then he told me to write this note. He told me what to write and everything, so I did." Sonny wiped his nose with the back of his hand. "He made me do it twice. I didn't know how to spell unnerstand."

249

"Then what?" I asked.

"Then he made me promise I'd do it, and he gived me the money. So I brought the note, and then that pretty lady said she'd give it to you." He looked at the paper, still clutched in Jimmy's hand. "Guess she did."

Jimmy frowned. "How come you didn't just keep the money and throw away the note?"

"Because he said he'd know if I didn't do it." Sonny shoved the twenty back in his pocket, as if he were afraid we'd take it from him. "I didn't want to give the money back."

"What did he look like?" I asked.

Sonny shrugged again. "He was white."

"What else?" I asked.

"I dunno."

"Think," I said. "It might be important."

"He was rich."

"What made you think he was rich?" I asked.

Sonny thought for a moment. "His car was new."

"What kind of car?"

"I dunno. Green, I guess."

"Anything else?"

"He had lots of money in his wallet. I never seen so much all at once." Sonny touched his pocket as if it held a talisman.

"You don't remember anything else?" I asked. "His hair color? Whether or not he had a scar or wore jewelry? His name?"

"He didn't say his name," Sonny said. "I didn't say mine neither. I'm not dumb."

"Yes you are." Jimmy slid away from my hand. The tension I'd been feeling burst out of him. "Didn't nobody tell you not to take money from strangers?"

"Twenty bucks, Jim!"

"He didn't have to give it to you," Jimmy said. "He got you right next to the car. He could've held it out, and when you grabbed it, he grabbed you."

"What would he do with me?" Sonny's eyes widened.

"Hurt you." Jimmy's voice lowered. "Other stuff. Guys like that, they can do all kinds of stupid stuff."

I frowned, remembering Jimmy's mother. He'd watch her pick up men and take their money. Had any of her johns done stupid stuff to him? I had never thought to ask before.

"You don't go near guys like that no more, promise?"

"Jim, twenty bucks," Sonny wailed.

"Promise?" Jimmy was fierce.

"No!" Sonny said. "You're not my dad. You don't got the right to tell me what to do."

"Ask your dad what he'd do if some guy offered him money to come near a car," I said.

Sonny glared at me.

"Just ask him."

"You said you wouldn't get me in no trouble," Sonny said.

"I'm not going to talk to him. You will." I gave him what I hoped was a reassuring smile. "And you don't have to tell him about this. Just ask him what to do if something like it should ever happen."

Sonny started to cross his arms, then remembered his precious twenty-dollar bill. He hooked his thumb on his pocket instead. "You're not going to tell him nothing?"

"No," I said.

"That white guy, he's not going to get you, is he?" Apparently Sonny was beginning to realize the seriousness of what he'd done.

"I don't know," I said. "I hope not."

Jimmy was shaking with anger. I kept my hand on his shoulder.

"Do me a favor, though," I said. "If you see him again, come get me or Marvella. Remember? The woman who gave you cookies?"

He studied me for a moment, then his gaze passed over Jim, as if he couldn't quite face him. "I was waiting for him," Sonny said quietly.

"What?" Jimmy nearly shouted the word. I tightened my grip on his shoulder slightly.

"What do you mean, waiting?" I asked, hoping that this boy knew more than he'd been willing to say.

Sonny's fingers curled over his pocket. "Leon Gantz and some of the guys said that this white guy in a new green car gave them all five bucks to take a note to some guy's house on your block. They showed me where they saw him and I kinda been hanging out there all week."

"For the money," I said.

He nodded.

"Did he offer you five or twenty?" I asked.

"Five, but I told him I knew he paid four guys five each, so he could afford to pay me twenty if I done it all by myself."

"You son of a bitch!" Jimmy launched himself at Sonny, but I still held Jimmy's shoulder. I pulled him back.

"Go outside," I said.

"He set us up, Smoke."

"Go outside, Jimmy. I'll finish here."

"No." Jimmy lowered his shoulder, moving it away from my grip, then crossed his arms.

I looked at Sonny. "Just let us know if you see him again."

"Okay." Sonny bowed his head, his cheeks flushed. He was blinking hard, and I suspected he was fighting tears. He'd seen easy money and he had been thinking of the upcoming holiday, not of us. "I didn't mean nothing, Jim, really. I'm sorry."

"You're a dork," Jimmy said and stomped out of the building.

"Thanks for talking to us," I said.

Sonny snuffled, nodded, and backed into the apartment. I followed Jimmy outside.

He was leaning against the rusted iron railing. It bent sideways with his weight, threatening to collapse. I put my hand on his back to let him know I was there.

"I thought he was my friend," Jimmy said without turning around.

"I know," I said. "I think he still is."

"Friends don't do stuff like that."

"Jim, you know what it's like to have to make choices. I don't think he even considered us—"

"I don't need no stupid lecture!" Jimmy whirled and faced me. "I don't care what you think. He was supposed to be my friend. Friends don't do stuff like that!"

Then he crumpled the note and tossed it to the icy ground with the force of a basketball player trying a slam dunk. He kicked the note once as he started down the sidewalk, walking so fast that I would have to run to catch up to him.

I didn't try. I knew this was just one more betrayal for Jimmy in a whole lifetime of betrayals, and there wasn't much I could say to make things better.

I bent down, picked up the note and smoothed it out.

Grimshaw!!! Stay out of stuff you don't understand.

What stuff? If this came from a white man, as Sonny had said, then it had nothing to do with the Blackstone Rangers, like I'd initially thought. The boys who'd found Louis Foster's body had seen a white man in a blue car drive away from the scene, but not a lot of people knew I was working on that case.

Besides, the note-writing didn't fit. Foster's killer had shown he had no compunction against killing large black men. If he thought I was too close, he would come after me, not leave me notes.

That left only one other case, a case so unimportant I'd almost forgotten about it.

I put the note in my pocket and went back to the apartment to call Laura.

TWENTY

I don't understand, Smokey," Laura said, her voice amplified through the phone's receiver. "Why would they threaten you?"

I was sitting on the arm of the couch in my living room. Jimmy was in his room with the door slammed shut. I had checked on him when I'd come in and he'd told me to go away.

"They want to isolate you, Laura. They still don't believe that you're the threat. They think that if McMillan and I leave you alone, you'll drop this whole notion of participating in the company." I unzipped my jacket and struggled to get it off while cradling the phone between my ear and shoulder.

"I'm not going to participate," she said. "I'm going to run it."

"I know that and you know that. They haven't figured that out yet." I tossed my jacket on the couch. The apartment was still hot and the radiator was clanking beside me. "But they are scared. They're scared of what you could do."

"You mean kick them out?"

"Maybe," I said. "Or maybe they just don't want you to see the various things they've been involved in. I'm pretty sure that Sturdy's above board these days, but that doesn't mean it always was."

"Who do you think these guys are?" she asked.

"You mean the people threatening me? I don't know." I slid onto the couch, crossed my legs and rested my feet on the coffee table. "But so far, they're only doing rinky-dink stuff."

"Do you think it'll get worse?"

"If you lay low until the board meeting, no, I don't think it will."

"They still haven't delivered the information I asked for," Laura said. "I'm going to go back to court on Monday."

"That's not laying low," I said.

"I told them I'd do that. I can't back down now."

"What does McMillan say?"

"He says we can wait, but he's willing to do what I ask."

"McMillan and I are both counseling the same thing, Laura. I say leave it go until January."

Jimmy's door opened just a crack. He was listening.

"And let them think they've scared us off? What does that gain us, Smokey?"

"It doesn't matter. The tables turn in January. Tell McMillan not to file on Monday."

There was a long silence. I saw a movement behind Jimmy's door.

"He filed today," she said softly.

"Damn," I said. "Can't you cancel the suit?"

"It's not really a suit," she said. "We've notified the court that they're not complying with the judge's orders. Now that the judge knows about it, I don't think it's something we can take back."

I sighed, closed my eyes, and leaned my head against the back of the couch. "I wish you hadn't done this, Laura."

"Why? What do you think will happen?"

"I don't know," I said, opening my eyes and peering down the hallway. Jimmy's door was open wider. "I don't like the threats. That implies something I really don't want to think about."

"Implies what?" she asked.

Jimmy stepped into the hallway.

"It implies that they have something to protect and they're willing to use muscle to do it."

"I wish I'd known about these notes before," Laura said. "I thought all they were doing were strange legal games."

"That's all I thought," I said. "I hadn't realized they were behind the notes until this afternoon, and even now I'm not one-hundred-percent sure."

Jimmy reached the edge of the hallway and leaned against the wall beside the TV.

"Has anything else been happening?" I asked Laura. "Anything out of the ordinary?"

"What do you mean?"

"Have you gotten any notes, had any conversations that could be perceived as threats? Has McMillan?"

"No. Besides, no one could leave notes on my door. They'd have to get past building security," Laura said. Then her breath caught.

"What?" I asked, knowing her well enough to recognize that sound. She had remembered something.

"Nothing," she said. "It's nothing."

"I'm asking you to be paranoid, Laura. Nothing is not nothing at the moment."

"All right." She sighed. "I've had a few hang-ups."

"Hang-ups?"

"The phone would ring, I'd pick it up, and there was clearly someone on the other end. I'd say hello a few times and they'd hang up."

The equivalent of notes. "Do they make you uncomfortable?"

"I think they would if I didn't live in such a secure building." She sounded uncomfortable still. Last August, she had nearly died in her secure building. Although she'd fixed the problems, I knew she no longer felt safe there. She'd talked about moving in the fall and I'd talked her out of it. She wasn't going to find a safer place to live in the entire city.

"Well, take notes about the calls. Keep accurate records of

anything that bothers you. And don't go anywhere alone."

"Smokey—"

"Laura, you're threatening some important people here and they have shady connections. Don't be complacent."

Jimmy's mouth thinned. I recognized the look. He was scared.

"If you can," I said, "get McMillan to do some kind of legal trick to make it seem like you're backing down on getting those materials. If—"

"But Smokey, these people have known me all their lives."

"They may not want to hurt you," I said, "but you have no idea who they're in bed with. There were rumors that your dad was connected to the mob."

"That's not true." She sounded like the defensive woman I'd met in Memphis.

"You've always said that, but have you checked on it? He was a small-time crook in Atlanta. People like that don't change just because they moved to a new city."

She was silent again.

"I haven't been in Chicago very long, Laura," I said, determined to make this point, "but even I know that the mob has its fingers in several big construction firms around town."

"Sturdy's legitimate," she said. "We've got stockholders. We have to make our records public."

"All of them?" I asked. "Even for the subcontractors and all the corporations in which Sturdy has a controlling interest? What about the smaller businesses that funnel jobs to Sturdy? Do you know who is in charge of those?"

"That's why we want the records, Smokey."

"Doesn't the fact that they're fighting you so hard on even the simplest stuff tell you something, Laura? Yes, they don't want you to have a hand in, but you're going after them with an out-of-town attorney. What did they do? They answered to your dad's attorney, an old Chicago boy who knows what's going on. They're sending you messages. Through me, through McMillan, and even through your dad's attorney. They're warnings, Laura. Back off."

Jimmy sank down the wall, folded his arms over his knees, and hid his face. I wanted to go to him, but didn't.

"You're scared, aren't you, Smokey?"

Worried was probably more accurate, but I answered, "For you, yes."

Another silence. Jimmy didn't move.

"January second isn't very far away, Laura," I said. "Once you take over the company, they can't touch you. Just be patient."

She sighed. "I'm not good at patience."

I smiled. "I know that. But you have to be, and you have to be cautious, too."

She didn't say anything for a moment, and I thought she was going to argue with me. But I said nothing more. If she didn't agree to my suggestions, I would call McMillan myself. Maybe she would listen to him.

"Smokey," she finally said, "do you ever feel like the world's a place you no longer recognize?"

"I'm not sure I ever recognized it, Laura," I said and hung up. Then I went and joined Jimmy on the floor.

"Them notes are for her?" he asked, not lifting his head.

"I don't know for sure," I said.

"How come people hate her?"

"She's doing something very risky," I said, and explained what she was trying in as simple terms as I could.

"You're helping her?" Jimmy asked.

"I'm guarding her," I said.

"But you never see her. How can you watch her without seeing her?"

"I'm here when she calls me," I said. "She's safe most of the time."

"That's not what you said on the phone."

"I was trying to scare her, Jim," I said. "I want her to be as cautious as possible."

"Like you want me to."

"Yes," I said.

He nodded, his head still buried in his arms. "You think that white guy who sent the notes is from Memphis?"

I kept my hand on his back. "No, I think he has something to do with Laura."

"But he'll tell all the police people about you and me."

"No he won't, Jimmy."

"But Sonny told him where we were!"

"Sonny thinks we're Grimshaws. He doesn't know who we are or where we're from."

"He—"

A sharp rap on the door made us both jump. Jimmy raised his head, eyes wide.

"Who's there?" I shouted.

"Jack," Sinkovich shouted back.

"It's open."

He came in, a duffel bag over his shoulder and a grocery bag in his arms. He pushed the door closed with his foot, then set the grocery bag on the counter.

"Figured I'd help a little," he said.

"I thought you couldn't get into the house," I said.

"I still can't, the bi—" He stopped himself when he saw Jimmy. "This stuff is from my locker. They let me in to get some clothes."

"The groceries, too?"

"I keep some money in my locker, just in case. Good thing, huh?" He dropped the duffel on the floor, then reached into the grocery bag. "I'm cooking tonight, if you don't mind burgers and homemade french fries."

"You don't have to do that," I said.

"And you don't have to give up couch space." Sinkovich put food on the counter, then reached inside the bag and pulled out a six-pack of Old Style. "Besides, you don't have the good stuff. Figured we needed something to take the edge off."

"I can't drink that stuff," Jimmy said sullenly. He did not look happy at Sinkovich's appearance.

"I know, sport," Sinkovich said. "I got you a Coca-Cola. Unless you can't drink that neither."

Jimmy looked at me. I'd been trying to get him to drink milk with every meal. "This time," I said.

"How long's he gonna be here?" Jimmy asked, not even trying to lower his voice.

"Till Sunday, sport. Then I get to reclaim the family homestead." Sinkovich took off his coat and hung it on the rack. Then he looked at Jimmy, his expression serious. "I'll do my best to make this as pleasant as possible for all of us, okey-doke?"

"Okay," Jimmy said, sounding unconvinced.

I wasn't convinced either, but I was glad Sinkovich was at least making an effort.

Sinkovich hadn't had time on Friday to do any research, so he got up early Saturday morning and went to the main library. I tried Delevan again and got no answer. Jimmy's mood hadn't improved, and since I finally had help on the Foster case, I decided I could afford one day off.

At my insistence, Jimmy and I went tree shopping. Amos Bonet had been right; most of the trees sold in the Black Belt were so old that the needles fell off. I knew we'd have trouble shopping in the white areas, but just when I was about to suggest it, we stumbled on a black-owned tree lot. These trees were freshly cut that morning, small but pretty.

We bought one. That, plus the tree stand and two strings of lights, took most of my cash. I didn't have decorations, so I had to rely on the old-fashioned methods.

After we got the tree up, I taught Jimmy how to string popcorn and make rings out of construction paper. The finished product wasn't pretty, but it was festive—and it even made my little Grinch smile.

Sunday we returned to routine. I got Jimmy to the Grimshaws' in time for church, then returned home for my meeting with Johnson and Sinkovich.

As I walked in the door, the phone was ringing. Sinkovich was hovering over it as if he wasn't sure if he should answer it.

"Expecting a call, Sinkovich?" I asked with a grin. He

flushed and went into the half-kitchen, apparently to give me some privacy, not that it would work.

I picked up the phone. Mrs. Weisman was on the other end.

"I'm sorry to call so early on a Sunday," she said, "but I had to speak to someone."

I braced myself against the couch. I wasn't sure I wanted to hear this news. "What is it?"

"Elaine's sister. You spoke to that girl, didn't you? She's unreasonable."

"What's happened?" My voice must have sounded odd, because Sinkovich gave me a strange look.

"I finally reached the girl just a few minutes ago and she tells me there won't be a memorial service."

"That's the family's choice," I said.

"Family. That sister doesn't deserve to be called family. She came to Chicago, buried her sister, and left without telling anyone. She didn't even put a notice in the papers. I'm sure Elaine's friends don't even know she's dead."

I sat down. It explained so much: Elaine's attempts to be a free spirit, her utter devastation when Saul, whom she cared about, was hurt because of her. He was probably one of the few people who had ever really loved her.

"If I had only known, Mr. Grimshaw, I would have spent as much time with Elaine as I did with my Saul. But she seemed so tough. I thought she'd survive the attack. She was so strong."

"It's not your fault, Ruth," I said, purposely using her first name. "How's Saul taking this?"

Sinkovich snuck past me, carrying a bundle of clothes and a fresh towel toward the bathroom.

"Terribly. It's just one more blow in a series of them. We found out this morning that the surgery didn't take. He's losing the eye."

That would be as devastating to him as the loss of Elaine. "I'm sorry."

Mrs. Weisman sighed. "He says he doesn't want to see anyone right now. Maybe that'll change when I get him home this afternoon."

"They're letting him out?"

"They can't do anything else. They tell me he has to heal before they even consider other options. They want to talk about glass eyes. I won't let them near him with that idea. Not yet."

"Probably wise," I said, not sure what to say.

"I think you should come visit him," Mrs. Weisman said, and I had a hunch this was the real reason behind her call.

"I thought you said he doesn't want to see anyone right now."

"He may change his mind if someone shows up," Mrs. Weisman said.

I knew she was manipulating me, but I had grown fond of her. Besides, I had another reason to stop by.

"All right," I said. "I'll use the photographs as an excuse."

"Photographs?"

"The reason I was coming to the house last Sunday."

"Oh," she said. "I'm not sure he can find photographs."

"Maybe you can help, then. I need them for a case I'm working on."

"I'll ask," Mrs. Weisman said. "If he wants you to have them, I'll make sure you get them."

"Thanks," I said. "I'll come by tomorrow. If he's ready to see me, fine. If not, I'll still pick up the pictures."

"That sounds good," she said. "I'll do my best to get him to talk with you."

She thanked me again for listening, and then she hung up. I stared at the receiver for a moment before slowly putting it back. Elaine was already buried. Put away, hidden, deemed so unimportant by her family that she didn't even get a memorial.

She was done, her life over and gone.

Only I would remember her. And so would Mrs. Weisman. And Saul.

I took a deep breath and stood. I had to focus on other things, just like Mrs. Weisman did.

Sinkovich had folded his sheet, blanket, and pillow and

placed them on the edge of the couch. I carried them to Jimmy's room. Then I put on a fresh pot of coffee, took out the donuts Sinkovich had brought the night before, and grabbed the morning paper.

The news was charming, as usual. Statistics covered the front page. Since 1961, over thirty thousand U.S. soldiers had died in combat in our undeclared war against Vietnam. Chicago teachers still planned to strike, even though agreement had been reached on three of the union's two hundred and fifty contract demands.

The sports page didn't bring any relief either. The main article was about Muhammad Ali starting his jail term for draft evasion.

Sinkovich came out of the bathroom, drying his hair. He grabbed a yellow legal pad from his duffel and came to the table. "I found five more possibles," he said, handing the pad to me.

The dates came from 1967 and early 1968. Sinkovich had found them in obituaries, which I hadn't bothered to look through.

At that moment, someone knocked on the door.

"It's open!" I shouted, hoping it was Johnson.

He came in, also carrying a box of donuts. I didn't want to tell him or Sinkovich how clichéd their fondness for donuts was.

"You know," Johnson said, "this isn't the best neighborhood to keep your door unlocked."

"I usually don't," I said. "I was just expecting you."

He set the donuts on the table, then went back outside. After a moment, he returned carrying a large box.

As he shut the door with his elbow, he said, "This meeting never happened. None of you saw this stuff and if you did, you don't remember how or why. Got that?"

"I'm a little confused by it," Sinkovich said with a grin. "If I never saw it, how could I not remember it?"

"Don't go there." I took a twist out of Johnson's box. The donut was still warm.

"These are the files." Johnson set the box down between us. "It took me a while to find them. These cases are supposed to be open, but guess where the files were."

"Records," Sinkovich said.

Johnson nodded. "No one's following up on these things, so I don't think anyone's going to notice they're missing."

"Have you had a chance to look through them?" I asked.

"Not really," he said. "Mind if I have some coffee?"

"Help yourself." I folded the newspaper together, then put it on the floor.

"They got anything in common?" Sinkovich asked.

"Nothing besides the obvious," Johnson said. "We're going to have to dig."

And dig we did. We each went through three files, and after some consideration, we threw out one of the old ones because it didn't seem to conform to the pattern. Johnson kept it on the table, though, just in case.

He said, "Sometimes these guys don't develop a routine until the second or third killing."

"These guys?" Sinkovich asked. "What've you been studying?"

"People who kill strangers," Johnson said. "Usually it's pretty random, tied to another crime. But we're getting a whole new group, like the Strangler, people who kill for the thrill of it. We got some study through the department—I don't know if you got it or not in Vice—saying that these types of random stranger killings with multiple victims are becoming more and more common."

"Why?" I asked.

"They think all the publicity around the *In Cold Blood* killings, not to mention the Strangler and Speck, are inspiring copycats." Johnson reached for his third glazed donut.

"You don't believe that, though," I said.

"I think these sick bastards have always been with us," Johnson said. "They just usually pick targets that no one notices."

"So why are we noticing now?" Sinkovich asked.

Johnson looked at him as if he had just remembered that Sinkovich was in the conversation. "*We* aren't just noticing now. *You* are."

Sinkovich frowned. "What does that mean?"

"It means that in the past twenty years, the victims have changed," Johnson said. "Now everyone's noticing because a lot of them are white."

TWENTY-ONE

The files were less revealing than I had hoped. The victims did not live in the same neighborhood. The two nearest lived blocks apart in areas where blocks were the same as miles. They did not work in the same parts of the city, and they seemed to have no friends in common.

In most of the cases, the investigating detectives did an admirable job of interviewing friends and family. Johnson suggested that perhaps the black community had lied to the white detectives, but even if that had happened, we could redo the interviews. We still had the names of the interviewees.

None of the interviewees crossed from one case to the other either. The only way we'd find connections—if there were any obvious ones—between these victims would be to interview every name on the list. That would take a lot of time, and a lot of footwork. We all knew it, and we weren't looking forward to it.

Something had brought all of these very different victims to the attention of the killer. That something just wasn't obvious, like we had hoped it would be.

By the time I went to pick up Jimmy, we knew a lot more than we had when we started, but not much of it seemed relevant. My frustration had grown. I would have to prepare Mrs. Foster for a long investigation. I would try to keep my expenses down—she didn't need to bear the burden of the related investigations—but I would still have to make a living and this case would take time from others.

I didn't really favor telling her I suspected that her husband was a random victim of some sick creep, but I would have to. Otherwise, she might wonder whether I was being up front with her.

We packed up everything and stored it in my office. Sinkovich wanted to go home to see if his wife had reconsidered, and Johnson had some family business to take care of as well. We agreed we'd start through our lists and get together again on Wednesday afternoon before Jimmy got home.

I could tell we were all settling in for a long investigation. We had to be methodical so that we didn't miss an important detail. But we all felt time pressure. We had to catch this guy before he killed again.

By the time I got to the Grimshaw house, it was twilight and someone had turned on the Christmas lights. The place glowed, including the tree up front that Malcolm had decorated. I had never seen so many lights. They surrounded the windows, the porch, the doors, and the edge of the roof, as well as several shrubs in the front yard. I hoped Franklin had thought about the added electric bill, then realized he probably didn't care.

I didn't even have to get out of the car. Jimmy bounded off the porch and got in, slamming the door behind him. He was angry that I hadn't joined them for dinner for the second week in a row, even though we had already fought about that on the drive to the Grimshaws' that morning.

"Hello to you, too," I said, trying to sound more cheerful than I felt.

He made a snorting sound and didn't speak to me for the rest of the drive home.

Once we got inside, Jimmy turned on the television and settled on the couch. I couldn't even yell at him about it. He didn't have any homework. He was free to waste his time all he wanted.

I made myself a sandwich, since all I'd eaten were donuts. I still had a number of things to do that evening. I wanted to make some calls, and I wanted to get my notes organized for the week ahead. I sat at the table, determined to eat and work. As I bit into my ham-on-rye, the phone rang.

"Got it!" Jimmy leaned across the couch and grabbed the receiver before I could set my sandwich down. He said hello and then grinned.

He chatted for a moment, mostly about pinball, and I frowned. I had no idea who he was talking to. Then he extended the receiver toward me.

"It's Laura," he said.

I wiped my mouth, got up and took the phone. "Everything all right?"

"Yes and no," she said. "You got me thinking, so I talked to Drew. He wants us to meet with you tonight. Can you come over here in an hour?"

I looked at Jimmy, spread out on the couch. I'd already shoved him at the Grimshaws several times this week, and I'd imposed on Marvella once as well. I almost wished Sinkovich was still here, even though I was relieved to have his snoring out of the apartment. At least he would have been able to baby-sit for a few hours.

"If I absolutely have to," I said. "But to be honest with you, it's a school night, and I'd like to get Jim in bed on time."

He looked up at me, a frown on his face. He didn't like to be talked about as if he were a child.

"Can we meet early tomorrow morning?" I asked.

"Let me see." Laura put her hand over the phone. I heard her voice, muffled, and the squeak of her skin against plastic. Finally she pulled her hand away. "No. It needs to be tonight."

I didn't answer her right away. I felt a deep annoyance and I wasn't sure what it was at: either the fact she had to consult with McMillan—who was clearly in her apartment on a Sunday evening—or the fact that I felt like I was constantly at someone else's beck and call, when all I wanted to do was have a normal night with a boy who'd become my child.

"He could stay the night here," Laura said. "I haven't changed his room at all."

He'd spent part of August with her, and she'd kept his room the same, apparently hoping he'd come back.

I looked down at him. He had his arms wrapped around a pillow and was staring at a stopwatch that dominated the screen, ticking away its sixty minutes—the logo for the new "news magazine" that had started in the fall. He hated that show, so I knew he was listening, not paying attention to the TV.

"Why don't you come here?" I said. "That would be easiest for all of us."

"Oh, good idea," Laura said.

I gave her directions, and then we hung up. Jimmy was staring at me over the back of the couch.

"Here?" he said. "You seen her place and you're asking her here?"

I was having the same reaction myself. At least when she'd seen my home in Memphis, it had been *mine*, not a dumpy rental with furniture so old that the upholstery was frayed. Still, she was bound to see it at some point, and the fact that she hadn't was a tribute to my ability to find ways around any visits.

"Yes, I invited her here," I said, "and you're still going to go to bed on time so that we can have a chance to talk."

He grinned. "Yeah, talk."

"Her lawyer will be along," I said. "This is business."

"Oh." He got up and shut off the television. "I got the dishes."

He usually didn't volunteer for anything, so I knew this meant that her visit was important to him, too.

We cleaned the apartment until it glistened, then I put on some coffee. I still had some of Sinkovich's beer left, but I doubted Laura and McMillan were the Old Style type. Jimmy was going to change clothes, but I discouraged that, even though it was another sign that he wanted to impress Laura Hathaway.

Then I heard voices in the hallway. One rose. A woman's. Marvella's.

"We don't cotton to no white folks here," she was saying, affecting an accent I'd never heard her use before.

I pulled open my door. Marvella was blocking the stairs, one hand on the railing, the other pushed against the wall, her magnificent legs bare beneath the shortest skirt I'd ever seen. The blouse she wore over it revealed the strength in her arms.

Laura was standing just inside the door, McMillan beside her. She was wrapped in a brown cloth coat I'd never seen, and she wore her flower-appliqued blue jeans beneath. McMillan's heavy black coat, black pants, and shiny black shoes made him look as if he were dressed for court.

They looked up when I opened my door, but Marvella didn't move.

"It's all right, Marvella," I said. "They're coming to see me."

"On business, Bill?" Her voice had an edge I didn't like.

Laura's cheeks stained pink.

"Tonight," I said.

Marvella glanced over her shoulder at me. There was fury in her face. "Awfully fancy piece, Mr. Grimshaw."

"Awfully crude mouth, Miss Walker," I said.

She let one arm drop. The movement was obvious and theatrical. Then she stepped toward the banister, not relinquishing her place on the stairs.

"Come on," I said to Laura. "Sorry about my neighbor's hostile reception."

Laura took a deep breath and started up the stairs. Marvella blocked her way again.

"So this is the one," she said, loud enough for me to hear. "Somehow, I thought you had better taste than that."

"Marvella," I said, "stay out of my business."

McMillan was a half step behind Laura. Marvella placed one foot on his stair and touched his sleeve.

"Although this one's pretty, too. You sure they're not a couple? We're fun to fuck, but that's about as far as these whities—"

"Marvella," I snapped. "Shut up."

She turned her magnificent face toward me. "I don't know why you're wasting your time, Bill. She's clearly made her choice. She—"

"Come on, Laura," I said. "Drew. Ignore her. I usually do."

Marvella's eyes narrowed. Laura hurried up the stairs. I extended my hand to her and pulled her to my side. McMillan followed, throwing Marvella a look that implied she was crazy.

"Go inside," I said to them.

Laura squeezed my hand and walked into the apartment. Mc-Millan followed. I pulled the door closed and went down the stairs, stopping one step above Marvella.

"I don't care how many favors you've done me," I said, my voice low. "I don't care who your cousin is. I don't even care about the friendship I thought we had. You stepped over a line, Marvella."

"You don't need her, Bill. White women are not status symbols. They're just trouble. You—"

I raised my hand and pressed it against her lips, silencing her. I pushed hard, letting all the anger I felt express itself in my rigid fingertips.

"You don't know who I am," I said softly, "or what I need."

Her eyes grew wide. For the first time, I saw fear in them.

"Because of the work I do," I said, "a lot of people you do not know or like will come into this building. You will not interfere with any of them again. Are we clear on that?"

She stared at me, then she nodded.

"Good." I let my fingers drop. They left white impressions against her lips.

I turned around and walked up the stairs without sparing her another glance. Then I entered the apartment, closing the door behind me.

McMillan was standing near the coatrack, his hands in his pockets. Laura held Jimmy's hand. They were looking at the Christmas tree, and he was pointing out the construction-paper chains he'd made.

"What was that all about?" McMillan asked.

Laura leaned forward, her free hand brushing the popcorn string. She looked engrossed in Jimmy's recital of our Saturday, but I knew she was listening.

"For the past six months, Marvella's been trying to find a way into my bed. Apparently she thought this would work."

McMillan studied me for a moment, assessing me. Then his eyes crinkled. "It wouldn't be my first tactic."

"Believe me," I said. "It's not hers either."

He smiled, and I thought I saw some sympathy in the look.

"Take off your coat and stay a while," I said. "I've got coffee, beer, milk, juice, Coca-Cola, and some very fine bourbon."

"Bourbon," McMillan said, just like I expected him to. "Neat."

"Nothing for me," Laura said as she turned to me. "Do these tree lights work or are they just here to tease us?"

Jimmy and I had been forgetting to turn them on. So much for the festive mood in the house.

"Go ahead, plug them in, Jim. Show the lady our beautiful tree." I went into the kitchen and reached into the top cupboard for the bourbon.

"I wanted real ornaments," Jimmy was saying to Laura, "but Smoke says this way is more fun."

"It is," Laura said. "I've always wanted to do a tree like this."

"You have?" His voice rose.

"Yeah," she said. "Ours was always so overdecorated and perfect. I wanted to throw tinsel on it and mess it up a bit."

"We don't got tinsel," Jimmy said.

"You don't need it. It's pretty just the way it is."

The tree lights came on. I saw them reflected in the glasses I had taken out for McMillan and me.

"Spectacular," Laura said.

"Me and Smoke spent all day Saturday looking for this tree," Jimmy said.

"A man of hidden talents." McMillan came into the half kitchen and leaned against the counter. He had taken off his coat. "You know, Laura won't tell me anything about you. I find that fascinating."

I handed him his glass. "Why?"

"Because of the way she feels about you."

I picked up my own glass and walked into the living room. "Hey, Jim," I said. "Why don't you give our guests a tour?"

We'd already discussed this. After he showed off the apartment, he was supposed to go to his room.

He shot me a pleading look, but I ignored it. Then he smiled at Laura—his charming smile, one I hadn't seen in a while.

"This is the biggest place I ever lived," he said to her as he led her down the hall. He completely ignored McMillan, who didn't follow them.

Instead, McMillan sat on one of my kitchen chairs and propped an ankle on his knee.

"What's so urgent?" I asked before he could say anything.

"You finally convinced Laura of something I've been trying to tell her all week. I have no idea how you did it, but I'm glad you did." He sipped the bourbon, then his eyes widened, and he nodded appreciatively. Apparently that, too, wasn't what he had expected.

"I've been getting threats and so has she," I said. "I don't like Sturdy's history or its connections. I figure they know the right people to make good on their threats, and I also figure these guys are smart enough to know that if something happens to Laura in the next few weeks, their troubles are over. I told her to take the threats seriously. I'm glad she has."

"I was telling her that as well, but she was determined to move forward." He looked amazingly comfortable in that chair. "You have more clout than I do."

I wondered at the second mention of my relationship with Laura. McMillan seemed more attentive than the average lawyer, although I was basing this on a sense rather than on experience. I couldn't tell if he was honestly curious about me, or if he wanted to know where I stood with Laura before he let her know how he felt about her.

I gave him a tight smile. "Maybe it was the fact that we both agreed that convinced her."

"Or maybe," Laura said from the hallway door, "I figured it out all on my own."

McMillan and I both watched as she came into the room. She had taken off her coat before I had come into the apartment. She was wearing a bulky cable-knit sweater over her jeans, and the combination was a lot sexier than Marvella's short skirt and sheer blouse.

Laura smiled at me and sat on the couch. "This is a nice apartment for the two of you, although I have no idea how Franklin lived here with his entire family."

I'd forgotten that she'd found Franklin and Althea's house for them. "It was a tight squeeze." I said as I sat beside her.

"How many lived here?" McMillan asked.

"There were nine last summer," I said.

He whistled softly.

"That's not unusual around here," Laura said. "Rents are too high. Sturdy's one of the worst offenders. It's one of the many things I want to change."

McMillan sipped his bourbon and studied her. Then his gaze met mine and slipped away.

"We have to get you to that stockholders' meeting," I said.

"That's what we wanted to discuss." McMillan set his bourbon on the table. "We're going to withdraw the lawsuit tomorrow."

"Good," I said.

"But I'm worried that won't be enough. Laura's drawn attention to herself in exactly the ways we wanted to avoid."

Laura's lips thinned. "You make me sound like an unruly child."

I sighed. I hadn't touched my bourbon, but I picked it up now, just to hold onto the glass. "I have another case that's taking some of my attention. I can't be with you twenty-four hours a day, although I could find people who can help me with that if we need it."

If I had to set aside the Foster case to protect Laura, I would do it for the next three weeks. But there was Jimmy to consider as well. His life had been in danger too often this past year and I wasn't about to see it risked again.

"That's not our first option," McMillan said. "Although our first one does concern you."

"We ruled that out, Drew." Laura used her upper-class, control-the-servants voice with him.

"Let's give Grimshaw a chance to decide," McMillan said. "You don't have the right to say no for him."

"I trust Laura," I said.

McMillan's eyes crinkled again, but I got the sense he wasn't about to smile. Instead, he seemed annoyed. "Hear me out."

Laura glared at him. "Sometimes you treat me no differently than they do."

He ignored her, looking directly at me. "Right now, if Laura dies, her stocks go to a bunch of different charities. The group at Sturdy would continue to vote those stocks same as they did before. All they'd have to do is approach the various charities, tell them the arrangement, and explain that it's simpler if the group continues to operate the way it always has. No over-worked charity is going to say no to this."

"I know," I said. "That's not why you wanted to talk to me."

"Actually, it is." He put his feet on the ground, then leaned forward, resting his elbows on his knees. "If we can make Laura more valuable to them alive, then they'll stop coming after her and no one will have to watch her back."

In spite of myself, I was intrigued. "How would you do that?"

"When we withdraw the lawsuit, we notify Sturdy. And when we do, we also send them the clause out of Laura's new will, the clause that makes you inherit the voting shares of her stock."

"Me?" I felt cold. "Because I'm black."

"Yeah, I'm afraid so." He said this without apology. "You also would support her vision, and you wouldn't be controlled by any outside forces."

"Of course, they'd come after me," I said. "Or hadn't you thought of that?"

"I had. With your help, we pick a black-run organization like Operation Breadbasket to inherit the money if you die. If one organization has that much money in stocks, they're not going to let a group of white bigots run their company."

"Thus keeping me alive as well."

"Yes." McMillan leaned back, obviously proud that he'd thought of this.

Laura's hands were clenched in her lap, her knuckles white. He had embarrassed and angered her, and hadn't even realized it.

I put my hand on her back and felt the tension in the muscles. I had been as silly as Marvella, worrying that this man would interest Laura. He had no idea who she was or what she wanted from her life. He tried to understand, but he had no clue.

"Sorry," I said, "but Laura was right. I'm not interested."

"I thought you wanted to protect her."

"I do," I said. "Just not like this."

"You're one of those guys who doesn't like money, right?" McMillan frowned. "That's what keeps you and Laura apart. She knows it and she doesn't want to embarrass you any further. So you refuse from pride, and put her at risk."

I should have gotten angry, but I didn't. It was clear to me that he was speaking out of frustration and his own desire to protect Laura. Of course, he'd thought of a way to do so using his strength—his ability to manipulate the law.

"In case you've forgotten," I said, "there's a little boy in the next room who means a lot to me, and your plan puts him in danger. I'm all he has. If anyone comes after me, they hurt him. And I'm not going to risk that. Not for all the money in the world."

McMillan looked at Laura, confusion on his face. She didn't meet his gaze, but I felt the tension in her back increase. She had told him I wouldn't do this and wouldn't tell him why. Then I offer a reasonable explanation, one that he understands.

Only Laura and I knew that the truth I just gave McMillan

was a partial one. Yes, to protect Jimmy, I wouldn't put my name in that will, but there were several other tiers to that protection. Even if we could write a valid legal document using a name other than my real name, giving that document to Sturdy meant that they would start investigating me. And we couldn't allow that for any reason. Right now, they saw me as a nameless, faceless black bodyguard whom Laura trusted a little too much. If we put me down as her backup, then I become a whole lot more—and a lot bigger threat.

"We can't put me on that will," McMillan said. "Even if it weren't a conflict of interest, they're not going to be threatened by me. They're the kind of guys who believe any lawyer can be bought. They need someone they'll take seriously, someone with integrity, someone they can't just push around."

I ignored his attempt at a compliment. "There is another way, but Laura's not going to like it."

"In case you men hadn't noticed," she snapped, "I am sitting here."

"I noticed." I slid my hand up to her shoulder and turned her toward me. Her gaze met mine, and it was as if McMillan wasn't even there.

I captured her hands and held them like a man about to propose. Her fingers were cold.

"I can guard you twenty-four hours a day if you want," I said. "Or we can figure out a way to make McMillan's plan work. But I have a simpler, easier suggestion, one that will probably get all of us to the meeting on the second with no trouble at all. In fact, I think Cronk and the rest will relax if we do it this way, and won't try to figure out ways of preventing you from taking over Sturdy."

A small frown creased her forehead. "What won't I like about this?"

"Drop the lawsuit," I said. "Then go to Sturdy and lie."

"Lie?" she asked.

I nodded. "Tell them you've fired McMillan and you've fired me. We gave you bad advice. You've been thinking about it, and of course Cronk and his cronies were right. They've done just fine with the money. Tell them you're really sorry that you were so harsh, but you were only doing what McMillan told you to do."

Her skin had paled so much that I could see the blood vessels in her cheeks.

"In other words," I said, "pretend you're the young, dumb woman they think you are."

She yanked her hands out of mine and stood so fast that she knocked the coffee table over. It crashed to the floor and she didn't seem to notice.

"Would you do that, Smokey?" She wasn't shouting, but her voice was penetrating all the same. "Would you pretend you can't think without some white person telling you what to do? Would you meet all those horrible, horrible stereotypes?"

"If I had to." My hands were still open, in the same position they'd been in when she let go. "To save my life, or Jimmy's. Or yours."

"I can't believe you're asking me to do this. You know how demeaning this is."

"I do," I said.

"It's a good idea," McMillan said. "All week, those men implied that we were controlling you. This would simply confirm their own prejudices."

"I don't want to confirm their prejudices. I have never acted like that, not for anyone. I've been naïve, I've made mistakes, but I've never pretended to be a stupid woman who can't think for herself."

"I know what I'm asking you to do," I said. "I know how it'll feel, Laura. But it's only for a few weeks. Then you'll go into that meeting, and you'll show them what you're really made of. You'll strip them of their power and their prejudices. You'll win then, Laura, if you do this now."

Jimmy had come out of his room, probably drawn by the raised voices and the knocked-over coffee table. But he didn't interrupt us. He just stood in the dark hallway, watching, thinking that no one saw him.

Laura had her back to him. She was looking at me. "What

if they decide to go after me anyway to hedge their bets?"

"They won't," I said, "if you take the meeting and then become difficult to find."

"Why don't I just do that anyway?" she asked. "Without going through the damn game."

"Because Sturdy has the connections to go after you. If they want you dead, they'll kill you, Laura. But if they believe you're not a threat, and you become hard to find, then they won't expend the energy if you're outside of Chicago. Do you have a passport?"

"Yes, of course, but—"

"Then use it. See some sights. Have an exotic Christmas, somewhere unexpected." I reached for her, taking her fist in my hand and pulling her back to the couch. "It's real easy to disappear for a few weeks, Laura. You don't even have to change your name to do it."

I said that last so softly that I knew McMillan couldn't hear me.

She gave me an anguished look, a look that was more about me and what I'd been through than what she was facing. Then she touched my cheek with her free hand. The caress sent a pleasant shiver through me.

"Won't they still come after you?" she asked.

"Not if you tell them I've been fired." I caught her wrist and brought her hand down, holding it. "Same with McMillan."

"They'll think it's over?"

"Yes," I said.

"But I have to stay away. Even for the holidays."

"I think it's best."

"Me, too," McMillan said, and Laura jumped. I think she had forgotten he was in the room. Her entire body stiffened, and I followed her gaze.

She was looking at Jimmy.

He took that as an invitation to join the conversation. "You're going away?"

"I think I have to," she said.

He nodded once, started to turn toward his room, and then

stopped. "If somebody wants to hurt you, maybe Smoke should go with you. He's real good at saving people."

It cost him a lot to offer my services without including him. Laura squeezed my hand. "I know."

"Laura and I would be pretty conspicuous, Jim," I said.

"Pretty what?" He frowned at me.

"Easy to find."

"Oh." He stared at her for a minute. "I'm not gonna see you again, am I?"

My heart ached. Everyone he'd ever cared for in his short life had gone away and left him behind.

"Yes you are," Laura said. "I'll be back right after New Year's. Then you and I will have a special holiday all our own."

"Okay." Jimmy nodded, but it was clear he didn't believe her.

"I promise, Jim."

He gave her a brave little smile. "I know."

She stood up and walked to him, putting her hand on his shoulder. "Come on," she said. "Let me help you back to bed."

He went with her, looking smaller than he had a moment before. They disappeared through the door to his room, and I could hear her voice, faint and warm.

McMillan was watching me. "Such a simple plan. I've been a lawyer too long."

I picked up the bourbon again, and this time, I had a larger sip. It didn't help. "One of us should go with her, you know."

He shook his head, his expression sad. "Don't throw me in the middle of your little domestic drama. Laura can take care of herself. You know that."

I nodded.

"She's a lot more complicated than I initially gave her credit for." He smiled, then picked up his glass, saluted me with it, and downed the rest. "I made the same mistake with you. I'm beginning to think I'm not a lot better than the guys at Sturdy."

"The fact that you're even thinking that proves you are." I grabbed both our glasses and went into the half kitchen to refill them.

280

"Maybe," he said, looking down the hallway.

I could still hear Laura's voice, very faint, and Jimmy's rising and falling with distress. He was the one we always seemed to hurt, no matter what we did. I shouldn't have let him overhear the discussion. But we had been so loud the entire building had probably heard us. Fortunately, no one here had any connections to Sturdy beside the three of us.

I handed McMillan his drink, then returned to the couch. "How serious do you think the threat to Laura really is?"

He swirled the liquid in his glass. "Her father's old lawyer came to me yesterday and made some of the same insinuations you did on the phone to her."

"Insinuations?"

"About mob connections, messing with the wrong people, watching her back. It might be all talk." He sipped. "It might not."

At that moment, Laura came out of Jimmy's room, looking wan.

"I'm sorry that you had to take care of him," I said.

She shook her head. "It was good. No one's told him they were coming back before. And I'm going to. We have a date, he and I, for the Saturday I get back. We're going to do our own Christmas then."

"Good," I said. "Am I invited?"

"Always, Smokey," she said, her tone implying that she meant more than just a Christmas celebration. "Always."

TWENTY-TWO

We made our plans for the next day before they left. I would accompany Laura to Sturdy, but I wouldn't go inside. Then we'd get her to the airport, and I'd make sure she wasn't followed when she got on her plane.

I put the glasses away, stored the bourbon in the cabinet, and checked on Jimmy. He was asleep, hugging his pillow as if it were a lifeline, his cheeks tear-stained.

I hoped Laura was right. I hoped it would be good for him to have her return, to keep her promises. All I knew now was that the next few weeks would be rougher than I imagined—and not just for Jimmy.

Her visit had left me restless. I went into my office and stared at the files on the floor. If I thought she would have been safer traveling with me and Jimmy, I would have left these cases with Johnson without hesitation.

But Laura could disappear into a crowd and go a thousand places without us. With us, she'd be noticed in every city in this country. A few well-placed questions, and she'd be found.

Besides, it would send the wrong signal to Sturdy. They wouldn't believe that she had changed her mind. If I stayed here and if McMillan went back to his old life, even for a few weeks, Sturdy would believe the crisis was over.

And then she would shock them, just like we planned.

I sighed and moved some papers aside. Then I saw Delevan's phone number. I had never called him this late. It was worth a try.

I dialed, then counted the rings on the other end. On the fifth, someone picked up.

"Yeah?" a sleepy male voice said.

"Oscar Delevan?" I asked.

"Yeah? Who is this?" He had a thick Chicago accent.

I said, "My name is Bill Grimshaw. I'm sorry to call so late, but I've been having trouble getting ahold of you."

"My company sent me to Thunder Bay for a couple of weeks, and I just got back, thank God. It's colder than a witch's patutie up there."

I slipped the information about his company and his trip to Canada into my memory to ask him about them later.

He asked, "What can I do you for?"

"I'm investigating the death of a man named Louis Foster. Apparently you were one of the last people to see him alive. I'd like to talk with you about that. In person, if possible."

"You got the wrong Oscar Delevan," he said. "I don't know anybody named Foster."

"You met him only once," I said. "He looked at the house you're trying to sell."

"Oh, jeez. I saw a lot of people about that. House ain't moving. Neighborhood's going through a change folks don't like."

I straightened. He thought I was white. "I'll bring some photos and see if that jogs your memory."

"Crap," he said. "I was gonna suggest doing this on the phone. Guess that rules that out. How soon do you need this?"

"As soon as possible," I said. "I've been trying to reach you for more than a week."

He sighed. "Okay. I'm in the city most days for work. I'm guessing that's where you are."

"Yes."

"Then it'd be easier to meet at the old house. This new one's great, but it's a bitch to find, and it's a heck of a drive from the Loop."

"I don't mind meeting at your old house," I said. "In fact, it's probably better. You won't have to describe as much. You can just show me what you showed him."

"If I can remember," Delevan said. "This won't take more than an hour, right?"

"I would hope not," I said.

"Okay. Tomorrow's my first day back, so I don't got much time during the day. We'll have to meet after work—around five. That work for you?"

"Yes, it does. Let me give you my number in case anything changes between now and then." Not that I would be home, but he didn't know that. This was always a good ploy for getting information from an unsuspecting person. "And why don't you let me have your work number in case I'm running late."

"I'm a new muckety-muck at Chicagoland Shipping. Don't have my personal number yet, since they sent me to the boonies on a test, to see if I had the balls to deal with our Canadian partners. You'll have to call the switchboard and I don't got that number here. But tell 'em we have a meeting, and they'll patch you through."

"Thanks," I said and hung up.

I picked up Delevan's home number and placed it inside Foster's file. I hoped that whatever Delevan had seen—or whatever he knew—would be worth the effort it had taken to reach him.

Laura set up a meeting at Sturdy for noon, which gave me the morning to go to Rogers Park. I was dressed for the meeting at Sturdy—navy pants that looked like they could be part of a security guard's uniform, and a long coat that hid my sweater. I wore an old pair of shoes that were so scuffed they were nearly worn through.

I felt odd going to Mrs. Weisman's dressed like that, but I knew I would have no time to go home and change.

Mrs. Weisman's neighborhood didn't seem like the street of horrors it had been the Sunday before. There were no haphazardly parked cars, no emergency vehicles, no people in uniform.

Instead, the houses had that same quiet appeal they'd had

when I first visited. They might even have been more appealing since none of them had the ubiquitous Christmas decorations, although many had menorah in the front windows. Some of the ones with artificial lights were already on, casting a glow on the dismal morning.

Mrs. Weisman's menorah had only two candlesticks in the eight-branched holder. She had it set in the window of her porch, where it looked more obligatory than festive.

She had clearly been watching for me, because she opened her front door as I parked. I got out and went up the walk. She was smiling as she wiped her hands on her apron.

"Mr. Grimshaw," she said with obvious pleasure. "I have coffee on if you can stay."

"I'd love to, but I'm afraid I don't have a lot of time," I said. "I have another meeting in the Loop around noon."

"I thought that might happen." She led me through the enclosed porch into the house.

I looked into the living room. The floor where Saul had nearly been beaten to death was clean, as if no blood had been spilled and nothing had ever happened.

The kitchen was spotless, although there were clearly fewer decorative dishes on the counter than there had been before. The room was warm and comfortable, with no hint of the violence that had ultimately cost a woman her life.

"My neighbors brought me this table," Mrs. Weisman said, putting her hand on it. "They cleaned everything up, found a new tablecloth, and even managed to find me some replacement dishes. Still, I sit in here at night and I think I can hear her screaming."

"She wouldn't want you to dwell on it," I said.

"But I do," she said. "I replay that afternoon every day in my head, trying to figure it out different. Sometimes I think it's all my fault."

"It's not your fault. It's Owens' and Mattiotti's. They have a lot to answer for."

"I know. They have attorneys now, but the prosecutor, he's been calling. He made me take pictures of Saul. He says we

285

have a good case." She peered up at me. "I don't suppose you want to testify."

How perceptive she was.

"I'd prefer not to," I said.

She nodded. "It's a shame I never learned your last name, Mr. Grimshaw. Saul can't remember it either, or how to find you. The police officers never wrote it down. I did promise, though, that the next time I saw you, I'd let you know that the prosecutor would like to speak with you."

Then she grinned at me, and I saw an impishness that must have made her irresistible as a young girl.

"How is Saul?" I asked.

Her smile faded. "Throwing a pity party, not that I blame him. He has a lot to overcome. But he is up and around. Let me see if he'll talk to you."

She untied her apron and hung it on a peg near the sink. Then she opened the door to the upstairs and started to climb, closing the door behind her.

The stairs creaked and so did the floorboards above. I could hear her footsteps, faint against the wood. But this house was well-made and solid. No voices carried to the kitchen. I had a hunch Mrs. Weisman hadn't heard Elaine's screams that afternoon. That might have haunted her even more.

I shoved my hands in my coat pockets and peered out the kitchen window. A huge garden, covered in mulch and prepared for winter, filled the backyard. A large oak tree, its leaves gone, provided shade on this side of the house.

After a moment, Mrs. Weisman rejoined me.

"He doesn't want to see anyone right now," she said. "But he told me to give you these."

She handed me two manila envelopes brimming with photographs.

"He has the negatives if you need them," she said, "although he says you'll have to get someone else to blow up any area you need. He doesn't think he'll use his darkroom again."

"You disagree?"

"I think he can do anything he sets his mind to," she said. "He's just not ready to face that yet either."

"Do you think he will?" I said.

"Yes, I do," she said. "He's like us, Mr. Grimshaw. He's a survivor. He just hasn't realized it yet."

I made it to the Loop with plenty of time to spare and waited in the lobby for more than an hour while Laura had her meeting upstairs at Sturdy Investments. I got a lot of uncomfortable stares while I read the *Chicago Tribune* and shot casual glances at the elevators.

A couple of times, I slid up my left sleeve and looked at my wrist, cupping my hand so that people would think I was checking a watch.

We had agreed that if Laura thought she was being followed when she left this meeting, she would enter the lobby and yell at me, reminding me I was fired. I had convinced her to make a big scene, which would allow her to get out and meet Mc-Millan, leaving me behind to deal with whoever followed her.

The three of us would hook up at O'Hare when I was through.

After the first hour, I got restless. There were only so many times I could read that today was the day the presidential electors cast their ballots. Just once I wished the electors would forget their parties and their mandates and take some initiative. But I knew after the year we'd had, with the assassinations and the disaster at the Democratic National Convention, that this was not the election in which my wish would come true.

Finally, the elevator door opened and Laura emerged, walking fast. She wore her rich, society-girl outfit—rabbit-fur coat, wool pants, and an expensive sweater. She had on more makeup than I'd ever seen her wear, and her hair had been styled into its fashionable flip, but none of that masked the fury in her eyes.

My stomach churned. Had I been wrong? Had this ploy backfired in a way I hadn't expected?

"Come on, Smoke," she said quietly as she passed me, just

like she was supposed to do if she thought she was in the clear. She headed to the wrought-iron doors. I waited until she went through them. No one followed her off the elevator, and no one followed her through the doors.

I hurried across the lobby and into the crowd. No one seemed to notice her as she ducked into the diner where McMillan waited. I watched for a good five minutes before joining them.

McMillan was at the counter, paying the bill. Laura stood beside his table, her shiny leather boot tapping against the tile. When she saw me, more color suffused her cheeks.

"Let's get out of here," she said.

"We're going out the back," McMillan said, joining us. He put his hand on Laura's coat, propelling her toward the kitchen. She let him push her forward, and I followed, still trying to see if anyone was watching us.

No one seemed to be. The people inside seemed to be mostly city workers on breaks. The crowd walking past the windows were a mixture of business people and holiday shoppers, their heads down against the wind. No one so much as glanced inside.

I hurried through the kitchen, the smells of fried onions and grilling hamburgers making my stomach growl. McMillan held the back door open for me.

We went to McMillan's car and he handed me the keys. I was to drive while he and Laura sat in back, so it would look like they had a chauffeured ride to the airport. That, too, had been my idea when I had seen McMillan's new black Cadillac.

I was just backing up when Laura burst out, "I will never do anything like that again. Do you know how humiliating that was?"

I glanced into the rearview mirror. McMillan's gaze met mine. Laura's face was mottled, her lips compressed with fury.

"They believed me. They believed I couldn't think for myself. Cronk told me that it was perfectly understandable, and Eugene! Eugene put his arm around me and told me not to worry about it, that he'd make sure everything was all right. They even offered to find a new lawyer for me, one who wouldn't be so power-hungry."

Her speech took us to the Expressway. The car handled like a dream. It floated on the pavement. I'd never driven anything so fine.

"Power-hungry," McMillan said, a smile in his voice.

"Don't laugh," she said. "It was all I could do to keep up the pretense, not while I was talking to them, but when they all decided to take care of me, to let me know that I was in good hands. I never want to see Cronk smile again."

"He won't," I said. "Not when you're done with him."

She flounced back in her seat. "I didn't expect it to be this easy."

I had, but I didn't tell her that. It was always easier to appeal to people's prejudices. That was why I insisted that I drive the car. People's prejudices. Laura and McMillan hadn't thought of that.

"Just focus on January second," I said. "Then they'll understand how wrong they were."

"Do you think it'll work?"

"They won't know what hit them," McMillan said.

"Oh," I said, smiling, "I think they'll have an idea. They'll remember this past week and be furious at themselves. That'll make your victory even sweeter, Laura."

She sighed. "I hope you're right."

I had never been out to O'Hare before, and I was startled at all the newly built luxury hotels that filled the area around the airport. The traffic here was thicker than it had been in the Loop. When I asked about it, McMillan explained that a lot of meetings were held near the airport because of the convenience.

By the time I'd parked and gone inside, I had trouble finding them. I scanned the lines of passengers, their piles of luggage beside them while they waited to board. A lot of them smoked, making the air inside the terminal blue.

Laura was at one ticket counter, talking with a dark-haired

young man in a blue uniform. McMillan was at the next counter, handing some cash to a middle-aged woman whose hair had been pulled back so severely that it hurt to look at her.

I had told Laura to buy a ticket under a false name. It was ridiculously easy. All she had to do was pay cash. No one ever asked for identification. But I hadn't told McMillan to buy a ticket. He had obviously come up with something on his own.

The initial plan was for Laura to fly to another major city, buy a ticket there under yet a different name, and to do this until she felt comfortable. If she went directly to Europe, she would have to travel under her own name, but if she bought the ticket in New York or Los Angeles, no one from Chicago would be able to track her down.

The only luggage she had was an overnight bag. She would buy more clothes along the way.

McMillan finished first and joined me. He scanned the terminal, as I had done when I first entered, and like me, seemed to see nothing unusual.

"What were you doing?" I asked.

He held up two tickets. "My wife and I have to see family in Boston over the holidays."

Very clever. Even if someone who recognized Laura overheard the destination she was buying a ticket for, that person wouldn't realize she had gone on a different flight with McMillan.

I tried to remain calm about it. After all, I had been the one who had suggested he go with her. Apparently he had changed his mind.

Laura joined us, shoving her ticket in her purse. "I don't think I've ever flown into Denver."

McMillan smiled at her. "Let us walk you to the gate, Miss—?"

"Hamilton," she said. "Debra Hamilton."

"Miss Hamilton." McMillan glanced at me over his shoulder. "Joining us?"

I decided I might as well. We walked through the terminal, following the gate signs attached to the walls. Even the corridors were wide here, but the air was clearer. Apparently few people smoked as they walked to their planes.

Halfway to Laura's gate, McMillan stopped. He patted his pockets like he was looking for something. Laura and I stopped, too. People flowed past us like water around a rock.

"Here it is!" he said after a moment, and handed Laura a ticket. "I thought we'd lost your ticket, darling."

She looked confused.

"Don't you remember?" I asked. "You two have family to visit this Christmas."

"Actually," McMillan said, "Suzy's going to have to go without me. I called the office and the shipment we were expecting arrived a short time ago. I'm going to have to go back."

"Oh," Laura said.

He leaned over and kissed her cheek. "I'll see you on the second, darling."

She frowned at him.

"You'll see that she gets to the gate safely, Charles?" he asked me, his eyes twinkling.

I finally understood his little ploy. "Yes, sir," I said with complete seriousness.

Then he put a hand on my shoulder, leaned forward slightly and said softly, "I'll wait for you in the loading zone outside the baggage area. But I will need the keys."

I dug into my pocket and handed them to him with some reluctance. His car had spoiled me.

He kissed Laura again, a casual, husbandly peck on the lips, and headed back up the corridor. My stomach clenched, and Laura's cheeks were flushed.

"G-guess I'd better double-check the gate," she said, opening the ticket folder and looking at the ticket. It was handwritten in blue ink. On top, the gate was listed and underlined.

We were nearly there, but neither of us moved.

"I'm going to keep an eye on you," I said, "but I'm not going to sit with you. That would be a bit too memorable."

She nodded. "I don't want to go."

"I know. But it's best, and you'll be back soon."

"Strong until the last." She grabbed my hand and squeezed it, hiding our fingers beneath her coat as she did so. "I'm going to miss you, Smokey."

"I'll miss you, too," I said. More than she would ever know.

TWENTY-THREE

By the time McMillan dropped me at my car in a parking lot near the Loop, it was almost three-thirty. Because of traffic, I didn't get home until four. I was feeling out of sorts and frazzled, and very happy that I had asked the Grimshaws if Jimmy could stay for dinner.

I had no idea when I'd be through that night.

I had to meet Delevan in an hour. I changed clothes so that I didn't look like someone's hired man. I didn't have time to look through the photographs, so I locked them in the bottom drawer of my desk. Then I made myself a quick snack because I knew I'd need all my strength to face that neighborhood again. Before I left, I opened the glove box of the car, pulled out my gun and tucked it under my jacket, just in case.

I arrived at Delevan's old house at five. It was fully dark and the streetlights were on, creating pools of light in the mostly empty street. Driveways were still vacant, but neighboring houses had lights on inside. The white paint on the FOR SALE signs cast eerie reflections up and down the block.

The lights were on in Delevan's house as well, but they only emphasized its lack of occupancy. No curtains covered the windows, and the empty rooms were visible from the street. A light over the front door revealed a man standing on the enclosed porch. He was tall and balding, with sloped shoulders and the bulk of a former college wrestler. When the car shut off, he opened the screen door and started down the stairs to the sidewalk.

I got out and walked around the car toward the house. As I did, the man said, "What can I do for you?"

He was abrupt, his tone cold. Even though the words were warm, the emotion behind them wasn't. He didn't want me there.

"I'm Bill Grimshaw," I said. "I have an appointment with Oscar Delevan."

"You're Bill Grimshaw?" He stopped where he was.

"Yes," I said, knowing the reason for his surprise. From our conversation the night before, he had expected a white cop in uniform, not a black man in plainclothes.

"You're investigating a murder?"

"Yes." I stopped on the curb. At this moment, it was prudent to stay close to the car.

"I take it this Foster fellow was a ni—Negro?"

"He was black," I said.

Delevan nodded once, then sighed. "All right." He seemed resigned. "What do you need to know?"

"Can we go inside?" I asked, not wanting to stand here with my back to the street.

"I suppose." He climbed the stairs and went inside the enclosed porch. He walked over to two folding chairs that stood beneath the picture window and sat on one of them. As I entered the porch, he kicked the other chair toward me.

I didn't sit down. Instead, I leaned on the picture window's external sill, determined to make it seem as if his hostility didn't bother me at all.

"Louis Foster was as tall as I am," I said, "but thinner. A real estate agent named Jane Sarton brought him here the Friday afternoon before Thanksgiving."

"Jesus, Sarton," he said. "She's half the reason we're in this trouble."

"Trouble?"

He waved a hand toward the street. "This used to be a good

neighborhood. Families lived here for generations, handing the houses down to the kids. But for some reason, bitches like Sarton think a place like this don't have an identity. You live with people who're like you. That's the American way. You know that."

I didn't answer him. Across the street, a car pulled into a driveway. A man got out. He was wearing a suit and carrying a briefcase. He walked into his garage as if he were exhausted.

"But this Sarton woman and a handful like her seem to think that just because someone can afford the house, they deserve to live in it. She don't think of community, she don't think that people should be with their own type. She just wants to make a buck."

My hands gripped the wooden sill so tightly paint chips bit into my palms. "Did you tell her this?"

"Oh, I let her know. I put the house on the market about six months ago because I get a company house as one of the perks of my job. I say I don't want no niggers, pardon my French, moving into my house, and she says then maybe I should rent the place so I can control who's in and out. Like I got time for that bullshit."

"Did she offer to manage the place for you?"

"Hell, no. She don't do stuff like that, and the people who do charge an arm and a ball, so I wouldn't make no profit anyhow. And they couldn't promise me they wouldn't rent to no coo—Negroes. Said they couldn't make that promise by law, though they'd try to do what I wanted."

"I'm sure they wouldn't have had a problem," I said, anger creeping into my voice despite my best efforts. "They don't elsewhere in the city."

"I know that." He hooked the metal leg of the other folding chair with his left shoe and dragged the chair toward him. "I just figure we'd have a nice arrangement, then some federal investigator would stick his grimy nose in and things would get messed up all over again. I'd be paying that arm and a ball and still not getting what I wanted."

"Why would you care?" I asked. "After all, as you said, you have a company house in Lake Forest now."

And it had to be rather grand. Companies around here didn't give small houses to their executives.

"I grew up here. I hate the changes going on, and I'm not going to be a part of them."

"Yet you let Mrs. Sarton show Louis Foster the house several times."

"She'd been bringing in all kinds of folks to see this place. Started spouting something about Fair Housing regulations and talking to her lawyer. I told her what I wanted and that's when she said I should rent the place."

It sounded like she had been angry. I had a hunch it took a lot to make Jane Sarton angry, especially over an issue like this.

"She told me that you were going to meet Mr. Foster and show him around," I said. "It sounded like you had an amiable relationship with him."

"I didn't have no relationship with him." Delevan put his feet on the folding chair across from him. It creaked under their weight. "I only met him the once."

"Then why were you willing to introduce him to the neighbors?"

He shook his head. "You don't get it, do you, boy?"

The word made me stiffen. Somehow that one was worse than all the others, maybe because he had used it deliberately. "What don't I get?"

"I thought he was white. It wasn't until he walked up the walk, sure as you please, that I realized my mistake."

Just like I had done.

"But Jane Sarton said she left him here with you." I was no longer resting on the sill. My hands were braced there, ready to launch me forward if I had to move quickly, my feet firmly beneath me. "She said you were going to introduce him around and she was pretty convinced she'd get a sale out of this."

"Shows you just how dumb that bitch truly is." He wasn't looking at me any longer. He was staring at the street. The streetlights were so bright that the shadows around them seemed even darker than they should have. "She wasn't going to get no sale."

"Because he died." I said that softly, every muscle in my body taut, prepared to move if he so much as turned toward me.

"Hell, no," he said. "I was real polite to that boy. He was a smart one. Had a good job, seemed pretty decent, you know. That's what made him perfect."

"Perfect?" My mouth was dry.

"For proving my point."

"Which was?"

"You people don't belong here." He kicked the second chair away and it clattered against the porch. I stood up, hands down and open at my sides, but he didn't get out of his chair. I didn't think he even saw my change in posture.

"How would Foster have proven that point?" I asked.

"I figured he'd go talk to the neighborhood association and they'd let him know him and his wasn't welcome here. Then he'd go back to Sarton, tell her that his Friday night maybe wasn't the most pleasant one of his life, and she'd get the idea."

"What exactly did you think they'd do to him?" I asked.

Delevan sighed as if he were dealing with a recalcitrant child. "Why, put the fear of God into him, of course."

"The fear of God," I repeated, shaking my head. "And in doing that, they accidentally killed him?"

"You're awfully quick to make accusations." He put his hands on his thighs and twisted his elbows outward. "These are people I've known all my life. Good, decent people who have good, solid jobs and live good, quiet lives. All they want is a nice home with like-minded neighbors. They don't kill to get that."

"How would they get it then?" I asked.

He pushed himself up and turned to face me. I tensed. "By talking to you people," he said, emphasizing each word. "By letting you know that you do not belong, that your family would not be welcome, not threatening any physical harm, but making it clear that life here would be unpleasant."

I let out a short, humorless laugh. "That sounds so reasonable and we both know it isn't. We also know it's not effective. There are black families living in this neighborhood now. They must have had the fear-of-God talk. They moved in anyway."

He walked toward the screens and stared into the street. "After the riots in April, people down here got scared. They thought we were next because we're not far from your damn ghetto. Some folks just left. They sold their houses to anyone who'd buy. They didn't care. They wanted out. I don't think most of them met the buyers. I don't think they knew they sold to Negroes, or they just didn't care."

"Oh?" I said. "Shouldn't your vigilantes have protected you from the black invasion? Didn't they know who the buyers were ahead of time?"

He didn't move. "I don't like your mouth, boy."

"I don't like yours either," I said. "But you can answer my questions or you can go to the police station to do so."

I figured Johnson or Sinkovich would back me up on this if I needed them to.

"You know, you never showed me no identification."

"No, I never did, and I don't plan to now. We're a little past that. You've answered enough questions to make me suspicious of you and your friends. You may as well keep talking to clear their names."

He looked at me over his shoulder. I couldn't see his face in the thin porch light, only the shape of his head.

"None of us did anything," he said.

"That's not what you told me," I said. "You said you threatened a man so that he wouldn't move into this neighborhood. I'm just trying to figure out the extent of that threat."

Delevan turned back toward the street. "I don't know. I wasn't there."

"You just told me you took him to the meeting."

"No I didn't. I said I wanted them to put the fear of God into him, that he was the perfect person to do it to. He was respectable, you see. He'd tell his friends that this isn't a good place to live, not for your people, that we didn't want him here. I thought it worked, too, when he never came back."

"So what happened after Jane Sarton left him with you?" I asked.

Delevan's shoulders slumped further. "He went to the meeting."

"Without you?"

"A friend of mine took him."

"When was this?" I asked.

"That evening. Just after that real estate bitch left."

"Then explain something to me," I said. "If you weren't there, how would you know these neighbors of yours carried out your plan?"

He reached down, grabbed the metal folding chair and sat on it, facing me. The anger seemed to have left him. I wasn't sure why.

"I told them to," he said.

"In front of Foster?"

"Hell, no." He sighed. "That boy told me Sarton had warned him that we wouldn't get along, and he'd laughed about it, said she probably misread me. He trusted me."

There was no heat on the porch and the wind whistled through the screens. Goose bumps rose on my arms.

"You never said anything."

"Not to him."

"Then to who?"

"The friend who walked him to the meeting."

"Who was that?"

He rubbed his hands along his knees, his head down.

"Who was that?" I repeated.

"I think I said enough."

"If you believe your friends are innocent," I said, "then there's no harm in telling me. If you don't tell me who they were, I'm going to assume that you believe they had something to do with Foster's death."

"You never told me how he died," Delevan said.

"He was murdered," I said, finding the timing of his question fascinating.

"I know, but how?"

I debated telling him. If I said nothing, he might not answer my questions. "What are you afraid of?"

He shook his head.

"Afraid that they got a little overzealous?" I asked. "Afraid that someone hit him one time too many, a little too hard?"

His head moved up as if he were beginning a nod, then thought the better of it. "Accidents happen."

"Is that what you think this was?" I asked.

He gave me a one-shoulder shrug.

"I can assure you, Mr. Delevan," I said. "What happened to Louis Foster was no accident."

His gaze met mine, his skin fishbelly-white in the thin light. I thought I read fear in his eyes, but I wasn't sure. They seemed so pale that they were almost clear.

"These guys would never do anything deliberate," he said. "And so far as I know, they'd never hurt anybody. They've used words you probably don't like, and they would make it real clear that you don't belong, but they'd never touch anybody. If he started something, sure, they'd defend themselves, but they'd never hurt anyone. Not willingly."

Footsteps on the concrete made him stop. We both looked toward the street. A white man walked south, hands stuck in his pockets. He wore a uniform that looked familiar, but I couldn't place it.

Delevan waited until he was gone before turning back toward me. "I don't know who was at the meeting," he said quietly. "I haven't lived in this neighborhood for six months. The association elects new members in July."

He glanced toward the street again, as if he wasn't sure he wanted anyone to see us together.

"But I'll tell you this. The guy who walked your friend to the meeting is Rudy Hucke. He's a good guy. He'd never hurt anyone. I'm telling you this so you know that I believe he's not involved with anything. I'm sure your boy went to that meeting, got the bejeezus scared out of him, then headed for home. Something happened to him somewhere else, not here."

"Rudy Hucke," I repeated. "How do I reach him?"

"I don't got his number on me, but he's listed."

"I assume he lives nearby," I said. "I can just walk over there."

Delevan shook his head. "Call him first."

"So you can warn him about me?"

"Someone's got to. This ain't the kinda neighborhood where you can knock on doors."

I was trying to filter his words, trying to make sure I heard what he was saying and what he really meant. "You told me this was a good neighborhood."

He kept staring into the street. Another man walked by, then turned into a driveway, obviously heading home.

"It is," Delevan said. "For me."

"But not for me?" So I had heard him right. "What would happen to me if I knocked on doors?"

His entire body tensed. The reaction was quick and involuntary. It took him longer to respond verbally. He was clearly choosing his words. "They would call the cops."

"That wouldn't bother me," I said, still playing my role as a plainclothes detective.

"Really? That ain't what I heard. I heard you people ain't really part of the force, that you get beat up just like the rest of your kind."

That had a grain of truth to it. I'd learned in the last few months that the African-American Patrolman's League had been formed as a response to several such incidents.

"If you're worried that the neighbors would call the police, I don't consider that a threat. So you don't need to call ahead and warn anyone."

He leaned forward and put his head in his hands. He rubbed his face once, then he stood.

It was my turn to tense as he turned around. But he didn't make a move toward me.

"Look," he said. "I ain't gonna lie to ya. Tension's gotten really bad down here. I may get a few calls tonight because you're here. Your kind's not wanted down here at all, and these folks make that plain. They're not the killing type, but they might rough you up a bit, make you remember that every time you come down here."

"I can handle myself."

"Maybe," he said. "You're a big guy. But even big guys don't got a chance against a bunch of folks."

A chill ran down my back.

"What are you saying?"

"I'm saying I don't know what happened to your friend. I know my neighbors couldn't've killed him. That's not what they do. They might've scared him, though, and they'll do their best to scare you. Or hurt you. I'll call them, let them know you're coming. That way, it ain't my fault if something happens to you."

The speech was probably more revealing than he had intended. He thought Foster's death might be his fault, in one way or another. Or was Delevan smart enough to lead me astray, to make me think that his friends had beaten up Foster, when, in fact, he had taken care of the situation for them?

And if that was the case, why wasn't he going after me now? I could be a complication.

"You've already given me the name of your friend Rudy," I said. "Just show me where he lives and I'll go there now. I need to talk to him anyway, since he saw Foster after you did. I might not need to talk to the rest of the committee."

"I told you. Rudy didn't do—"

"I'm not saying he did," I said hastily. "He might have scared Foster off and never taken him to the committee. If that's what happened, I need to know that, too."

Delevan's eyes narrowed. He seemed to be trying to see through me, to know what I was really about. After a moment, he appeared satisfied with what I'd said.

"Rudy Hucke lives two doors down, this side. You go to the front door. Rudy's awful protective of his garage. Thinks of it as part of the house."

I understood the warning. If I went inside anywhere without Rudy's permission, he'd see that as a threat.

"If he's not there, is he going to be upset if I talk to his wife?"

Delevan shook his head. "Wife left fifteen years ago. Best if you don't mention her at all."

"All right," I said. "I'll call if I have other questions."

"I told you everything I know," he said.

Probably not, but I didn't tell him that. Instead, I thanked him for his time, and stepped off the porch, my back prickling. I knew he was watching me walk away. I felt relieved when I turned onto the city sidewalk. Out of the corner of my eye, I could see Delevan standing where I'd left him, facing the street.

He wasn't the only one. Curtains up and down the block twitched, the movement visible because of the window-shaped squares of light that fell on the street. Only a handful of houses were dark—and one of them was Hucke's.

It was a small house, the kind that real estate agents sometimes called a starter. A single-story white house with a gray roof and a one-car garage. The house itself probably had no more than eight hundred square feet on the interior—two bedrooms, a bath, a tiny living room, and an even tinier kitchen. The way the house's foundation was built up suggested that there wasn't even a basement. If I went around back, I had a hunch that I'd find a slatted wooden door at a thirty-degree angle to the house and the ground, a door that led into a combination root and storm cellar.

I mounted the cheap concrete stairs that someone had illadvisedly painted deep red. The colors seemed even darker in the thin light from a makeshift lamp above the garage door. That door was closed and Hucke had even put shades over the windows.

The shades in the house were drawn, too, and I could tell even before I knocked that no one was home. Still, I pounded the thick wooden door with my fist, listening to the thuds reverberate inside. As I did, I stood so that I could see the street as well as the house. I didn't want anyone to sneak up behind me.

No one did. The entire street seemed to be holding its breath, watching me. I expected to hear doors open, or shoe heels clicking on concrete, coming toward me, but none of that happened.

The residents of this street were content to spy, probably hoping that I would go away.

During any other investigation, I would have walked around the house, checked the windows and the back door, but I wouldn't here. The night was too dark and so was I. Hucke's neighbors were paranoid enough. I didn't need to give them an excuse to come after me.

I sighed as I walked down his steps. Now he would be warned that I was coming to visit him, not just by Delevan, but by his other neighbors, too. He'd have time to make up a story if he needed one, and he'd also have time to help the neighborhood association contrive a group story as well.

I was almost to my car when a man came down the street toward me. He was wearing a heavy coat, unzipped over his denim work shirt, and denim pants. I felt the reassuring presence of my gun under my coat, and made certain my right hand was in position to grab it quickly.

As he got closer to me, his stride did not slow down, but we made eye contact. "You ain't thinking of moving to Delevan's house, are ya?"

I almost said no, and then I realized that I would find out nothing if I denied it. But if I let him believe I might move here, I might get the same reaction Foster had. If Foster did die here, I might find out. I was safer than Foster was: I had a gun. I could defend myself against a knife. And unlike Foster, I was prepared.

All those thoughts went through my mind in an instant, as I heard myself say, "It's a nice neighborhood."

"Won't be," he said as he came up alongside of me, "if there's too many fucking jigaboos in it."

My hand went for my gun, finding the grip, hard and firm beneath my palm. I whirled, but he was already past me, not looking back. I kept him in sight, kept the gun under my coat.

He was already several yards away. He hadn't done anything more than deliver his message.

But it was a chilling message, one I'd gotten over and over again in this part of the city. Ethnic white neighborhoods on

Chicago's far South Side did not want middle-class blacks— hell, any kind of black—to move in.

And it was becoming clear that they'd do anything to prevent it.

TWENTY-FOUR

The drive home seemed to take forever. The threats had unnerved me. It took me a few blocks to realize that my reaction didn't come from fear, but from anger.

Usually, I responded to such threats in two set ways. Often
those threats came before a physical confrontation, which I was
more than suited for. Other times, they were a single one-shot
comment, which I could respond to verbally.

I had done neither here, and it felt uncomfortable.

As I left the neighborhood, I approached the grocery store
where I had received such harassment. To my surprise, it was
still open, its red neon sign ablaze, and white fluorescent light
pouring out of its front windows. I glanced at the clock on my
dash.

No wonder the store was still open. It wasn't even six
o'clock. Most stores closed between seven and eight.

My encounter with Delevan had lasted less than an hour.

It had seemed like a year.

As I drove up, I noticed a black woman standing by the open
trunk of a new Oldsmobile. She wore a knee-length cloth coat,
obviously expensive, and a pair of high heels that looked too
thin to protect her from the cold. Her black hair was pulled
away from her face, accentuating her delicate features.

A full grocery cart sat beside the car, and as I approached, I toyed with stopping to help her load them into the trunk. I almost drove by but in the end, some instinct made me pull over.

This woman shouldn't have been alone, not near this store, in this neighborhood so late at night.

I wasn't able to stop near her. I was half a block back. I started to get out of the car when a man came out of the store, pushing another grocery cart. I didn't recognize him, but he hadn't moved away from the door. He was short, his face in shadow.

He spoke to her, but I couldn't make out his words. She laughed in response, and I realized that she didn't need me after all. She had come with someone else, and she didn't seem to have had trouble shopping there.

Maybe evenings were the best time for blacks to shop, or maybe the butcher had managed to get store policy changed after all. Maybe the problem was the manager, who would probably have left by now.

I got back inside my car and drove on, somewhat relieved that I didn't have to go over there. A year ago, I might have gone despite the other man's presence. The woman was pretty, and obviously doing well at her work. It would have been worth my time to find out if she were single.

But Laura had changed that. I really didn't want to meet anyone else. Marvella was right; my heart was taken, whether I wanted it to be or not.

I picked up Jimmy at the Grimshaws', took him home and made us both dinner. He wanted to know about Laura, and I told him that she had flown out safely. I promised she would return, but I knew he still didn't believe me.

When we finished eating, I left him with the dishes and the television while I went into my office. I unlocked the file cabinet and pulled out the packets that Mrs. Weisman had given me. I poured the photographs out of the manila envelopes and spread them out on my desk.

There had to be about one hundred photographs in front of me. Their edges curled upward and they smelled of developing fluid. I sorted them into thematic groups before examining them.

Just as Saul Epstein had told me the day before he was beaten, most of the photographs were useless to me. There were a few gang pictures, but on close inspection, it seemed not to be a meeting of rival gangs but of Van Spillars and Gus Foley talking to some gang members their own age, trying to get the watch back.

The gang shots hadn't held him for long. He took only one roll of that. He'd taken more shots of early morning ground fog against a pair of twisted tree trunks in the center of the park. The effect he was going for appeared to be both Gothic and artistic—in the best shots, the trees looked like they were coalescing out of the mist.

Then the photographs changed. There were a few shaky shots of the crime scene—obviously taken while the photographer was moving toward it. Two photographs caught the matching looks of horror on the faces of Gus and Van. A series of candid shots followed them as they ran out of the park to call the police.

No one else appeared in those photographs. The park seemed empty, but I caught a glimpse of the blue car that the boys had mentioned. Its front end disappeared off the last two photographs in that series. Try as I might, I couldn't make out the license plate. Even with the small magnifying glass I kept in my top drawer, I couldn't see much more than the plate's shape. I couldn't even tell what state issued it.

The bulk of the photographs were of the crime scene and they were beautifully done. Epstein hadn't taken the most informative ones to the *Defender*—he had taken the most interesting artistic shots.

He started his photographs from a good twenty yards away from the body, proceeding closer. I could almost imagine him walking forward, the camera in front of his face, as he snapped shot after shot.

He got pictures of the ground leading up to the body, complete with cigarette butts and beer cans and, most informative of all, footprints still remaining in the early morning frost. I studied the prints for a long time.

There were four sets. Two sets matched. They were small, not quite child-sized, but the size of a woman's shoe, or a young boy's. They had no tread; their smooth bottoms marked them as sneakers or well-worn regular shoes.

I glanced back at the long-range photographs of the boys. Sure enough, they both wore sneakers. In one shot, Epstein had managed to get the back of one boy's shoe as he ran, revealing no tread at all.

The other two sets went in different directions. One came toward the body; the other veered away at a sixty-degree angle. After a few moments of study, I realized that these footprints were made by the same pair of boots—men's boots, judging from their size. I couldn't get a sense of the exact size, but it was clear that these boots were much larger than the boys' shoes.

The reason it took me some study to realize that the boots belonged to the same person was because of the way the footprints looked. On the way to the crime scene, the heel marks were so deep they actually broke through the frost into the ground. On the way from the scene, the footprints were fainter, in some instances, vanishing completely.

One man had carried the body to this place. Alone. One very strong man.

I set down my magnifying glass and rubbed my eyes. From the living room, the television rang with laughter, and a voice crying, "You bet your bippy!" echoed down the hallway. *Laugh-In* was on.

I usually joined Jimmy for it, but tonight I couldn't bring myself to do so. Looking at these photographs after meeting Delevan that afternoon brought the murder closer to me than it had ever been. Even after meeting Louis Foster's friends and coworkers, I hadn't felt this sense of urgency that I felt now.

I slid another pile of photographs toward me. This group had surprised me when I had first seen it. Epstein had gotten close to the body—as close as a crime-scene photographer would get—and had taken precise, somewhat ghoulish pictures.

Several focused on Foster's face—the flaccid look of the features so common after death. He had no bruising, no cigarette burns like last summer's copycat victim. If it weren't for the slight slit in his coat just over his heart, marked only by blood as the knife exited the wound, he wouldn't have seemed injured at all.

I especially studied his hands: no defensive wounds. Like the other victims, Louis Foster had been surprised by his attacker, dying swiftly and silently with a minimum of fuss.

Something about the poses was supposed to tell us something. The killer was leaving a message we were missing, a message we should somehow have understood.

No matter how long I stared at the photographs, I couldn't figure the message out.

I skipped the duplicates of the photographs that Epstein had given the *Defender* and focused instead on the last set of photos. He had taken those after the police had arrived on the crime scene.

He'd used only one roll's worth, but that was enough to tell a tale of evidence destruction that was even worse than usual. The footprints—including Epstein's own—were obliterated before the cops reached the body. Police officers searched the victim, moving his clothing, reaching into his pockets and patting his sides, searching for what, I could not tell. They had not followed their own department's rules of evidence.

The most shocking photograph was also the most artistic, almost as if it were posed, although it was clear it was not. The composition was of award quality. It was a shot of a detective, his shield on his blazer, leaning against the other side of the tree. Epstein had pulled his lens back far enough to encompass the entire trunk, and Foster's body still splayed in death. The cop had a cigarette in his right hand. Smoke blew out of his mouth as he casually flicked ash on Foster's coat.

I made myself set the photograph down slowly, restraining the urge to crumple it. I pushed away from the desk and stood, clenching my fists as I walked toward the window. I hadn't even closed the curtains, although my neighbor in the building next door had closed his. I wondered if he could see inside, see the anger that was beginning to fuel me, whether I wanted it to or not.

I had to remain calm. That photograph was evidence—evidence of a lot of things, none of them good. Epstein would have to make copies of this one himself, or instruct me on how to use his darkroom. I wouldn't trust this photograph to any other developer, professional or not.

When I was calm enough, I returned to my desk and gathered up the photographs. The Foster case could no longer be mine. I would have to share it completely with Johnson and Sinkovich.

I wondered if they'd do anything about it. After all, the man with the cigarette was one of their colleagues. Perhaps they were inured to things like this.

But I wasn't—and I hoped I never would be.

The next morning, the phone woke me. It invaded a dream in which I was talking to Laura. She was reassuring me that she was all right, and I was yelling at her for contacting me at all. The ringing phone, I kept saying, is proof that someone is listening, someone knows where you are.

And then, in my dream, I hung up.

The phone continued to ring, and somehow I realized that the sound was real. I grabbed my robe and hurried toward my office, where our only extension was.

"What?" I said as I picked up. The room was dark. The sun hadn't risen over the buildings yet. I squinted at my clock. Not even 6:00 A.M.

"Get dressed, Grimshaw." It took me a moment to wake up enough to recognize Truman Johnson's voice. "I need you here, and fast."

"Where?" I asked, my mouth cottony from sleep.

"Oak Woods Cemetery," he said. "We have another one."

TWENTY-FIVE

Somehow, even with all the things I had to do—dress, make calls, and get Marvella (who demanded an apology from me, of all things) to watch Jimmy until Franklin took over my school duties—I still managed to make it to the cemetery in fifteen minutes.

The morning was cloudy and cold, the lightening sky the only way to tell that the sun was coming up. I wore my heaviest jacket and a pair of thick gloves, but I still felt chilled. Part of me hadn't yet left the warm comfort of my bed, believing all of this to be a horrible dream.

It wouldn't have been hard to find the crime scene even if Johnson hadn't given me specific directions. Police cars, their lights revolving, were parked on the dirt access road. The gravestones were turning red and blue in the alternating light, a parody of color worthy of a *Smothers Brothers* spoof.

Men in and out of uniform examined the scene, but unlike the Foster investigation, they did not appear to be compromising the evidence. I couldn't see Johnson, but the gray light made everything seem diffuse.

I also couldn't see the body, and no one seemed to be standing near any of the trees. It took me a moment to realize they were working near one of the monuments.

It was huge, standing at least forty feet tall, its edges gray against the gray sky. If it weren't for the dark rivulets of dirt running down its sides, I wouldn't have been able to make out details at all.

As it was, the monument seemed somewhat generic. A bronze soldier stood on top of a large spire that trailed down to a base covered with plaques. On one side, a row of old gravestones was lined up like chess pieces. Clearly, this was some kind of war memorial, but from a distance, I couldn't tell which war was being remembered.

I walked closer and no one tried to stop me. They didn't even seem to notice me as they worked in relative silence, gathering evidence off the manicured lawn and marking off areas with great precision. About five men worked the scene, while two uniformed officers stood on the side of the access road, talking to an elderly white woman who seemed very distressed.

The closer I got, the odder the monument seemed. Concentric trenches surrounded it, and the base, or mound, that the plaques covered, seemed to go on forever. The base's shape was rectangular and I approached it along one of its long sides. It wasn't until I reached a shorter side that I saw the body.

It looked tiny against the aging stone, but I knew that had to be an optical illusion. Any human being would look small against that base.

A man looked up from his position near the body. He dusted himself off, walked around one of the trenches and came toward me.

Johnson. He looked like he hadn't slept at all.

"How'd you call me from out here?" I asked.

"Dispatch patched me through."

I hadn't even noticed. His voice should have had an odd quality—probably did—but I had been so sound asleep that it hadn't even registered.

"When did you get here?"

"Uniforms called me about forty-five minutes ago."

"They knew you were working on cases like this?" I asked.

Johnson shook his head. "It's my turf. And even if it wasn't, brass would probably figure that it's safer to have a black detective at this cemetery than a white one."

"What about the Gang Intelligence Unit?"

"Not even an amateur would think this is a gang killing."

"Why?"

He nodded toward the monument. "Because of that."

"What is it? World War One?"

His eyes widened, then he shook his head slightly. "I keep forgetting you're new around here. It's Civil War."

"So? I don't—"

"Confederate," he said. "It's a Confederate monument."

"In Chicago?"

"It's the largest Confederate memorial in the North."

I frowned. "What're you saying? There was a battle around here? A lot of Southern sentiment?"

"No." He sighed. "There was a Confederate prison camp not far from here. Six thousand Confederates are buried here, and in eighteen ninety-five someone felt they deserved a monument."

I let out a small snort of surprise. "I will never understand white people."

"It gets even more interesting," Johnson said. "I guess the old lady there has a grandfather buried here. She brings him flowers every December. She was a little surprised this morning."

I glanced at the body, still an undistinguishable mass of flesh, hair, and coat from this distance. "Can I see?"

"Wouldn't have asked you this far if I didn't want you to."

He led me past the trenches. The monument was clearly marked. The bronze plaques on the sides looked like they had been added later—they weren't built into the monument, but attached.

A shiver ran down my spine. The South was full of monuments like this. I'd trained myself not to study them, because they honored a cause that was a centuries-long atrocity, an atrocity that was, in some ways, still continuing.

I had never, ever, expected to see something like that this far north.

As we stepped onto the concrete apron, I made myself focus on the body. A purse sitting on the top of the base, above the plaques, told me that this was a woman long before I saw her features.

Johnson led me to the front of the body, keeping me away from areas that he didn't want trampled. Her position was right—on her side, arm sprawled before her like a supplicant, one high heel dangling off her foot.

The high heel made me uneasy. I scanned her nylon-covered legs to the expensive cloth coat and felt my breath catch. The coat was closed, the knife slit and faint bloodstain easily visible against the camel color.

I was already holding my breath when I looked at her face. Even before I saw her delicate features, I knew.

I knew.

Not twelve hours before, she'd been loading groceries into the back of a brand-new Oldsmobile. I'd stopped, but I'd moved on because I thought she was safe.

"Know her?" Johnson asked.

"I should have," I said. "It might have saved her life."

"You want to explain that cryptic statement?" Johnson asked.

But I wasn't ready to. Her purse sat on top of the monument like a beacon, but I didn't see the groceries or anything else that seemed to belong to her.

"Where's her car?"

"Car?" Johnson shrugged. "Hell, it could be anywhere, if she even had a car. I don't know why a woman that fine would have come to this cemetery—"

"She didn't, Truman," I said. "She was dumped, like the others."

"Probably," he said. "But you're making an assumption, and you know that we can't do that at this stage of the investigation."

"I'm not making an assumption," I said. "I saw her last

night. She was loading groceries into a late-model Oldsmobile."

Johnson looked at me, eyebrows raised. "She was that obvious? Or do you always notice pretty women at the grocery store?"

He wasn't joking. He was sincerely interested.

"She was that obvious," I said. "I had just gone to investigate a house that Louis Foster had been . . ."

My voice trailed off. I stared at her sightless eyes, her slack mouth. She looked so much like Foster, not because they were related, but because everyone looked the same in death. Facial muscles relaxed, expressions were lost, the things that made a person unique vanished as the last breath left the lungs.

"Had been what?" Johnson prompted.

"We have to check the files," I said.

"What?" He looked confused.

"I think we may have our link."

"What link?"

I finally pulled my gaze from her, this unknown woman who had seemed so vibrant the day before. "The neighborhood. She was at a grocery store in the same neighborhood that Foster had been in when he was last seen."

Interest flickered across Johnson's face. "Tell me what you know," he said.

By noon, we had a police-department map of the South Side spread across my kitchen table. Using different-colored inks, we charted the places where the murder victims lived, where they were found, and where they were last seen.

All points converged on the very neighborhood I had been in the night before.

Sinkovich and I had done most of the work while Johnson finished up at the crime scene. Sinkovich had arrived at my apartment around nine, complaining that we hadn't called him to the cemetery.

I was pretty certain that Johnson wanted to keep their association a secret, not because of Sinkovich's actions the previous week, but because he didn't want either of them getting in trouble for doing work that didn't exactly follow departmental regulation.

When he arrived, Johnson brought burgers and root beer from A&W. The greasy smell of meat and fries filled the room.

"I didn't expect you to have this done," he said as he came in.

"It was easy once we knew what we were looking for," Sinkovich said.

Johnson set the food on the counter. "Any other links beside the neighborhood?"

"Nothing obvious," I said. "Louis Foster contemplated buying a house there, Matthew Gentz had just gotten a new bicycle and friends saw him taking off in that direction, and Viola Stamps was visiting her grandson, who had just moved in with his white father."

"The other little boy, Allen Thomason, was doing a solicitation for his church, raising money for the War on Poverty," Sinkovich said. "And Otis Washington, the homeless guy, often fell asleep in doorways. I think he might have picked the wrong one."

"That's not everyone," Johnson said, handing me a paper-wrapped, lukewarm burger.

"No," I said. "Some of these people don't seem to have obvious ties to the neighborhood. But they were all doing something unusual the day they died. One was job-hunting. Another was doing lawn work. We have no way of knowing where they last were, because they never checked in with anyone."

"What about today's victim?" Sinkovich asked Johnson.

Johnson set the fries on the counter and handed Sinkovich his burger. The root beers remained on the counter as well. I toyed with taking the map off the table, but I really didn't want to.

"Didn't Grimshaw tell you?" Johnson asked.

"About the grocery store, sure," Sinkovich said. "But not who she was or what was going on."

"Her name was Bonita Henderson. She had just been transferred here from New York. She rented an apartment on the cusp of the neighborhood, about a block north."

"Still an all-black area," I said.

Johnson nodded. He took a bite out of his burger and closed his eyes, as if it were the best food he'd ever tasted. It took him a moment to chew and swallow. "The store you saw her at was between her apartment and her new job with an all-black insurance company."

"Secretary?" I asked, thinking it odd that they would transfer her.

"Claims adjuster. Apparently one of the best in the company." This time, Johnson spoke around his mouthful of food.

I took a bite of my hamburger as well. It was flat and tasteless. There appeared to be more mustard than beef between the bun.

"Anyway," Johnson said, "I talked to one of the grocery store clerks. She said that Miss Henderson had come in three weeks in a row and that the previous week, the manager had asked her not to come back. The clerk said Miss Henderson had laughed at him and asked why she had to drive farther to pay higher prices when he was nearby."

"That's odd," I said.

"Why?" Johnson asked.

"She was with a man last night. He was helping her with her groceries."

"Black guy?" Johnson asked.

"I don't know," I said. "I didn't get a good look at him."

"Think she brought him as protection?"

I shrugged.

"Think he's our killer?" Sinkovich asked.

"She seemed comfortable with him," I said. "So no. I don't think he did it."

"There's a racial component to these killings," Johnson said. "Maybe if she was with a white guy, someone decided to punish her for it."

"What about the white guy?" I asked. "Wouldn't he have gotten killed, too?"

"Maybe someone followed her home," Sinkovich said. "Waited until he left, then went after her."

So many maybes. We still had a lot of work ahead of us, and we had a new victim. The more time we took, the more lives could be lost.

"It would make sense for her to bring a bodyguard of some kind." Johnson finished the last of his burger, then got up and grabbed some fries. "Last week, the manager talked to her. Told her that if she didn't go away, someone would put the fear of God into her. It was better if she just left—"

"What?" I asked.

"The manager talked to her," Johnson said.

"No," I said. "Did you use the phrase 'the fear of God' as a description or did the clerk actually say that?"

"She actually said that. Why?"

"Because Delevan mentioned the same thing. He told Rudy Hucke to put the fear of God into Louis Foster."

"He told who?" Sinkovich put his still-wrapped burger on the map. Johnson, obviously irritated, took the burger off and leaned his chair back to set it on the counter.

"Rudy Hucke," I said. "You know, the neighbor who was supposed to take Foster to the association meeting."

"I didn't think you knew his name." Sinkovich was frowning.

"Is there a problem?" Johnson asked.

"Yeah." Sinkovich stood up and stuck his hands in his pockets. "I don't think we can do this."

"Do what?" Johnson said.

"Investigate this neighborhood," Sinkovich said.

Johnson's face flushed. "Why the hell not?"

"Rudy Hucke," Sinkovich repeated, as if the name would conjure an image. "He's a precinct captain."

I had spent nearly three months in Chicago before I had learned that a precinct captain was not a police officer. In Chicago, a precinct captain was a person who was in charge of a voting precinct. Precinct captains had close ties with the city's Democratic machine. Mayor Daley had been a precinct captain as a young man.

The other important fact about precinct captains was that they were supposed to form a close personal relationship with every voter in their territory. If a voter needed a job or a good apartment, the precinct captain made sure the voter got that job—in exchange for a vote. If a voter got into trouble, a precinct captain could get him out—for a price.

"So?" I asked Sinkovich.

"He has ties to the mayor," Sinkovich said.

"Yeah, so?" I asked again. "We have no idea who committed these killings. Why should we care about Hucke?"

"He knows everybody in the neighborhood," Sinkovich said. "He might even know who's doing this, but he's not going to let us close to that guy. From what you said, Hucke's in the neighborhood association. Even if we find the killer, Hucke's not going to let us arrest him. The neighborhood association is affiliated with Hucke and Hucke is affiliated with the machine. That's too much scandal. We won't be able to crack this."

"We're not talking about cracking anything," I said. "We don't even know if the neighborhood association is involved. All we know is that they might be the last people to see Louis Foster alive."

Johnson tapped the map. "But we know someone in the neighborhood did this."

"Yes, we do. Or someone who frequents the neighborhood. But that's all we have," I said. "That and some anecdotal evidence, and a catch phrase."

"Doesn't matter," Sinkovich said. "Precinct captains protect their own."

"Like cops," I said.

Sinkovich nodded.

But my own comparison reminded me of something. I got up and went into my office, grabbed the photographs out of my desk, and returned. I kept the photographs in their envelopes, but thumbed through quickly until I found the batch I wanted, the ones of the police investigation.

I pulled them out, along with the ones that Epstein had originally taken of Foster's body, and handed them, in order, to

Johnson. "You ever seen a murder investigation like this?"

"Where the hell did you get these?" he asked.

"What are they?" Sinkovich leaned forward, taking photos away as Johnson looked at them. When Sinkovich saw the first one, he whistled. "Who did this?"

"A photographer I know," I said. "He was one of the people to find the body."

"And rape the corpse," Sinkovich said. "Jesus. How much did he make selling these fuckers?"

Both Johnson and I looked at him. Sinkovich was getting more worked up than we were. But his emotions were closer to the surface. His wife had already started divorce proceedings. He wasn't sure he had enough money to hire his own lawyer, and he was afraid he'd never see his child again.

"He didn't sell these pictures," I said. "I'm not even sure he showed them to anyone but me."

"But he developed them."

"To give to me."

Johnson was still looking through them, his expression grim. Without comment, he handed a photo to Sinkovich. Sinkovich studied it, two spots of color rising on his cheeks.

"Is this what you were talking about?" Sinkovich turned the photograph toward me, showing the police searching the body.

I nodded. "There's another."

Johnson found it and slammed the stack on the table. Then he got up and walked away, just like I had when I saw it.

Sinkovich reached for the stack and searched until he found the photograph of the cop flicking his cigarette ash on Foster.

"I even know this prick," he said. "He's one of the ones who pushed for me getting kicked off the force."

"Who is he?" Johnson asked.

"Ed Joravski," Sinkovich said. "We went to school to-gether."

"He's from your neighborhood?" I asked.

"Naw. A couple of blocks west and about a mile south. He moved out, but he hasn't really left. No one does . . ." His voice trailed off and then he stood, bending over the map.

After a moment, he put his finger on an intersection just inside the neighborhood we were studying.

"There," Sinkovich said. "He grew up there."

"You think the police did this?" Johnson's hands were braced on the sink. His head was down, but his body shook with repressed rage.

"Naw. These guys think they're honest. They're upholding life as we—they—know it."

Johnson raised his head and slowly turned to face Sinkovich. We both caught the slip, only I was willing to let it go. Apparently Johnson wasn't.

"We?" he asked.

Sinkovich's jaw worked. The spots of color in his face had grown to encompass his cheeks and were starting to move down to his chin.

"Look," he said holding out his hands as if he expected us to attack him and he was going to fend us off. "I was raised a certain way. It ain't pretty and I ain't proud of it, but I didn't think nothing of it until that boy died last summer."

"Why would that change anything?" Johnson asked, his voice harsh. "You've seen dead black children before."

"Sure. But I could always explain it away, you know? The gangs or the drugs." Sinkovich apparently realized what position his hands were in, because he brought them together and interlaced the fingers. "Then this kid—and you guys, wanting to stick with your own because you didn't trust white detectives."

"Why should we?" Johnson whirled, grabbed the photo of the cigarette smoker and shoved it in Sinkovich's face. "You people do this."

Sinkovich held his position. He didn't even unclasp his hands. "I never did nothing like that."

"No?" Johnson glanced at me. "Bill tells me you enjoyed doing riot control at the Democratic National Convention. You beat college students with nightsticks."

The color drained from Sinkovich's face. "And I can't stop thinking about it. I dream about it every night, the way that stick sounded when it hit a kid's head. I could feel the shot move in my glove, scraping my fingers, when I punched somebody. I sat up most nights smoking because I couldn't sleep, then the wife took my cigarettes away. Hell, I still can't sleep. Then Grimshaw here, he tells me that I violate people's rights all the time, and now all I'm trying to do is help, and my wife steals my kid, and you guys treat me like I'm the goddamn enemy."

He grabbed the photograph out of Johnson's hand and stood so that they were eye to eye. "I would never, ever, violate a person like this. It's wrong. I don't care if I hated the dead guy for doing something to me personal, I'd never ever do this to a corpse. You can't just blame me because I'm the only white guy in the room."

"Why the hell not?" Johnson asked. "That's what you people do to us."

"That's enough." I stood, grabbed the photographs and stacked them. "I didn't bring these pictures out here so you guys would start reenacting Birmingham. I brought them because of what Sinkovich said about Hucke. If he's a precinct captain, then he's got friends on the force, right?"

"If some precinct captain tried to hide some murderer's trail," Sinkovich said, "no cop would cover for him."

He was still glaring at Johnson, who hadn't moved either. I put my hands between them and pushed them apart.

"Concentrate, Truman," I said. "We have a dead woman on our hands and she's the tenth victim that we know about."

Johnson didn't seem to hear me. "Maybe the problem's the definition of murder. Any man who would do that to a corpse doesn't see the victim as human."

Sinkovich moved away from us. "Give us some credit. There's something else going on here."

"What could that possibly be?" Johnson asked.

I frowned, let my hand fall. "Delevan said something yesterday."

Both men looked at me.

"He was fighting me, saying no one would deliberately kill

Foster. But after a while, he got nervous. It was pretty clear to me that he knew his neighbors were capable of beating someone to death and calling it an accident."

"He said that to you?" Johnson asked.

"Not quite that plainly, but yeah."

Sinkovich nodded. "If these cops think someone they know is involved, and they think it's accidental, then they'll cover it."

"Especially if the victim isn't human," Johnson said.

"Even if the victim is white," Sinkovich said.

They stared at each other.

"A knife wound isn't accidental," I said, "and it was really clear that Foster wasn't beaten."

"But by the time they found that out, they'd already mucked up the corpse. See, guys who beat up black guys, if they're good, they don't go for nothing that'll show. They'll fight dirty, break some ribs, but stay away from the face," Sinkovich said.

"Like you used to do?" Johnson asked.

"I never did nothing like that," Sinkovich said.

"Except at the Convention."

Sinkovich's shoulders drooped and he stopped looking at both of us. After a moment, he said, "Guess I done all I can here, Grimshaw. I'm gonna head back. You need something, you call."

"Stay, Jack," I said.

Sinkovich shook his head. "I'll catch ya later."

And then he was gone.

I whirled toward Johnson. "Jesus, Truman, we need him. He has connections that we don't have. He can go in and out of that neighborhood with no problem. He can talk to people and they'll talk back without being suspicious."

Johnson's eyes narrowed. "Maybe you believe that little sob story, but I don't. How do we know he's not just passing our information on to all his little buddies from high school?"

"Why would he do that after last week? After all he's been through?"

"To get back in their good graces." Johnson said this so flatly that I knew he believed it.

"Look, Truman, I think he's actually been going through some kind of change. He had no idea I was working this when he stopped here last week. And he has been extremely helpful."

Johnson shook his head. "Sometimes your idealism surprises me, Grimshaw, it really does. You look down the ass-end of humanity and come up with gold."

I didn't like the analogy. "I don't think you understand—"

"No." His voice was firm. "I don't think you do. Chicago's not Memphis. We have a long-standing tradition of graft and corruption. Either you flow with it or you lose."

"Do you flow with it?" I asked.

"I ignore it a lot," he said, "and when you ignore it, it ignores you. But when you buck against it, you could get killed."

"You're saying that's what happened to these people?"

"No, I'm saying that with a precinct captain involved—"

"We don't know that."

"—and the appearance of some police involvement, the stakes have gone way up. You ever hear of Benjamin Lewis?"

"No," I said, feeling wary.

"Lewis was one of Daley's house niggers. Daley still has them, aldermen who say, 'Yasuh, Mistah Daley,' and 'Nosuh, Mistah Daley,' and never once think about the people they represent."

I crossed my arms. I was beginning to hate the way people kept telling me that I didn't understand Chicago.

"At the end of sixty-two, Lewis starts believing his own press. He starts easing the white precinct captains out of the ward. Some say he was talking about keeping a larger share of the ward's gambling money, but I don't think Lewis was that smart."

"Gambling money?" I asked.

Johnson held up a finger to keep me quiet. "Next thing you know, Lewis is murdered, found in his office handcuffed to a chair with three slugs in the back of his head."

"Mob hit," I said.

"Looked that way, but no one got arrested. And the white

precinct captains stayed, and control stayed in the hands of those guys who always had it."

"You think Daley did that?" I asked.

"Mayor Daley." Johnson gave me a cold smile. "Mayor Daley denies that any of this goes on, and I think he actually believes that. He knows about the machine and uses the machine and turns a blind eye when it makes a mistake."

"So did he give an order and turn a blind eye?" I asked.

Johnson shook his head. "Daley's too political for something like that. He must have been mad, though. Someone wasn't thinking. There was a tight mayoral primary coming up in a few weeks, and this created a minor stink. Not a major one because, as the Democrats kept saying, 'Thank God Lewis wasn't a white guy.' "

"Why am I supposed to care about this right now?" I asked.

"Because it shows that those precinct captains have a direct route to the seat of power. If we bring any one of them down even by implication, we're attacking the mayor. He'll quash us like nothing. He'll throw me and Sinkovich out of uniform and find a way to get rid of you without touching you at all."

"We don't know that this guy Hucke covered up anything," I said. "We're making assumptions."

"I'm making an assumption," Johnson said.

"And you warned me about that just this morning."

He nodded. "But I know how this city works, and even though this isn't evidence that'll stand up in court, it more than convicts Hucke in my eyes."

"Not mine," I said.

"So you're going to go after him."

"No," I said. "I'm going to meet him and his neighbors and treat them all like suspects. Maybe that'll lead us to the real killer. Or maybe it'll just eliminate them and force us down a different route."

Johnson leaned against my stove and crossed his arms. He looked like a professor about to chastise a student who hadn't studied. "What will you do when you get your proof?"

"What do you mean?" I asked.

"Let's say I'm right. Let's say Hucke is covering for someone. Hucke represents the entire machine, and he's not going to let go. Who will arrest our killer?"

"You," I said. "Maybe Sinkovich."

"Why?" Johnson asked.

"People are dying, Truman."

"*Black* people, Grimshaw. They die every day. Why should we care?"

If I hadn't known that he did, I would have been shocked at his tone of voice. I knew he was baiting me.

"Because this is murder, Johnson. Murder on a large scale, and someone's got to care."

"There it is again," Johnson said. "You're staring down the shit hole and expecting to find gold. Where did that idealism come from? You should know better."

"Stop patronizing me," I snapped.

"I'm not," Johnson said. "I'm just telling you that we can't do anything. If we get evidence and we find out that Hucke has been covering for our guy, then no one will arrest him—or if I do, I'm done, out of this job, *finito*. And I like to think that I do some good on occasion. Not all the time, but some of the time."

"What about the FBI?" I asked, feeling uncomfortable as I did. I hated the FBI, but they had their uses. However, if they were on any case, I'd have to make sure Jimmy and I stayed far out of their way. "They're supposed to look at multiples."

"The Chicago branch of the FBI?"

"C'mon," I said. "Not everyone in this city's corrupt."

"Not everyone," Johnson said. "But some of us are practical. No one connected with this town will go after anyone who is protected by a precinct captain. Not even the high and mighty *Tribune*. The *Defender* might, but no one in government or anywhere else cares what the *Defender* prints. More paranoia from the Negroes, they'll say, and that's what it'll be."

"So we let this go on?" I couldn't keep the shock from my voice.

"That's one choice," Johnson said.

"You sound like there's another," I said.

He raised his eyebrows at me. "How do you know our copy-cat's gone?"

My breath left my body. I felt it disappear, like I felt the warmth leave my skin. Johnson had known, even though I never told him, that I had killed the man who menaced Jimmy and Laura. I had had no choice. In the year of assassinations, I too had become an assassin.

And it wasn't a role I cared to repeat.

"Be clear," I said.

Johnson tilted his head slightly. "I'm just saying that no one would care if a slimeball like this got taken out."

"Not even his cronies in the government? Not even the mayor?"

Johnson shrugged. "Stuff would leak about him, just like it did about Lewis. Someone would assume that the last victim turned the tables and killed the killer instead."

"Or they'd investigate and find the man who took him out."

"Not if that man was good at moving around," Johnson said.

I stared at him, unable to believe what he had just said. He was encouraging me to kill another human being, and him a cop, a cop whom I had mistaken for a good man.

"You can get out of my house," I said.

"Grimshaw, look—"

"Jesus, Johnson, I came to you for help. I came to you because we have a problem we need to solve legally. And then you throw this at me."

"Sometimes that's the only way," he said.

It certainly had been for me last August. But I had arrived to find Laura's and Jim's lives in danger. I had acted in the heat of the moment, not with the cold, rational calm that Johnson now had.

"Sometimes it is," I said, "but not this time. We haven't explored all our options yet."

"Explore, then," he said. "You'll see that I'm right."

I shook my head. "I thought you were a cop."

"I am a cop."

"A cop who wants a vigilante partner on the side, some killing machine he can let loose when he's afraid the system will fail him."

"The system will fail us," Johnson said. "You know that. No one's going to care about these people and no one's going to act."

"So I should?" I said. "Every time I find injustice against black people, I should take matters into my own hands because you're not strong enough to fight the system that you're part of, the system you claim to believe in? Do you know what you're asking?"

"Yes," he said.

"No you don't." I took a step toward him. He actually stood up straighter. I must have looked menacing. "You're asking me to become no better than this nameless, faceless creature who is out there murdering people for God knows what reason. I'm sure it's rational to him. I'm sure it makes perfect sense, and I'm sure he believes the system would fail him, too."

"It's not the same," Johnson said.

"Isn't it?" I asked. "Tell me how it's different."

He stared at me. His mouth moved, then he shook his head. "These killings can't continue."

"So stop them, Truman. That's your job."

He shook his head slightly. "You know, I thought I'd finally found someone else who knew what we're up against every day, every moment, of our lives. Someone who actually had a sense of the way the world works."

He pushed off the stove and walked toward the coatrack.

"But?" I asked.

"But I should have realized how naïve you are when I found out that you and Franklin Grimshaw were related. You still think the system works sometimes."

"You sound no different than that Black Panther I heard a week ago Saturday," I said.

Johnson shrugged on his coat. "Sometimes," he said, "the revolutionaries have a point."

TWENTY-SIX

I was still shaking with fury as I drove to pick up the kids. When I pulled into the parking lot, I saw that the playground was full of young Blackstone Rangers, their red tams dull in the twilight gray. They seemed to be having some sort of rally, although I couldn't see a speaker. They didn't seem to be threatening anyone else, even though part of me wished they were.

That same part of me wanted to vent this anger, to let it loose and do harm while also doing good.

In essence, do exactly what Johnson was suggesting.

Jimmy and the Grimshaw children were not outside. I had to go inside the school to get them. They were watching the playground through the window, the expression on their faces the same—fear.

I had no solution for any of this, save a fantasy one in which I waved my arms and all things were equal—schools, justice, friendship. But I didn't have that power. No one did. And I couldn't think of anyplace to go to find it.

Jimmy saw me and smiled. He didn't hug me, although I could see him check the impulse in front of Keith. The boys moved the younger children forward, and they all marched in a clump toward the car, just like Franklin and I had instructed them.

No one on the playground noticed. It was as if we weren't even there.

330

I stopped at the Grimshaws' when I dropped off the children. I wanted to talk to Althea, to thank her for taking over every time I'd asked her to. As yet, I didn't know how to repay her or Franklin, but I would think of something.

For the sake of my own pride, I would have to.

As I followed the children to the door, Malcolm came down the walk. His eyes twinkled as he caught my arm and kept me from going inside.

"I found it," he said.

I had no idea what he was talking about.

"I found the watch."

Even after he had clarified, it took me a moment to remember. He had found the watch that the Stones had stolen from Gus and Van and then pawned. Even though I had given him the assignment ten days before, it seemed like an entire lifetime ago.

"Are you sure it's the right one?"

"It matches the description," he said. "Besides, it was in the pawnshop near the Stones' headquarters on Sixty-seventh. Word is, they use it a lot."

"Word?" I asked.

He grinned at me. "I still have friends in low places, Smokey."

"The kids see the watch yet? Have they confirmed it?"

"No," he said, his grin fading. "And we have another problem, too."

"What's that?"

"The watch is selling for fifty dollars, no negotiation."

"None? It's a pawnshop." My stomach sank. I couldn't afford fifty dollars for a good deed. Not right now.

Malcolm nodded. "I got him down from seventy-five, but he won't go lower. The guy behind the counter wasn't acting like it was his idea."

I sighed. "All right. But I don't want to take the boys down into Stones country. It doesn't seem safe."

"There's lots of little kids there," Malcolm said.

"All wearing suns, I'll bet."

"Most."

I shook my head. "Let's see what we can do first. If we need Gus or Van, we'll bring them back."

"All right," Malcolm said. "You want to go now?"

"I can't," I said. "I have to take Jimmy home. I've been imposing on Franklin and Althea too much as it is."

"I don't think the watch's going to be there long."

"At fifty bucks, it will be," I said.

Malcolm moved closer to me. "I think a couple of Stones have their eyes on it. I think if they push hard enough, they might get a gangland discount."

In other words, they might take it and no questions would be asked. But if they could do that, so could I.

"We'll go tomorrow. I'll meet you about three," I said. "And you'll play along with me, no matter what. Got it?"

"Yeah," he said, then bounced a little. "Hey, Smoke. Does it always feel this good to crack a case?"

"I wish," I said, and went inside.

The next morning, I awoke tangled in my sheets. The heat was up again, the radiator clicking away beside me. In my sleep, I'd continued the argument with Johnson and Sinkovich, screaming at them to get along, to find another way to handle their differences while we tried to solve this puzzle.

As dawn filtered through my thin curtains, I realized that the dream was telling me something as well. There had to be another solution, a way to take care of this murderer without becoming murderers ourselves—and I had an idea how to do it.

I got out of bed and grabbed my robe, feeling confident for the first time in days. I had a lot to set up, but I had a hunch my idea would work, given enough time and planning.

I took the kids to school to make up for Franklin covering for me the day before. After I had dropped them off, noting once again the large group of Stones in the playground and no Gang

Intelligence Unit van, I drove north to Rogers Park. Once again, I needed Epstein's help.

I normally didn't drop in on white people, particularly before ten in the morning, but this time, I thought it was best. If I called ahead, Epstein could refuse to see me or leave the house. This way, I might catch him by surprise.

The neighborhood seemed even quieter than usual. Most of the houses seemed dark and empty with the men off to work and the children off to school.

I parked in my usual place in front of the Weisman house. As I got out of the car, I reflected on how comfortable I was in this neighborhood versus Hucke's neighborhood. Here, despite the attack, I didn't feel the need to take my gun out of the glove box.

The weather had warmed from the day before, but the clouds overhead were dark and menacing. The air smelled damp. I pulled my coat closer, went to the outside porch door and rang the bell.

There were four candlesticks in the menorah, and they had dried wax drips down their sides. Mrs. Weisman was adding candles to mark the days of Hannukah, trying to keep some semblance of normal, at least.

Footsteps, then the curtain swished on the interior door before it opened. Mrs. Weisman saw me and waved as she unlocked the porch door.

"Mr. Grimshaw," she said with pleasure. "To what do we owe this honor?"

"I need to see Saul, Mrs. Weisman."

Her smile faded. "He doesn't want to see anyone right now."

"I know, but I need his help."

She put a hand on my arm. "I don't think he's in the position to help anyone, Mr. Grimshaw."

"Let's let him decide that, shall we?"

She took a deep breath, squared her shoulders, then led me inside.

The house smelled of coffee. Yesterday's *Chicago Tribune* sat unread on the dining-room table on top of a pile of mail. A man's jacket hung on the back of one of the dining-room chairs. Mrs. Weisman picked it up by the collar as she went past.

"He's upstairs," she said quietly. "He goes up there now when the bell rings."

Leaving his grandmother to take care of any problems that arise. He probably didn't even realize the position he was putting her in. The phrase she had used the day before—a pity-party—rose again in my mind. That was the precise word for it. Right now, Saul Epstein couldn't see past himself.

"Thanks," I said to Mrs. Weisman.

She gave me a small, nervous smile, then pulled the upstairs door open and I looked at the narrow, old-fashioned steps. They had a carpet runner going down their middle, held in place by little gold dowels. The carpet was so old and thin that I could see the wood beneath it.

These stairs creaked, and as I climbed, I braced myself for Epstein's reaction. Somehow I would have to get through his anger, confusion, and fear, something his grandmother hadn't been able to do.

The ceiling was low on the second part of the staircase, following the slope of the roof. As I stepped into the hallway, I realized that most of the second story was a converted attic, with rooms extending all the way to the eaves. There was a musty smell up here, like old mothballs, and I suspected that no matter what Mrs. Weisman did, that smell wouldn't leave.

Three closed doors faced me—two on the long side of the hallway and one at the end. I knocked on the first. "Saul?"

He didn't answer, so I turned the glass knob and pushed the door open. The room was small and dark, with the shades pulled down and the bed made. It looked like no one had been in that room for a long time.

Then I went to the next door and knocked on it. "Saul, I know you can hear me. Open up. I'm not going away."

There was no answer here either, but I heard a shuffling inside the room. I knocked again, then opened the door.

The shades were drawn here as well, but the overhead light was on, the old-fashioned bulb sending yellow light throughout the room.

Saul sat on the edge of a narrow, twin-sized bed, his feet barely touching the floor. His right arm was in a sling, which surprised me because I hadn't heard of any damage there. A thick bandage covered his left eye and the shaved part of his skull. The rest of his face was varying shades of purple and black, but not as swollen as I would have expected.

"Leave me alone," he said without turning toward me.

"I'm sorry to bother you, but I do need to talk to you."

"I told Gram I'm not seeing anyone." His voice was flat.

"I know," I said. "I bullied my way past. I said it was important."

"You have the pictures. We're even now."

Even? It took me a moment to realize what he meant. Those photographs in return for saving his life.

"I'm not coming to make any kind of claim on you, Saul."

"Good." He turned toward me, then gasped, and clutched his left side with his left hand. The broken ribs probably pained him more than the other injuries. "Get out."

"I want to give you a chance at a story, something that will—"

"I can't fucking see anything!" He screamed the words. "Think about it! How can I do a goddamn story if I can't see?"

"You can see," I said. "You're looking at me now."

"Human beings measure depth of field and perspective with both eyes. I only have one now. I'm not a photographer anymore. So find someone else."

"I wasn't coming for your photographic skills," I said. "I came because you're the only national reporter I know."

He turned away from me. "I'm not working right now."

"What about later?" I asked. "When do you plan to go back to work?"

"I don't know. I'm not thinking of that."

"So you're living off your grandmother's charity?"

His lips twitched, but he didn't say anything.

"Tell you what," I said. "I'll explain what's going on and you can tell me if you want to participate."

"I don't. Go away."

"This is an opportunity to make your name as a reporter, Saul. Maybe put you on the staff of a national paper like the *New York Times*."

He didn't say anything. I took his silence as encouragement and walked deeper into the room, hunching over, until I reached a rocking chair so old that the paint had peeled off its arms. I sat, turning it so I faced him.

His single eye met mine, his expression both hostile and filled with pain. I did not look away.

"The man whose body you found last month," I said, "was one of a series of victims, all of whom died like he did, their bodies posed just as his was."

Epstein remained still. I figured as long as he didn't protest, I had his attention.

"These deaths have two other features that link them together. All of the victims were black, and all of them had visited a certain neighborhood just before they died." I lied about that last, since we still weren't sure about some of the victims. "The homicide detective who has been working most of these cases and I have reason to believe that the local precinct captain might be involved, probably protecting the perpetrator."

Epstein's single eyebrow went down into a frown. He winced, but leaned forward, his free hand bracing his sore ribs.

"If we're right, then an arrest won't do any good. His friend will be back on the street within hours. The local papers won't touch the story—"

"*Daily News* might," Epstein said. "They're not fond of the machine."

Got him. I kept the smile off my face, and worked to keep the pleasure at his response out of my voice. " 'Might' being the key word. We need someone who will cover it—or who will work the story until someone picks it up."

"What can an outside newspaper do?" Epstein asked.

"Shed a little light on the darkness. Your photographs also show some police involvement in the cover-up. We have evidence of crimes of long-standing. If these were white victims, you and I wouldn't be having this conversation. The cops would be taking care of it, and the machine would be behind them. But these killings have gone on for more than two years."

"Light on the darkness?" Epstein asked. "What the hell does that mean?"

This was the crucial part of the argument. He had to understand what I was after. "Chicago is not a very popular place right now. With the Walker Report declaring the events at the Convention a police riot, the national mood is ripe to hear more about police corruption in Chicago. If we bring out the fact that the police are allowing a murderer with multiple homicides to go free—maybe even collaborating with him because they're not fond of the victims—the story will get national press."

"So?" Epstein said.

"If it gets national press, outside pressure will be brought to bear on the city. They'll have to prosecute this guy."

"Outside pressure from whom? Elaine—" His voice broke. He took two deep breaths and began again. "Elaine pretty much educated me on how much white people don't care about black people."

"Well, black people care about black people," I said, "and some organizations have national clout. The national NAACP and the Southern Christian Leadership Conference will jump all over this. And if we move it out of Chicago's insular world, we give people like Jesse Jackson a chance to speak out as well. He wouldn't dare if we just stayed within the city."

"Elaine said he's an opportunist."

"That's what we need right now," I said. "Besides, there are white groups that will take up this cause, seeing it as theirs because of the events of last summer."

Epstein shook his head slightly. "This would have appealed to me two weeks ago."

"Why doesn't it now?" I asked.

"Because it sounds naïve. Newspapers don't change the world."

"No," I said. "Information does. Right now, this city has a stranglehold on information coming out of the Black Belt. No one really knows or cares what it's like down there, and when the news does come out, it comes out in distorted ways, ways that make it seem like our fault that we live in terrible conditions or our children are killing each other in gang wars."

"You don't want me to write about that, though."

"I'm asking you to help us stop a single person or a single group of people who are using murder to forward their own ends."

"Gangs do that."

"Yes, they do," I said. "But a series of newspaper articles wouldn't stop the Blackstone Rangers. It will stop a small group of white killers because those people can be put behind bars."

There was a light in his eye for the first time since I'd come up here. "I'm no good to you. I can't take photographs—"

"You already took the photographs," I said. "A number of the ones you gave me from the Foster crime scene tell the entire story."

"Then what do you want from me?" he asked.

"I want you to write this up in an article or a series of articles. I want you to come with us tomorrow when we get the proof we need against these guys. And I want you to write about the victims, people who were just going through their daily lives when someone attacked them for being different."

"Like me and Elaine," he said softly.

"Yes," I said.

"You asking because of me and Elaine?" he asked and this time, his voice had an edge to it.

"I'd be lying if I said that wasn't part of it, but that's not all of it. I need the national connection."

He rubbed his left hand on his thigh, thinking. "I can barely move."

"You wouldn't have to get out of the car."

"This is a lot of work to do on spec."

"Yes, it is," I said. "But what else are you doing right now?"

His neck got red. I couldn't tell if the rest of his face colored as well, because the bruising was so bad on his skin.

"All right," he said after a long moment. "Tell me what I have to do."

TWENTY-SEVEN

When I got home, I called Jane Sarton and asked her to meet me at Delevan's house at one o'clock. Then I hung up and stared at the phone on my office desk for a long moment.

I needed the help of at least one police officer, and only two knew of this case. Sinkovich, whom Johnson said I couldn't trust because of his links to that neighborhood, and Johnson, who had asked me to rationally consider the unthinkable.

I was more inclined to call Sinkovich. He seemed uncomplicated and sincere. But I wasn't uncomplicated, and I'd been known to be sincere when I was lying to get someone else to do something I wanted them to do. In the short time that I'd known him, he hadn't been consistent. He'd been helpful and barbarous, and for a while, hadn't understood the difference.

I wasn't sure that he understood the difference now, either.

With a sigh, I sat down behind my desk and pulled the phone toward me. Its hard plastic shell felt like a weapon. My fingerprints coated the black surface, and there was an ink stain on the clear rotary dial. The choice I made now was the most important one of the day.

If I were completely honest with myself, I would have to admit that Johnson had scared me. I understood his arguments; I would have to be a hypocrite not to. But his willingness to turn, so fast, to a solution that had nothing to do with law and order, that had everything to do with the kind of vigilantism that we were fighting, made me distrust him more than I distrusted Sinkovich.

I needed to try this my way. If it didn't work, then Johnson could find someone else to settle it his way.

I picked up the receiver and called him. And as I listened to the phone ring, I wondered if I would have to apologize, even though I felt like I hadn't done anything wrong. I wondered if Johnson would even speak to me after our encounter the day before.

The dispatch answered and informed me that Johnson was out on a case. I told her it was urgent, but not an emergency, and that he should call. She promised to have him call back as soon as he got my message.

I pressed the button and hung up, leaving the receiver beside my ear. I could call Sinkovich, but I knew, in that instant, that I wouldn't. I knew that Johnson wanted this perp. I wasn't so sure about Sinkovich.

Maybe I would call him in the morning.

I knew it would take at least twenty-four hours to put all the pieces in place. I also knew that I needed to go over the notes one last time to make sure I wasn't missing anything obvious.

I spent the afternoon reviewing photographs and reading the police files.

A little after three, Malcolm arrived, just like we had arranged. He was still in a good mood, and he was dressed just like I had asked him to be—in dark colors, looking as sedate as he could.

"You ready?" he asked at my office door.

I closed the last of the files. "I guess."

"Tough case?" Apparently he noticed that I wasn't smiling.

"Yeah," I said, and didn't add anything else. "I'll meet you in the living room."

He nodded his understanding and went down the hall. I opened my bottom drawer and took out my shoulder holster, slipping it on. Then I grabbed the lightweight jacket I'd purposely left on the chair across from the desk and put it on.

I didn't bring any gloves. I wanted to have full use of my hands, and the cold wasn't bad enough to slow me down.

Earlier, I had cleaned the cash out of my wallet, not that I had much. I made certain that I had a twenty-dollar bill, though, the most I would contribute to the cause of the lost watch. I didn't want to be tempted to spend more, and deny Jimmy a good hot meal or one of the Grimshaw kids a Christmas present.

By prearrangement, Jimmy was staying with the Grimshaws until I dropped off Malcolm. I hoped we could get Grace Kirkland to teach the kids after school. Otherwise, I might have to hire someone to watch Jimmy from three until six or seven.

When we reached my car, Malcolm got in the passenger side. I got in the driver's side, closed the door, and then leaned across him, pulling the glove box open.

His eyes widened when he saw my gun. "What the hell?"

"I don't like the neighborhood we're going to," I said, and stuck the gun in my shoulder holster. Then I started the car and we were off.

Malcolm kept glancing at me as I drove south several blocks to Sixty-seventh and Blackstone. Most of the South Side, even the gang sections, had a vibrancy to them—a lot of people filling the streets, going about their business, even though many of them wore tams.

But this neighborhood didn't. In the approaching darkness of the late afternoon, it looked abandoned. On one side of the street, an empty lot was covered with brown grass and broken bottles. On the other, wood buildings leaned together, so old and fragile that it looked as if a good shout would knock them down.

Three had signs—one was a pool hall, the other a pawnshop, and beyond that, a bar. The rest were homes, or what had once been homes. They looked pretty empty now.

Beyond the empty lot was the back of a warehouse. The huge

wall was covered in graffiti. Most of it was done in blue spray paint, the words unreadable at a distance. But someone had spent a lot of time on a central image, which dominated the wall.

The painting—and it was a painting—depicted a mountain with a red sun behind it. A blue four-pointed star filled the center of the mountain. Forming a circle around the mountain were these words: "Almighty Black P. Stone."

The Black P. Stone Nation, still commonly called the Blackstone Rangers. We were in the heart of their territory now.

Malcolm swallowed audibly. I glanced at him. "You came down here alone?"

"I wasn't alone," he said. "I had a few friends with me."

I didn't like it. Not a single car had passed us since we turned onto Sixty-seventh. The only other cars on the road were rusted-out hulks, some stripped for parts. In an alley, I noticed several cars cherried out and untouched. A white van, its engine running, appeared to be stalled two intersections down.

I parked in front of the pawnshop. "You listen to me," I said while I glanced in the rearview mirror. So far, no one was coming toward us. "If I tell you to do something, you do it, no questions asked."

"Okay," Malcolm said.

He was scared now, probably because of my mood. I didn't care. I got out of the car and he followed.

A drop of something wet and cold hit my forehead, startling me. I wiped it off, looked at my fingers, saw water. I wasn't sure what I had been expecting. Another drop hit me, then another, and another, thicker than rain, but not light enough to be snow.

Malcolm raised the collar of his coat and ducked inside the shop. I followed, shivering. My jacket wasn't good protection in this weather.

The pawnshop was small and dark. An overhead light barely penetrated the gloom. A reading lamp sat on one of the glass cases. It was on, but illuminated little else than the merchandise below it. The shop smelled of must and incense mixed with cigarette smoke so ancient I suspected it coated everything in a layer of yellow.

Directly behind the lamp, a man sat up. The reading lamp's glare hid his features.

"Help you?" he asked in a voice raspy from too many cigarettes.

I let the door bang closed behind us. "I understand you have my watch."

Malcolm stiffened beside me.

"I have a lot of watches," the man said. "Could be there's one for you here."

"You misunderstand me." I walked toward him. "You have *my* watch. It was given to my father. It's silver, quite old and distinctive, with an E and a G intertwined on the back."

His face become clearer the closer I got. He was thin and balding. He had a graying beard that was tobacco-stained around the mouth. A reddish-brown mole, large as one of my fingernails, protruded from the skin beneath his left eye.

"Got a watch like that," he said. "You got proof it's yours?"

"I don't need proof," I said. "It was stolen from my son a month ago on the El. We've been looking for it ever since."

"You're awful big to have something stolen from you," the man said, and it took me a moment to realize he was looking past me at Malcolm.

"His younger brother," I said.

The man's bushy gray eyebrows went up. He reached into the case in front of him and pulled out a pocket watch. It had been polished, the silver so shiny that it reflected the light.

"How'd I know your boy here didn't just tell you about it last night and you decided to make believe it's yours?"

I scanned his case. There were some other overpriced watches inside, several diamond engagement rings, and a ruby-and-pearl necklace that looked real.

"Because," I said, my voice low, "if I wanted to steal from you in that way, do you think I'd go for the stupid watch?"

His eyes widened a little. "I don't give stuff over without

344

proof. You want the watch, you pay for it, same as everyone else. I'm out cash for this thing, and I mean to get it back."

"Get it from the Stone who sold it to you," I said. "I'm not paying you."

"How're you going to avoid it?" he asked, and I watched his other hand move to a hidden part of the counter, probably going for his gun.

"There are a variety of ways," I said. "I could appeal to your good nature."

"Tried that just now, didn't you?" he asked. "Failed because I don't have one."

"I could reason with you."

"Nope," he said.

"Or I could call the police and tell them I have proof you're fencing for the Stones. It's illegal to traffick in stolen goods."

"Like the cops don't know what I do." But his hand shook.

"I'm sure they need proof, just like you said you do. And at home, I have proof that this watch is mine."

Behind him, something rattled. My eyes were becoming adjusted to the strange light. Someone had come through a beaded curtain strung across the back.

Malcolm still stood near the door. He nodded toward the curtain as if I hadn't noticed it.

But it was the man behind the counter who looked the most nervous. In fact, he looked terrified.

"Look," he said. "I'm out about fifty bucks on this watch. You pay me and we'll call it even, okay?"

"No," I said.

The other man stepped into the light. He wasn't much older than Malcolm. He wore his red sun down over one eye and a leather jacket so new that it was still shiny.

"I been hearin' 'bout an old man who been causin' trouble," the newcomer said. "Kids in the back, they tell me it's you. Threatenin' little boys, knockin' one in the nuts so bad he couldn't walk for a week. We don't like that shit around here."

So someone in the back had recognized me. "I don't like your shit either," I said. "I'm just trying to find a way to live with

345

it. But somehow you keep interfering with my life."

"Interferin', Gramps?"

"Messing with my kids," I said. "Stealing my possessions. I don't like any of it."

"You a one-man army? You think you can stop us. Cops can't even stop us."

"That's because they got rules to follow," I said, repeating what I had said at the playground a few days ago. "I don't."

"What you got with you, a bazooka? Because we got more guns on you than you ever seen all at once."

"I doubt that," I said, sounding calmer than I felt. My heart rate was up. The anger that I'd been suppressing was right below the surface, ready to serve as fuel for anything that came my way.

Malcolm shifted, then glanced at the door as if he wanted to escape through it.

The man behind the counter still held the watch. "Tell you what," he said to me, his voice two pitches higher from his fear. "Thirty bucks and its yours."

"No," I said. "I'm not paying for the watch because it already is mine."

"See?" said the younger man. "That's what I hear about you, Gramps. You ain't reasonable. The man gave you an offer."

"A bad offer, considering the watch was stolen from me."

"But if you take it, Gramps, maybe we can have us a little talk."

"What do you care about whether I pay him?" I asked.

The Stone shrugged. "You focus on stupid shit. Stupid and small. I don' like stupid or small. It bores me, man. And I hate bein' bored."

Malcolm shifted again. I wished I had explained my thinking to him before we arrived. I figured that if we encountered a few Stones, we could talk our way out of the problem. The Stones were still trying to look reasonable in the eyes of the law. If they weren't going to be reasonable with us, well then, that was what my gun was for.

"Why should I care about how you're feeling?" I said. "I'm

talking to this gentleman here about my watch. You've just butted into the conversation."

"Settle this," he said to the man behind the counter. "Or we got to deal with it."

The threat seemed like it was directed at him, but it was really directed at me.

"You want to deal with me?" I asked. "Fine. Let's deal. I have some information that you guys might be interested in."

He turned slowly, a move so calculated that it had to be practiced. "What kinda information?"

"Some things that the Gang Intelligence Unit is planning." I figured if he knew who I was, he would believe this. I'd been seen talking to the Unit more than once. "I'll trade that information for your guarantee that you'll leave my family alone."

Malcolm had come up beside me, his rigid young form guarding my back.

"Okay, Gramps." The Stone grabbed the watch from the pawnbroker and tossed it at me. I caught it with one hand, neatly, the way a pro ball player would snatch a fast-moving baseball out of the sky. "I ain't the one you talk to 'bout this. You come wit me."

I followed and so did Malcolm. The cigarette stench grew behind the beaded curtain, the smell so thick that the tobacco oils seemed to actually live in the air. An accumulation of junk, some of it decades old, was piled against a wall in the back. Boxes covered another wall, and a small table, obviously used to repair some items, sat near the door.

The Stone pushed open a wall panel that led directly into the next building. Malcolm and I followed.

We were in a dark, narrow hallway. The cigarette odor faded here, replaced by the faint, malty scent of beer, the kind of smell that old bars had. To our left, a boy with a short-cropped afro bent over a desk. From the back, he looked like someone doing schoolwork, but as I got closer, I realized he was cleaning a gun.

The Stone opened a doorway on his right and we entered a large room that had no furniture, only a stage built into one wall and murals covering the others. The murals had a pink background and depicted famous black faces. They seemed to move in some sort of progression, a progression that I didn't understand.

The largest faces belonged to Martin Luther King, Jr., and Jeff Fort, the leader of the Blackstone Rangers. The two men stood side by side, with Malcolm X in the background.

"You wait," the Stone said, then went back through the door.

Malcolm shifted. The wooden floor beneath him squeaked. "I don't like this."

I didn't reply. Instead, I stared at the painting of Jeff Fort for a moment. I'd seen him on television a number of times, and I'd passed him on the street. He could make logical arguments and he might listen to reason. But he had a coldness in his eyes that rational men didn't have.

While I waited, I walked around the room, studying the mural. It had clearly been painted by a talented amateur—or maybe a series of amateurs. There were words mixed into the flowered backdrop, and faces I didn't recognize. But the ones I did were famous—Nat King Cole, Aretha Franklin. Not something I would expect to find down here.

I heard a shuffling from the door before it opened, and I turned quickly.

Three young men entered. All were older than Malcolm, though not by much. None of them were Jeff Fort, but they clearly had some kind of power. One had a long, thin goatee; another hunched forward in his leather jacket; the last, the shortest one, had a pair of coke-bottle-thick wire-rimmed glasses.

Here in this room, without their friends behind them, they didn't seem that tough. But I wasn't going to take any chances.

I'd already noted two other ways out of this back area besides the door they used. The stage had two exits on either side, and I would wager one of them led to the back. I also thought I saw the outline of a door inside the mural.

The Stone who'd brought us in stepped into the room and closed the door behind him.

"I hear you gonna make us a deal, old man," said Goatee.

"It's real simple," I said. "I have some information you can use. If I give it to you, you swear to keep your people away from my family."

"Now why'd we care 'bout your people?" Glasses asked.

"I don't know," I said. "But you tried to recruit two of my boys. I protested, and now they and their sisters are being harassed."

Malcolm stood beside me, feet apart, face impassive. At least he was keeping up a good front.

"It's best for boys to join with us," said Leather Jacket.

"Maybe," I said. "But in my family, we take care of our own."

I was parroting a gang credo back at them, letting them know, as best I could, that we were a gang in and of ourselves.

"Ain't nobody take care of you on the street, bro. Jus' your friends. Maybe you should let your boys make some friends," Glasses said.

"We could argue this all day," I said. "Your organization serves a purpose in this community. I know that. I just choose not to have my children involved in it. We won't get in your way and we won't harm you, if you promise the same to us."

"In trade for what, old man?" Goatee asked. He was clearly the one in charge.

"Information," I said. "One-time information."

"One-time don't do us no good," said the Stone who brought them here. "We don't deal for one time."

"Fine. Your loss." I touched Malcolm's arm. "Let's go."

He looked startled, but to his credit, he didn't argue. We started for the door. The Stones watched us, until Goatee held out his hand.

"Hey, old man, we didn't give you permission to leave."

"I don't need permission," I said. "I thought you were going to deal, but you're not."

"Hang on. You tell us what you got," he said. "We'll tell you what it's worth."

I smiled. "Nice try."

"Old man, we don't make deals on information we ain't heard."

"I won't give you any information unless we have a deal. I already told you that it concerns the Gang Intelligence Unit."

"Like you'd know about that," Glasses said.

I didn't look at him. Instead, I said to Goatee, "Their van is parked two blocks down, motor running. They're trying to make it look like they've stalled on the street."

He looked visibly startled. The others moved closer together, their bodies tensing. So they had seen the van, too, and knew what it was. I'd been gambling on that.

"That what you want to trade?" Goatee asked, covering for his surprise. "That ain't worth nothing."

"I know," I said. "I'm just trying to show you that I know what I'm talking about. I'm trying to bargain in good faith."

"Why's it so important you keep your kids from us?" Leather Jacket asked.

Good question, one that put me in an awkward position. If I answered it honestly, I'd insult them, and if I lied, they'd see it.

"I think you know," I said. "I don't have to explain that."

Glasses nodded, then looked down at the floor. The Stone that brought us slipped a hand under his jacket, fingering his gun. He looked angry. Goatee seemed amused.

"Most old men, they got a layer of fat on 'em. Don't know nothing. Get scared when they see a brother with a gun. Think twice before messing with us."

"I'm not most old men," I said.

"You a cop?"

"No," I said. "I'm a father trying to find a way out of a difficult situation that my family is in."

Leather Jacket looked away. Glasses' mouth thinned. These boys understood family. Most of them lacked a true one and had come to the gang for a sense of belonging. I was trying to appeal to that. It was a delicate balance. If I pushed too hard, I'd make them angry, or worse, envious, and then they would no longer listen to me.

"You know why I hurt your friend," I said to the Stone who had brought us here.

"Because of your boy," he said.

I shook my head. "Because your friend took a doll away from a six-year-old girl, making her cry, and scared her sister. That's not what you guys are about. You're about protection, protection for the folks down here, not harassment."

Malcolm stirred beside me, but didn't look at me. Which was good. I didn't need to see the surprise in his gaze.

"Who did this?" Goatee asked the Stone.

"Li'l Cog," he said.

Goatee nodded once, then turned to me. "It won't happen again."

"Thank you," I said.

"Now you know how stuff works down here," Goatee said. "You understand protection. You know we get paid for it, right?"

"That's why I'm offering information," I said.

"Just so's you understand."

I nodded.

"We lay off your boys, them children that Charles here—" he nodded at the Stone who brought us in "—says you pick up ever' day and guard like they was worth more than that watch he give you."

So he'd told them about that, too. I didn't say anything. I could hear Malcolm breathing behind me—short, shallow breaths that spoke of his nervousness.

"We do that," Goatee was saying, "and you tell us what you think we need to know."

I straightened my shoulders. I was making this up as I went along, but they didn't have to know that—just so long as I didn't get caught.

"You know the Castle Church?" I asked. Castle Church was their term for the First Presbyterian Church in Woodlawn, the church they occasionally used as a base.

"Been there a few times," Goatee said.

"Gang Intelligence is planning a raid on the church this weekend. They're going to confiscate your weapons and they're going to see what they can find that's incriminating."

"They done that already," Goatee said.

I nodded. "A couple of years ago. But they're ready to do it again. They figure no one'll be worried about protecting the Black P. Stone Nation if they raid over Christmastime."

Leather Jacket let out a small whistle. Glasses shook his head. Charles crossed his arms.

"We can't do nothing about that, man," Goatee said.

"You can remove your stuff," I said.

"We don't got stuff there," Leather Jacket said.

"At least that's what Reverend Fry thinks," said Glasses, and they all laughed. I didn't.

"I don't care what you do with the information," I said, "but I know what I'd do."

"Take care of your stuff," Goatee said.

I shook my head. "I'd have the church defend its own property. I'd make sure they know about the threat. They're not too happy about the last time the cops raided."

"Hell, there's still bullet holes in the damn walls," Charles said.

"So let the church take care of it. They can use legal means to keep the police out. You can't. All you guys have to do this weekend is stay as far away from the church as possible."

Goatee tilted his head while I was talking, his small brown eyes assessing me. "You got brains, old man."

I shrugged.

"How'd we know this ain't no setup?" he asked.

"Don't do anything and see," I said.

He nodded his head, then smiled a little. "You know, sometimes the cost of protection goes up."

This was exactly one of my fears. If they liked my information, they would want more of it.

"I would expect that," I said.

"Just so's you know."

"And just so that you know," I said, "I'm not going to become your representative. If I overhear things, like I did this last time, that's one thing. But I'm not going to do any work for you. I may come back if I hear something, and that's it."

"You got strict rules, old man."

"Yes," I said, "I do."

"You know we could shoot you where you stand and no one'd care."

"A few people would care," I said. "But you're right. No one would touch you for the murder."

"Jesus," Malcolm whispered.

"So why ain't you scared?" Goatee asked.

"Right now, I'm too much trouble to kill. Especially with the Gang Intelligence Unit outside."

"They your protection?" He sounded surprised, maybe a little betrayed.

"Not in the way you think," I said. "They're looking for any excuse to shut you down. If they hear gunshots coming from this place, they'll be inside before you can dispose of my body. They'd go after the Main Twenty-one, and you know it. So I feel pretty safe this afternoon."

"What about tonight?" Goatee asked.

Voices shouted in the main room and all four of the Stones turned toward the door. They had their pistols out as the doors opened.

Twelve men walked in, carrying rifles and wearing ammunition belts over their shoulders. They were dressed like a military cadre: black leather jackets, black pants, and black turtlenecks. The black berets—worn rakishly down one side of their heads—marked them as Black Panthers.

"Shit," Malcolm said, so softly that I was the only one who heard him. I grabbed his arm and pulled him close.

I scanned the Panthers for familiar faces and thought I saw a few from the meeting where I'd met Epstein. But Fred Hampton wasn't with them, and neither, it seemed, were any of the men who'd been on stage with him.

More Stones piled into the room, pointing their weapons at the Panthers. I hadn't seen this much artillery in one place since Korea.

"We come for Mr. Jeff Fort," one of the Panthers said.

"You don't belong down here," Goatee said.

"We come in the spirit of brotherhood," one of the other Panthers said. "Chairman Fred Hampton wants to talk to you about joining the revolution."

"Shit, man, how stupid are you?" Glasses asked. "We don't give a flying fuck about no revolution."

"Hey, man," said the first Panther. "We're stronger together than we are separate. If we band together, build our own city out of these thin walls, then we can take down the white enemy, bring him to his knees."

I inched Malcolm backward, toward the side of the stage. No one was watching us. They were keeping the guns trained on each other.

"Enemy ain't always white," Leather Jacket said, glaring at the Panthers.

"It's the white capitalist system," said one of the Panthers.

"Born of slavery," said another.

"We can't let them continue to oppress us," said a third.

"We ain't oppressed," Glasses said.

I wondered how he could say that with a straight face. Then I realized that the gang was their protection against oppression. They grouped together and saw themselves as powerful. And right now, the threat to that power was the Panthers, not the cops.

Malcolm was right. We were in trouble. And I wasn't sure how to get us out of it.

TWENTY-EIGHT

"Chairman Hampton wants to have a meeting with Mr. Fort and the Main Twenty-one. He wants to discuss an alliance with them, not with you." The Panther spokesman, who seemed both older and taller than the others, spoke slowly, as if he didn't expect the Stones in front of him to understand.

Malcolm and I were close to the stage. The twelve Panthers stood in a semicircle, some with their backs pressed against each other's, near the door we'd come in. More and more Stones surrounded them.

"I don't care what your man wants," said Goatee. "We don't make alliances. Either you with us or you against us. That's all. Nothing more. You don't need Jeff for that."

Another door banged open and in the room behind the Panthers, screaming and shouting started, along with the sounds of crashing furniture and breaking glass.

"C-o-o-ops!" someone screamed.

The Panthers bolted through the main door, knocking down the Stones in their path. Their movements were so quick they caught everyone by surprise. There was more shouting from the front of the building.

Some of the Stones moved to the wall behind the door, holding their pistols ready.

I pushed Malcolm ahead of me. He nearly tripped climbing

355

the stage. He ran for the backstage area and I followed.

Strangely, the shouting was louder here. The stage opened into the hallway we'd entered through—and beyond that, I could see the main room. There had to be twenty-five police in uniform grabbing at Stones, looking in their faces, and then throwing them aside.

The cops weren't here to raid the Stones; they were after the Panthers.

There were no Panthers in sight. I supposed they had gone out through the pawnshop, but I wasn't certain. Cars started up outside, engines roaring, and I hoped no one was stealing my ancient Impala.

"Smoke!" Malcolm called. He'd found the back door. He peered through the glass window. "There's a cop out there."

I looked. Sure enough, a black cop in uniform guarded the back, his hand on the butt of his gun.

We couldn't go out the front because of the cops and Stones, we couldn't go out the pawnshop because of the Panthers and all their firepower. Our only hope was the back door.

My mind worked furiously. The only advantages we had were my age and the element of surprise. Twenty-five cops. That meant a lot of them had come from various parts of the South Side for this raid.

"Okay," I said. "Malcolm, put your hands behind your back like I've cuffed you. We're going to pretend you're my prisoner and I'm a cop."

"He'll know."

"He won't think about it, not in the amount of time we give him," I said. "You give me lip, fight just a little, but don't make it look out of control. Then when I tell you to run, you go for the car. If there are too many cops and weapons out there, you hit the deck. I'll figure out another way to get us out of here. You clear on this?"

"I think so," he said.

"Good."

He put his hands behind his back and I pulled my gun,

making certain the safety was on. Then I put it in the center of his spine.

"Smoke!"

"Trust me," I said, hoping that nothing went wrong.

Then I pulled the door open and shoved him outside. Cold rain dripped on us, covering us in an icy slime.

Malcolm started shouting, "You stupid, fucking Oreo! Ain't you got no sense? You cain't hold me, man. It ain't right!"

The cop at the bottom of the stairs looked startled. He pulled his gun.

"I got him," I said. "They need backup inside."

He was young, thank God, and he looked confused. "They told me to stay out here."

"And you should, you motherfucker!" Malcolm yelled. He was too good at this.

I shook him to shut him up. It worked for a moment. "Can't you hear what's going on around here?" I said to the cop. "It all went to hell. It's a war in there. They need backup."

"Should I call it in?"

"Shit, no," I said. "I'll do that when I put this asshole in the squad. Now, go. Go!"

Fortunately, the cop didn't second-guess me. Nor did he look at Malcolm's hands as he ran into the building. The door banged shut behind him.

"Let's go," I said to Malcolm, lowering my gun.

"You didn't say run," he said as he took off.

He was faster than I was, and moved with an effortlessness I could only remember. I followed, keeping my gun pointed at the ground because I had just taken the safety off.

More engines revved as we reached the street. There were two squad cars in front of the building, and the Gang Intelligence Unit van around the corner. But there were no cops outside, and no Panthers either.

Sirens blared and as I looked up Blackstone, I saw about six squads going after some cars. It looked like a scene out of a movie.

"What the hell?" Malcolm asked.

"Get in the car," I said.

He didn't have to be told twice. He got in the Impala and locked the door behind him. I climbed in, too, set the gun on the seat between us and started the engine.

No one came out of the building. No one seemed to care that we were taking off.

"Is this weird?" Malcolm asked.

"Very strange." I eased out of the parking space, then made a U-turn, heading away from the chase. In my rearview mirror, I saw two cops leave the Stones' headquarters. They didn't even look at us.

Some of the Stones came out, too. They looked like affronted citizens, gesturing and pointing. Their guns were gone.

"You looking at the road?" Malcolm asked.

I wasn't. I swerved to get back into my lane.

I drove several blocks south, then turned on Eightieth, cutting east until I reached State. Then I headed north.

My heart rate was beginning to slow down.

"You got the watch?" Malcolm asked.

It was a warm lump in my pocket. "Yeah."

"Was that worth it?"

"Worth what?" I asked.

"That confrontation with the Stones. Was it worth the watch?"

I glanced at him. His skin was gray, and sweat still dotted his forehead. "I was already on their radar, Malcolm."

"Yeah, and now they'll come after you," he said. "They're going to think you brought the cops there. Especially since we just vanished."

"If that's what they believe, then they'll think I did them another favor. The cops weren't after them. They were after the Panthers."

The sound of sirens had faded in the distance. The afternoon had grown dark. The snow-rain mixture was still falling, leaving large, wet splashes on the windshield, splashes that came with ice the size of diamond chips.

The road was getting slick. I slowed down, hoping my bald tires could handle the weather.

"So?" Malcolm said. He was still frightened. I had scared him, and I didn't know how to calm him.

"I wasn't lying about the Gang Intelligence Unit van out there. If they'd wanted to come after the Stones, they'd have done so long before the Panthers showed up. Did you see all the cops? They came in squads. Either they followed the Panthers down there or the Gang Squad called this in when the Panthers arrived."

"Why?" Malcolm turned to me.

I shrugged. "Maybe the cops see the Panthers as more of a threat. They certainly talk a tougher game than the Stones."

"I still don't see how all of this will get them to leave Jimmy alone."

"They're not going to mess with us for a while. Recruiting Jim and Keith and anyone related to us is too much trouble right now. It looks like they're going to have some problems with the Panthers, and they already have problems with the cops. They don't need us as a minor inconvenience."

Malcolm grunted and leaned back in his seat. The color was coming back to his face.

"You think it's all done then?" he asked after a moment.

"For now," I said.

"For now?" he asked.

I nodded. "Like the man said, sometimes the price of protection goes up. I just hope they'll have forgotten about us by then."

"What do you think the chances of that are?" Malcolm asked.

I smiled at him. "I wouldn't have gone into that building," I said, "if I hadn't thought the chances were pretty damn good."

TWENTY-NINE

On the pretext of having to do another interview about the Foster case, Malcolm and I returned the watch to Van Spillars. I'd never seen a happier boy. If he'd been younger, he might have hugged me. As it was, he grinned and bounced around his parents' yard like a Mexican jumping bean.

When he finally stopped, he tried to compose himself and act adult. "You just don't know what my mom woulda done," he said. "I'd've died."

As we walked back to the car, Malcolm nodded, once, as if he were having an argument with himself.

"Okay," he said after a moment. "You win. It was worth facing all those guns."

I grinned at him. Every once in a while, you got a chance to do it right.

That night, we had the neighborhood meeting to determine the children's after-school education. The meeting was at Franklin's house because he couldn't find any function room that would rent space to him this close to Christmas. I'd promised Franklin I would run the meeting since he'd done me so many favors the previous week, and he held me to that promise.

Fortunately, everyone brought food and no one seemed to

care that they had to sit on the floor. I felt crushed in my chair against the wall, next to the television. Althea had opened all the windows, and the cold night air barely managed to make the indoor temperature tolerable. I figured it would only get worse with all those people inside and all the conversation they would generate.

So much had changed since the week before that I could barely remember what my plans were. Grace Kirkland sat beside me, wearing her best dress and looking regal. Franklin had warned her that her offer to educate the children might be put to a vote—and that people might discuss her as if she weren't there.

She didn't care. She wanted to do this.

Franklin wanted to do it, too, and from the conversations I'd heard as I clawed my way to my chair in the tight corner, so did most of the parents.

I was the one having trouble. Here I was, forming a neighborhood group dedicated to watching out for its citizens, just like the group in Sinkovich's neighborhood, like the group I was going after tomorrow near Delevan's old house.

I'd managed to get ahold of Johnson, and he'd grudgingly agreed to meet me at my apartment at noon. I still hadn't completely decided about calling Sinkovich.

The meeting went better than I expected. A number of people testified to the need for additional education; Grace made a small speech, talking about her son at Yale and her credentials as a teacher, credentials I hadn't known about when I proposed her for the job. Then I talked about financing. One of the local businesses donated some unused space behind its offices rent free, and we finally agreed to pay Grace on a per-child basis. We set the base fee for each child, which Grace said could be paid either in trade or in cash. Franklin let everyone know that he would be monitoring payments, and he wouldn't allow anyone to be late.

When it was all over, I helped the Grimshaws clean up. Then I went upstairs, woke Jimmy up and drove him home. I should have felt vindicated by how easy that all had been, by the fact that we were actually moving to change something that hadn't been working.

But my mind was filled with the next day, the apologies I might have to make and the risks I might have to take. My plan for catching Foster's killer, which had seemed so fine this morning, now seemed like a lot of effort for a shaky return.

Johnson confirmed the feeling. He arrived at the apartment promptly at noon, did not demand an apology—nor did I—and seemed testy. When I told him the plan, he shook his head.

"How many times have I warned you, Grimshaw, not to interfere in a police investigation?"

"This isn't a police investigation," I said. "You made that abundantly clear with your little vigilante-justice speech the other day."

Johnson glared at me. "There's a whole number of things I can't do here. I can't involve a civilian. I can't do this without backup. And if I bring in backup, they'll just screw it up, especially if this perp has machine connections. You can't convict somebody with machine connections in this town unless the machine wants him convicted or the machine has washed their hands of him."

"Last point first," I said, grabbing my heavy coat. "Our reporter puts the pressure on the machine from outside the city. Second point, you'll have backup. And third, I'm a ghost. No one's gonna know I'm involved."

"Then you don't understand a sting, Grimshaw," Johnson said. "The purpose of the sting is to catch someone in the act of committing a crime."

"I know," I said. "And with luck, the evidence you get today will help you convict in the other crimes. You won't need me."

He frowned, his hands on his hips. "Someday you're gonna have to tell me exactly what it is you and the kid are afraid of."

"Someday," I said, making no real promise.

"You know," he said, "it would be better if I were the one pretending to house-hunt. We could have a few of my people back me up and then we wouldn't have to worry about you."

I shook my head. "Jane Sarton is expecting me. I don't think she would know what to do if you showed up."

"We could wait," he said in a tone that acknowledged how impossible that would be.

So far, my meeting with Johnson had gone better than I expected. I thought he might leave without considering the plan at all. I was also worried he might see the gun I had stashed in the waistband of my pants. I'd covered it with a bulky sweater, but if a gun was visible, an observant cop would notice.

And Johnson was an observant cop.

"Of course, there's a whole other matter you haven't thought of," he said.

"What's that?" I asked.

Then someone knocked on the door, and it opened without waiting for anyone to answer. Sinkovich came in, his cheeks red from the cold, his hair looking as if he'd been running his hands through it.

"You didn't tell me I was supposed to pick up a goddamn cripple," he said, pushing the door closed.

I put a finger to my lips, warning him to speak softly. Marvella wasn't home, but I didn't know if anyone else was, and loud voices carried in this building.

"Where's Saul?" I asked.

"In the car. Jesus, Grimshaw, you can hear him breathe. And how's he supposed to take pictures without a fucking eye?"

"Your journalist is blind?" Johnson asked.

"No," I said. "He's well-known, and he's already got pictures. He's just here to observe."

"Well, he brought a camera that weighs more than my kid," Sinkovich said. "Seems to think he can take pictures, even though he moans whenever he holds the damn thing."

"We'll find someone else," Johnson said.

"No we won't." I kept my voice even. I had everything planned, right down to the last detail. I even had Franklin picking up the children this afternoon in case something went wrong. I wasn't going to let these two screw me up.

"Okay, I'll find someone else." Johnson glared at Sinkovich. "Besides, I already made it clear to you, Grimshaw, I'm not working with this son of a bitch."

"Yes you are," I said.

"We can't trust him."

"You know, I should bust your face for that," Sinkovich said. "I put myself on the line here—"

"Nobody's busting anyone's face," I said. "I trust Jack. He won't tell anyone what's going on."

"Then you work with him," Johnson said. "Because I won't."

"Fine," I said. "You're the expendable one in this sting anyway."

Johnson froze. "What?"

I shrugged. "Sinkovich and Saul Epstein can sit in a car in that neighborhood all day and no one will ask them questions. If you so much as drive through, someone's going to notice you."

"So what were you going to have me do, hide in the trunk?" Johnson asked.

"No," I said. "You could do one of two things. You could sit in a squad a few blocks away and let Sinkovich radio you when we need you. Or you could stay low in the back seat and wait until they get the signal."

"You didn't tell me that part of the plan," Johnson said.

"I had a hunch you wouldn't like it."

"Well, you were right." He headed for the door. "Good luck."

"You know—" Sinkovich barred Johnson's way to the door "—I know some colored cops who got white friends in high places. Maybe you should listen to this guy, Grimshaw. Maybe someone already tipped off your target, and maybe it wasn't me."

"It couldn't have been either of you," I said, "since I didn't tell Johnson anything before he came here."

"Maybe that's why he's in such a hurry to leave." Sinkovich raised his eyebrows at me. "That what's going on, Truman?"

"You're a fucking son of a bitch," Johnson said.

"Yeah?" Sinkovich said. "Your point?"

"My point is that no one can warn Grimshaw's target because he forgot one thing. This sting is set up wrong."

"Oh?" I said.

"You already met with Delevan. He knows you're not interested in the house."

"Yes," I said. "So?"

"So, he was there that afternoon. You're basing all of this on what he said, on his version. There weren't any killings that we can find between the end of November and yesterday. During that time, you said, he was out of town. Seems to me he's a logical suspect, and he won't even be there today."

"That's right," I said.

Johnson frowned. So did Sinkovich. I wondered what would happen if I told them that they had identical expressions on their faces.

"I'm wagering that this sting comes to nothing. I'll meet with Sarton, she'll introduce me to Hucke, who'll take me to the neighborhood association, and they'll say that no one saw Foster that day. That leaves Delevan as our main suspect. If that happens, you guys can figure out a way to finagle the warrants and search his houses for evidence."

Sinkovich's frown turned into a grin. "He was ahead of you, Johnson."

Johnson's gaze remained steady on mine. "I get the sense he often is."

There was another faint knock on my door. Johnson pulled it open, but I couldn't see who was there.

"Is Bill Grimshaw here?" The voice was weak and tired, but I still recognized it.

"Saul! Jack said you were staying in the car." I stepped around Johnson so that Epstein could see me. He was leaning against the doorjamb, his face chalky. He wore a single eyepatch over his left eye and partially covered it with a stocking cap.

Sinkovich was right. Epstein's broken nose still whistled when he breathed.

"Come on in and sit down," I said.

Epstein waved a hand. "I thought we were going soon."

"We would be if these two would stop fighting," I said.

Johnson shook his head.

"They don't like your plan?" Epstein asked.

"They don't like each other."

Epstein gave them both a withering look. "If I can get out of bed today, you guys can play nice for a few hours."

"Come on," I said, putting my coat on. "Let's move. I've got to meet Jane Sarton at one, and you all have to be in position before that."

Sinkovich headed out the door before me, extending a hand to help Epstein, who ignored him. Johnson watched them go, and from the look on his face, I was certain he would back out.

After a moment, he said, "Ah, what the hell," and followed.

I closed the door behind us all and prayed that my idea would work.

THIRTY

When I got to Delevan's house, Jane Sarton was waiting for me on the porch. She wore a long white cape over a pair of black pants, and her boots, while stylish, couldn't be keeping her feet warm. She rubbed her gloved hands together, and if I hadn't met her before, I would merely have thought that she was impatient. But to me, it was clear that she was nervous.

I wasn't. I was ready to do this.

The weather wasn't cooperating. Even though I had chosen the lightest part of a winter day, it still felt like twilight. The combination of spitting rain and melting snow had continued throughout the night, making the roads slick and the visibility poor.

As a result, Sinkovich's car was parked closer than I liked. I'd noticed him and Epstein inside as I passed, looking as if they were waiting for someone at a nearby corner. I couldn't see Johnson, who had opted to wait in the back seat.

They had binoculars and Epstein's camera. They were supposed to keep me in sight at all times.

Before they took off, I'd managed to pull Epstein aside and ask him to keep me out of any photographs he took. He had looked surprised, but he promised to try.

I slammed my car door loudly and hurried up the walk. Jane

Sarton smiled when she saw me, throwing the porch door open and gliding down the stairs like a debutante.

"Mr. Grimshaw," she said, her clipped Chicago accent even more pronounced. "It's so good to see you. You haven't changed your mind, have you?"

For a moment, I didn't know what she was talking about, and then I realized she was playing her part even when we were alone. I supposed this would work better than waiting until someone was around. If she stayed in character the entire time, there was less chance of screwing up the possible sting.

"Mrs. Sarton," I said, carefully avoiding her outstretched hands, as any black man would do in this situation. "I just want to see the place one last time."

"Well," she said, speaking so loudly I was certain they could hear her in Memphis. "If you're truly interested, then I think you should meet the neighbors."

"I'm sure I will," I said, leading her back up the walk. I did not match the volume of her tone.

"No, no," she said. "I've learned when I've shown this house that the neighbors like to be involved. I've arranged a meeting with the neighborhood association. They all took a late lunch so that they could meet you. Mr. Hucke will be here to take you to the meeting shortly."

So she had reached Hucke. I was pleased. I was afraid we might just have to drop in on him, and I wasn't certain if surprise would allow my plan to work.

"Thank you," I said softly, while looking impatient in case anyone besides my team was watching. "May we go inside?"

I said that last a bit louder.

"Of course," she said, and scurried up the steps ahead of me, leaving a trail of Emeraude behind her. She unlocked the lockbox, removed the key and opened the house. This was also part of my plan. If Delevan was our suspect and he'd killed his victims in this house, there might be obvious evidence.

The house had the musty odor of a place that had been un-inhabited for some time. I sniffed carefully, trying to catch any foul odors that might remain, but there seemed to be nothing suspicious.

The main room was small, and the hardwood floor was dusty. There were patterns on the wood showing where Delevan's furniture used to be. An end table still sat in the corner, with a phone on top of it. As I passed by, I picked up the receiver to see if the phone still worked.

It did not.

The rest of the house was as empty. The faucet in the kitchen leaked, leaving a trail of rusty water down the side of the porcelain sink, and the second bathroom was as small as the one in my apartment. But the bedrooms were large and the small living room had charm. There was a garden in the back that looked like it hadn't been touched in years, but it had possibilities.

I was beginning to understand why Louis Foster thought this place would be the perfect gift for his wife.

When we finished our mock tour, we went back to the porch. Jane gave me her sales pitch, which was probably quite effective. I wasn't listening. I was pretending to look at the outside of the building, but I was really watching the street.

No one had bothered Sinkovich's car, and I thought I saw the flash of a lens. There were a few other cars parked along the street, and Sinkovich's seemed to blend in. The neighborhood was cheerier in the daylight, the houses neater and less threatening. But it was hard to forget how unfriendly this place had felt after dark.

"There he is," Jane said, and I turned slightly to see a man walking up the sidewalk. He was balding, with a square shape that seemed somehow familiar. It took me a moment to place him.

It was the guy from the grocery store, the one I'd seen behind the meat counter. The one who had actually tried to be helpful.

Fortunately, I saw him before he saw me. I had time to make certain the surprise did not register on my face. I kept my expression carefully neutral as he came up the walk. I was going to pretend I hadn't seen him before and see if he played along.

When he saw me, he gave me a wide, friendly smile, and my pretense at neutrality disappeared. This time, I let my shock show. I couldn't remember when a white man had smiled at me that way before.

I nodded to him as he came toward me, hand extended.

"Grimshaw is it?" he asked.

"Yes," I said, extending my hand. He grabbed it hard enough for me to feel the strength in his fingers, but not in any threatening way.

"I'm Rudy Hucke. Nice to meet you." He gave Jane Sarton a friendly smile. "Mrs. Sarton. Nice to meet you face-to-face as well."

She smiled and shot me a nervous glance, apparently not quite sure what she was supposed to do next.

"I'm going to take Mr. Grimshaw with me," Hucke said. "You're welcome to come, of course, but I have a hunch this'll be boring for you. Do you two need to finish up some business before we go?"

"No," I said. "We're fine."

Then, because I was playing a role, I put my hand on her shoulder, leaned in, and kissed her cheek, the way I'd seen white people do with female business acquaintances. I figured that little gesture would be enough to anger the calmest bigot. "Thanks, Mrs. Sarton. You've been wonderful. I'll call you."

She blushed to the edges of her wig. "Mr. Grimshaw, Mr. Hucke."

Then she hurried down the walk, nearly tripping in her high-heeled boots.

Hucke watched her go, and as he turned to me, I expected to see a change. Maybe his eyes would be colder, or his manner a bit forced. But when his gaze met mine, nothing was different.

"We're holding the meeting at my place," he said. "It's just a few doors down. Everyone's taking a late lunch."

The same words Jane Sarton had used. She was getting into her car, an old sedan that was covered in road grime. Something pinged at my memory, something Delevan had said about Foster.

He trusted me.

"Ready?" Hucke asked.

"Yes," I said.

"You'll like this place," Hucke said as he led me down the stairs. "The house is great. I used to help Oscar work on it. He loved it but he got a promotion and they moved him to Lake Forest."

"Must have been quite a promotion," I said. We sounded like possible friends. I had never had an off-the-cuff conversation with a white man like this, at least not this fast.

It threw me off balance, made me feel as if the world had tilted slightly. And I was surprised at my response to his friendly smile. It had warmed me, even though I was on alert.

How would it have felt to someone unprepared, someone like Louis Foster?

Probably like he'd walked into the one place where he could coexist with whites, where he and his wife could be happy for the first time in years.

He'd let his guard drop.

"What do you do, Mr. Grimshaw?" Hucke stepped over a root growing up through the sidewalk. We were closer to Sinkovich's car, and I had to work not to look at the men sitting in it.

"I'm a lawyer," I said, launching into the lies I had prepared in case the association meeting was just that—a sounding board for new neighbors.

"I thought you sounded educated."

There it was. The hint of bigotry, couched in such nice language.

But before I could react, he said, "Most folks here don't have much education. We're mostly blue-collar people."

And I found myself wondering if I was overreacting again.

"Well," I said, deciding to have the conversation I would have had if I were really thinking of buying the house, "if I had a blue-collar job, I wouldn't be able to afford to live here."

"No, I suppose not." Hucke's tone didn't vary. It was consistently friendly and interested. "I understand that black salaries are significantly lower than white salaries, especially in Chicago. I'm not quite sure what we can do about it."

His side of the conversation seemed genuine enough, and his use of the word "black" didn't sound forced.

"It'll just have to change company to company, I guess," I said.

"I take it money's not an issue for you, though?" He turned onto his sidewalk and kicked at some dried leaves as he went by.

"No, it's not," I said. "My business is doing very well."

"You own your own business?"

"Yes," I said.

"That's impressive." He mounted the red steps and opened his front door. "Anyone here?"

No one answered.

He turned toward me and smiled. "I told people to go in without me if I wasn't here. Guess no one else has arrived yet."

Then he went inside. I followed. This house was smaller than the Delevan house and smelled of furniture polish. The wood floors shone.

It was hot inside. I felt sweat bead on my forehead as I surveyed the room.

Hucke had rearranged the furniture for a meeting. Several kitchen chairs sat between the armchair and the couch. He had placed coasters on the coffee table in front of each seat.

He took his jacket off and hung it on a peg beside the door. "Take off your coat and make yourself to home," he said. "I'll go crank the heat down and see if I can find us something to drink. Want a beer?"

"It's a little early for me," I said. "Maybe some water would be nice."

"All right." He started for the kitchen. I turned, shrugged my coat off my shoulders, and started to slide my arms through the sleeves.

Suddenly, my coat twisted, trapping my arms behind my back. I tried to pull away, but couldn't. Hucke was beside me, the friendly look gone from his face. His eyes were as cold as I had expected earlier, maybe even colder, deader.

He was holding my coat with one hand. With the other, he held a knife and he was jamming it straight at my heart.

THIRTY-ONE

I butted his head with my own, feeling the sharp but expected pain shudder from my skull through my spine. At the same time, I rammed him with my shoulder, shoving him away from me.

His grip on my coat tightened, pulling me with him, but the knife flailed wildly, slicing my cheek and narrowly missing my eye. I could see the knife come back for a second attempt, and I managed to move out of its way.

My arms were hopelessly trapped in the coat. There was no way to free them without breaking his grip, no way to get to the gun pressing against my rib cage.

I caught my foot under his ankle, and he stumbled backward but didn't let go. The knife came for me again, slashing my left shoulder. I thought I heard something tear.

Blood dripped into my mouth, tasting of iron. I went for his feet again, and missed. He was quick, he was strong, and he was determined. I had never seen such rage in anyone's eyes, and I wondered fleetingly if I was the only victim who had had enough warning to be able to fight back.

I changed direction and shoved him farther back, slamming his hand against the wall so hard that a picture fell off and shattered. He uttered a guttural cry and stabbed at me, hitting but not penetrating the skin. I slammed him into the wall again, and again, until I felt his grip loosen.

Then I staggered away, dropping the coat and reaching under my sweater for the gun. He came at me, left hand clawing, right hand still stabbing. I managed to duck, and the knife swooped past.

He ran an extra step forward, carried by momentum, and by the time he turned, I had the gun out, cocked and ready to fire.

"Give me a reason," I said, spitting blood as I spoke.

His eyes were the only thing that moved. They gauged the distance between himself and the gun, between me and the knife. I could see him wondering if he could finish me off before I shot him, if he could disarm me faster than I could hurt him.

Not unlikely. Most people, even professionals like cops and soldiers, were afraid of knives. It was a gut reaction that was hard to train out.

But he'd already cut me, and I was alive. His knife didn't frighten me. And I wasn't afraid to use the gun.

"This is what they call a Mexican standoff," he said. "One of us has got to make a move, and if you shoot me, guaranteed, someone in this city will lynch you."

The word made me recoil. My parents were lynched. I had to fight to control my trigger finger.

"No they won't," I said.

At that moment, the door burst open and someone shouted, "Police! Freeze!"

Sinkovich came in beside me, his gun out. Hucke looked startled. Another door banged open and Johnson yelled the same thing.

Then there was a blinding flash of light, and I realized we weren't alone. Epstein had just taken a picture.

I turned. His camera was pointed at Hucke, bloody knife in hand.

Hucke was blinking, looking small. Sinkovich sidled toward him, one hand out as the other held the gun.

"Give me the knife," Sinkovich said.

I kept my gun trained on Hucke. Johnson came in through the kitchen. His gun was out as well. His gaze flicked to my face, to the blood dripping down my chin onto my sweater. My left arm was very tired. It took an effort to hold it up.

"Face me, you son of a bitch," Johnson said.

Sinkovich shook his head once. He knew what Johnson was going to do.

"Give me the knife," Sinkovich said again, desperation in his voice.

Hucke's mouth opened in confusion at the two different commands. Epstein took another photograph. Johnson didn't seem to care. All he seemed to be thinking about was making certain he didn't shoot Hucke in the back.

"Give him the knife, for crissake," I said.

"What the hell is this?" Hucke asked.

"Police," Sinkovich said again. "Give me your knife."

That seemed to get through. Hucke put the knife in Sinkovich's palm, then raised his hands just a little, palms out in front of his chest.

"Now, turn toward me," Johnson said, his voice cold.

Hucke started to turn.

"No!" I shouted. "Truman, he's unarmed."

My words made Hucke freeze. Johnson's eyes narrowed, and for a moment, I thought he was going to shoot. Then he lowered his gun and reached for his handcuffs.

"I said—" Johnson looked over at me as he spoke "—turn so that I can cuff you."

"Huh?" Hucke said.

Johnson grabbed one arm and pulled it behind Hucke's back, then grabbed the other. Epstein continued taking pictures of the arrest. Sinkovich didn't close his hand over the knife. Instead, he set it on the floor so someone could bag it later.

The handcuffs clicked shut. I still hadn't brought my gun down, but I wasn't sure if I was protecting anyone anymore or just unable to move. Black spots were rolling across my vision and my head felt heavy.

Hucke looked up at me. My left eye was closing, blood caking along the rim. "You're a cop?" he asked.

"I get that question a lot," I said as the floor came up to greet me. "I get that question a lot."

THIRTY-TWO

I woke up the next morning in the hospital, the entire left side of my face feeling as if it were on fire. Jimmy sat beside the bed, looking terrified, and I later learned that he'd thrown such a fit the nurses decided it was better to let him in my room than remain in the visitor's lounge.

"You ain't supposed to move your face," he said when he realized I was awake. He didn't move from his chair, nor did he let go of my good right hand. "Got stitches."

"Aren't," I mumbled.

"Huh?"

"Aren't supposed to . . ."

"Mr. Grimshaw," a woman's voice said from somewhere above me. "I see that we are awake."

A nurse. Only nurses spoke with that annoying royal "we." I tried to open my left eye further, only to realize there was a bandage around it. With my right, I could see Jimmy, the door, and the puke-green cinderblock wall. Whoever thought that color was healing I'd never know.

The nurse bent into my line of vision. She was younger than I expected, full-bosomed, and white. Her fingers found the pulse in my wrist and she timed it.

She wrote that down on my chart, then smiled at me. "Welcome back."

I tried to smile, only to feel a tugging on my cheek.

"No, don't," she said. "You have twenty very small stitches there. The doctor is hoping to avoid an obvious scar. So no smiling, and talk only through the right side of your mouth until the stitches come out."

"When?" I asked, carefully using the right side of my mouth as instructed. It made me feel like I was doing a bad Jimmy Cagney imitation.

"Just after Christmas."

"I can't stay here for Christmas," I said, trying to push myself up. That was when I realized that my left arm was in a sling.

"Oh, no. I suspect you can leave after the doctor sees you. I'll let him know you're awake."

And then she vanished out of my range of vision.

"You lost lots of blood," Jimmy said. "That's why you passed out. Then they gave you stuff while they stitched you up. That's why you didn't wake up right away."

I looked at him. There were deep circles under his eyes. "Were you here alone the whole time?"

He shook his head. "Althea's been here, and Franklin. They wanted me to go to school, but I wouldn't."

"Why not?"

"Because," he said, and I remembered how he had reacted last summer. *I thought you was gonna die.* But he wasn't saying that this time, even though the fear was evident.

I squeezed his hand. "Guess you can miss one day."

He started to smile, but then his eyes filled with tears. He leaned forward and pressed his face into the rubbery blanket, as if he couldn't hold himself up anymore. It was such an adult movement that it startled me.

I put my good hand on the back of his head and kept it there. I didn't die. But I nearly had. It would have been so easy, so quick. Hucke trapping my arms, shoving his knife into my heart. He had done some version of that with all the others. Charmed them, then when they least expected it, attacked them, and killed them with a single movement.

So easy. So quick.

I had been lucky, and I knew it.

It didn't take long for all the pieces to come together. Hucke had been doing the killings. There were even more than we had known about, beginning shortly after his wife left him fifteen years before. The killings had escalated in the last two years and he'd started leaving the bodies in public places.

The places got more and more obvious as well, culminating in the Confederate monument in Oak Woods cemetery. He would often wait in his car, watching the body until someone discovered it before he drove away.

Even though Hucke didn't start killing until his wife left, the warning signs were there. He used to beat up black children when he was a teenager. Then he went into the army and someone taught him how to use a knife.

He also got religion. The dangling shoe was a reference to something that Jesus had said—that if a town did not accept the word of God, the disciples should leave the town and wipe its dust off their shoes. Apparently, Hucke had twisted that quote to mean that the dust of his precious neighborhood shouldn't touch the shoes of the unclean.

After I passed out, Johnson made the arrest while Sinkovich got me to the hospital. Epstein did more than his share. The photographs were so stunning they went across the United Press International wire, which panicked me when I heard about it.

Then I saw them and realized I wasn't in them. Not a one. Johnson had seen to that. Epstein later gave me all the negatives with me in the shots, and never asked why I didn't want my face plastered all over the news.

He was having enough to deal with on his own. UPI had hired him as a stringer to follow up on this case, and to cover other Chicago stories that weren't being pursued by the city's major dailies. He was working hard and he still wasn't healed. Now his grandmother was worrying that he was doing too much rather than too little.

My plan did work, though. Epstein had gotten the photographs and a short version of the story to the wire services immediately. Word trickled through the upper echelons of the machine, and the lawyer Hucke had been expecting never materialized. Hucke's face was all over the next day's papers, and it was clear that his political cronies had decided to let him swing alone.

And swing he did. With story after story coming out in the national presses first under Epstein's byline, it soon became clear to all of Chicago that Hucke had been killing any black person who wandered alone into his neighborhood.

The prosecutor was putting together a case that didn't involve me. This had nothing to do with Johnson, but with logic. After arresting Hucke for assaulting me, Johnson called a forensic backup team. They found solid evidence linking Hucke to most of the murders.

A good portion of the evidence, besides the knife, consisted of car parts stored in the garage. Apparently, Hucke had driven the cars to another neighborhood, parked near an El line, and taken something from each car as a souvenir. Then he'd ridden the El home. Often the souvenirs were personal—an insurance card or the car's registration. He kept all the papers in a box that Johnson swore he found open on a workbench.

Johnson also said a lot of the other evidence linking Hucke to the crimes was in plain sight throughout the house, making them easy to trace. I had to wonder, and I hoped that in his zeal, Johnson hadn't done anything to jeopardize the case when it went to trial.

But that was no longer my worry. As long as I remained a forgotten incident, the reason for the arrest but not the reason behind the charges, I was happy. Jimmy and I were free to continue with our own lives.

Which we did. The Blackstone Rangers didn't bother us during the last few days of school, and I had hopes that they would leave us alone for good.

Mrs. Foster paid me a generous amount, plus a bonus, pleased to know what happened to her husband after all. I used some of the money for Christmas presents—even going to

Marshall Field's again to buy Norene her own Crissy doll. I probably spent too much, and I didn't adhere to Black Christmas principles, but I felt free for the first time in weeks. I put the rest of the money into an account as a cushion and felt some of the financial pressure ease.

Not all of it, though. I called the insurance company and reconfirmed our talk after the new year. If I could continue to freelance and find jobs that were a little less dangerous, both Jimmy and I would be happy.

I still had one job to wrap up. McMillan and I planned to meet in the week between Christmas and New Year's to pick the security team for the board meeting. I would bring in a few of my people, he would bring in some of his, and we would both review their backgrounds.

Until then, I concentrated on healing and the holiday. On Christmas Eve, Althea managed to guilt me into joining them for midnight services. The church was full, just like church had been during the Christmas Eves of my childhood. The smell of fresh pine boughs brought back that last holiday, when I'd stepped out in front of the choir and sang "Silent Night" in my pure boy's soprano. Martin Luther King, Jr., then just a child, stood in the row behind me, and there were all sorts of possibilities ahead of us.

On this Christmas Eve, in the last week of that horrible year 1968, Jimmy stood beside me, his face turned toward the altar as his raspy, untrained voice struggled with carols he had never learned. I kept a hand on his shoulder and didn't sing. My wounds ached. I hadn't been in a Christmas service in decades, and I always thought that when I returned, the feeling of warmth and security from the years before my parents died would return also.

It didn't.

I left the church, carrying a candle into the darkness with the rest of the congregation, feeling more bereft than I had in ages.

382

THIRTY-THREE

Laura returned on January second, as scheduled. McMillan picked her up at the airport while I assembled our security team. We met in the lobby of Sturdy's office building.

My bandages were off and my arm, while sore, was fine. The scar on my face hadn't puckered, thank heavens, but it was an angry red line that crossed from my temple to my chin. When I looked in the mirror, I didn't recognize myself, and I was beginning to understand the despair that Elaine had felt when she saw all the stitches running across her beautiful skin.

Laura saw my scar first, and reached to touch it, stopping herself just in time.

We had agreed that this meeting would be all business.

Although it was hard. I had missed her more than I wanted to admit. She looked tanned and fit, as if the trip had done her good. That afternoon she wore a mannish suit and little makeup. Her hair was pulled away from her face like a woman about to do battle.

We arrived at the eighth-floor conference room a few minutes late, by design. Laura marched in, McMillan beside her, and the five members of the security team flanking them, surprising all but a handful of the board members—the handful that Laura knew would vote with her as majority shareholder.

I stood near the arched windows, arms crossed, and watched

the proceedings. Laura handled herself beautifully. Cronk challenged her the moment she walked in, demanding that McMillan and the security team leave so that the board meeting could proceed. Laura calmly explained the threats she had received and said that she was not going to relinquish her security, especially since she planned to take over Sturdy Investments that very afternoon.

The meeting went from there. With several neat votes, Laura became chairman of the board, fired the team her father had put into place—including Cronk and the men who had insulted her at lunch—and established her own team to run Sturdy Investments.

In the space of a few hours, Laura had gone from the daughter of the company's founder to the head of the company. Cronk and his team didn't seem to know what hit them.

They'd figure it out soon enough. And by then, their jobs—and their power—were already gone.

After the meeting, we assembled again in the lobby.

"How much trouble do you think they're going to give us?" Laura asked McMillan.

"None," he said. "They don't dare. They wanted to prevent you from doing this, and you did an end run around them. Now that you're in, they can't get you out without calling attention to themselves."

He smiled at her, squeezed her arm, then said, "I have some public-relations announcements to take care of, but I think we need a victory celebration. Tell me when and where, and I'll meet you."

"Smokey?" Laura said.

"I have some errands to run myself," I said. A victory celebration would be easier without me, and I did have one errand I had promised Mrs. Weisman I would complete that afternoon.

"All right," Laura said. "My apartment at six. I expect both of you to be there."

Then she left us, skirting through the crowd, looking more regal than I had ever seen her.

"A hell of a lady," McMillan said, watching her go.

"A hell of a woman," I said, and headed to my car.

There was half an hour of daylight left when I parked my Impala on the access road leading into the newer part of the cemetery. Chicago was filled with graveyards. This one, on the northeast side, hid in a cluster of trees so old that they could have been part of the city's park system.

My dress shoes sank into the ground as I walked. The snow the day before had melted, just like it had done all winter. The ground wasn't yet frozen solid, which was why the tombstone Mrs. Weisman and I bought had been erected even though it was January.

My hands felt naked. I hadn't brought a flower or any token—I hadn't even realized until now that I needed one.

I stopped at the plot that had, until this morning, been marked by a small square number. The earth still looked disturbed, even though the grave had been there for weeks. I crouched beside the new stone. It glistened in the dim light, the carvings fresh and precise, not worn away by time—

Elaine Elizabeth Young
September 25, 1943—December 10, 1968

—followed by the single word that Saul had requested we place there:

Beloved

I touched the scar on my face, still tender, and then touched the ground before me. I knew the despair she'd felt, the hopelessness, and again it angered me that she hadn't even tried to overcome it. I couldn't imagine how Saul felt. Guilty, alone, lost.

He had loved her, and while she recognized it, she hadn't been willing to fight for it. Not really. She had lacked the courage for the everyday struggle, being unwilling to face the stares, the hatred, the fear, for something she believed in.

I lacked it, too. The everyday courage. What had Sinkovich called me? A holier-than-thou son of a bitch. A man who could handle the big crusades when whipped into righteous anger, but who could not seem to face the small ones.

Beloved.

Saul had that courage, returning to his work even though he was shattered. Jimmy had it, too, willing to go on even though he had lost everything.

So did Laura.

She would need it now so she could remember her goals, remember her mission, in the face of all the little business details that would flood her day after day.

Laura.

She would never make the choices Elaine had. She would never give up, no matter what she faced.

Laura would never let the bastards win.

But I nearly had.

For years, I had let the world step between me and the things I wanted, the things I believed in. There would always be men like Hucke, people like Sinkovich's neighbors, or boys like the ones who had attacked Saul and Elaine. It was easier to lash out, to destroy, than it was to stand and fight back.

Just like it was easier to remain invisible than challenge other people's preconceptions.

I traced the word one last time, feeling the cold stone sharp against my fingers.

Beloved.

Oddly enough, it meant something to me, too.

I arrived at Laura's apartment early. The elderly elevator attendant smiled at me as I got on, and watched me as if he saw something glorious in my face. I nodded to him when we reached Laura's floor, the penthouse. I waited until the elevator doors closed before walking the handful of steps toward Laura's door.

The silence up here was amazing. I noticed it every time I came. The walls were thick, insulated, protected from the world. The way Laura had been when I first met her. The way she was not now.

I rapped on the door with the back of my hand. It took a moment before I heard the locks snap open and the chain rattle. Laura pulled the door open, looking nothing like the woman I had seen at Sturdy Investments.

Her blond hair was down around her shoulders. She wore a baggy sweater and a tight pair of blue jeans. Her feet were bare.

"Smokey," she said, and this time, she did touch my scar, her fingers feather-light against my skin. "Are you going to tell me what happened?"

I caught her hand in my own. "Yes," I said, and the word was freeing. "I missed you."

"I missed you, too," she whispered.

Her hallway was still decorated for Christmas. Pine boughs had been draped over the picture frames, and a tiny tree stood in a pot by the door. Just inside the door, some mistletoe swayed in the breeze caused by a nearby heating duct.

With my free hand, I brushed the mistletoe. It was plastic. Then I stepped inside, beneath it, and pulled her close like I'd always wanted to do but never thought I dared. I cupped her face, slipping my hands beneath her warm, fragrant hair, and kissed her.

It felt like coming home.

After a moment, I rested my forehead against hers, black against white, skin against skin, feeling no difference between us at all. Her hands were wrapped around my back.

"Think it would be churlish of us to ask McMillan not to come to the victory party?" I asked.

"Who cares?" she said as she reached behind me and closed the apartment door.